epic!

CAT NINJA

Written by
Matthew Cody
Alejandro Arbona

Illustrated by
Chad Thomas
Derek Laufman

Colors by
Warren Wucinich

Cat Ninja created by Matthew Cody and Yehudi Mercado

Andrews McMeel Publishing
a division of Andrews McMeel Universal
1130 Walnut Street, Kansas City, Missouri 64106

www.andrewsmcmeel.com

Epic! Creations, Inc.
702 Marshall Street, Suite 280
Redwood City, California 94063

www.getepic.com

22 23 24 25 26 RR2 10 9 8 7 6 5 4 3 2 1

Paperback ISBN: 978-1-5248-7585-5
Hardback ISBN: 978-1-5248-7936-5

Library of Congress Control Number: 2022942037

Design by Dan Nordskog

Made by:
Lakeside Book Company
Address and location of manufacturer:
600 State Road 32 West
Crawfordsville, IN 47933
1st Printing – 8/29/22

ATTENTION: SCHOOLS AND BUSINESSES
Andrews McMeel books are available at quantity discounts with
bulk purchase for educational, business, or sales promotional use.
For information, please e-mail the Andrews McMeel Publishing
Special Sales Department: specialsales@amuniversal.com.

TABLE OF CONTENTS

Chapter 1
The Goldfather, Part 1

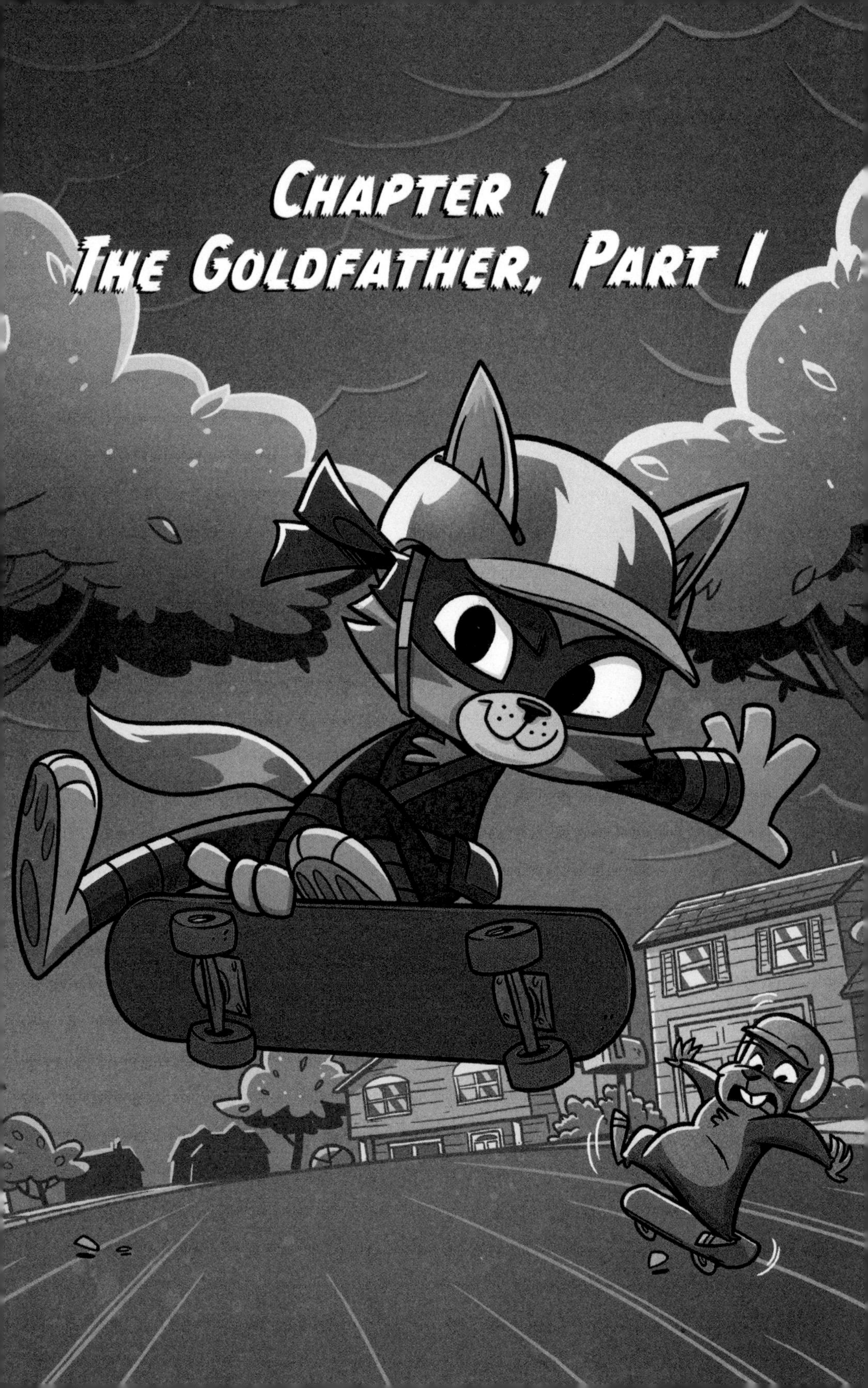

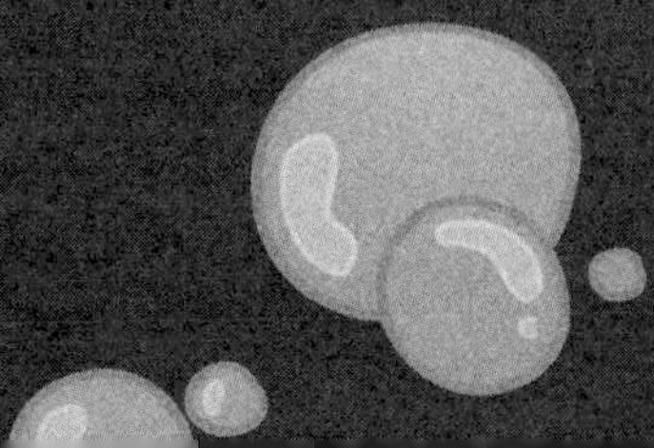

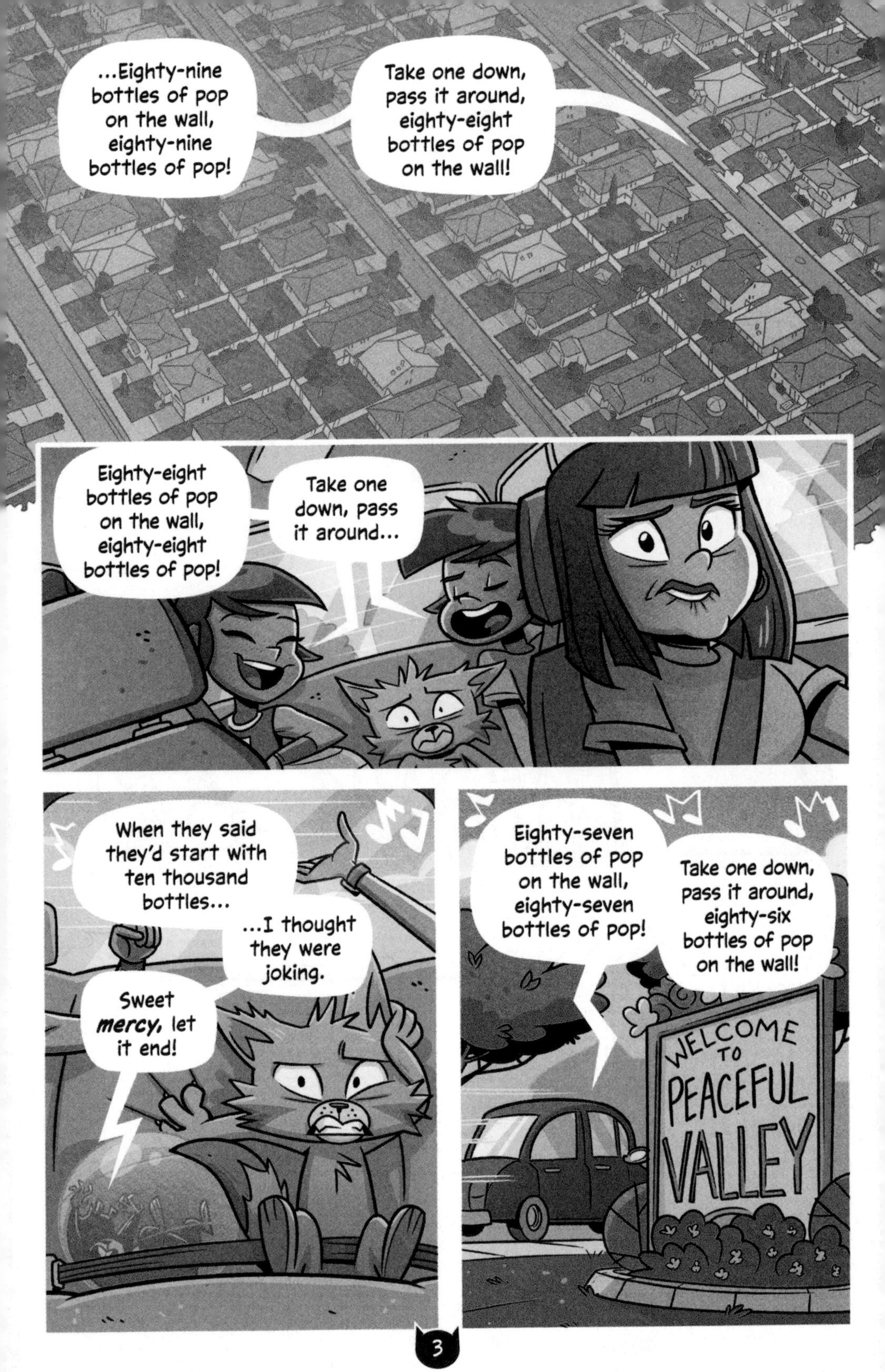
...Eighty-nine bottles of pop on the wall, eighty-nine bottles of pop!
Take one down, pass it around, eighty-eight bottles of pop on the wall!
Eighty-eight bottles of pop on the wall, eighty-eight bottles of pop!
Take one down, pass it around...
When they said they'd start with ten thousand bottles...
...I thought they were joking.
Sweet *mercy,* let it end!
Eighty-seven bottles of pop on the wall, eighty-seven bottles of pop!
Take one down, pass it around, eighty-six bottles of pop on the wall!
WELCOME TO PEACEFUL VALLEY

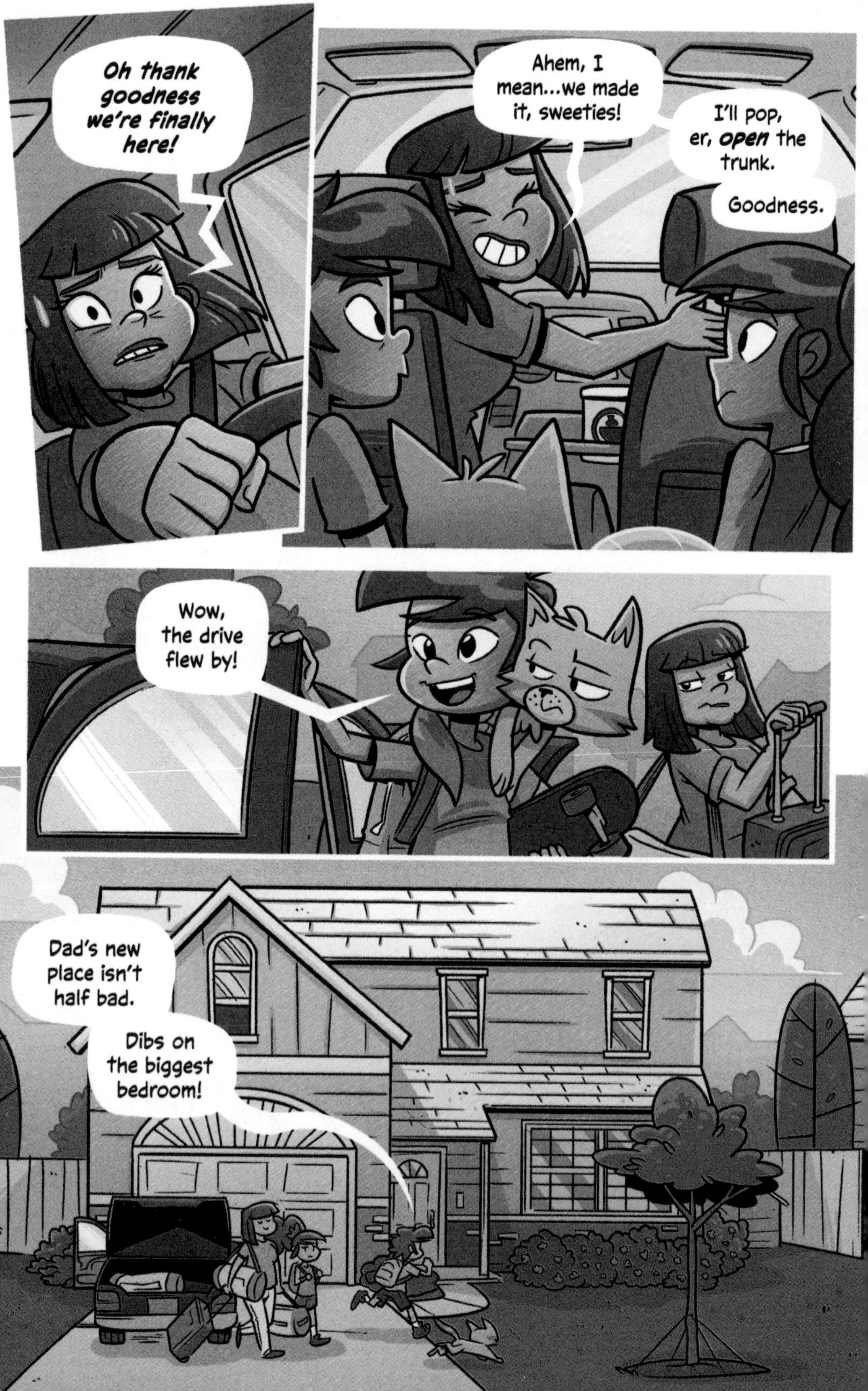

Oh thank goodness we're finally here!
Ahem, I mean...we made it, sweeties!
I'll pop, er, open the trunk.
Goodness.
Wow, the drive flew by!
Dad's new place isn't half bad.
Dibs on the biggest bedroom!

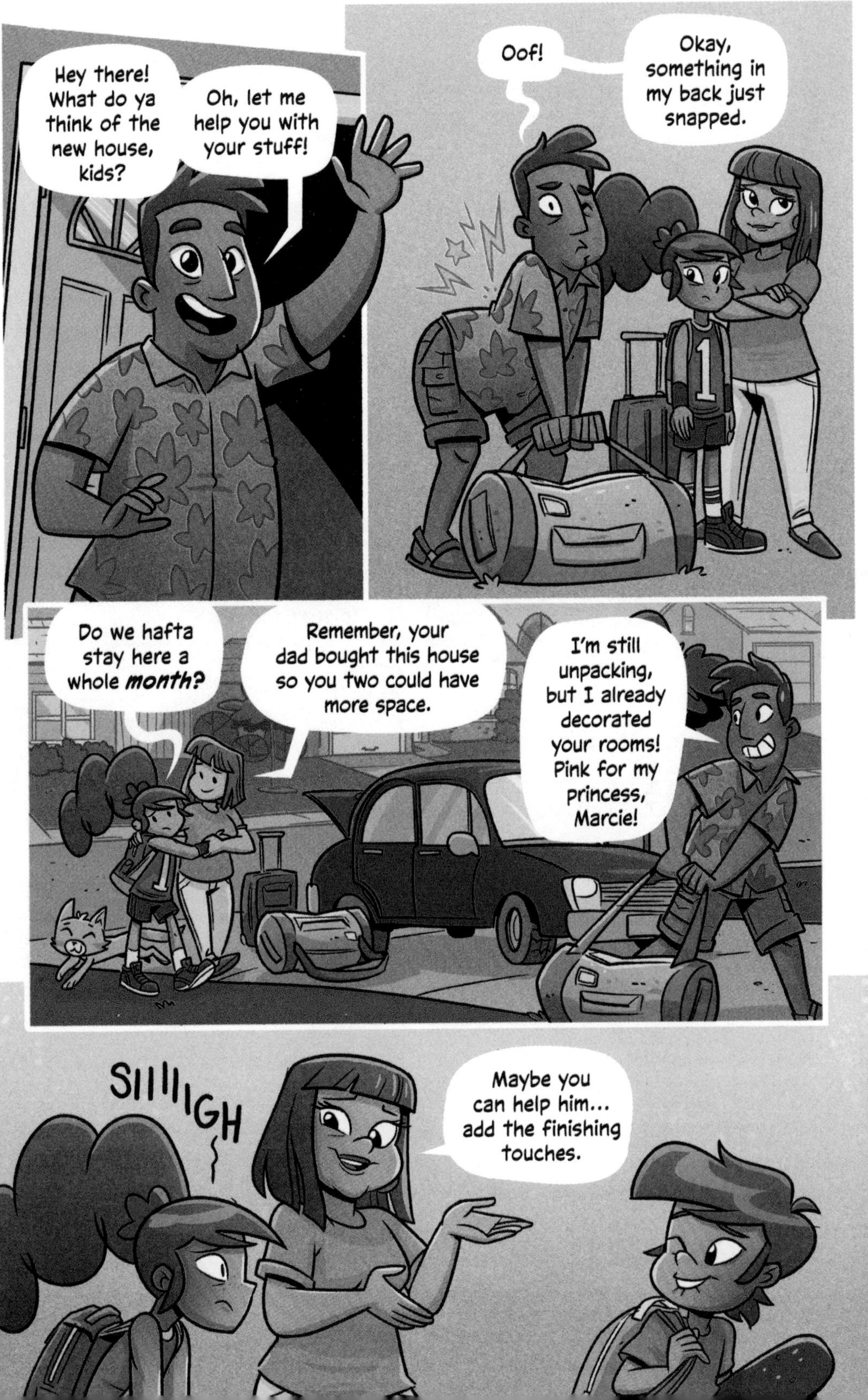
Hey there! What do ya think of the new house, kids?
Oh, let me help you with your stuff!
Oof!
Okay, something in my back just snapped.
Do we hafta stay here a whole *month?*
Remember, your dad bought this house so you two could have more space.
I'm still unpacking, but I already decorated your rooms! Pink for my princess, Marcie!
SIIIIGH
Maybe you can help him... add the finishing touches.

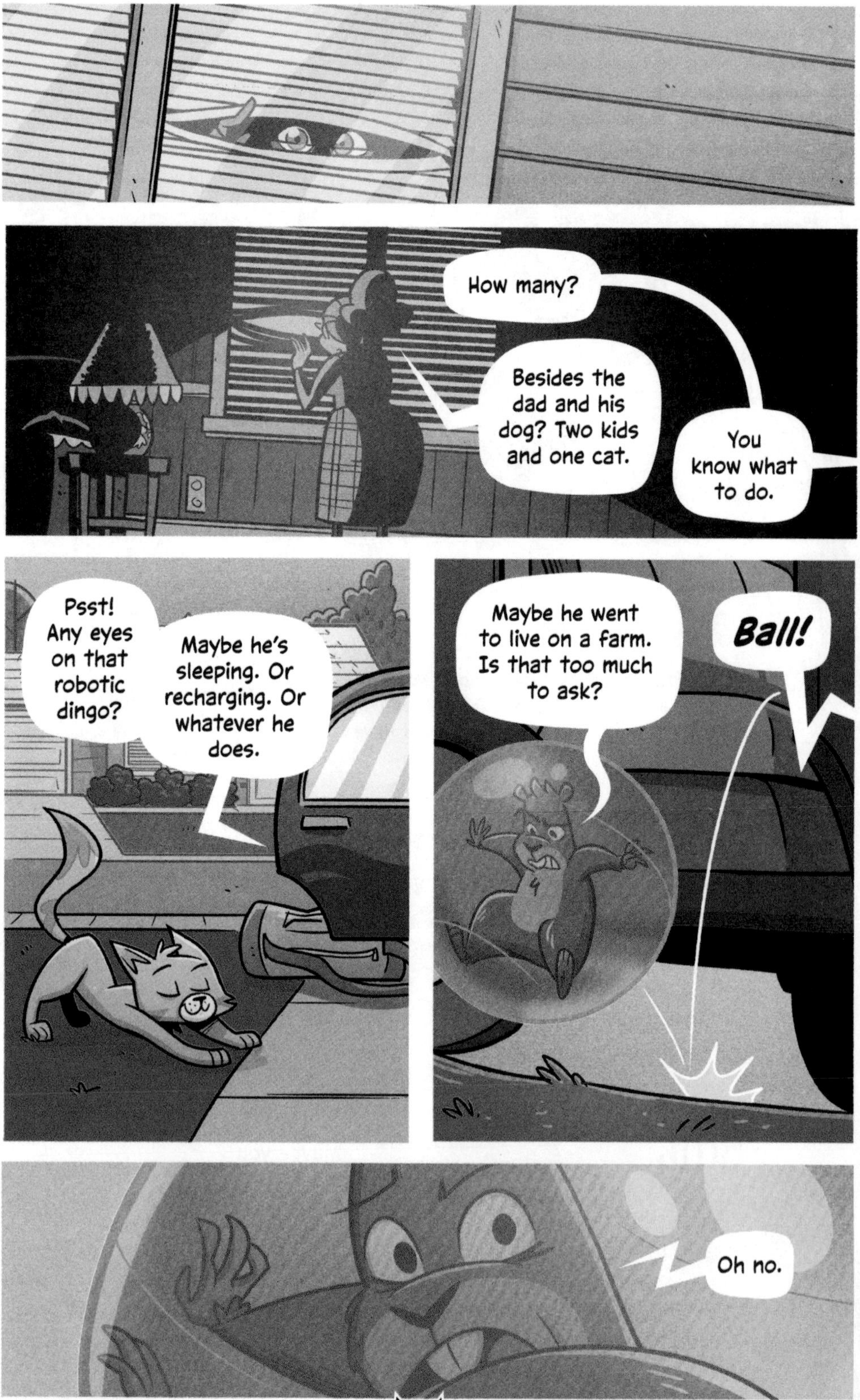
How many?
Besides the dad and his dog? Two kids and one cat.
You know what to do.
Psst! Any eyes on that robotic dingo?
Maybe he's sleeping. Or recharging. Or whatever he does.
Maybe he went to live on a farm. Is that too much to ask?
Ball!
Oh no.

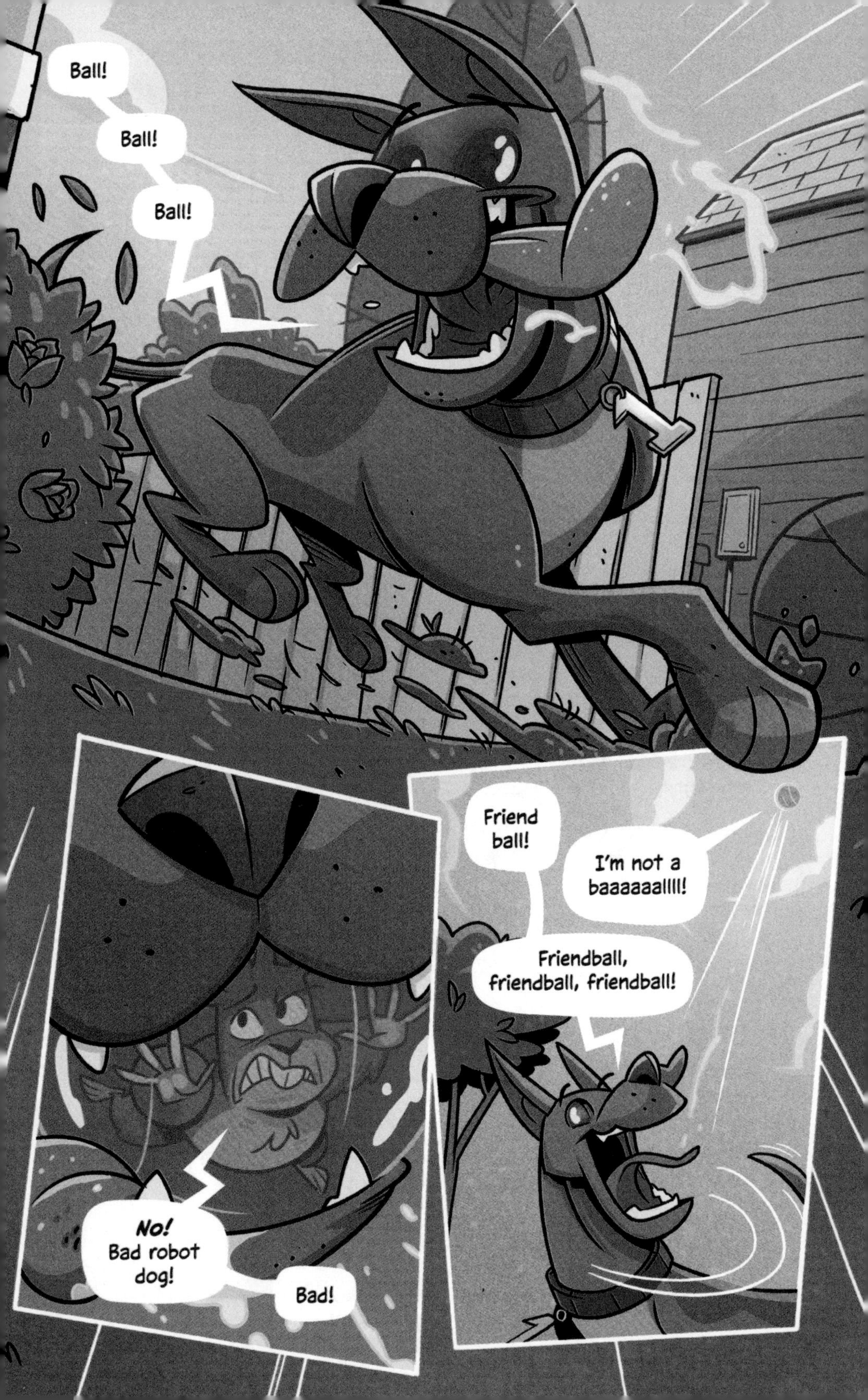
Ball!
Ball!
Ball!
No! Bad robot dog!
Bad!
Friend ball!
I'm not a baaaaaallll!
Friendball, friendball, friendball!

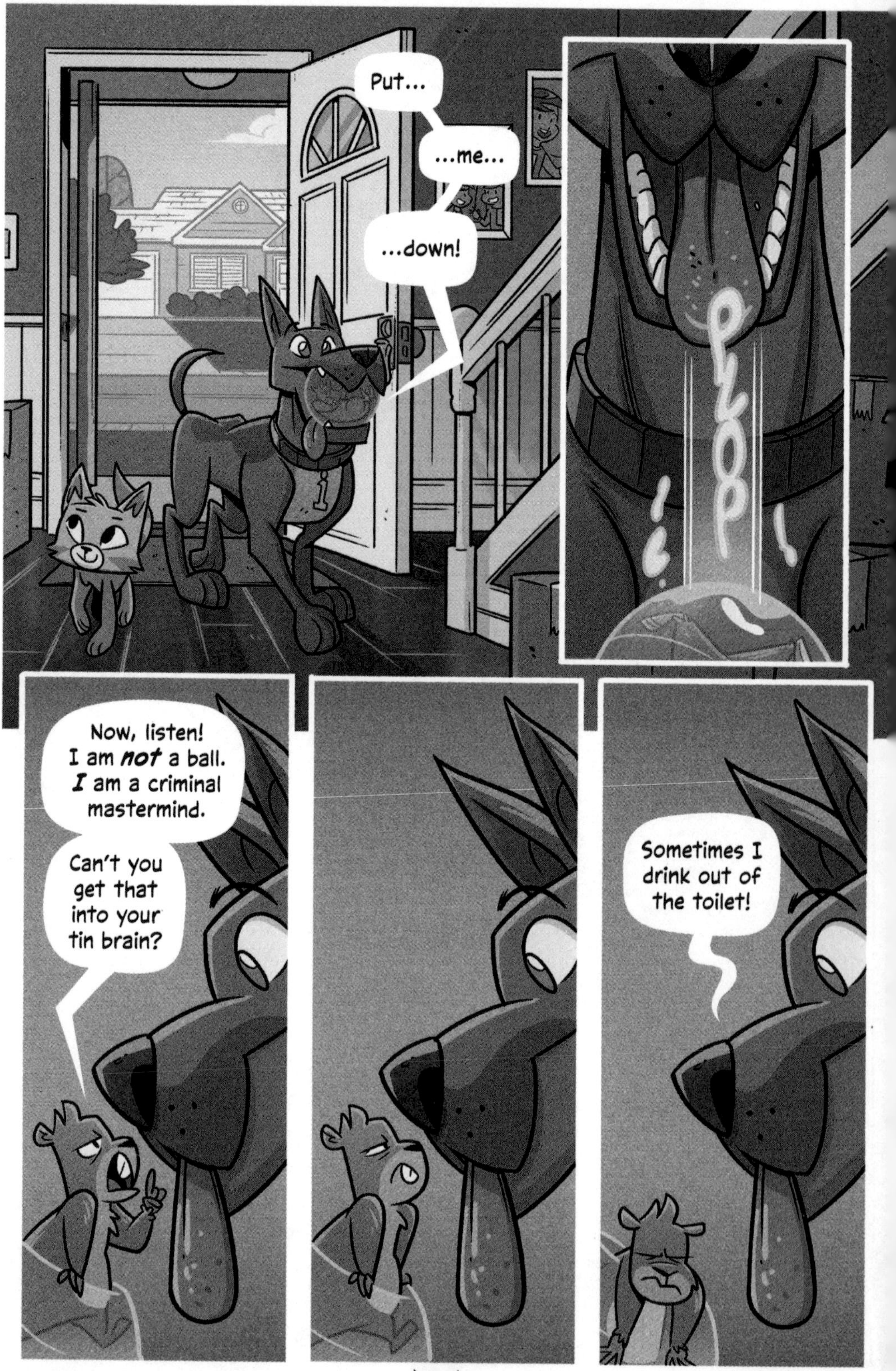
Put...
...me...
...down!
PLOP
Now, listen! I am *not* a ball. *I* am a criminal mastermind.
Can't you get that into your tin brain?
Sometimes I drink out of the toilet!

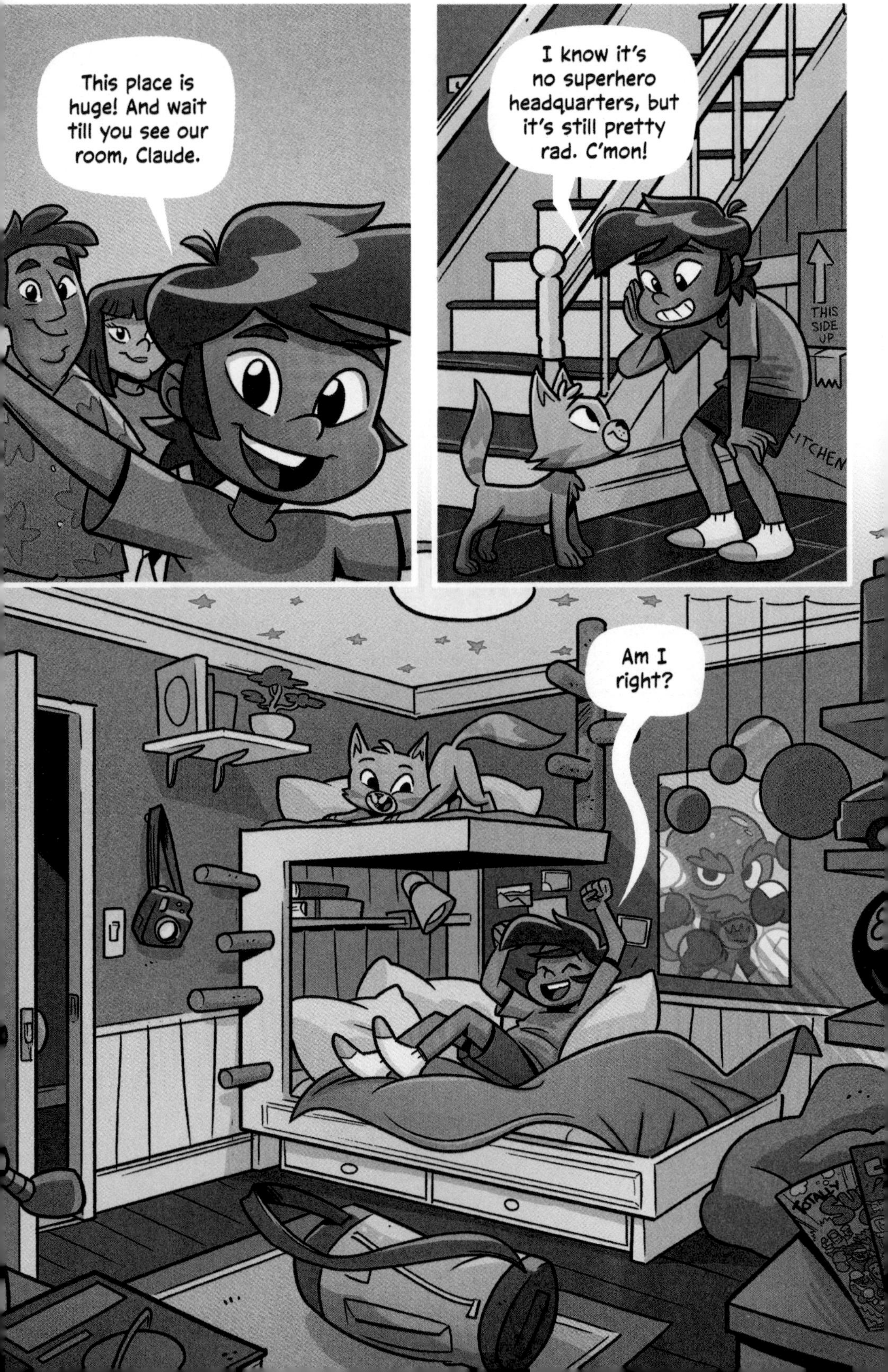
This place is huge! And wait till you see our room, Claude.
I know it's no superhero headquarters, but it's still pretty rad. C'mon!
THIS SIDE UP
KITCHEN
Am I right?
TOTALLY

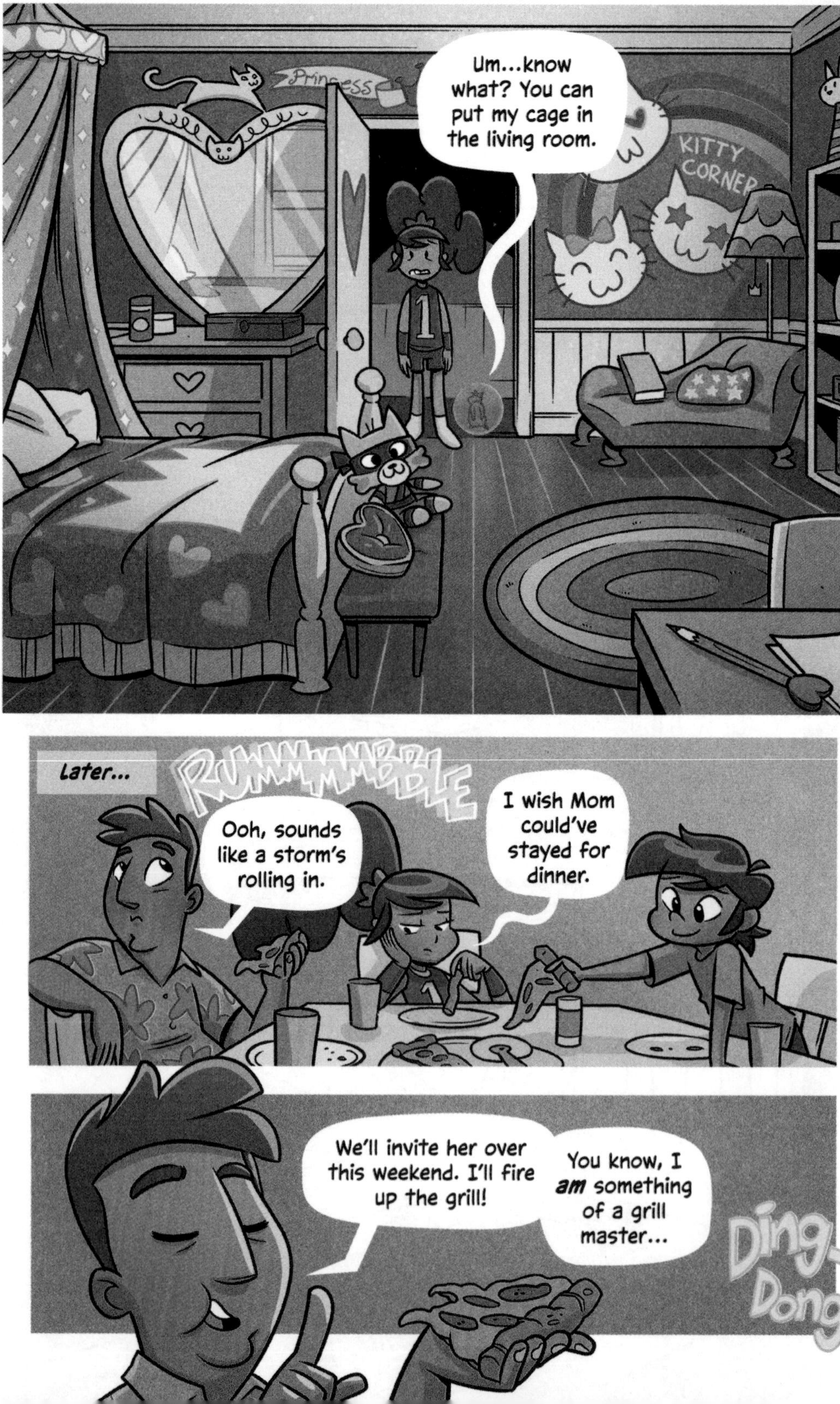
Princess
Um...know what? You can put my cage in the living room.
KITTY CORNER
Later...
RUMMMMMBBLE
Ooh, sounds like a storm's rolling in.
I wish Mom could've stayed for dinner.
We'll invite her over this weekend. I'll fire up the grill!
You know, I *am* something of a grill master...
Ding-Dong

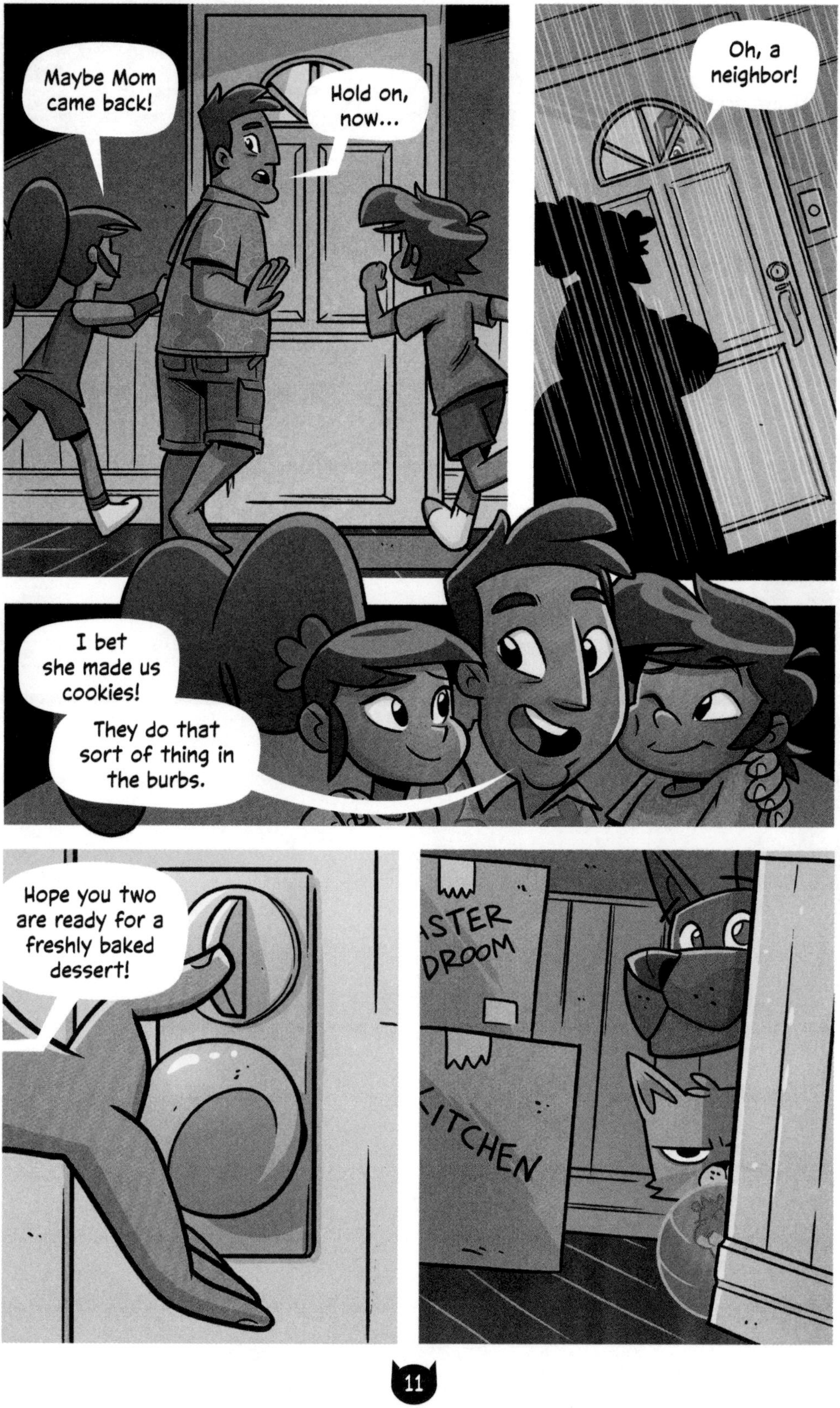
Maybe Mom came back!
Hold on, now...
Oh, a neighbor!
I bet she made us cookies!
They do that sort of thing in the burbs.
Hope you two are ready for a freshly baked dessert!
ASTER
DROOM
KITCHEN

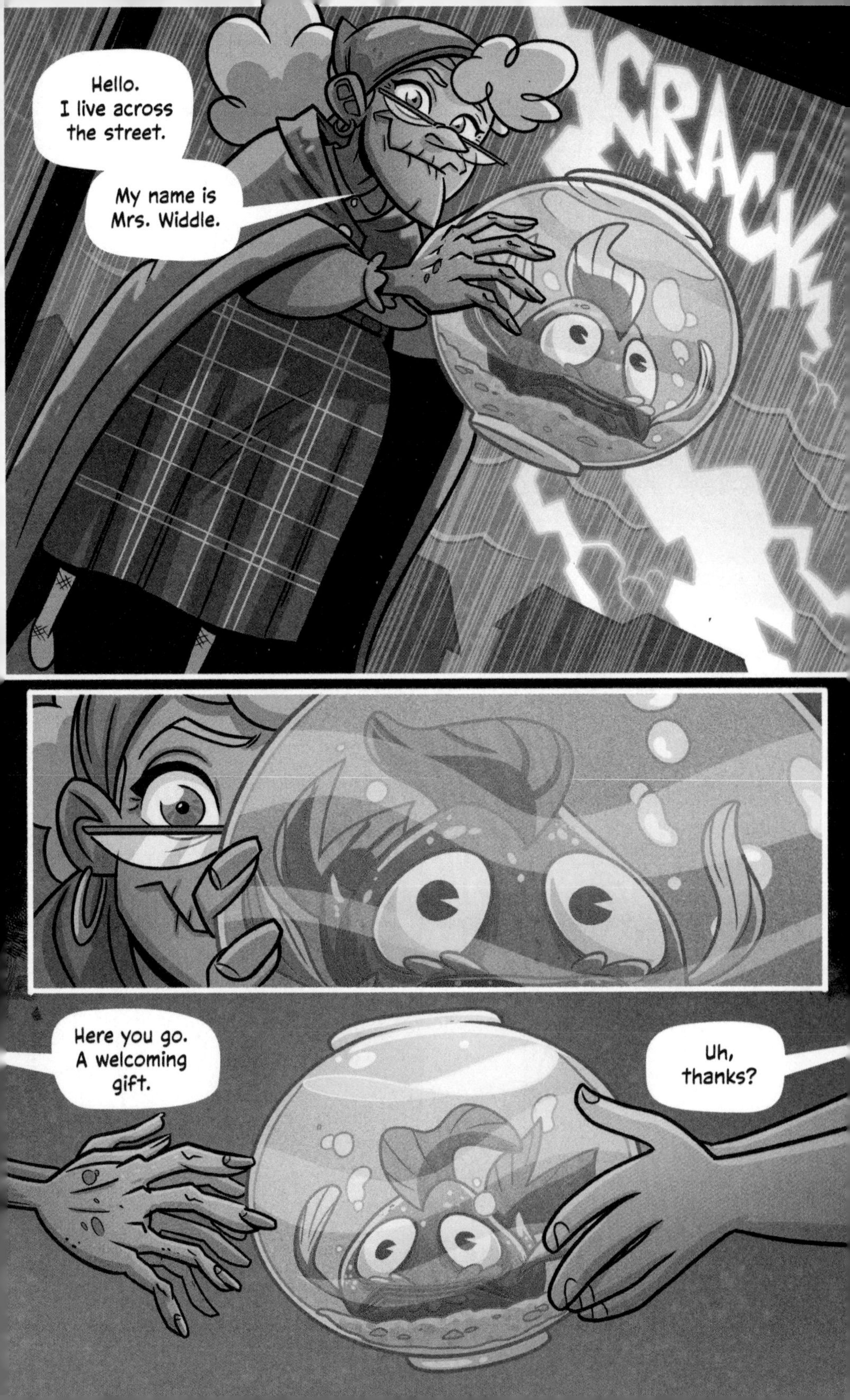
Hello. I live across the street.
My name is Mrs. Widdle.
CRACK!
Here you go. A welcoming gift.
Uh, thanks?

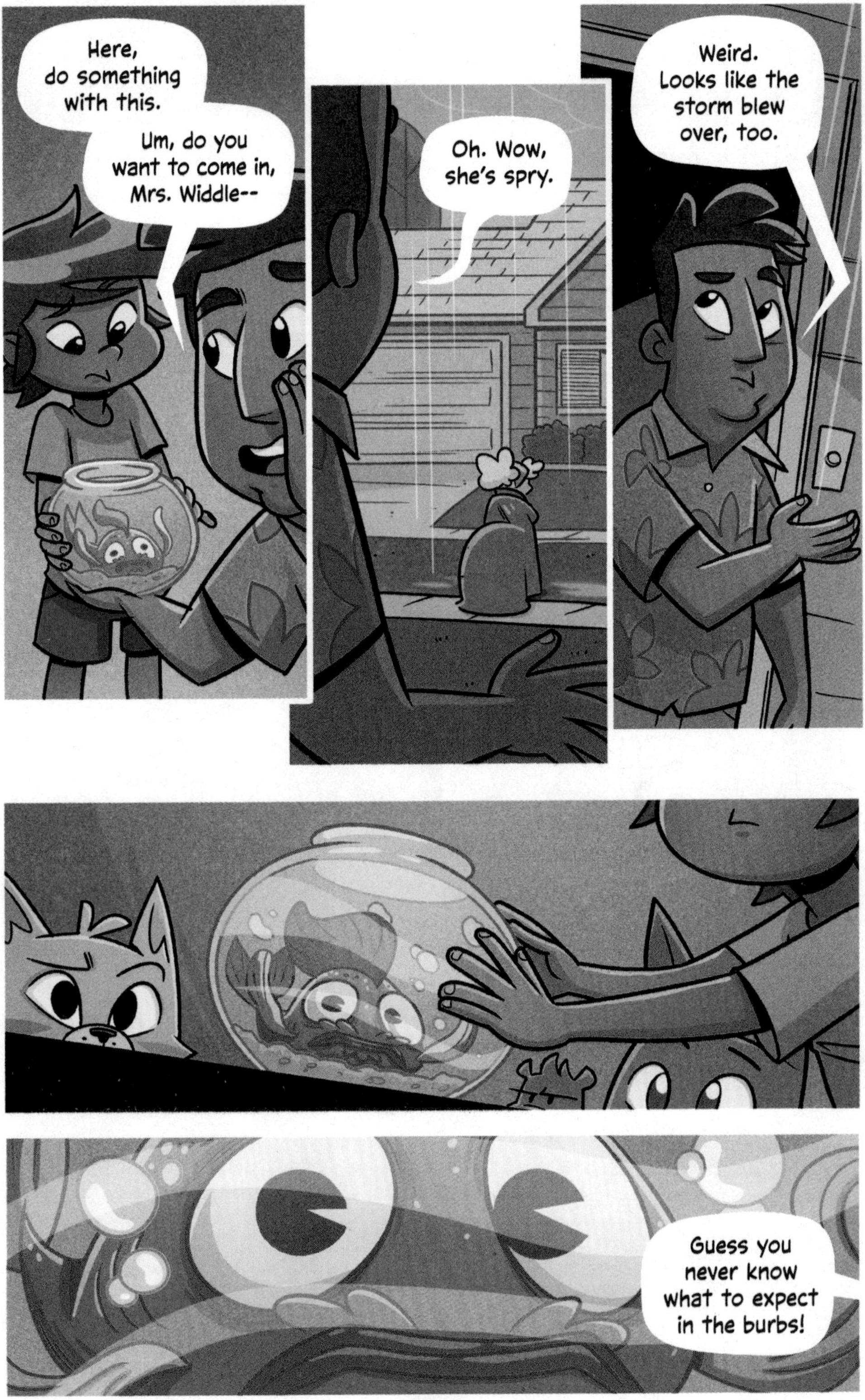
Here, do something with this.
Um, do you want to come in, Mrs. Widdle--
Oh. Wow, she's spry.
Weird. Looks like the storm blew over, too.
Guess you never know what to expect in the burbs!

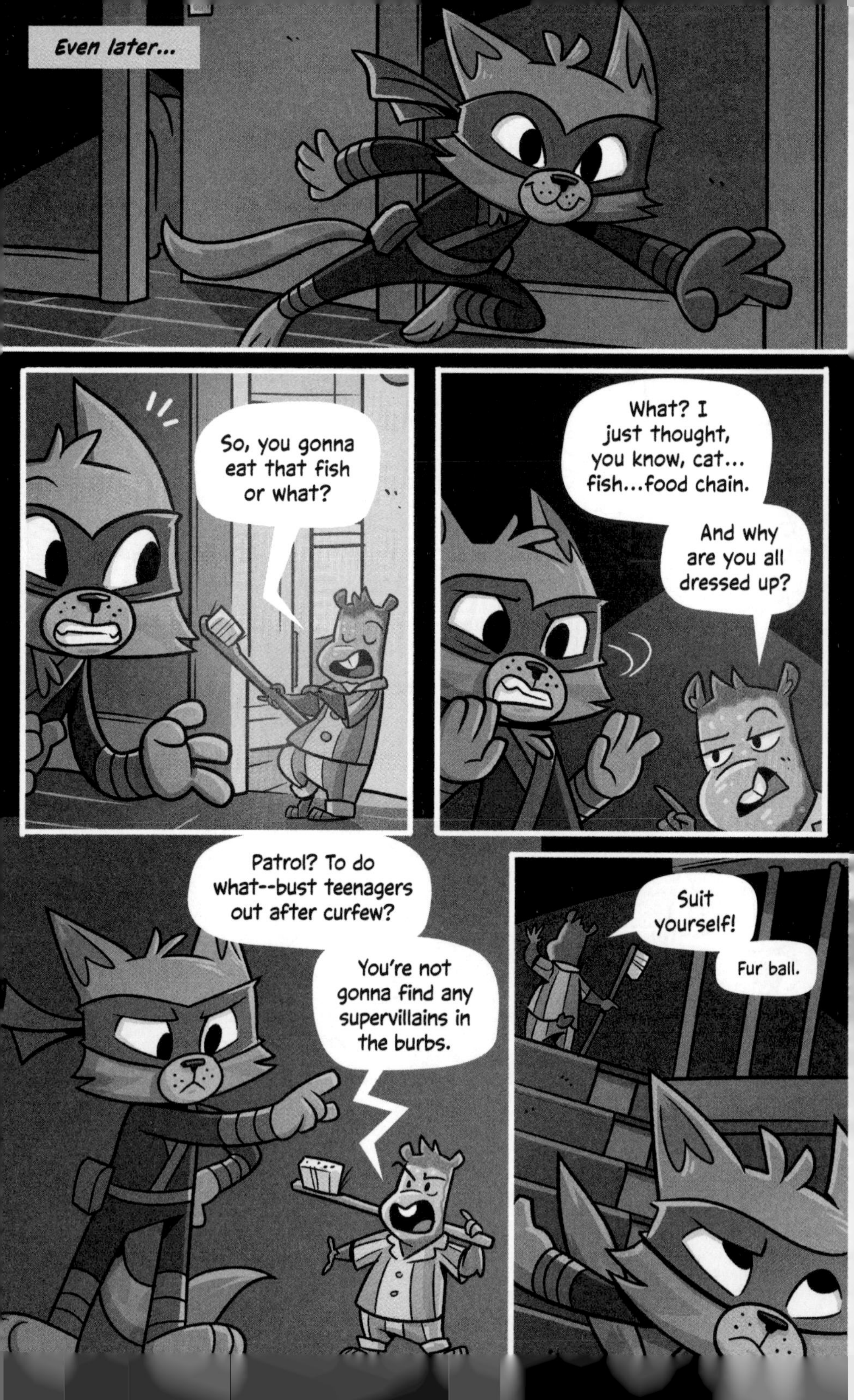
Even later...
So, you gonna eat that fish or what?
What? I just thought, you know, cat... fish...food chain.
And why are you all dressed up?
Patrol? To do what--bust teenagers out after curfew?
You're not gonna find any supervillains in the burbs.
Suit yourself!
Fur ball.

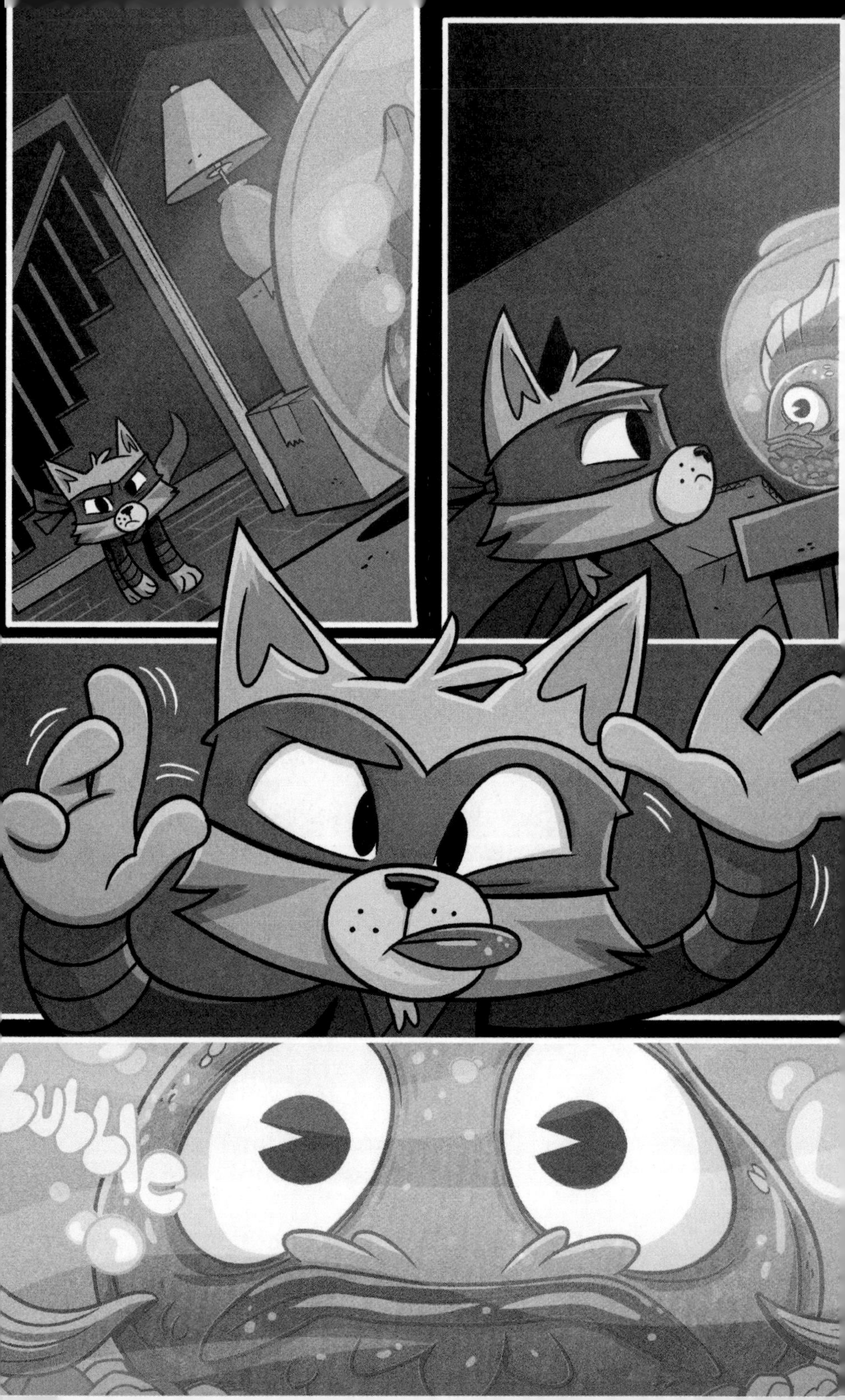
Bubble

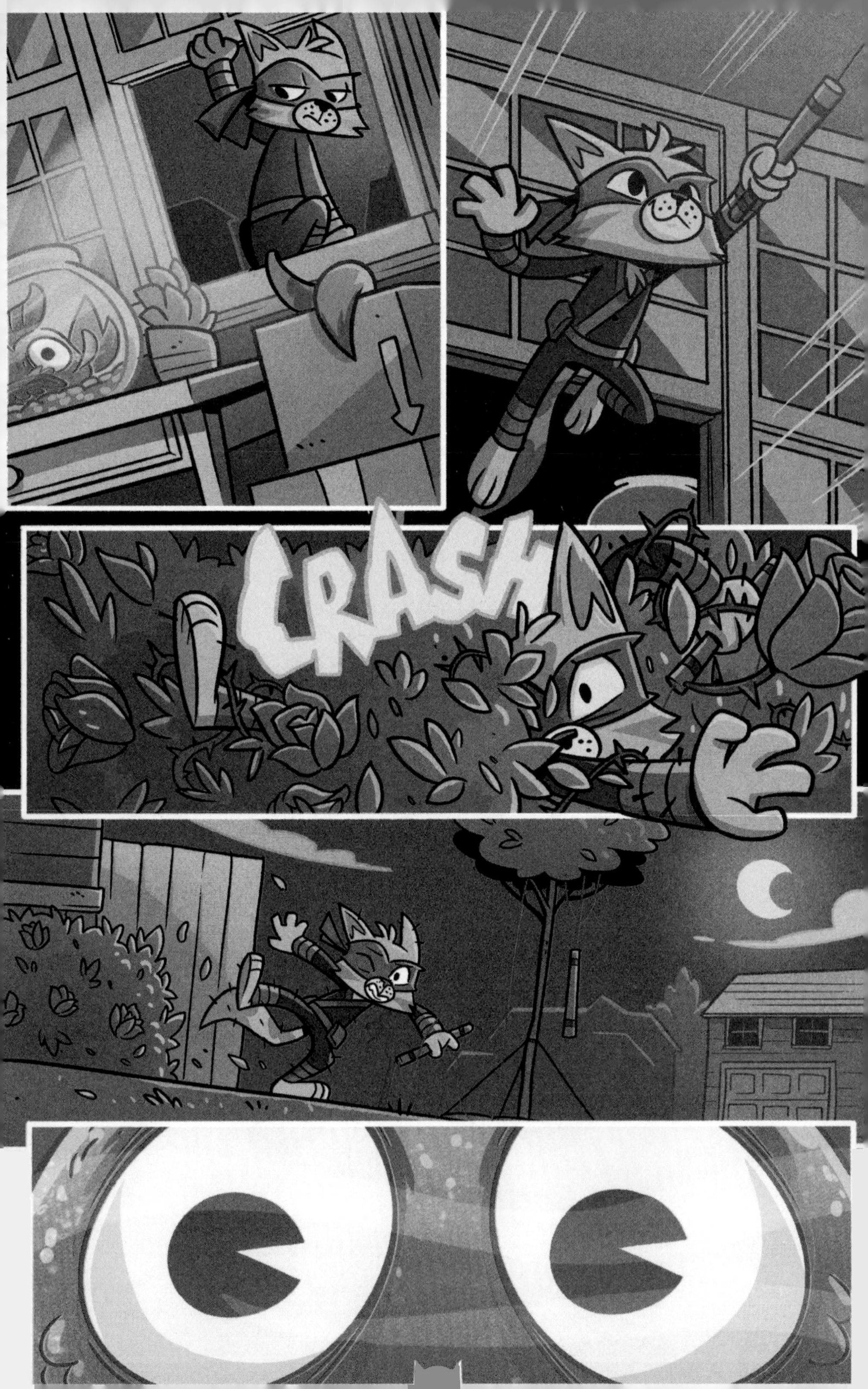
CRASH

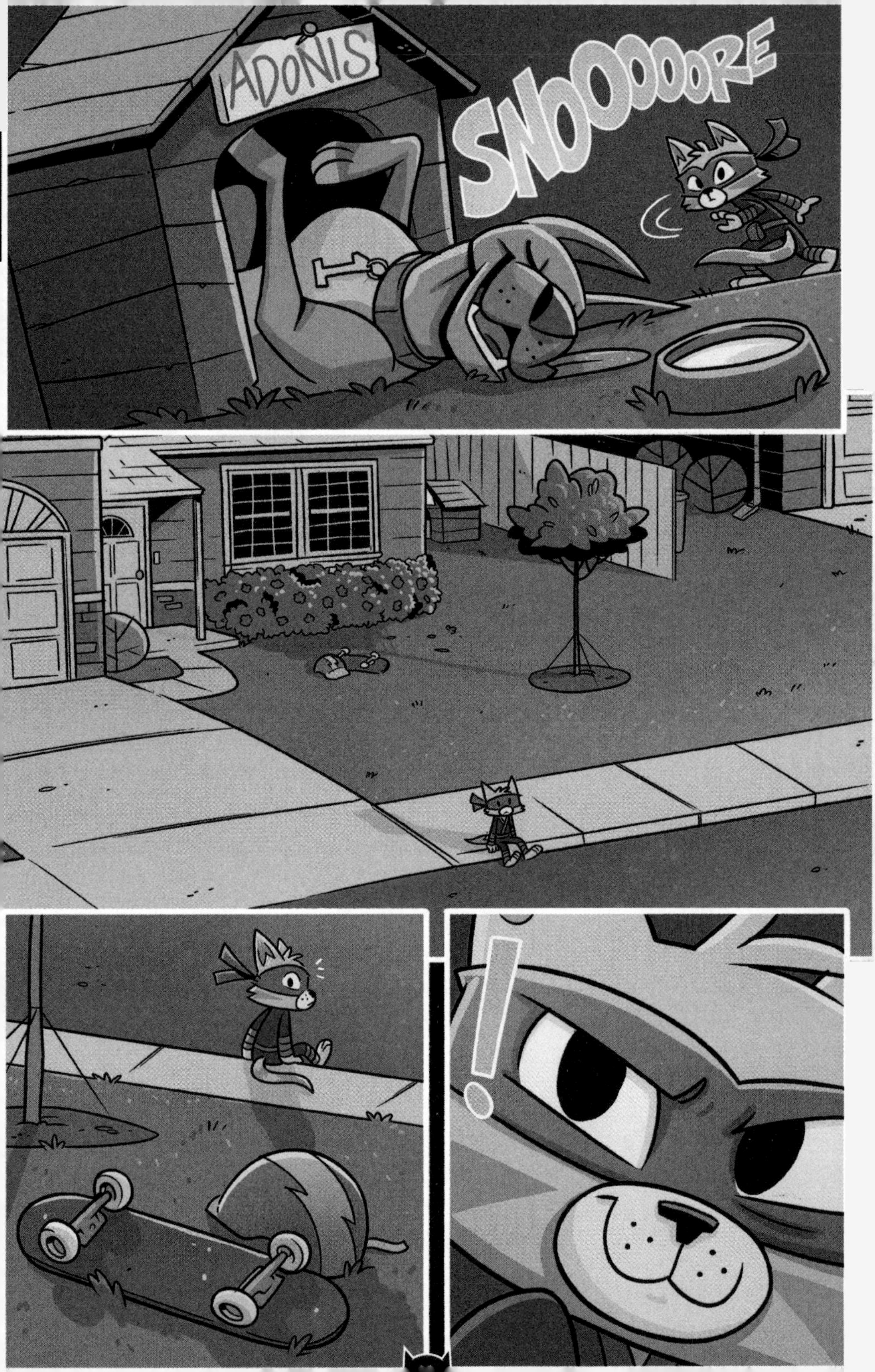
ADONIS
SNOOOOOORE
!

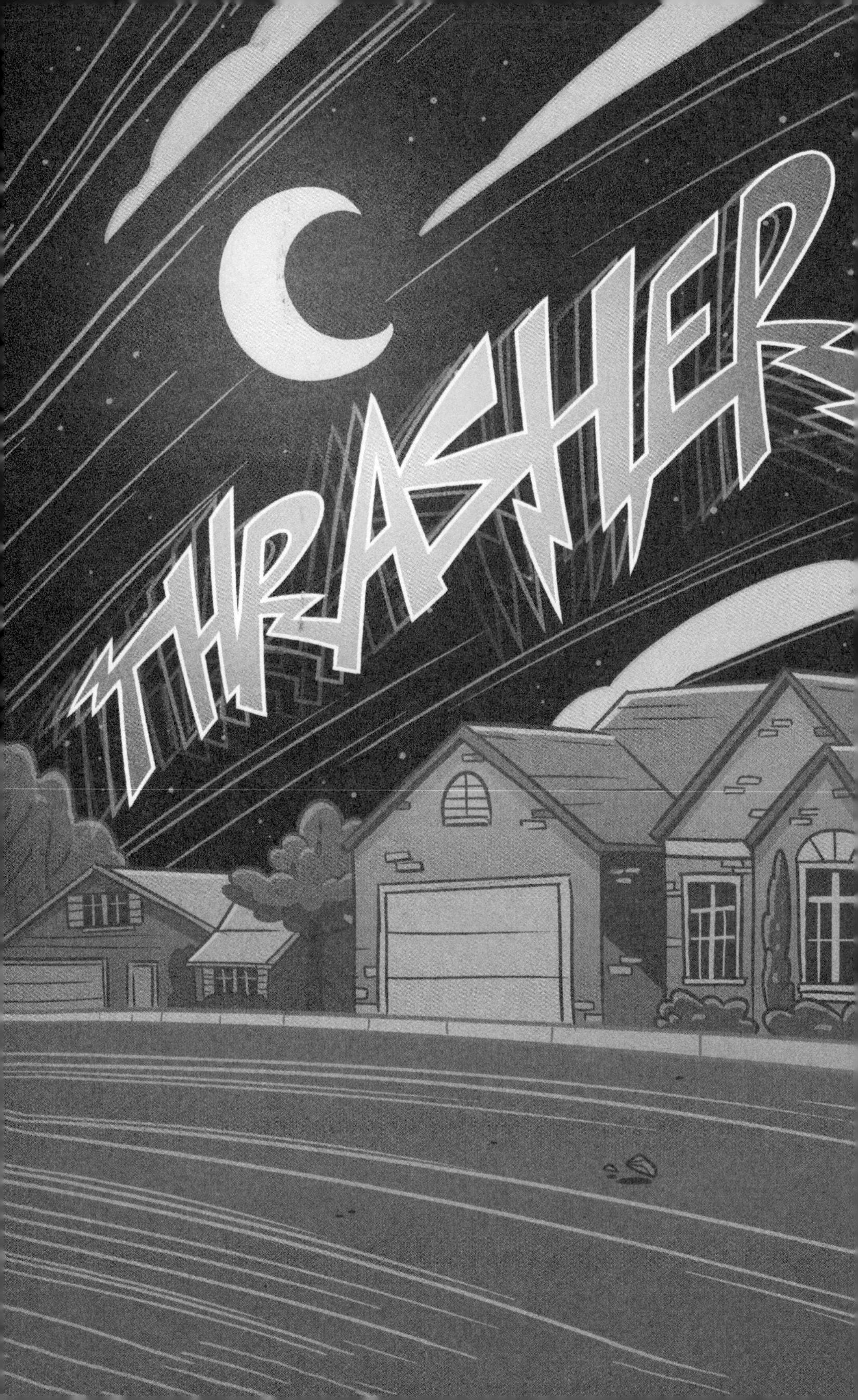
THRASHER

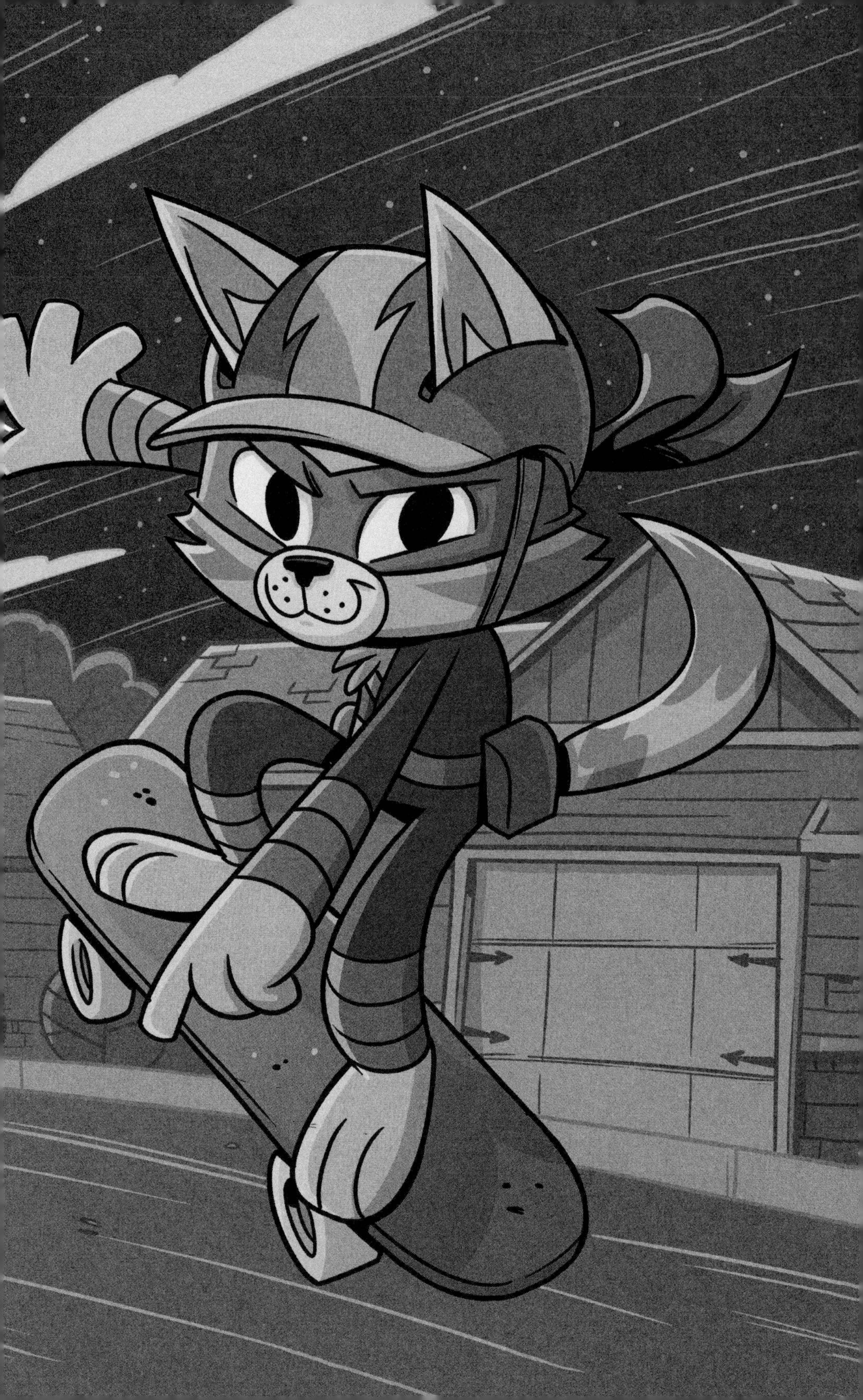

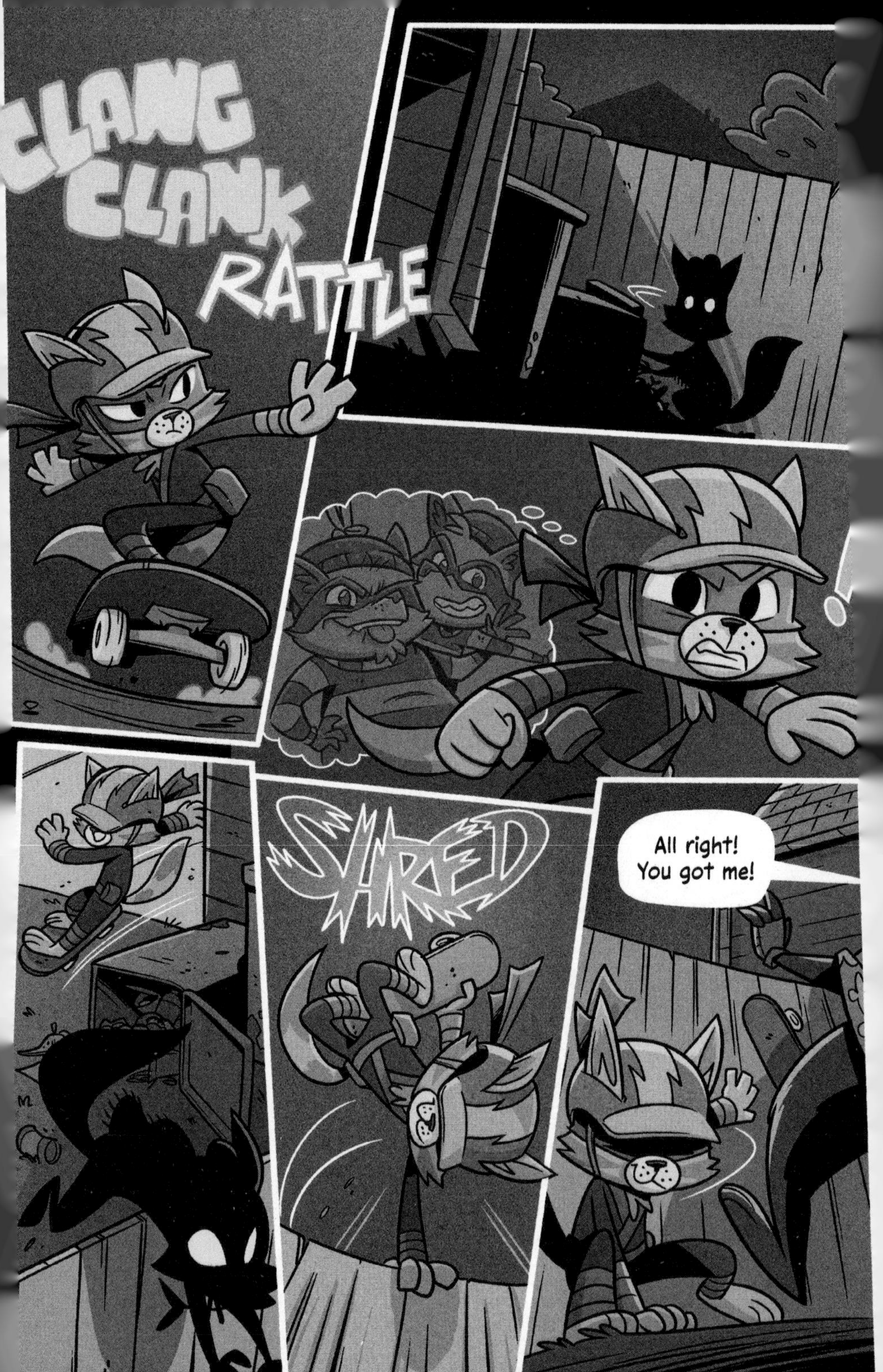
CLANG
CLANK
RATTLE
SHRED
All right!
You got me!

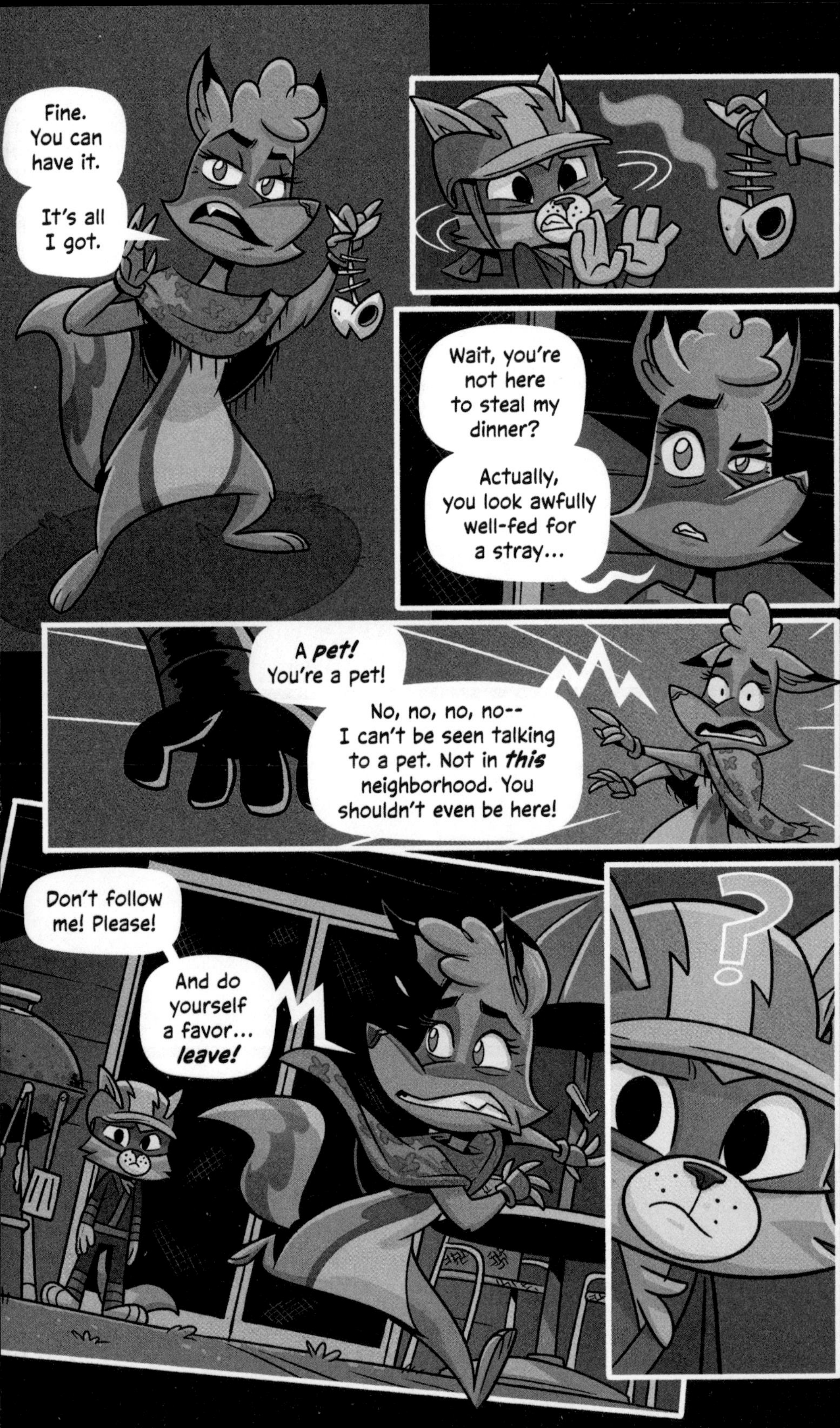
Fine. You can have it.
It's all I got.
Wait, you're not here to steal my dinner?
Actually, you look awfully well-fed for a stray...
A *pet!* You're a pet!
No, no, no, no-- I can't be seen talking to a pet. Not in *this* neighborhood. You shouldn't even be here!
Don't follow me! Please!
And do yourself a favor... *leave!*
?

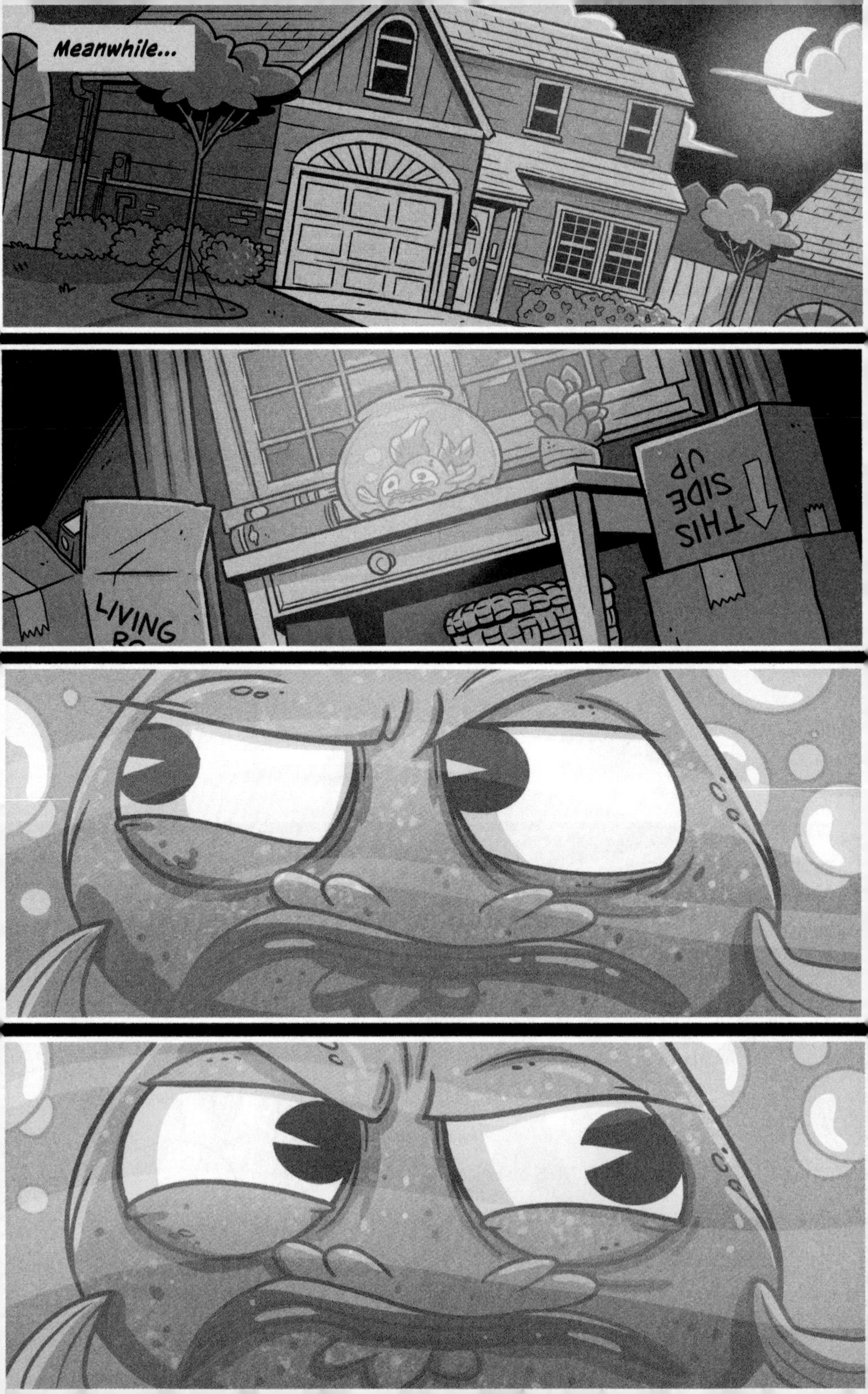
Meanwhile...
THIS SIDE UP
LIVING

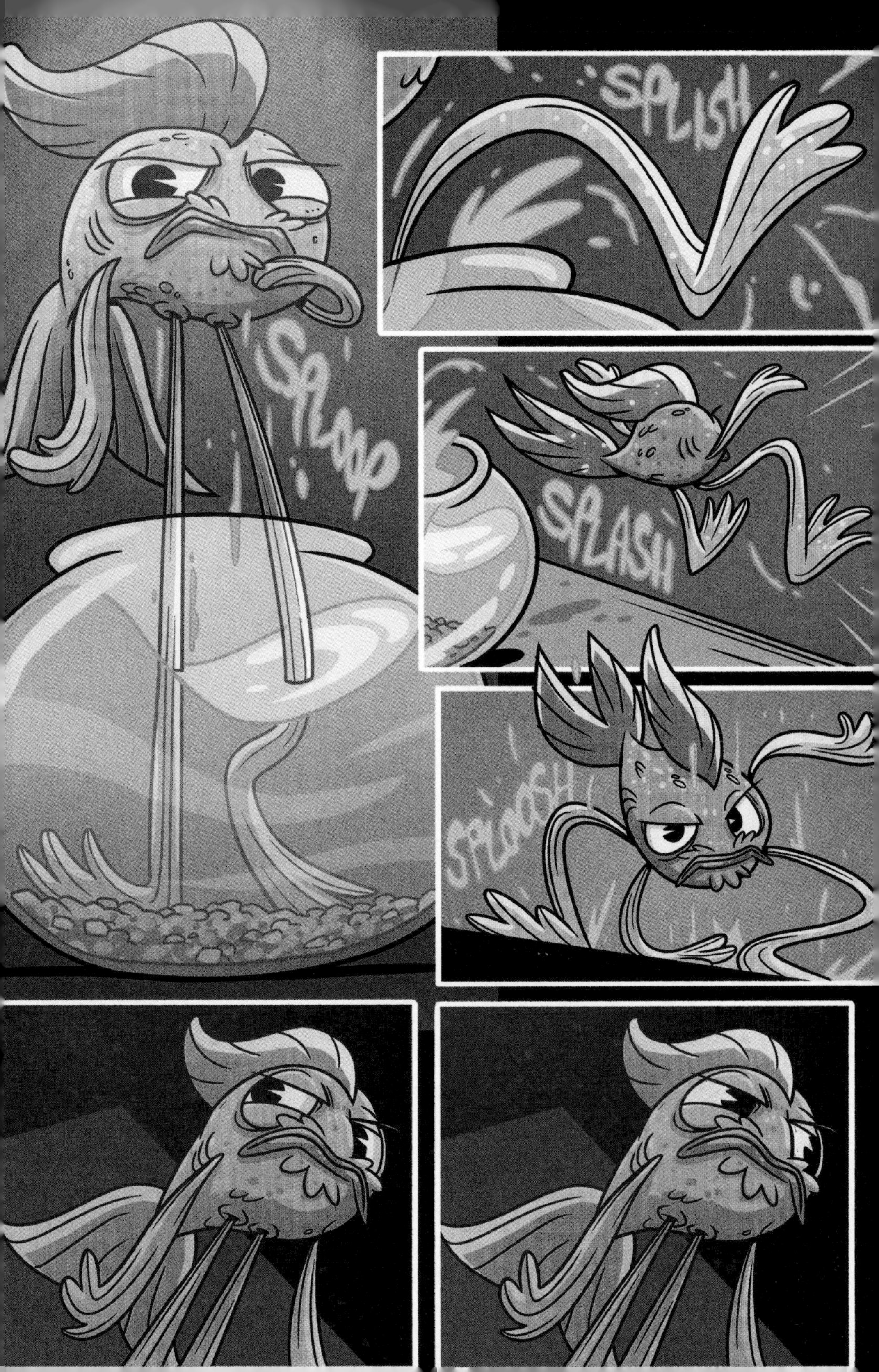
SPLOOP
SPLISH
SPLASH
SPLOOSH

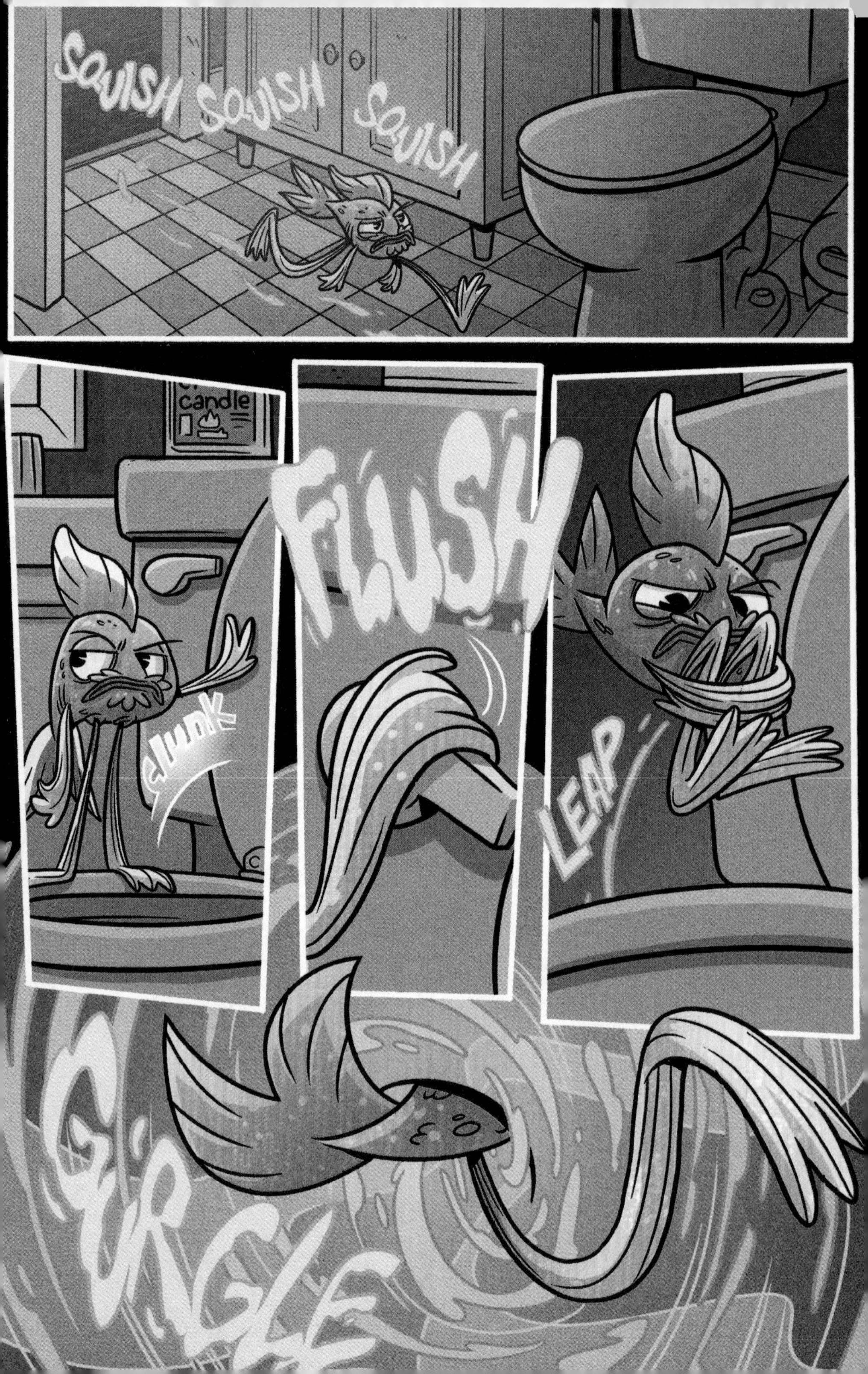
SQUISH SQUISH SQUISH
candle
CLUNK
FLUSH
LEAP
GURGLE

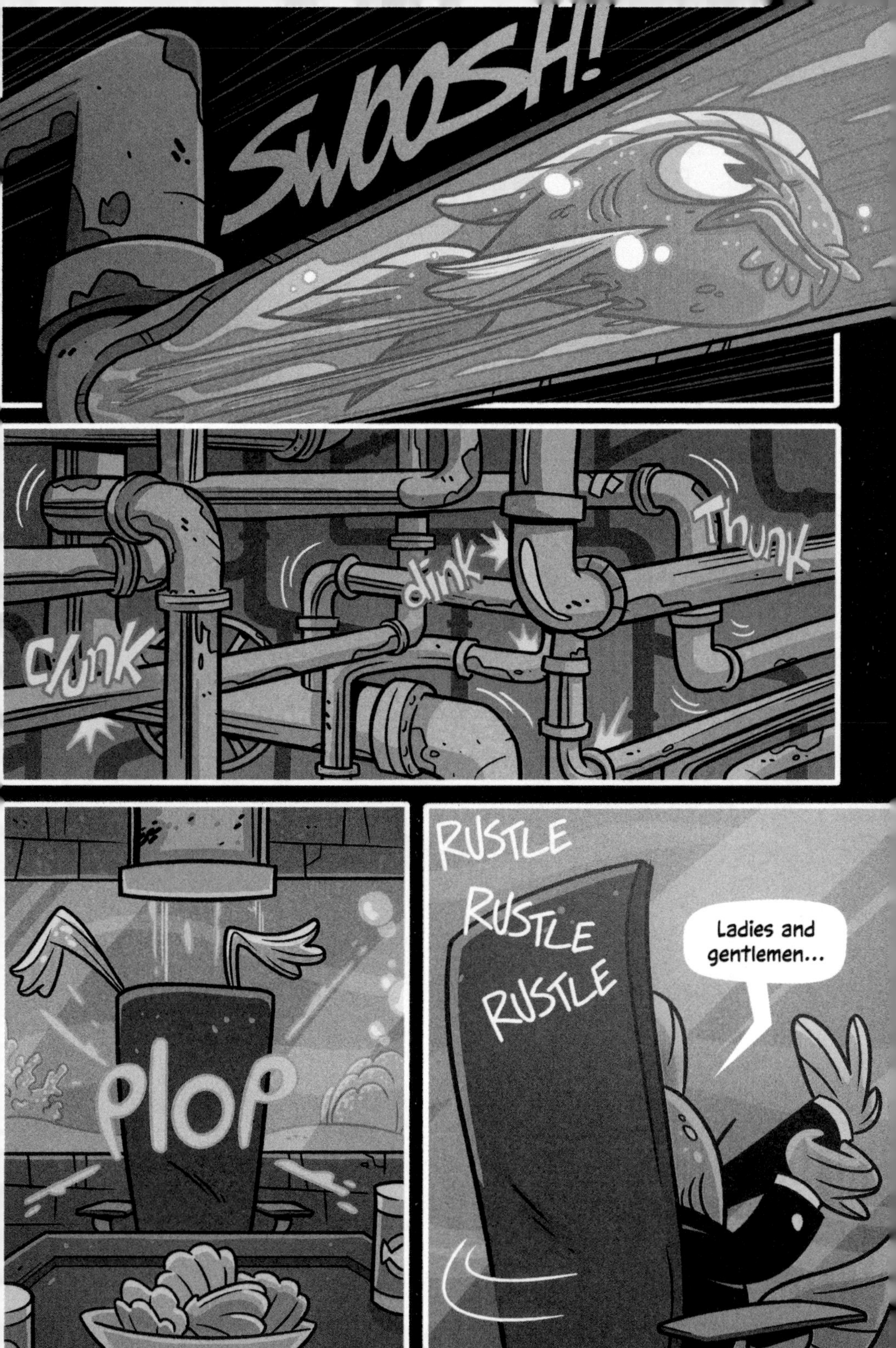
SWOOSH!
clunk
dink
thunk
plop
RUSTLE
RUSTLE
RUSTLE
Ladies and gentlemen...

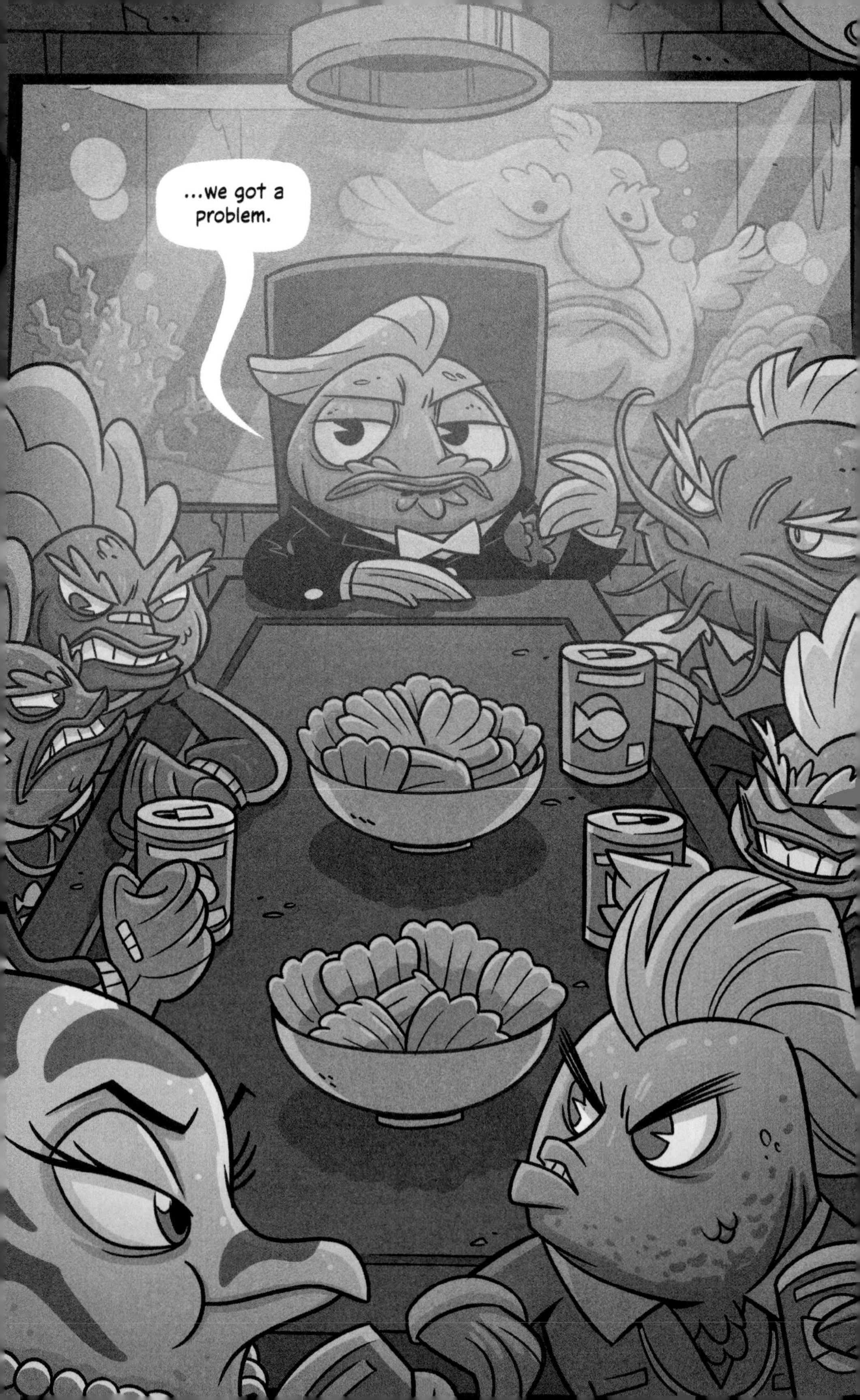
...we got a problem.

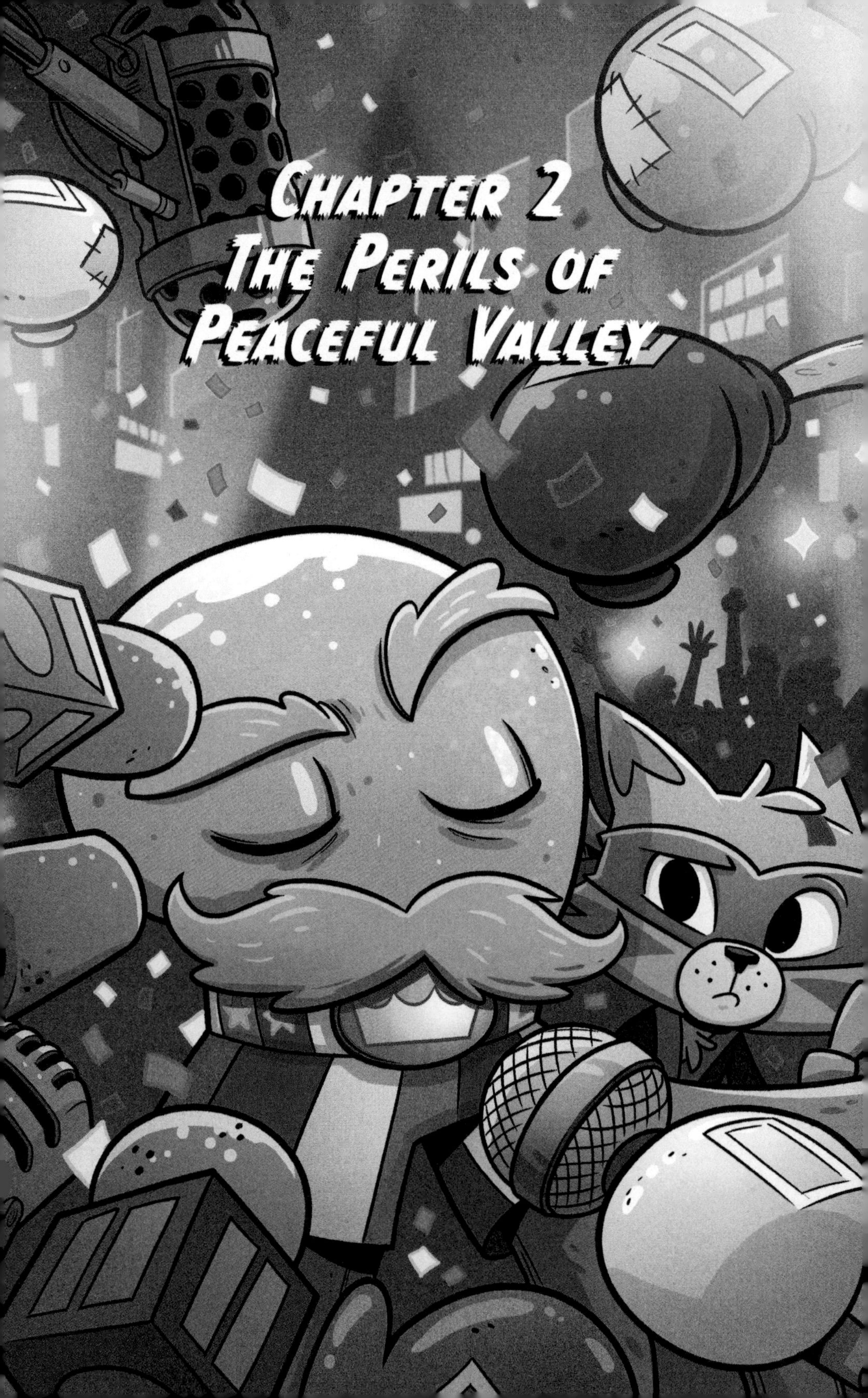
CHAPTER 2
THE PERILS OF
PEACEFUL VALLEY

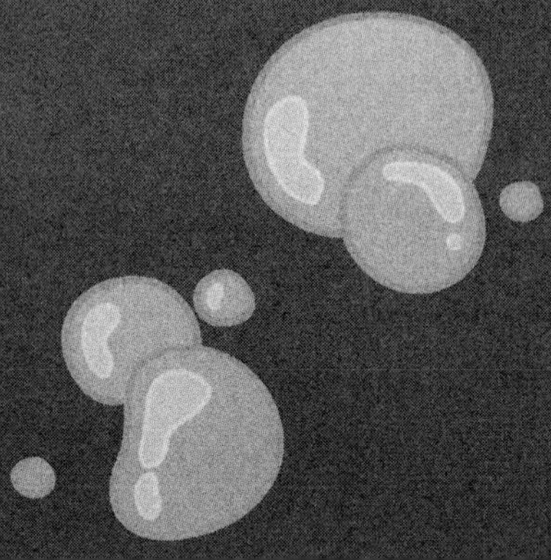

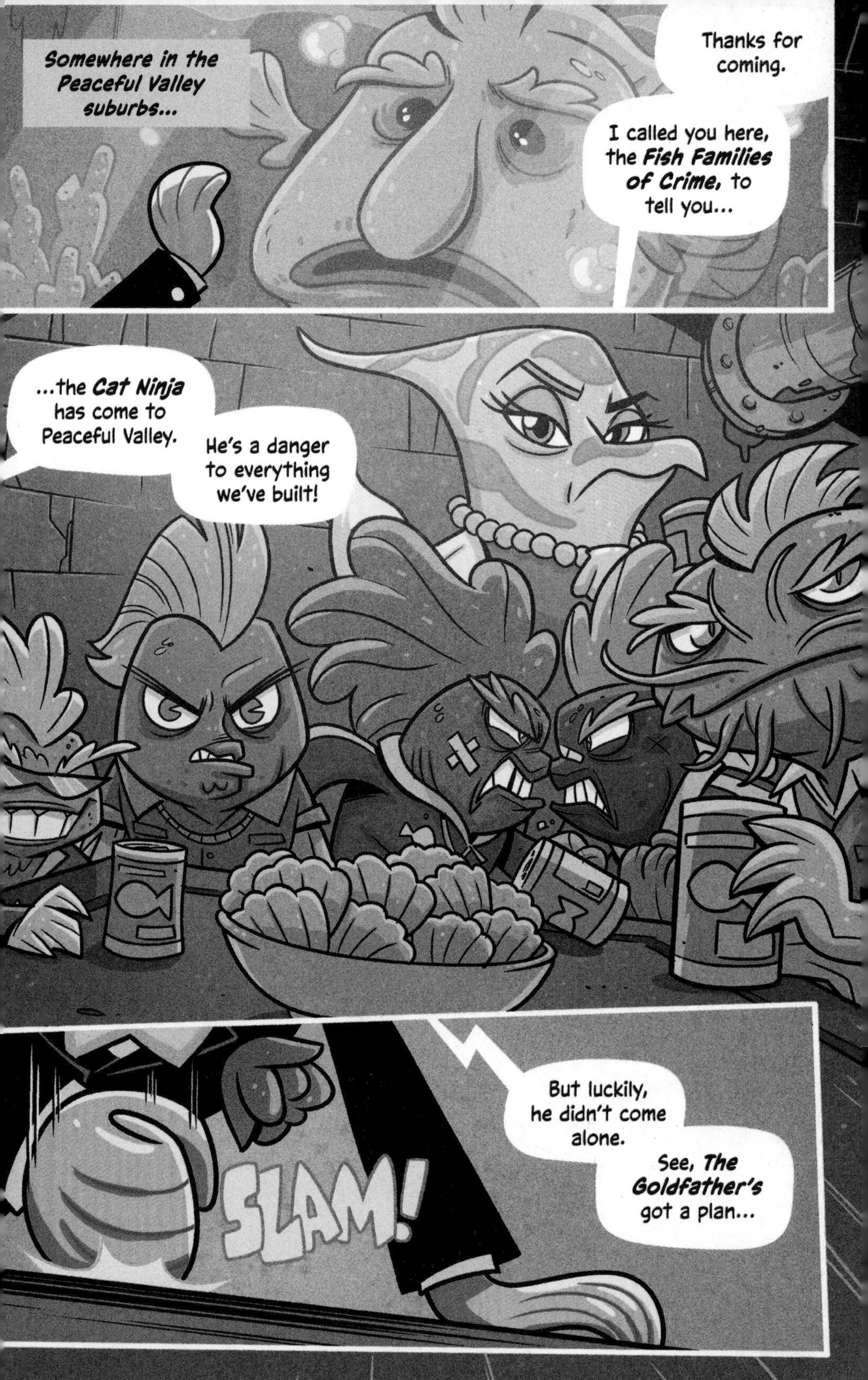
Somewhere in the Peaceful Valley suburbs...
Thanks for coming.
I called you here, the *Fish Families of Crime,* to tell you...
...the *Cat Ninja* has come to Peaceful Valley.
He's a danger to everything we've built!
SLAM!
But luckily, he didn't come alone.
See, *The Goldfather's* got a plan...

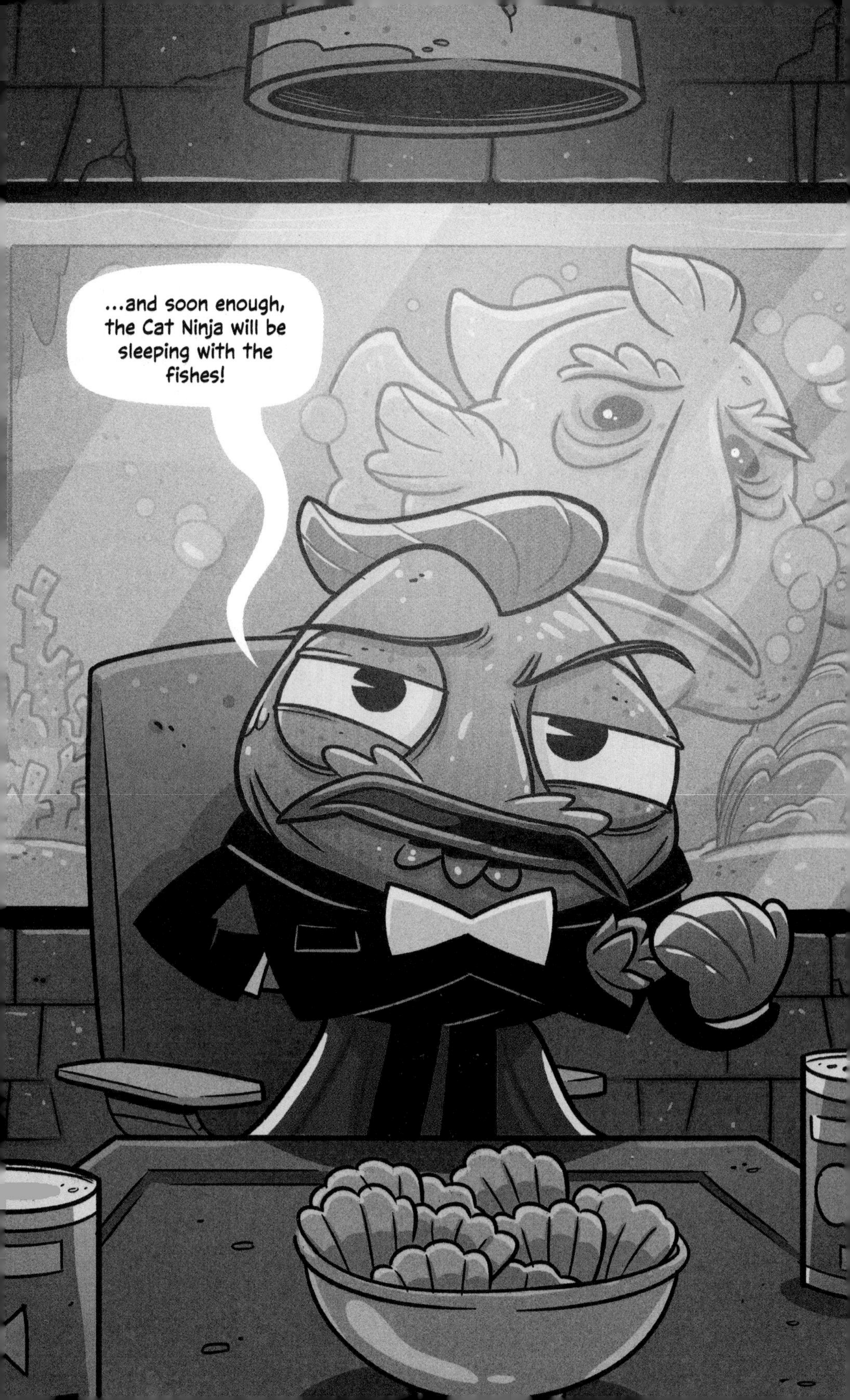
...and soon enough, the Cat Ninja will be sleeping with the fishes!

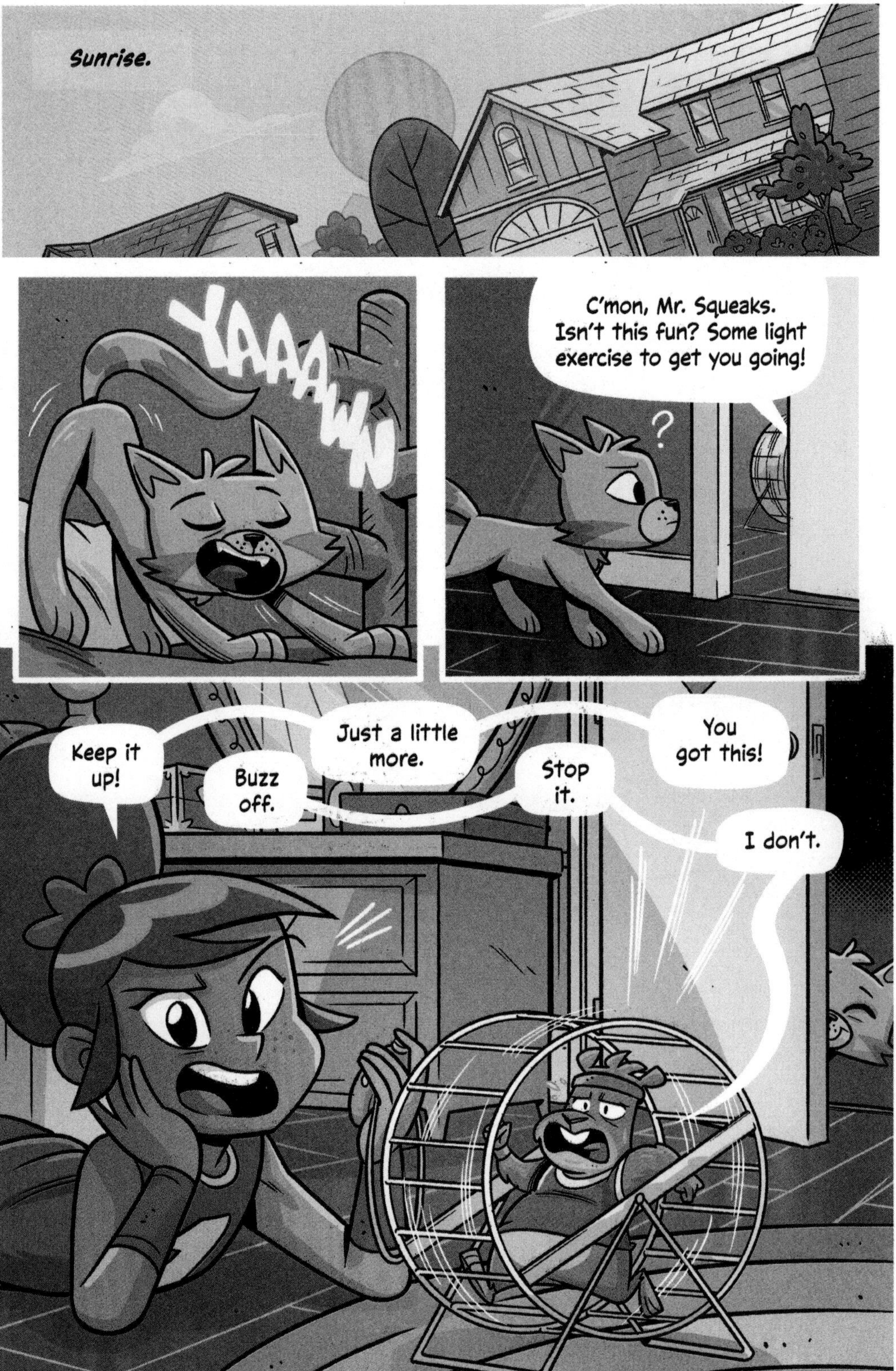
Sunrise.
YAAAWN
C'mon, Mr. Squeaks. Isn't this fun? Some light exercise to get you going!
?
Keep it up!
Buzz off.
Just a little more.
Stop it.
You got this!
I don't.

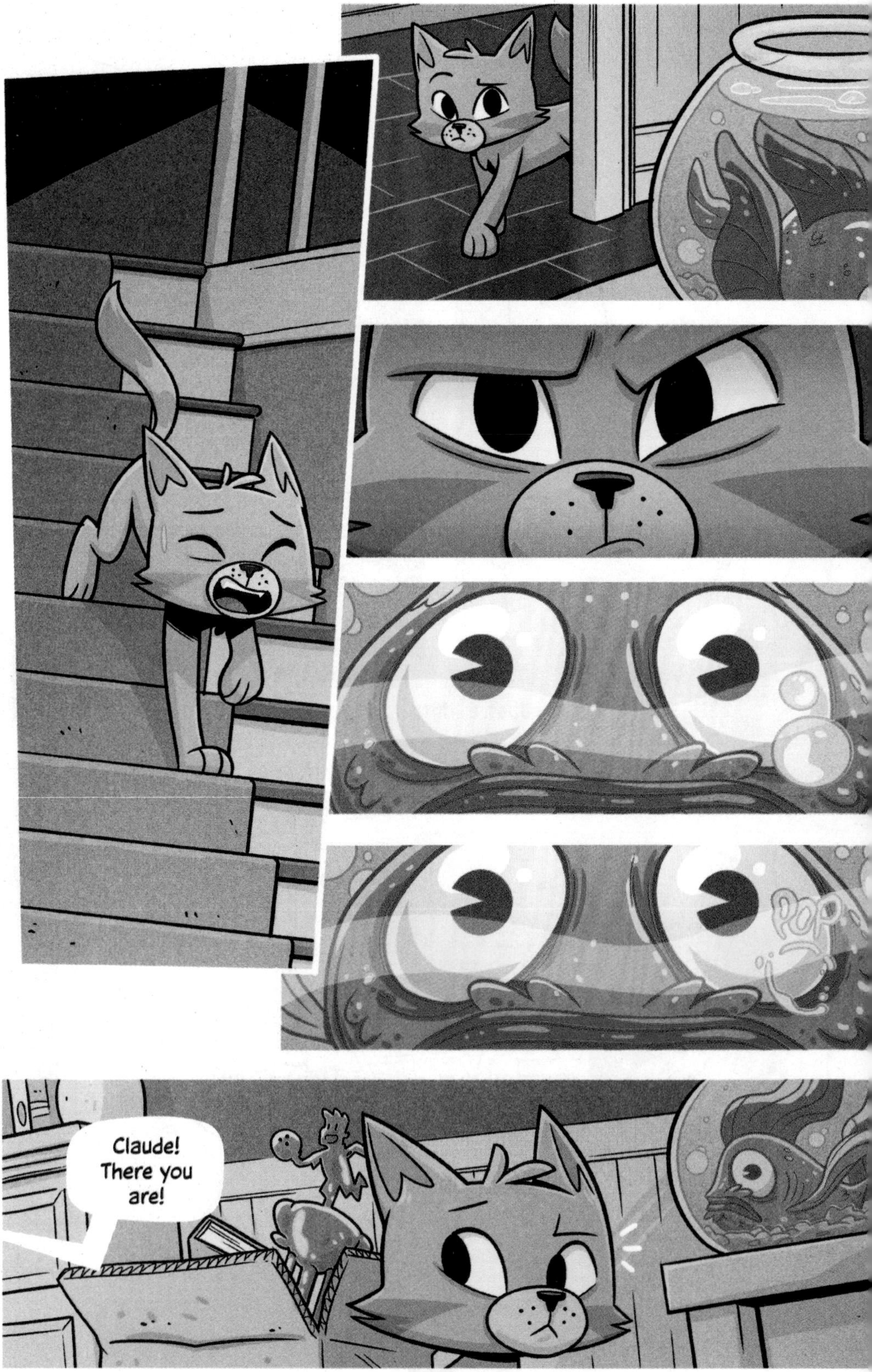
POP
Claude! There you are!

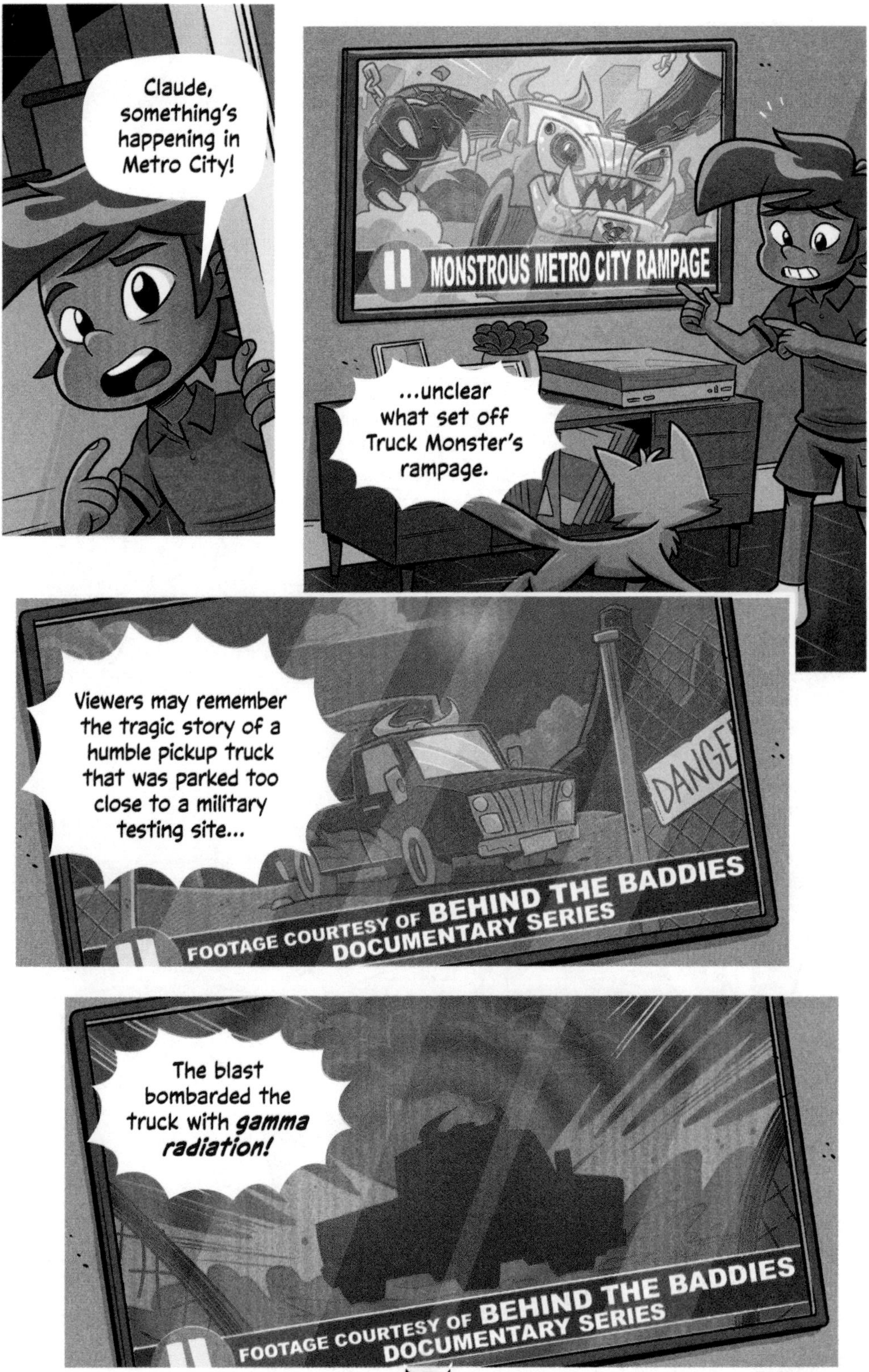
Claude, something's happening in Metro City!
MONSTROUS METRO CITY RAMPAGE
...unclear what set off Truck Monster's rampage.
Viewers may remember the tragic story of a humble pickup truck that was parked too close to a military testing site...
DANGE
FOOTAGE COURTESY OF BEHIND THE BADDIES DOCUMENTARY SERIES
The blast bombarded the truck with *gamma radiation!*
FOOTAGE COURTESY OF BEHIND THE BADDIES DOCUMENTARY SERIES

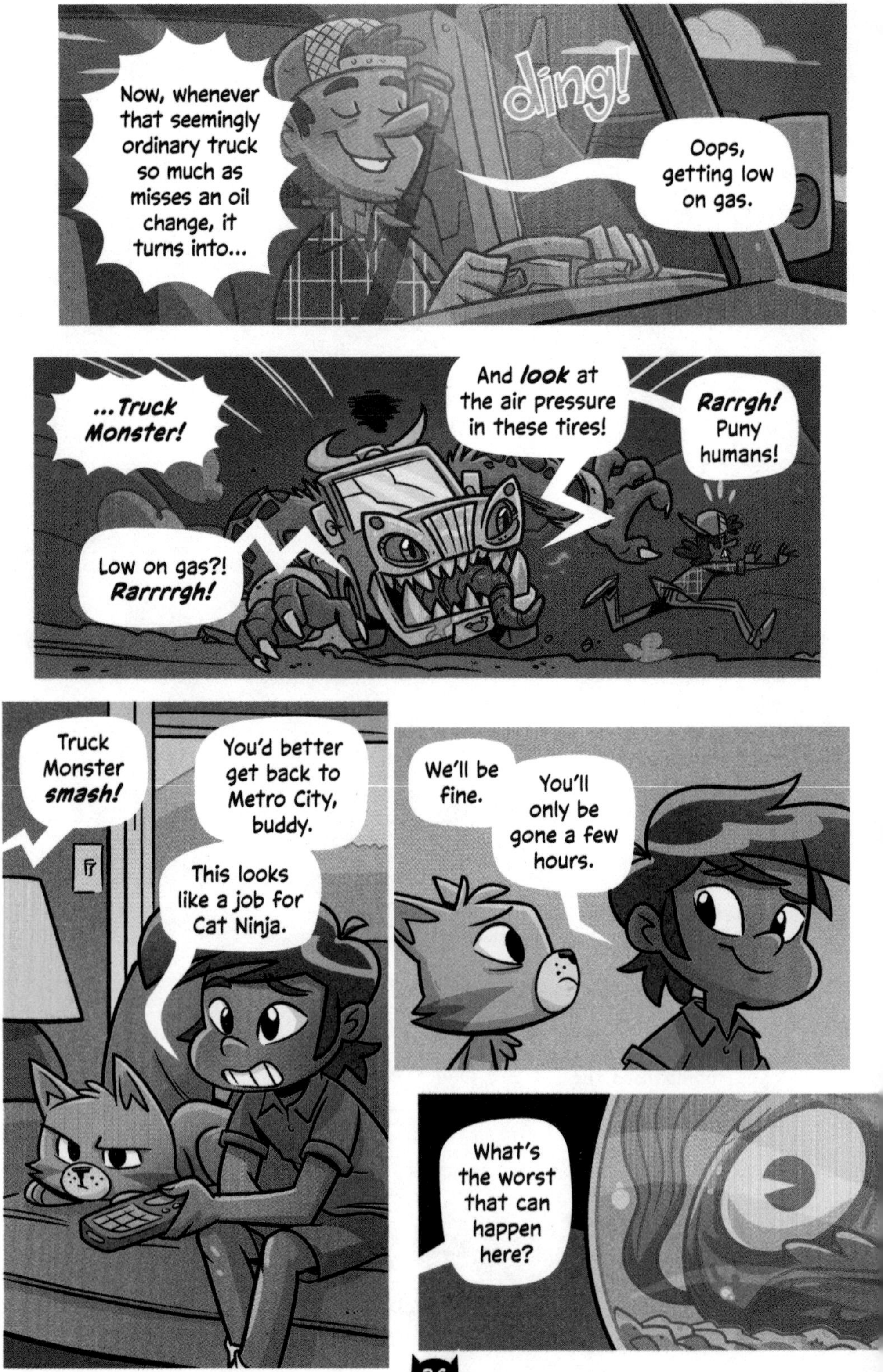

Now, whenever that seemingly ordinary truck so much as misses an oil change, it turns into...
ding!
Oops, getting low on gas.
...Truck Monster!
Low on gas?! Rarrrrgh!
And look at the air pressure in these tires!
Rarrgh! Puny humans!
Truck Monster smash!
You'd better get back to Metro City, buddy.
This looks like a job for Cat Ninja.
We'll be fine.
You'll only be gone a few hours.
What's the worst that can happen here?

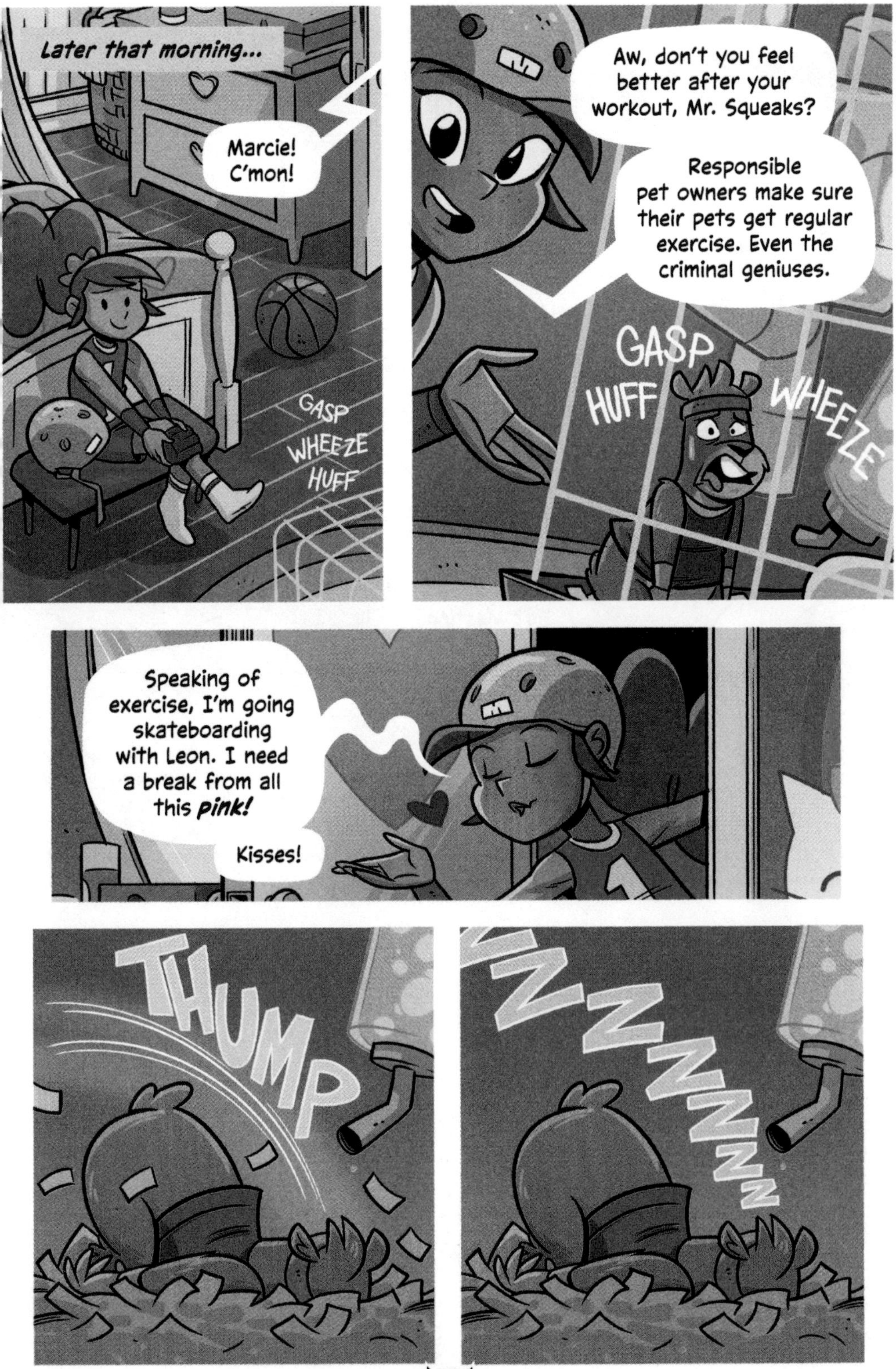
Later that morning...
Marcie! C'mon!
GASP
WHEEZE
HUFF
Aw, don't you feel better after your workout, Mr. Squeaks?
Responsible pet owners make sure their pets get regular exercise. Even the criminal geniuses.
GASP
HUFF
WHEEZE
Speaking of exercise, I'm going skateboarding with Leon. I need a break from all this *pink!*
Kisses!
THUMP
ZZZZZZZZ

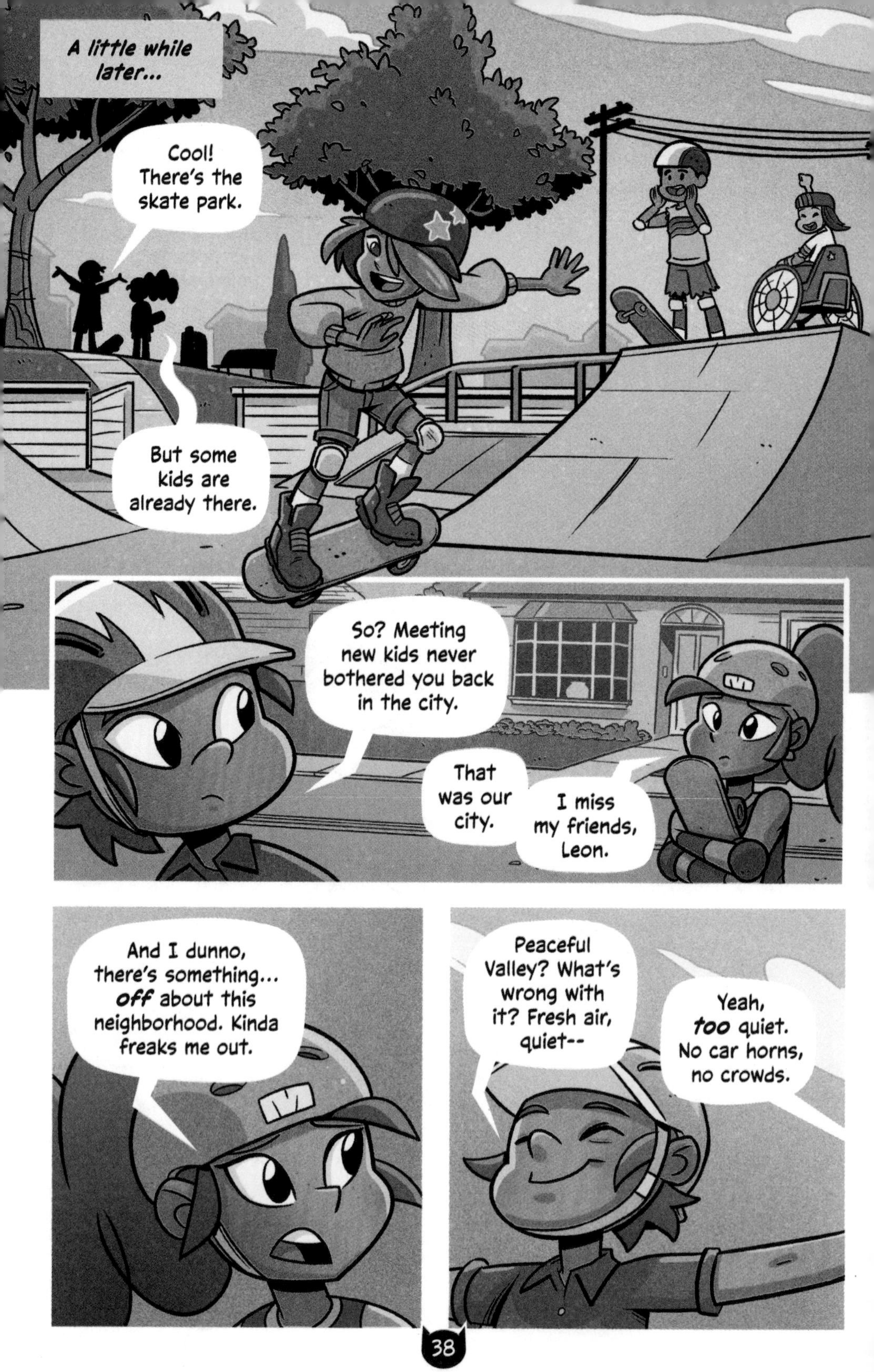
A little while later...
Cool! There's the skate park.
But some kids are already there.
So? Meeting new kids never bothered you back in the city.
That was our city.
I miss my friends, Leon.
And I dunno, there's something... *off* about this neighborhood. Kinda freaks me out.
Peaceful Valley? What's wrong with it? Fresh air, quiet--
Yeah, *too* quiet. No car horns, no crowds.

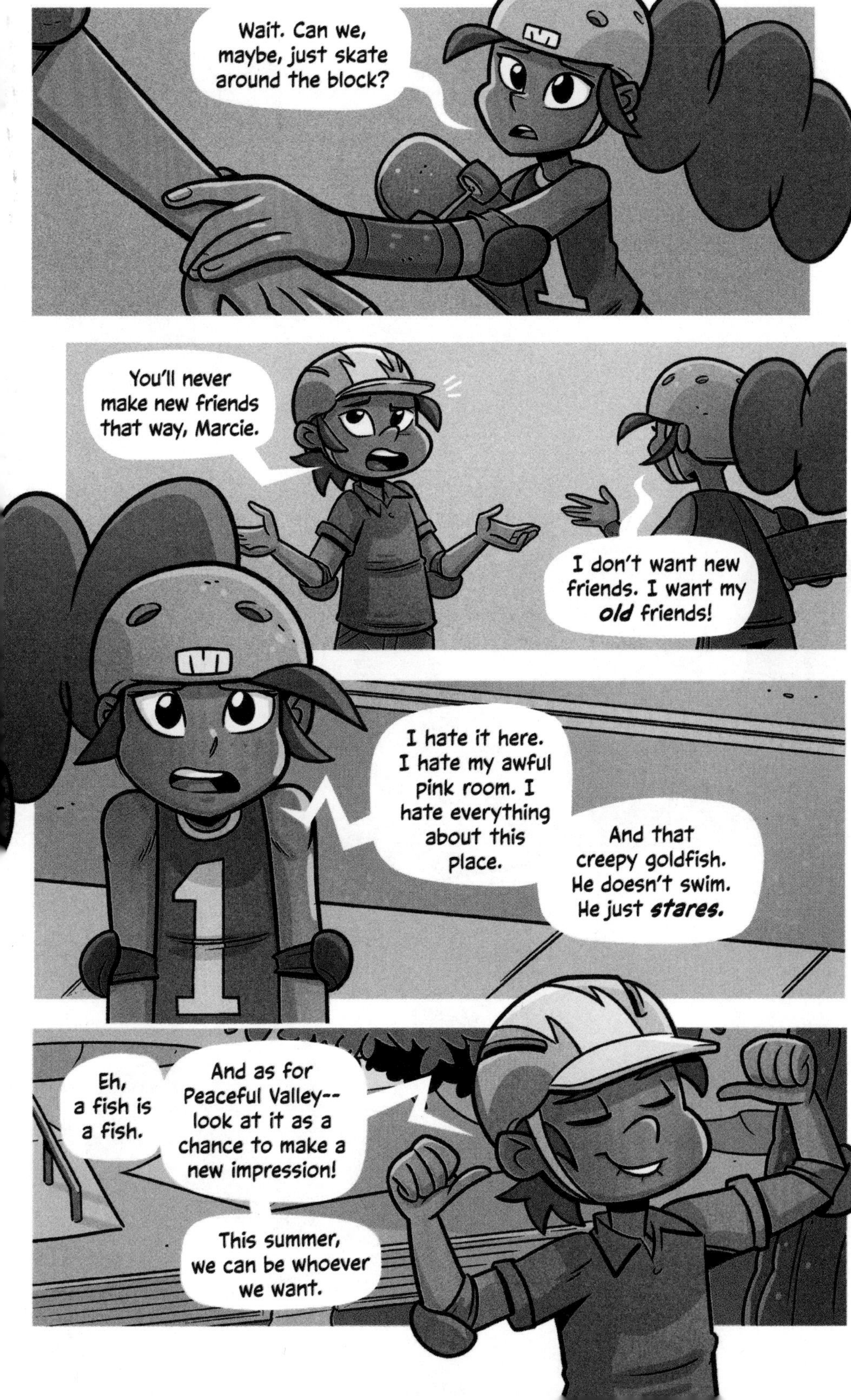
Wait. Can we, maybe, just skate around the block?
You'll never make new friends that way, Marcie.
I don't want new friends. I want my *old* friends!
I hate it here. I hate my awful pink room. I hate everything about this place.
And that creepy goldfish. He doesn't swim. He just **stares.**
Eh, a fish is a fish.
And as for Peaceful Valley-- look at it as a chance to make a new impression!
This summer, we can be whoever we want.

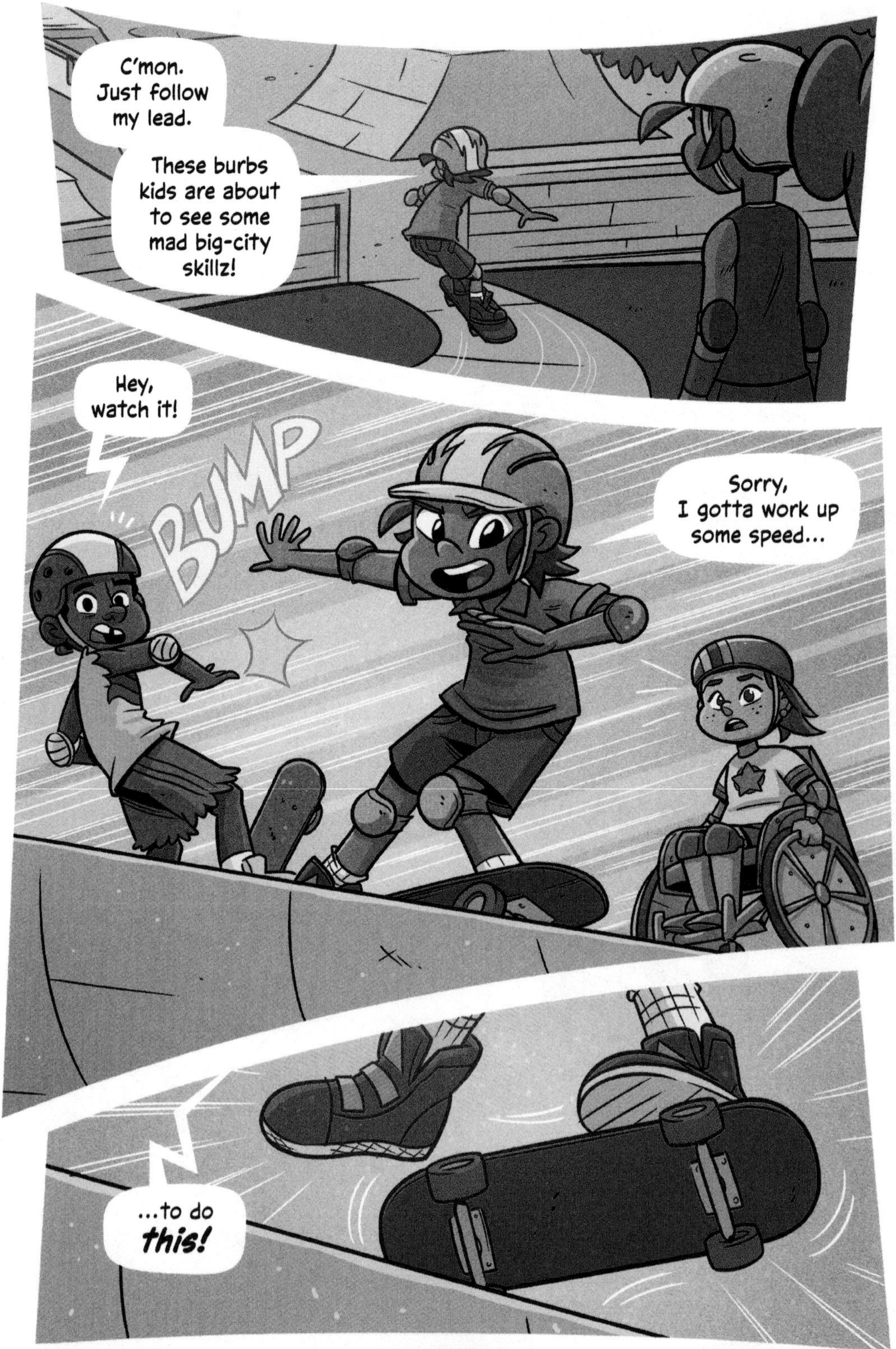
C'mon. Just follow my lead.
These burbs kids are about to see some mad big-city skillz!
Hey, watch it!
BUMP
Sorry, I gotta work up some speed...
...to do *this!*

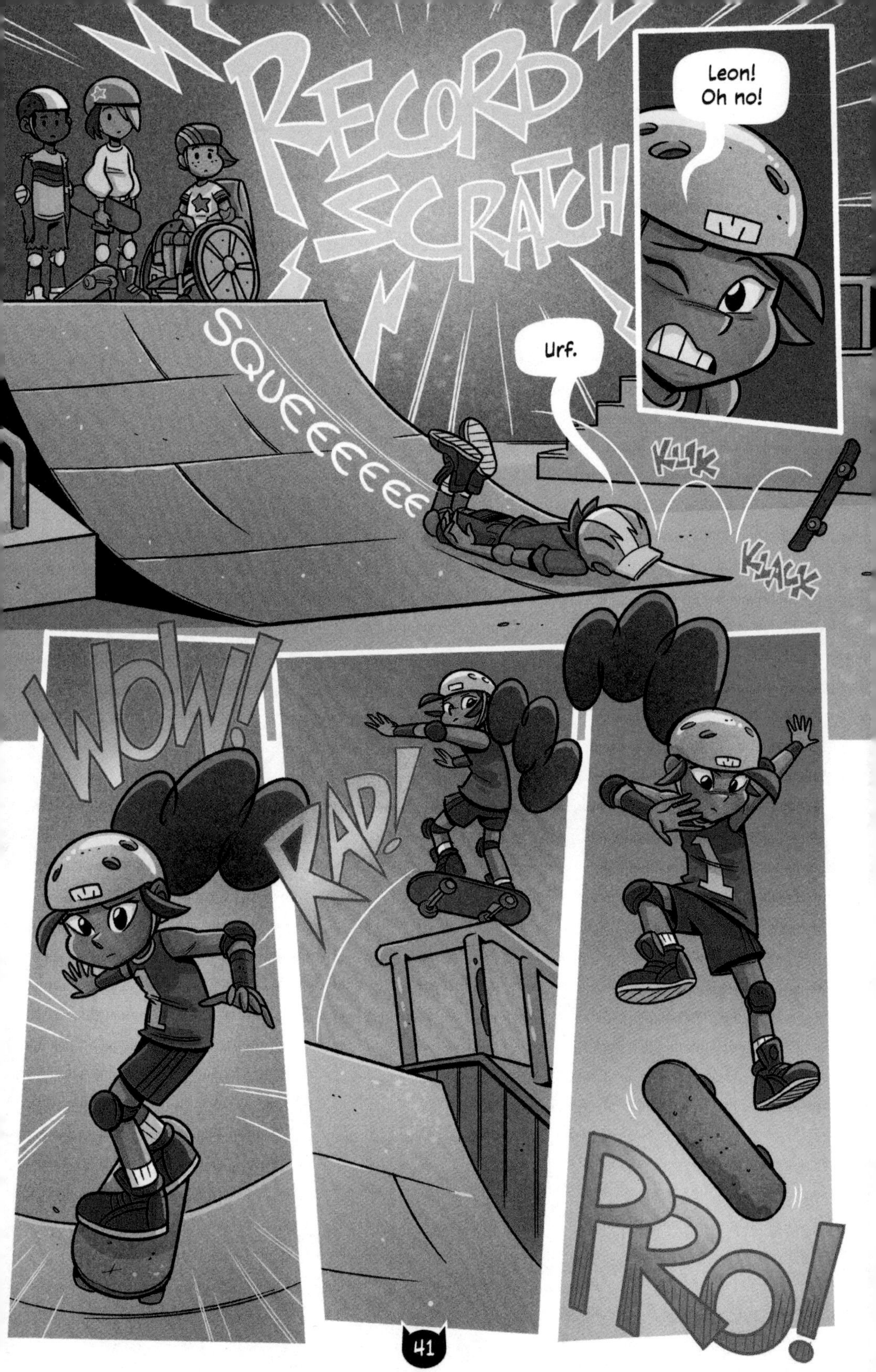
RECORD SCRATCH
Leon!
Oh no!
SQUEEEEEEE
Urf.
KLIK
KLACK
WOW!
RAD!
PRO!

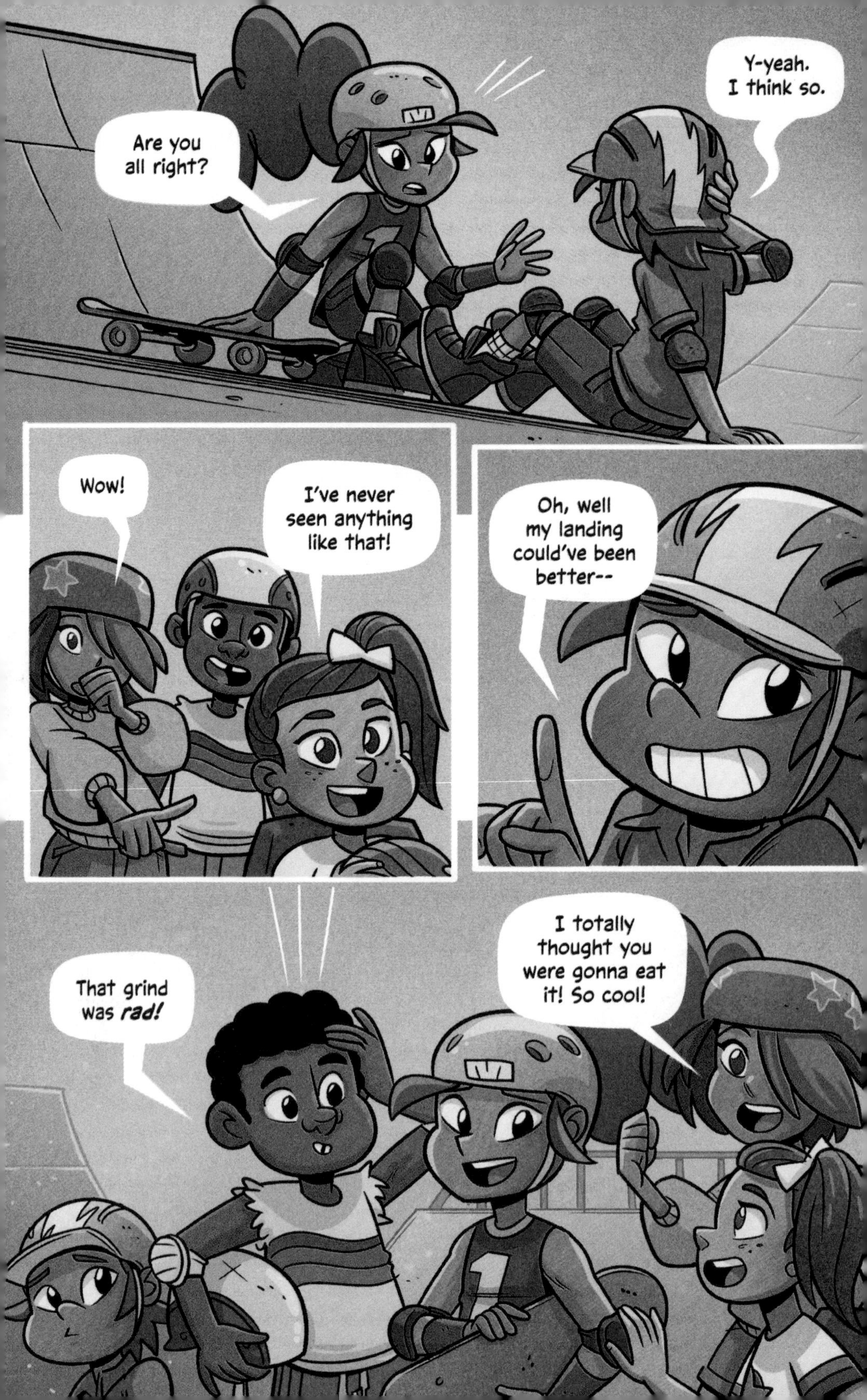
Are you all right?
Y-yeah. I think so.
Wow!
I've never seen anything like that!
Oh, well my landing could've been better--
That grind was *rad!*
I totally thought you were gonna eat it! So cool!

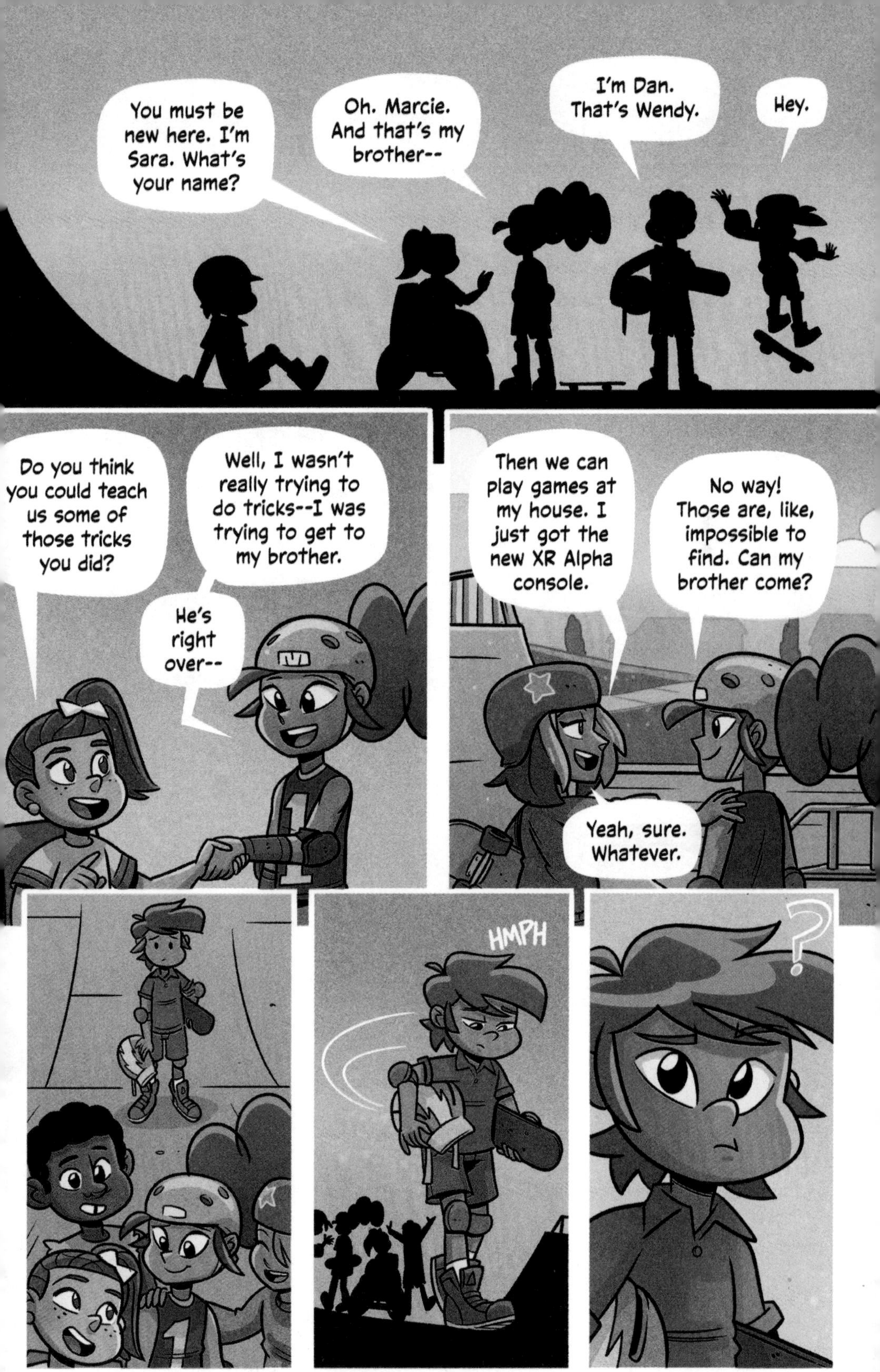
You must be new here. I'm Sara. What's your name?
Oh. Marcie. And that's my brother--
I'm Dan. That's Wendy.
Hey.
Do you think you could teach us some of those tricks you did?
Well, I wasn't really trying to do tricks--I was trying to get to my brother.
He's right over--
Then we can play games at my house. I just got the new XR Alpha console.
No way! Those are, like, impossible to find. Can my brother come?
Yeah, sure. Whatever.
HMPH
?

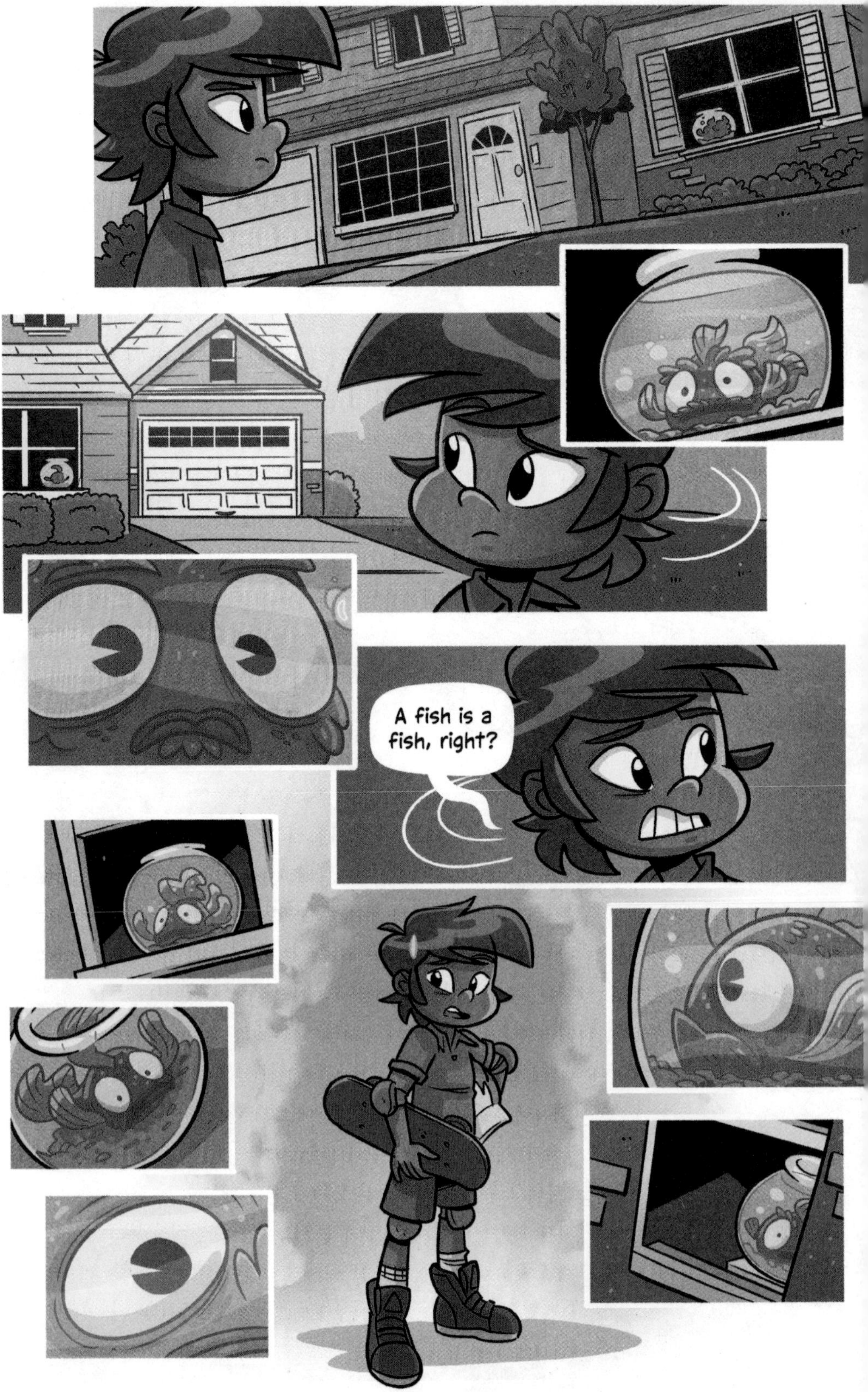
A fish is a fish, right?

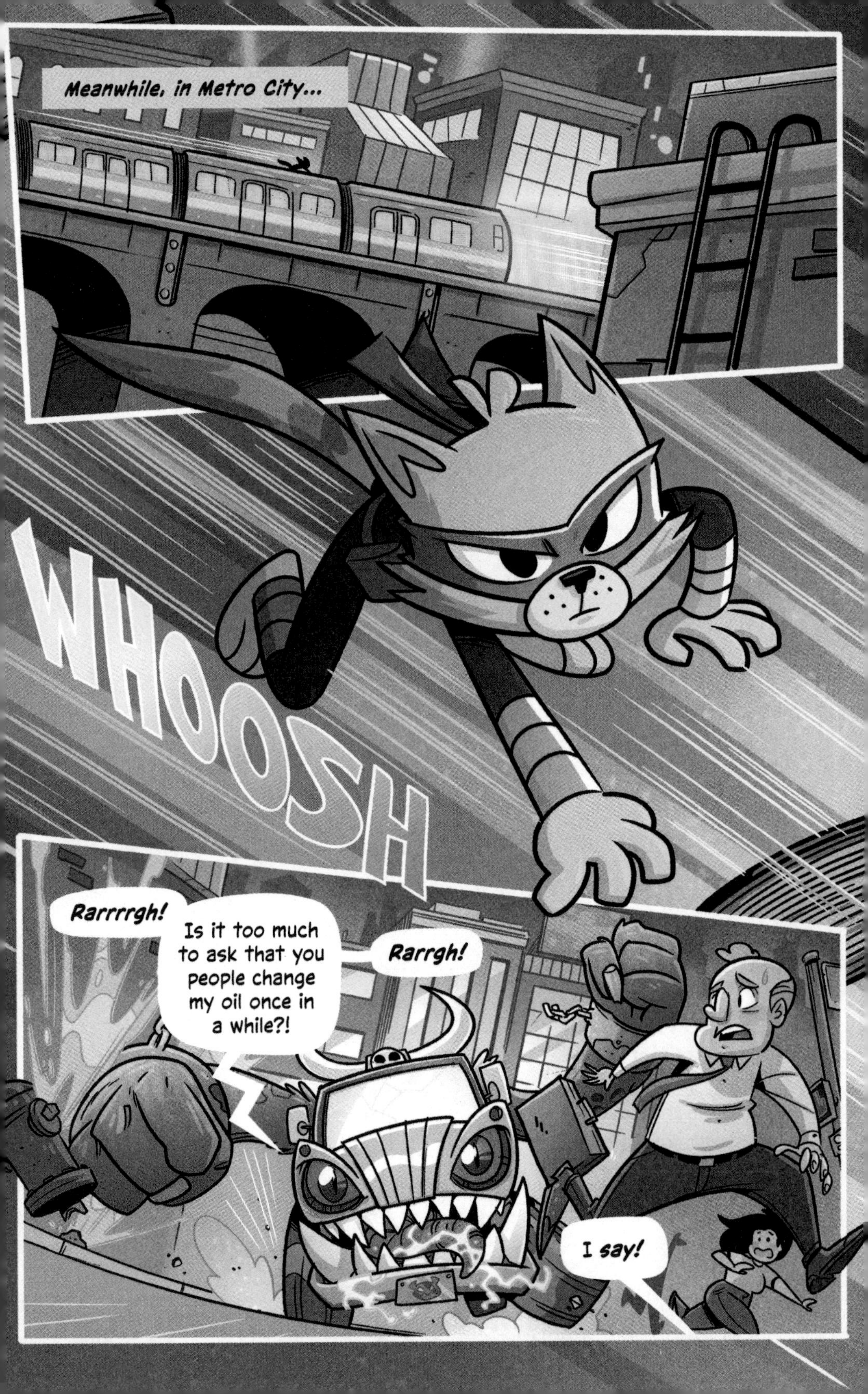
Meanwhile, in Metro City...
WHOOSH
Rarrrrgh!
Is it too much to ask that you people change my oil once in a while?!
Rarrgh!
I say!

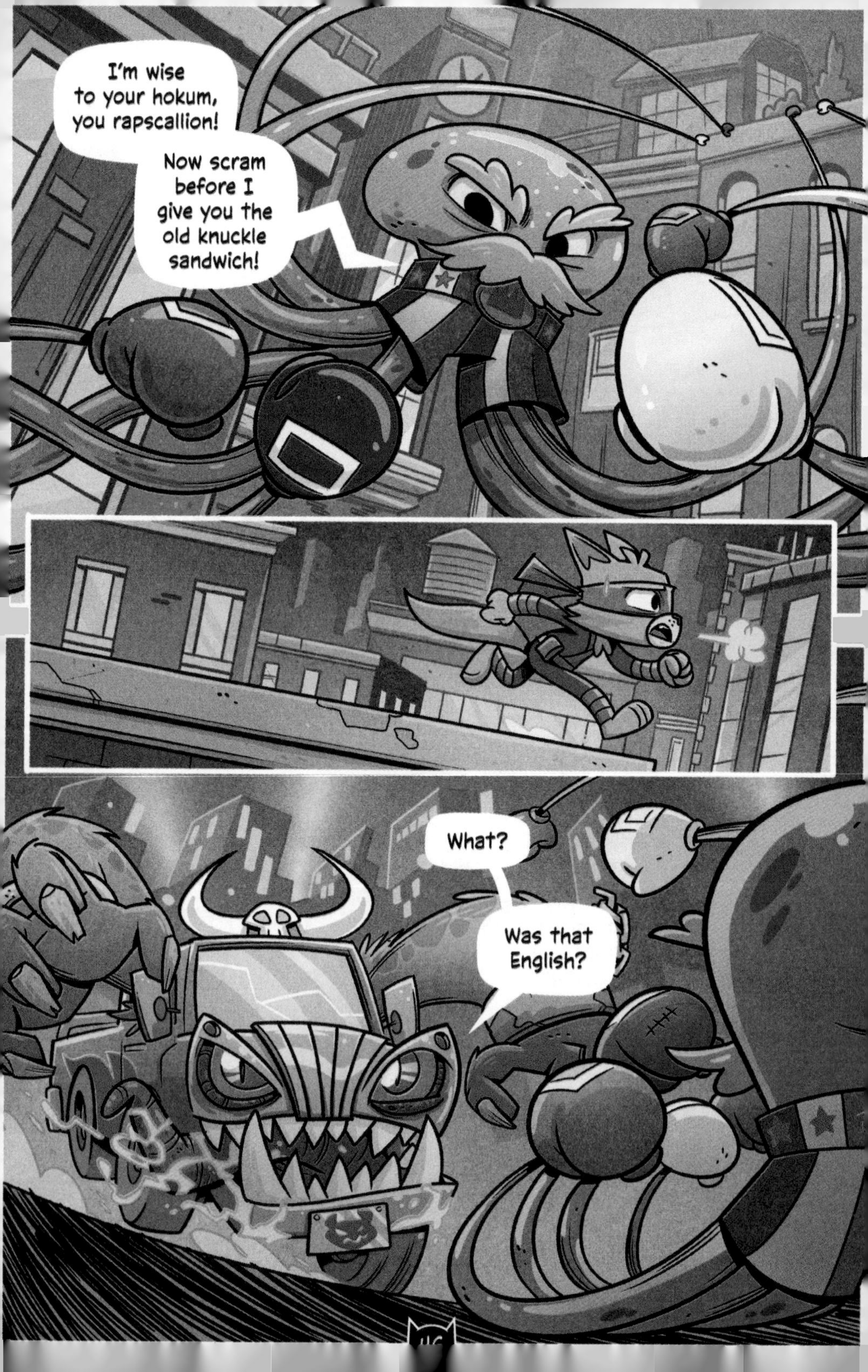
I'm wise to your hokum, you rapscallion!
Now scram before I give you the old knuckle sandwich!
What?
Was that English?

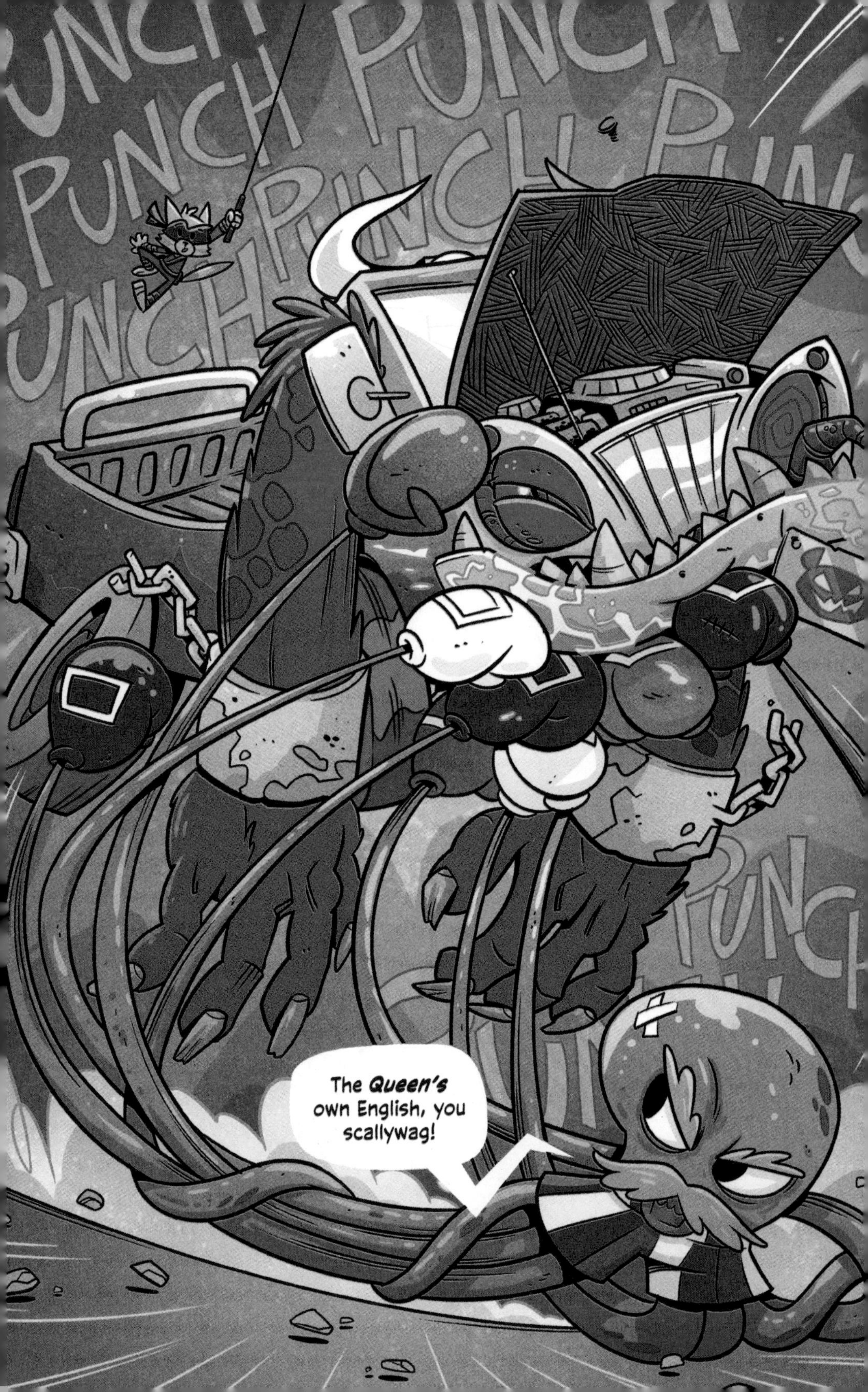
PUNCH
PUNCH
PUNCH
PUNCH
The *Queen's* own English, you scallywag!

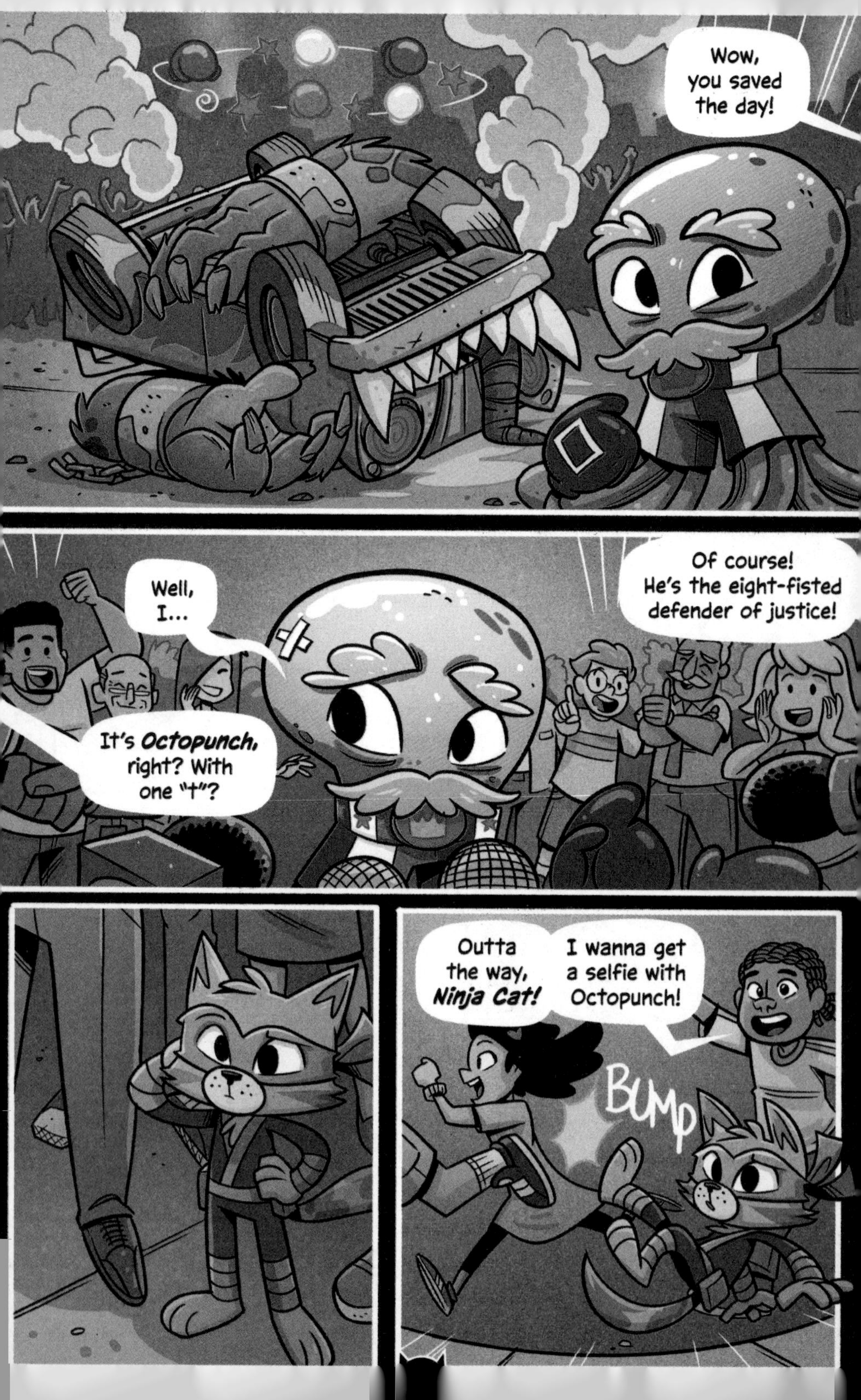
Wow, you saved the day!
Well, I...
Of course! He's the eight-fisted defender of justice!
It's *Octopunch,* right? With one "t"?
Outta the way, ***Ninja Cat!***
I wanna get a selfie with Octopunch!
BUMP

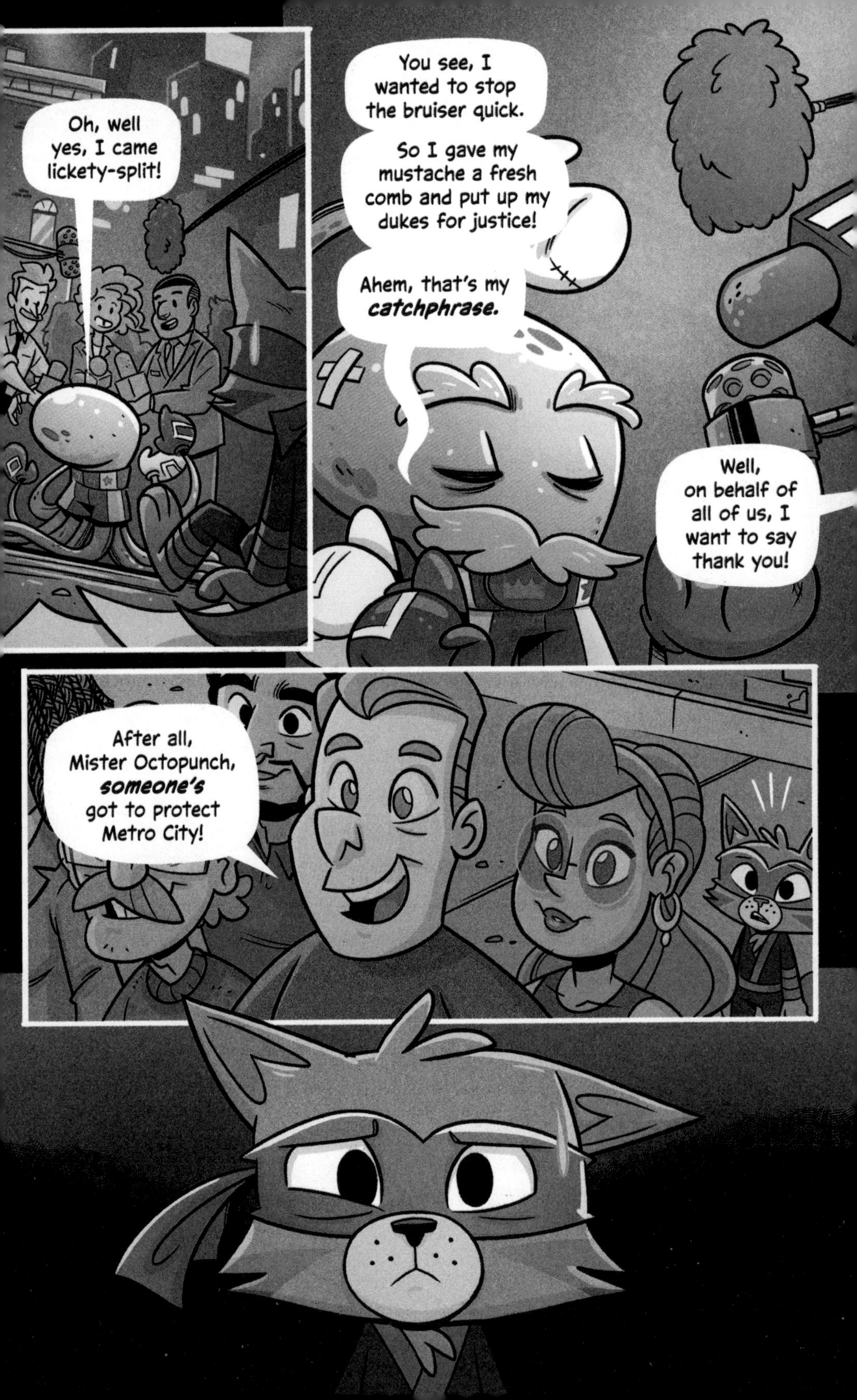
Oh, well yes, I came lickety-split!
You see, I wanted to stop the bruiser quick.
So I gave my mustache a fresh comb and put up my dukes for justice!
Ahem, that's my *catchphrase.*
Well, on behalf of all of us, I want to say thank you!
After all, Mister Octopunch, *someone's* got to protect Metro City!

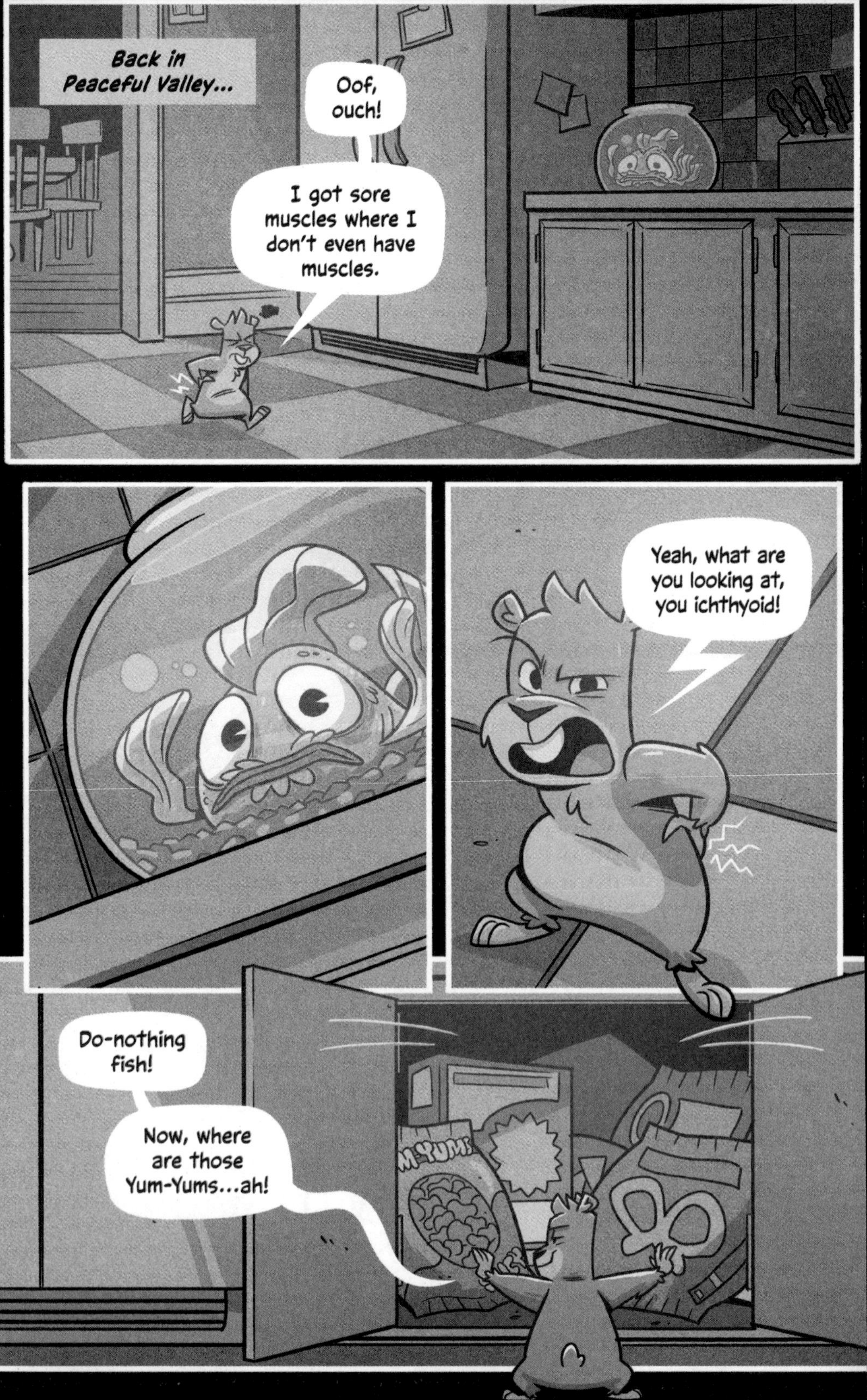
Back in Peaceful Valley...
Oof, ouch!
I got sore muscles where I don't even have muscles.
Yeah, what are you looking at, you ichthyoid!
Do-nothing fish!
Now, where are those Yum-Yums...ah!

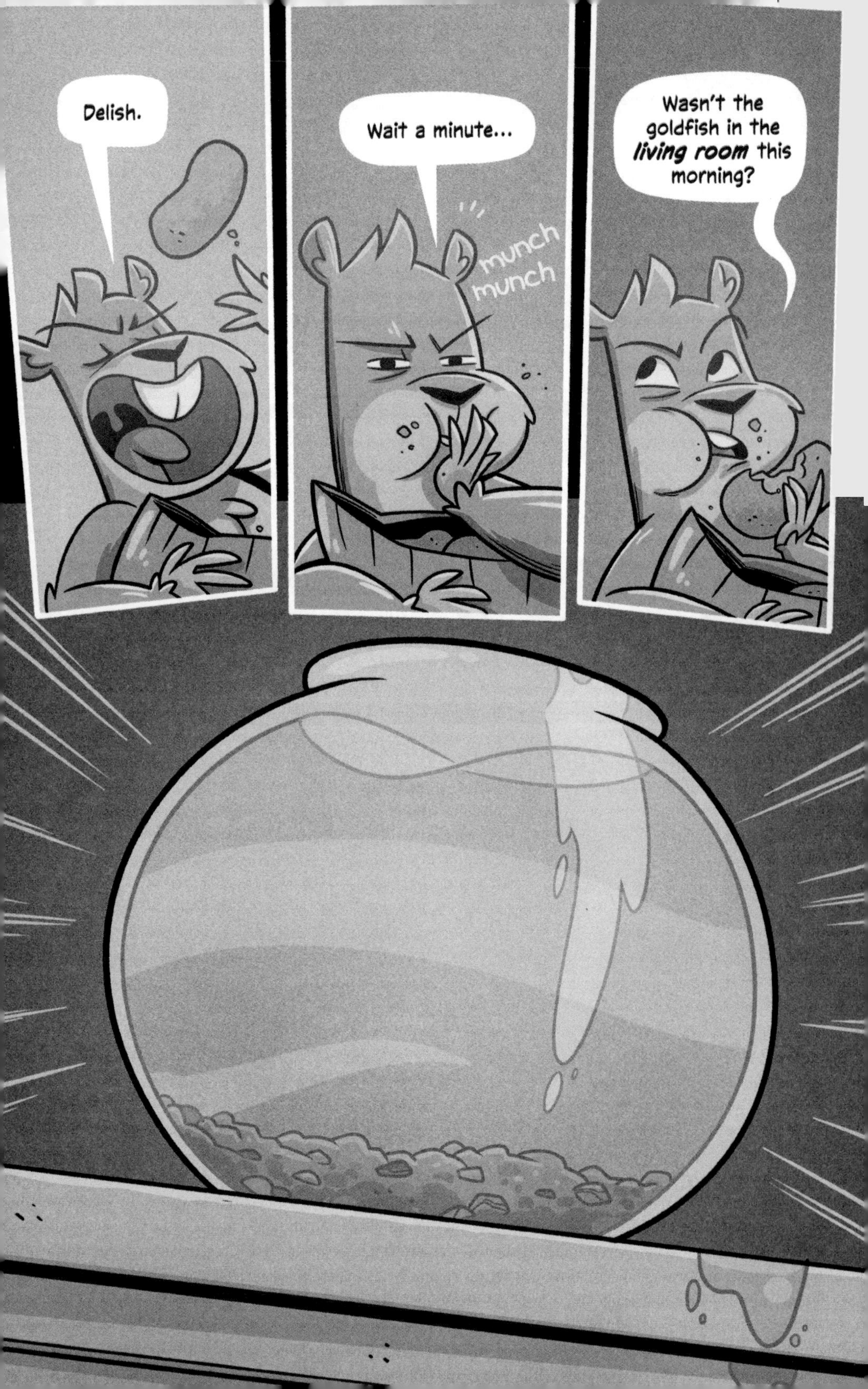
Delish.
Wait a minute...
munch munch
Wasn't the goldfish in the *living room* this morning?

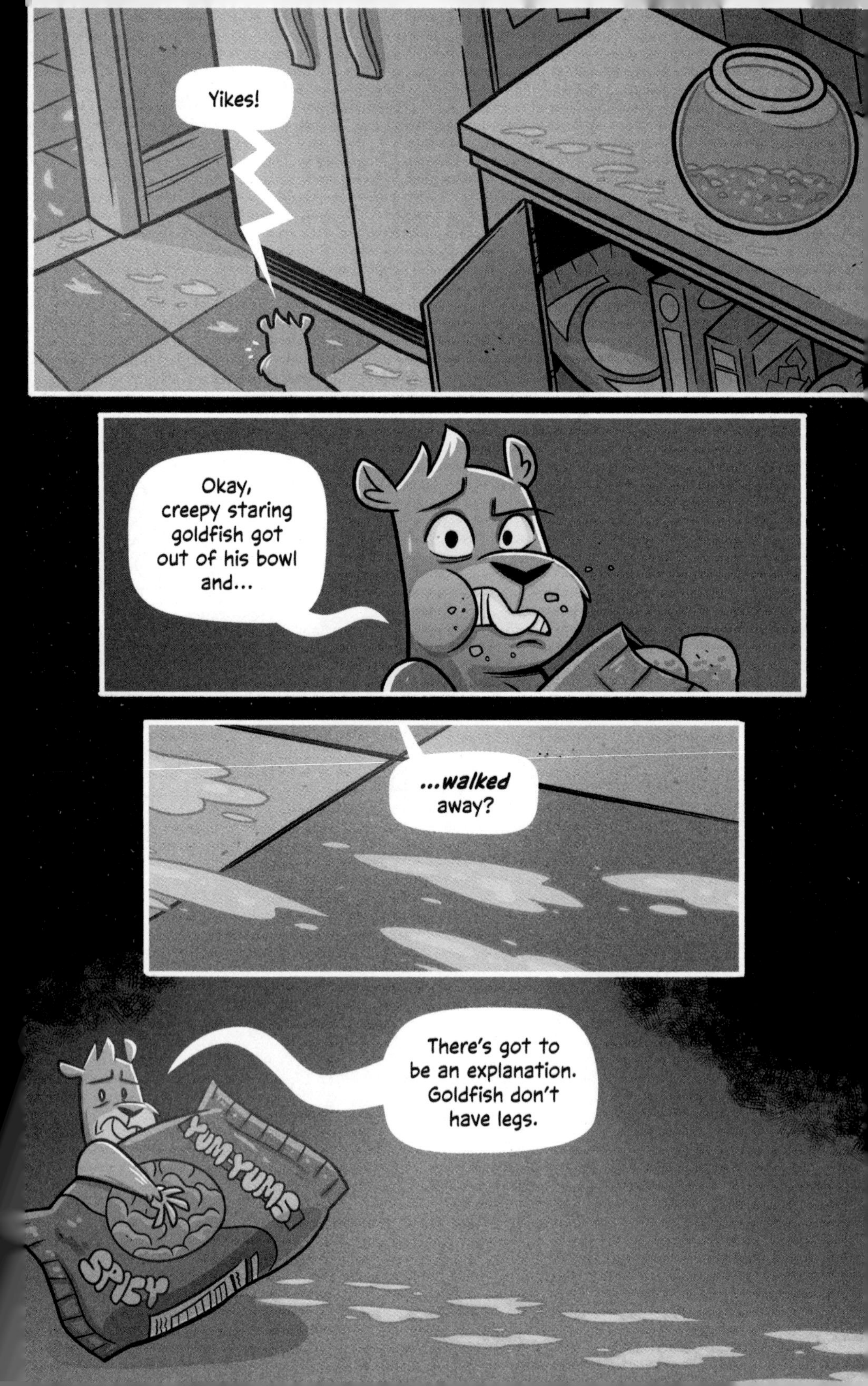
Yikes!
Okay, creepy staring goldfish got out of his bowl and...
...*walked* away?
There's got to be an explanation. Goldfish don't have legs.
YUM-YUMS
SPICY

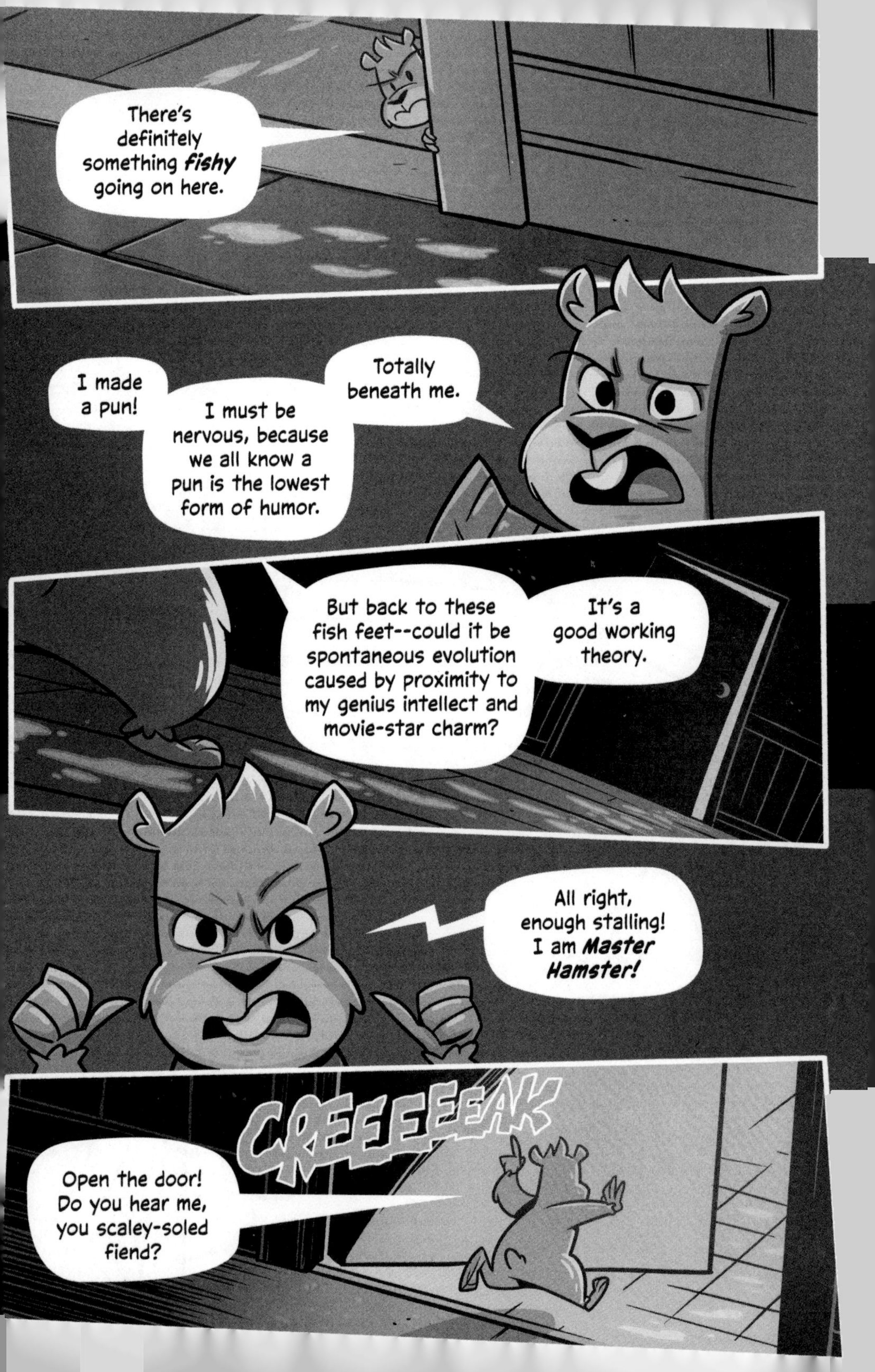
There's definitely something *fishy* going on here.
I made a pun!
I must be nervous, because we all know a pun is the lowest form of humor.
Totally beneath me.
But back to these fish feet--could it be spontaneous evolution caused by proximity to my genius intellect and movie-star charm?
It's a good working theory.
All right, enough stalling! I am ***Master Hamster!***
CREEEEEAK
Open the door! Do you hear me, you scaley-soled fiend?

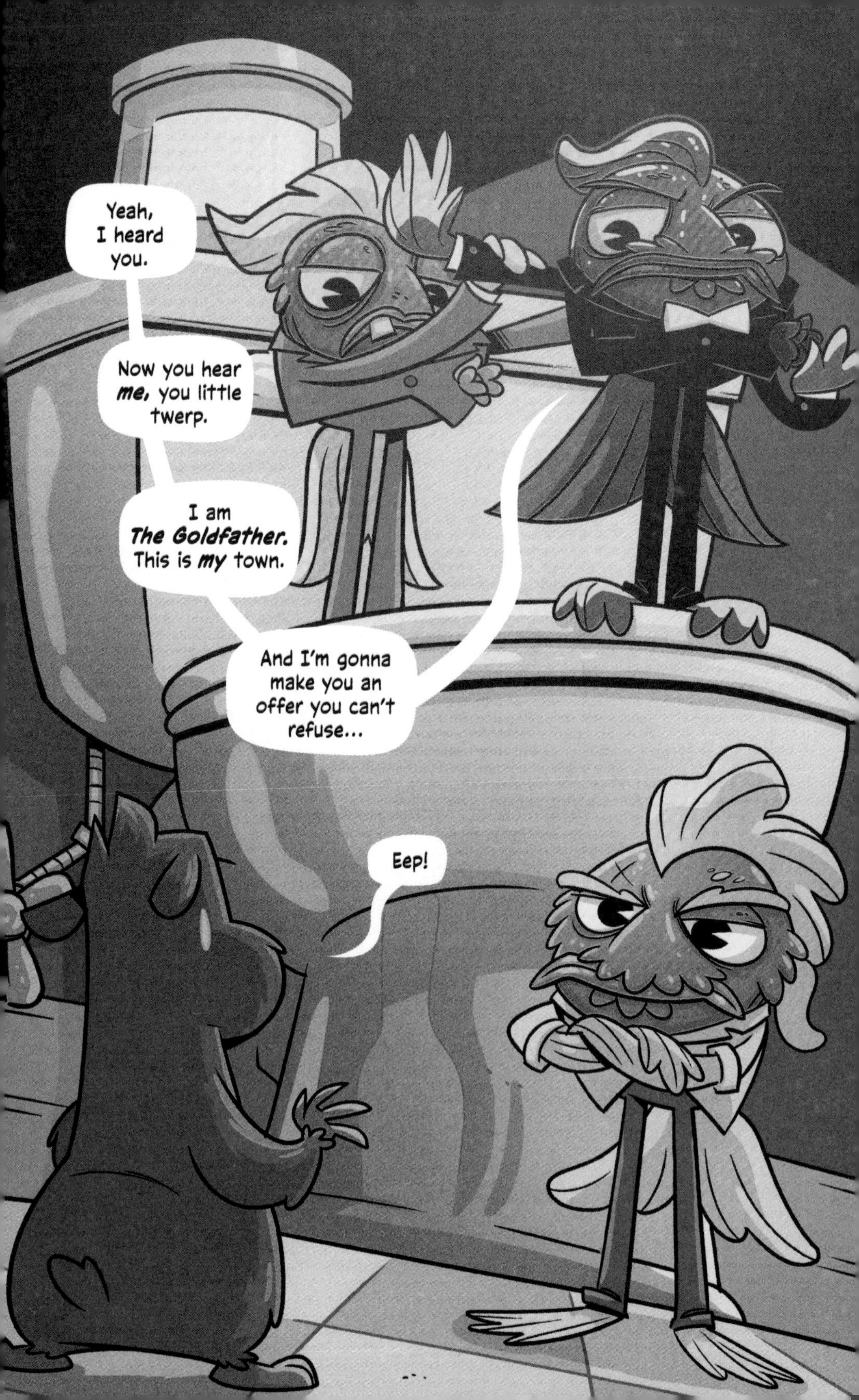
Yeah, I heard you.
Now you hear *me,* you little twerp.
I am ***The Goldfather.*** This is *my* town.
And I'm gonna make you an offer you can't refuse...
Eep!

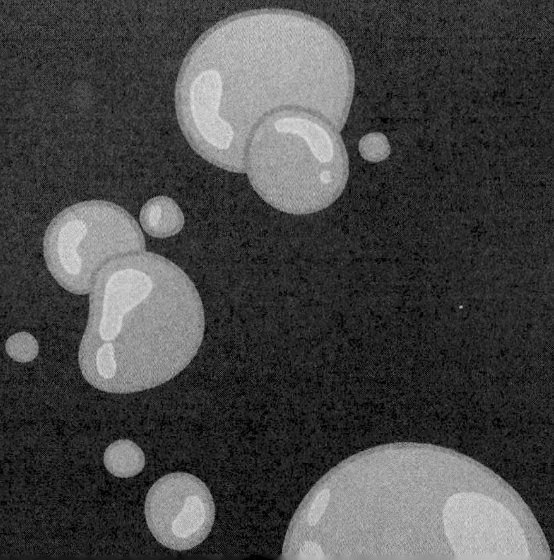

Chapter 3
The Goldfather, Part II

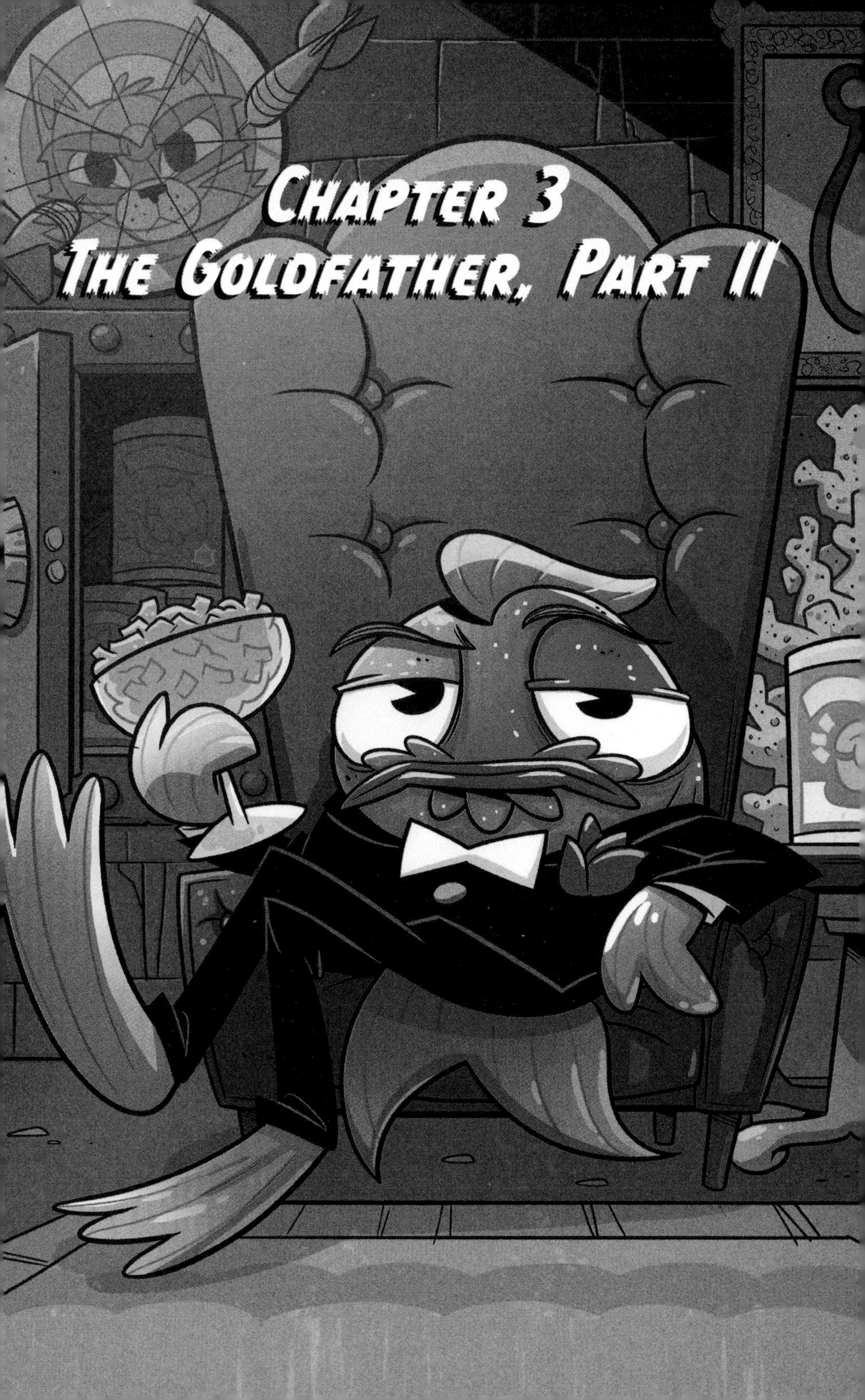

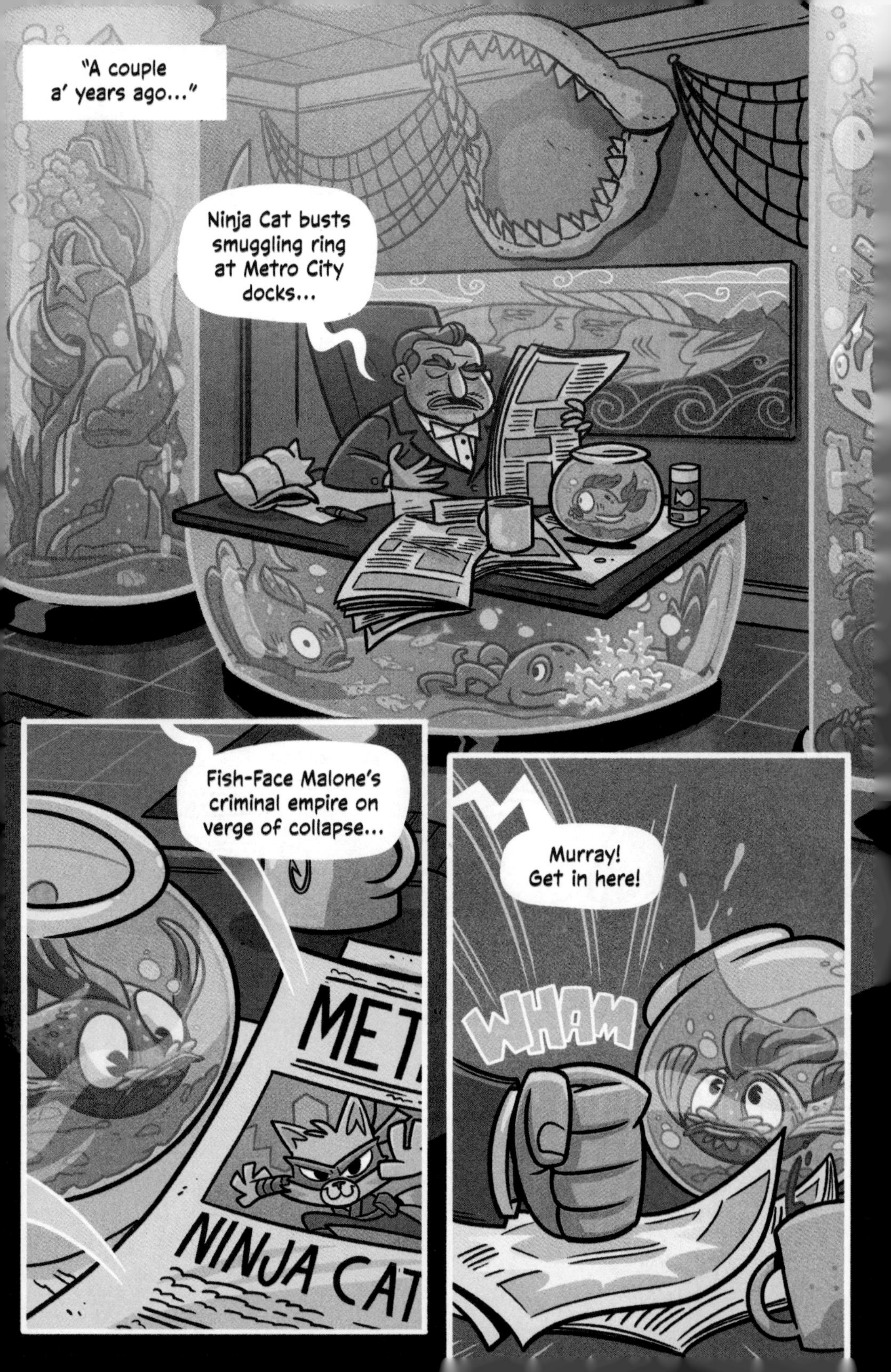
"A couple a' years ago..."
Ninja Cat busts smuggling ring at Metro City docks...
Fish-Face Malone's criminal empire on verge of collapse...
METR
NINJA CAT
Murray! Get in here!
WHAM

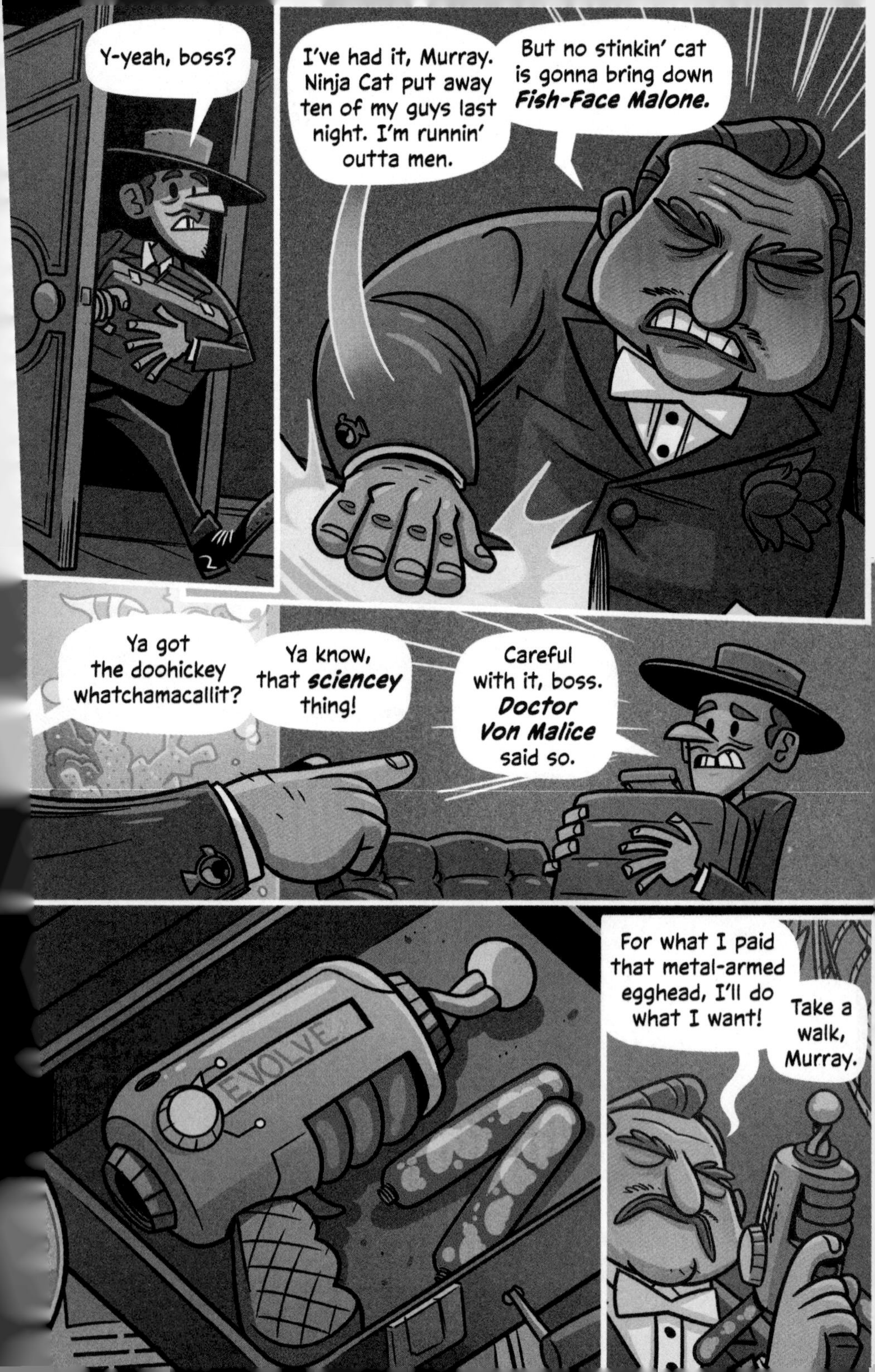
Y-yeah, boss?
I've had it, Murray. Ninja Cat put away ten of my guys last night. I'm runnin' outta men.
But no stinkin' cat is gonna bring down *Fish-Face Malone.*
Ya got the doohickey whatchamacallit?
Ya know, that *sciencey* thing!
Careful with it, boss. *Doctor Von Malice* said so.
EVOLVE
For what I paid that metal-armed egghead, I'll do what I want!
Take a walk, Murray.

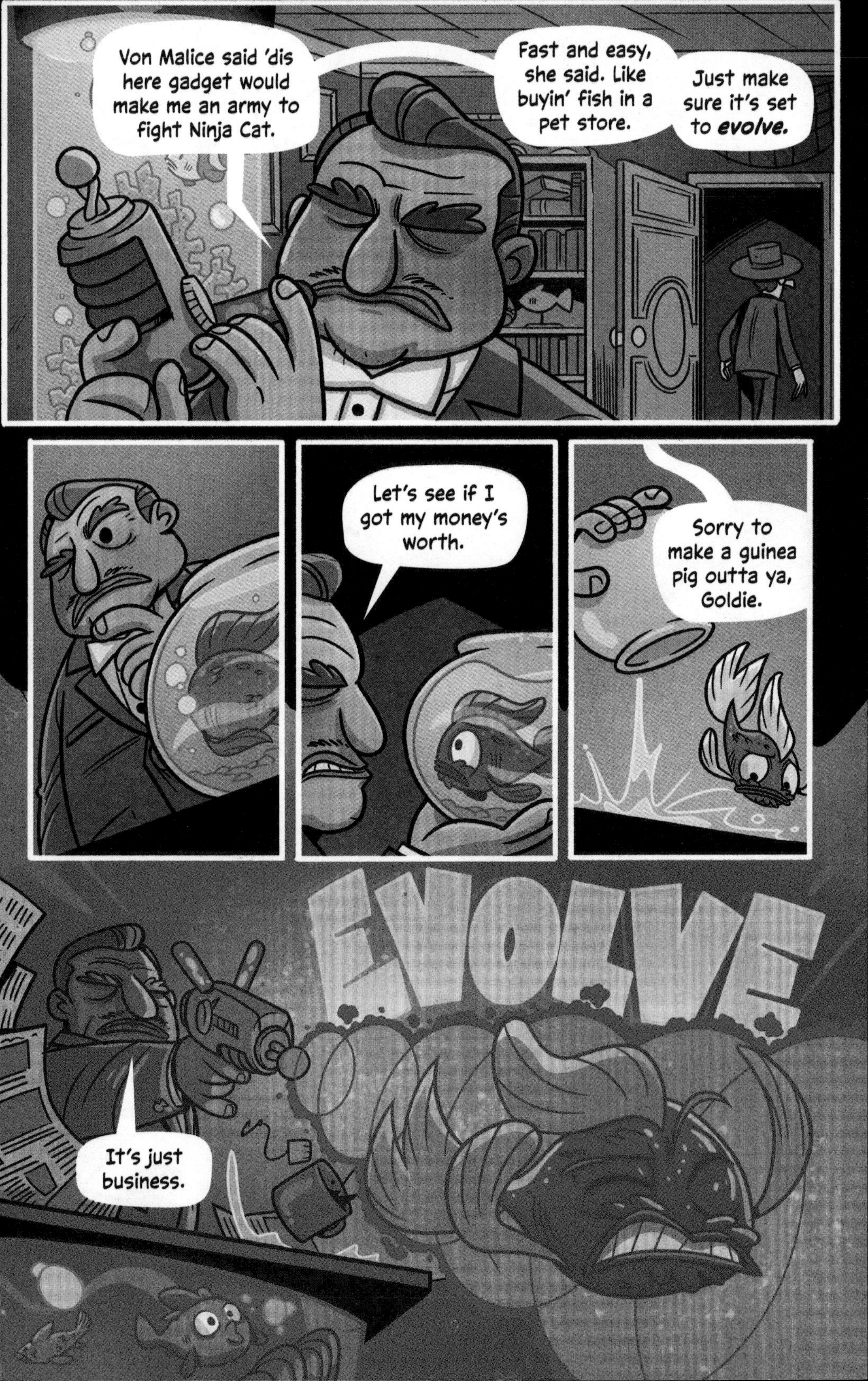
Von Malice said 'dis here gadget would make me an army to fight Ninja Cat.
Fast and easy, she said. Like buyin' fish in a pet store.
Just make sure it's set to *evolve.*
Let's see if I got my money's worth.
Sorry to make a guinea pig outta ya, Goldie.
EVOLVE
It's just business.

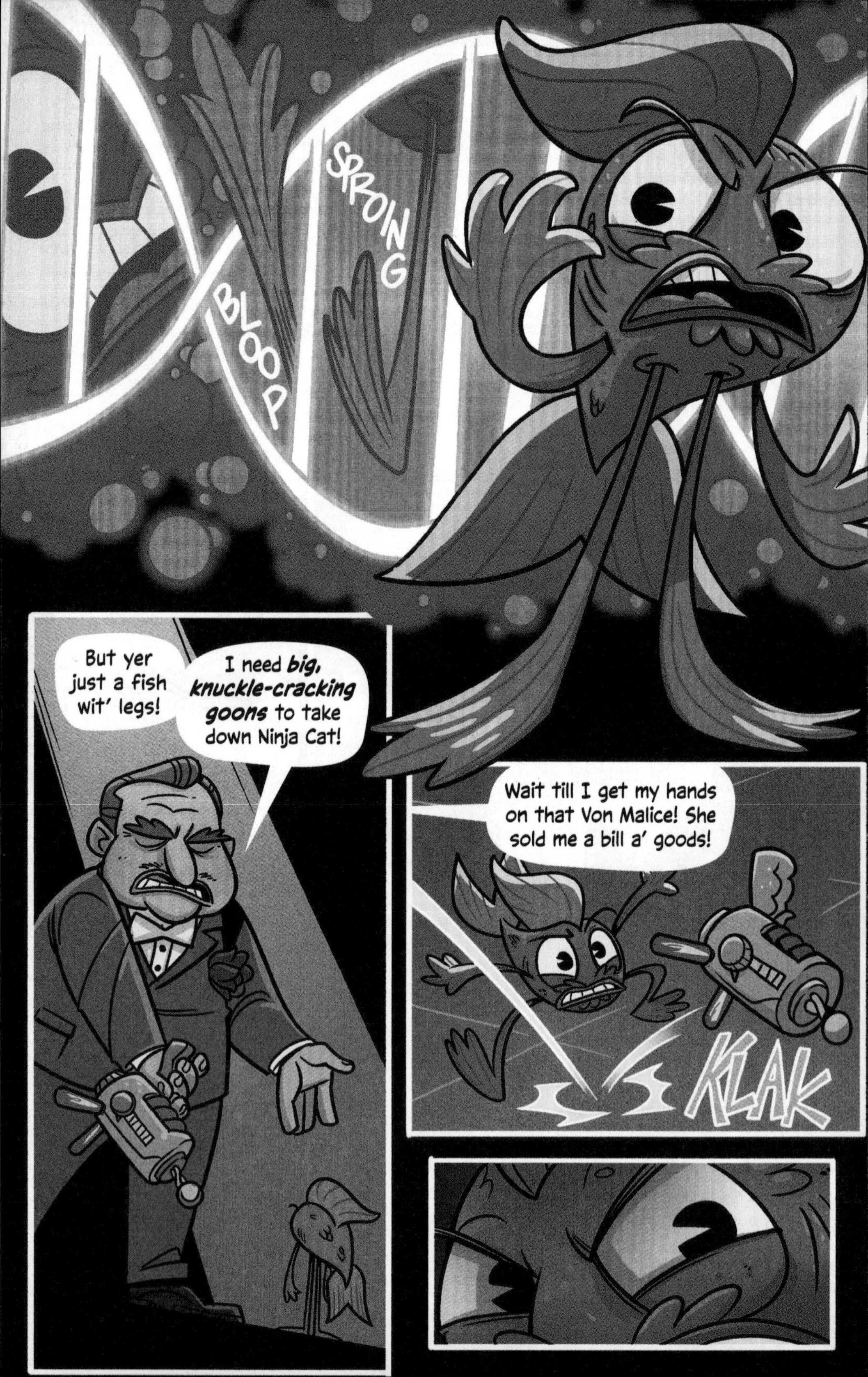
SPROING
BLOOP
But yer just a fish wit' legs!
I need **big, knuckle-cracking goons** to take down Ninja Cat!
Wait till I get my hands on that Von Malice! She sold me a bill a' goods!
KLAK

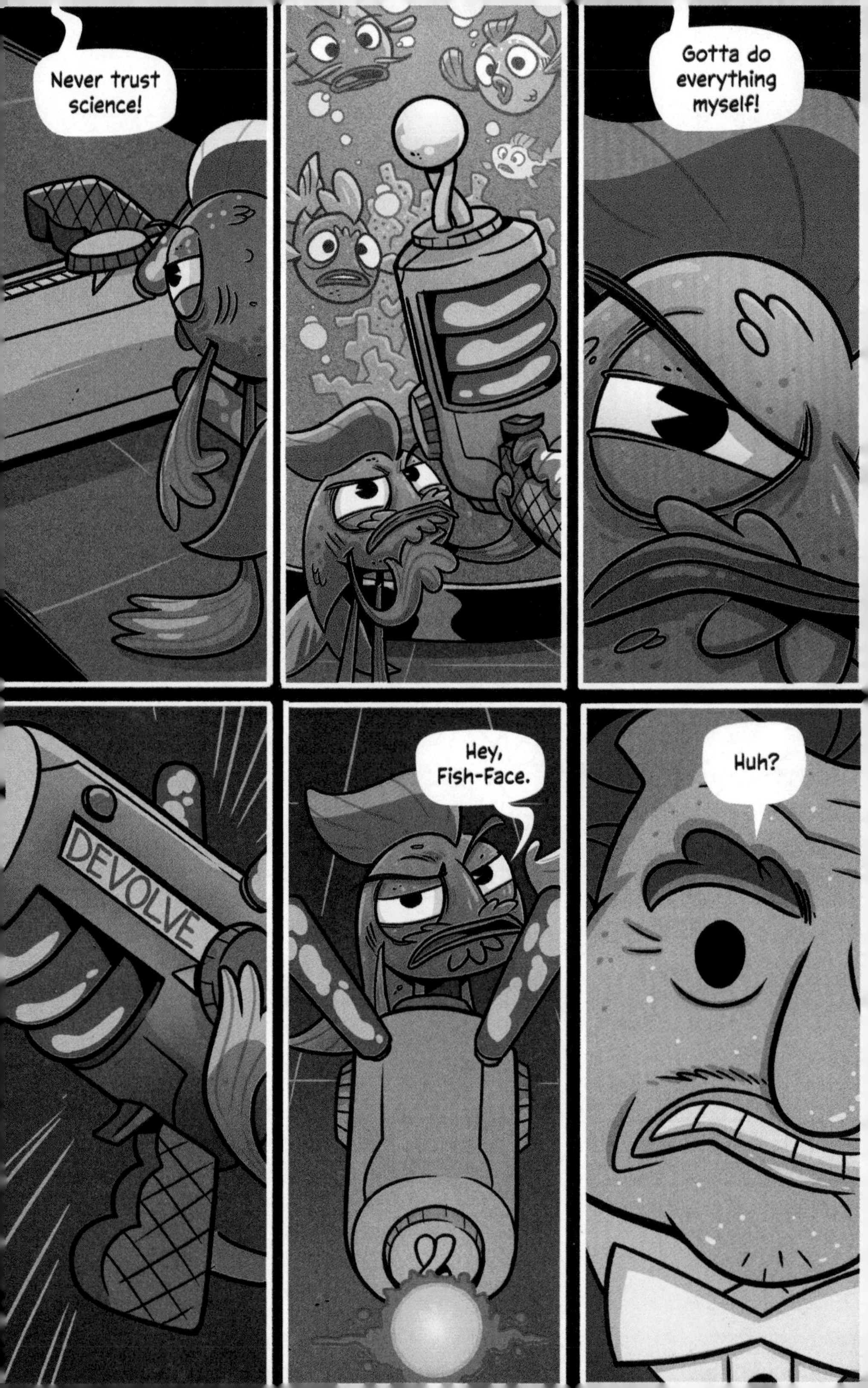
Never trust science!
Gotta do everything myself!
DEVOLVE
Hey, Fish-Face.
Huh?

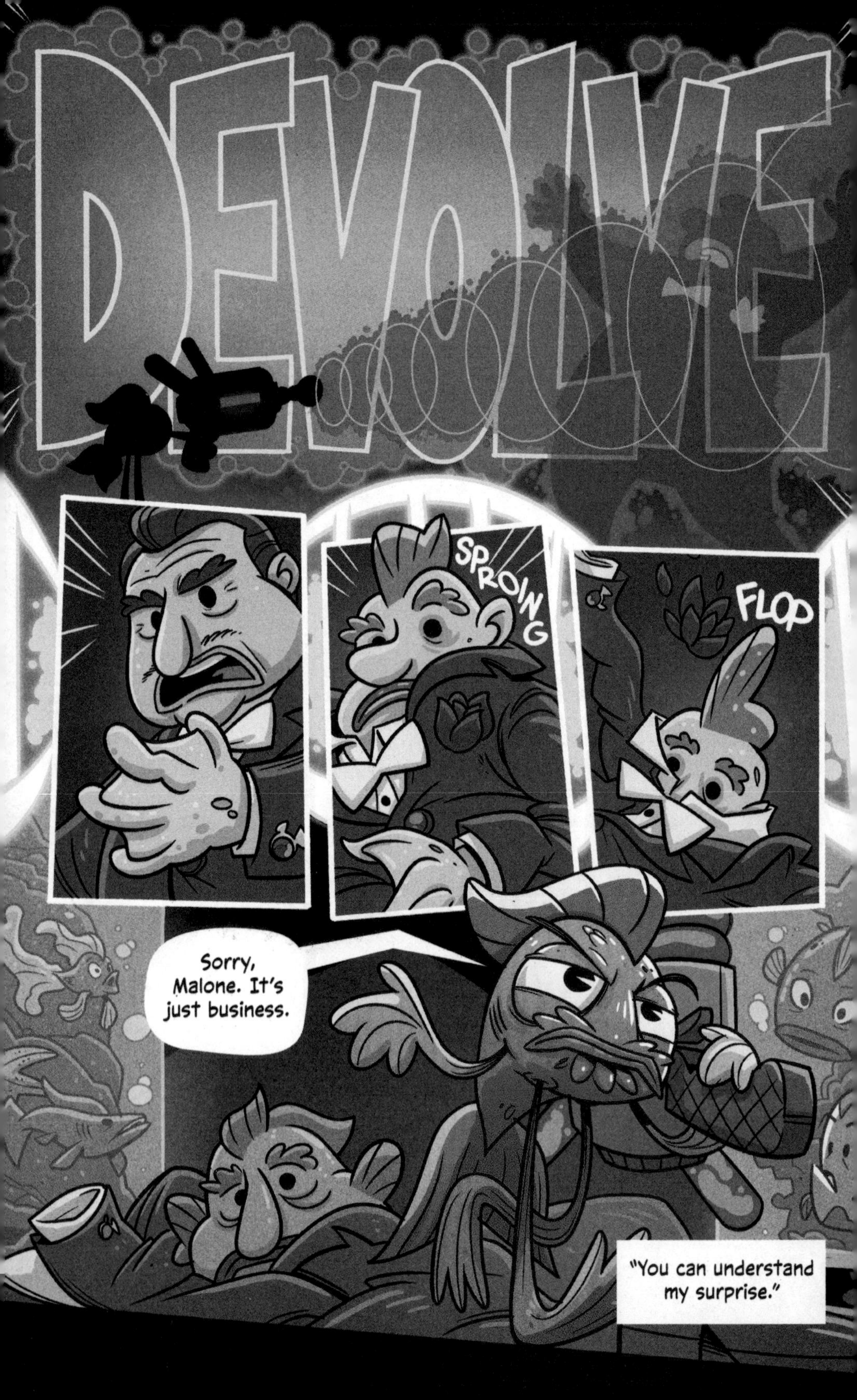
DEVOLVE
SPROING
FLOP
Sorry, Malone. It's just business.
"You can understand my surprise."

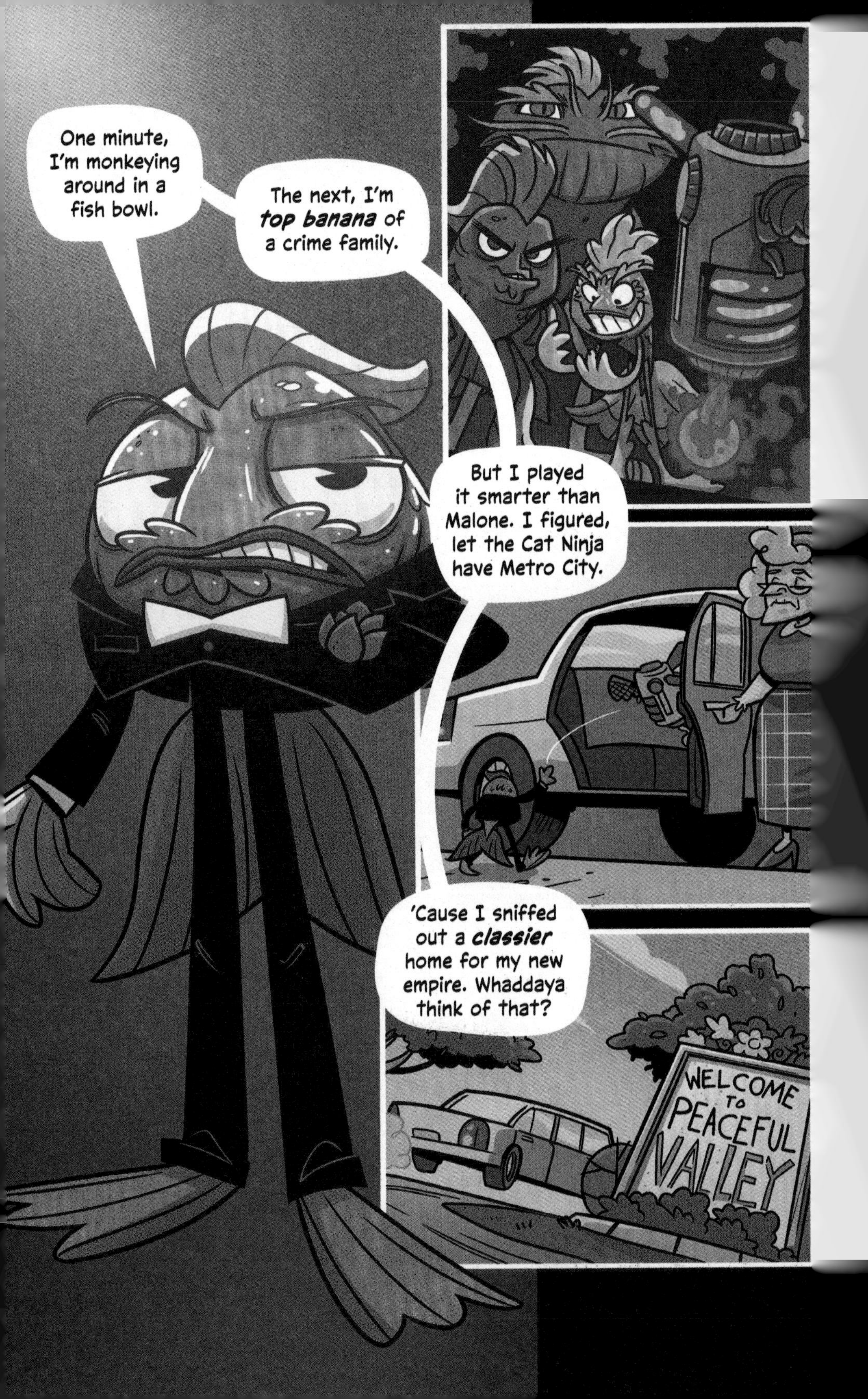
One minute, I'm monkeying around in a fish bowl.
The next, I'm *top banana* of a crime family.
But I played it smarter than Malone. I figured, let the Cat Ninja have Metro City.
'Cause I sniffed out a *classier* home for my new empire. Whaddaya think of that?
WELCOME TO PEACEFUL VALLEY

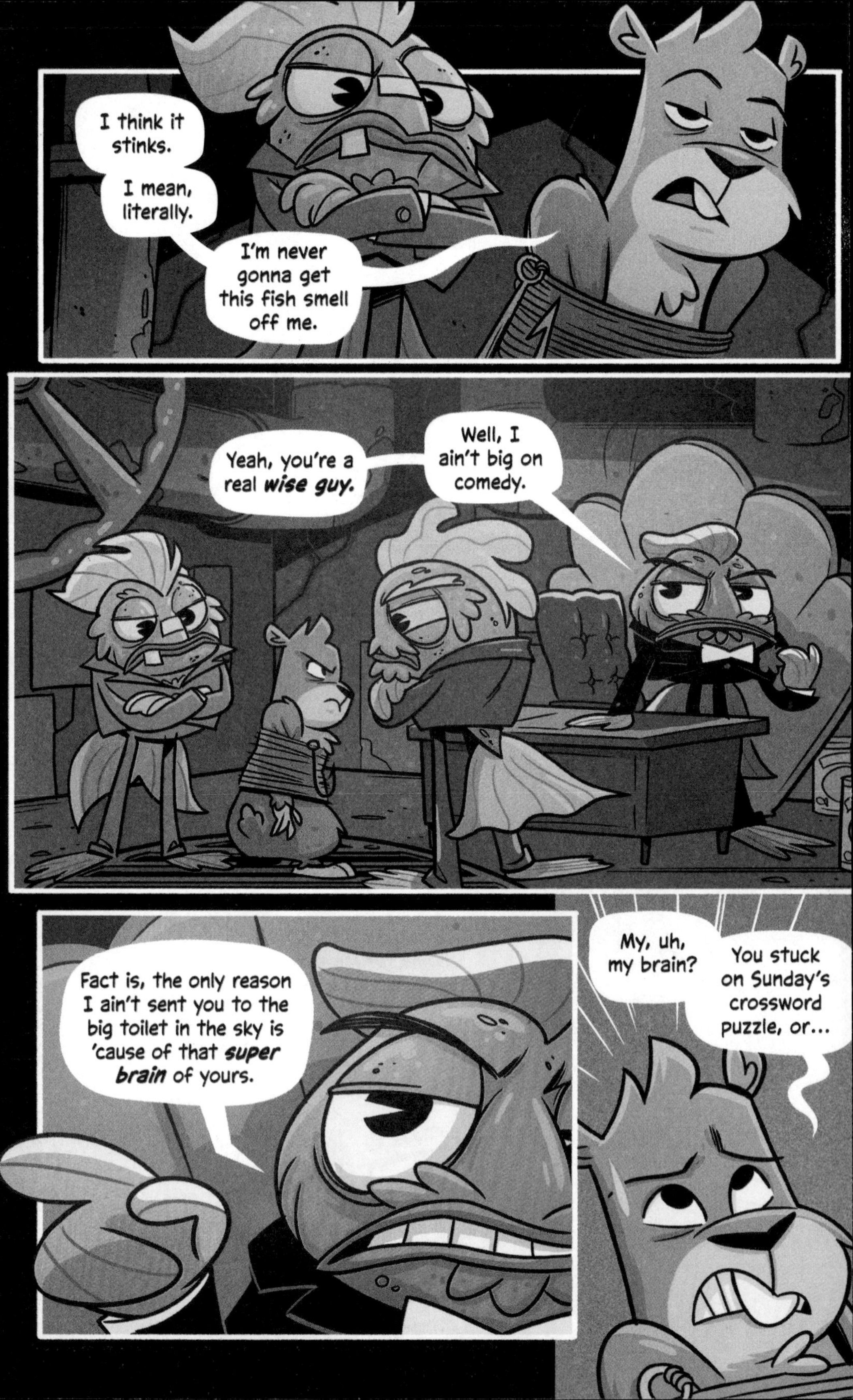
I think it stinks.
I mean, literally.
I'm never gonna get this fish smell off me.
Yeah, you're a real *wise guy.*
Well, I ain't big on comedy.
Fact is, the only reason I ain't sent you to the big toilet in the sky is 'cause of that *super brain* of yours.
My, uh, my brain?
You stuck on Sunday's crossword puzzle, or...

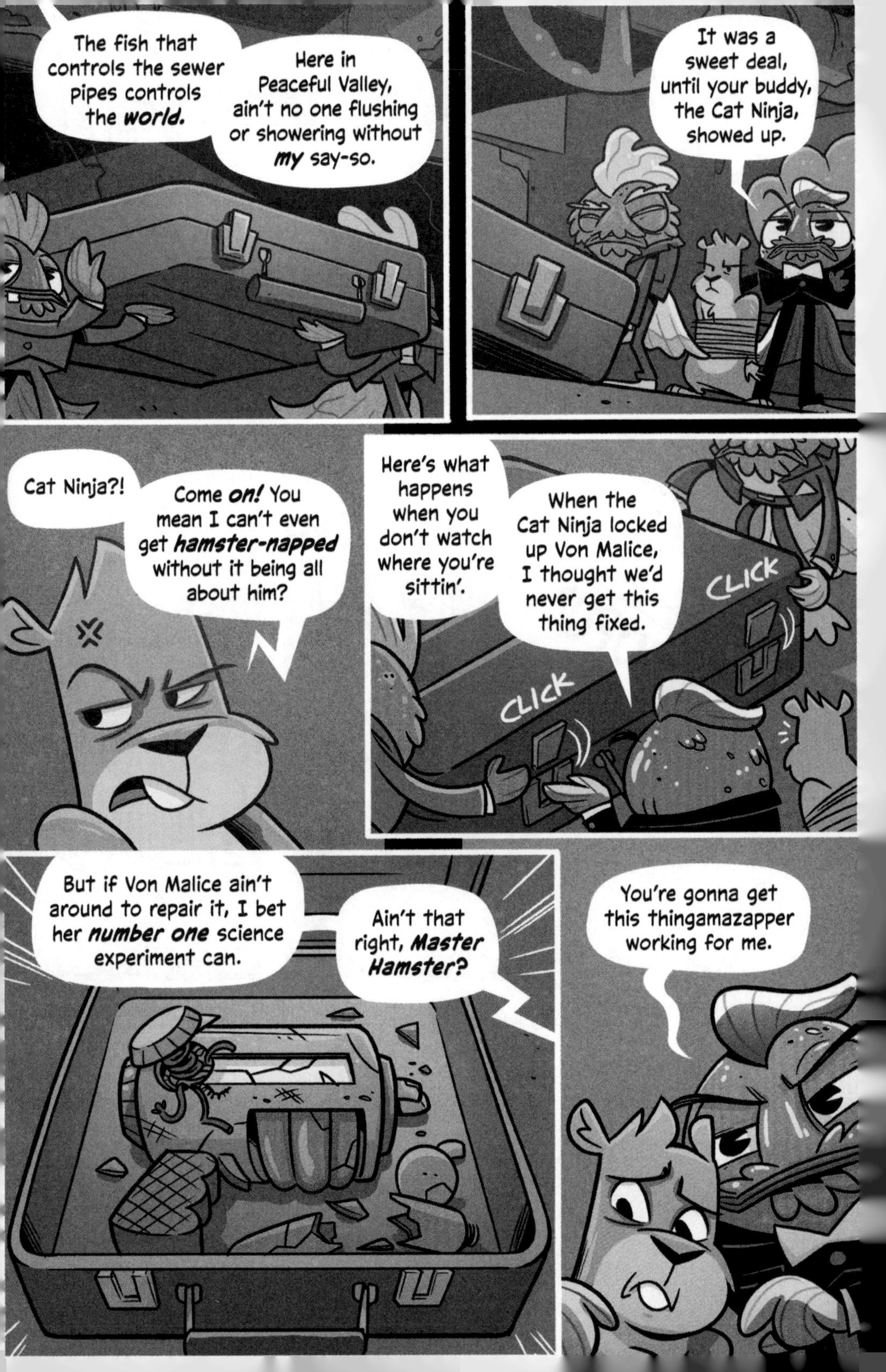
The fish that controls the sewer pipes controls the *world.*
Here in Peaceful Valley, ain't no one flushing or showering without *my* say-so.
It was a sweet deal, until your buddy, the Cat Ninja, showed up.
Cat Ninja?!
Come *on!* You mean I can't even get *hamster-napped* without it being all about him?
Here's what happens when you don't watch where you're sittin'.
When the Cat Ninja locked up Von Malice, I thought we'd never get this thing fixed.
CLICK
CLICK
But if Von Malice ain't around to repair it, I bet her *number one* science experiment can.
Ain't that right, *Master Hamster?*
You're gonna get this thingamazapper working for me.

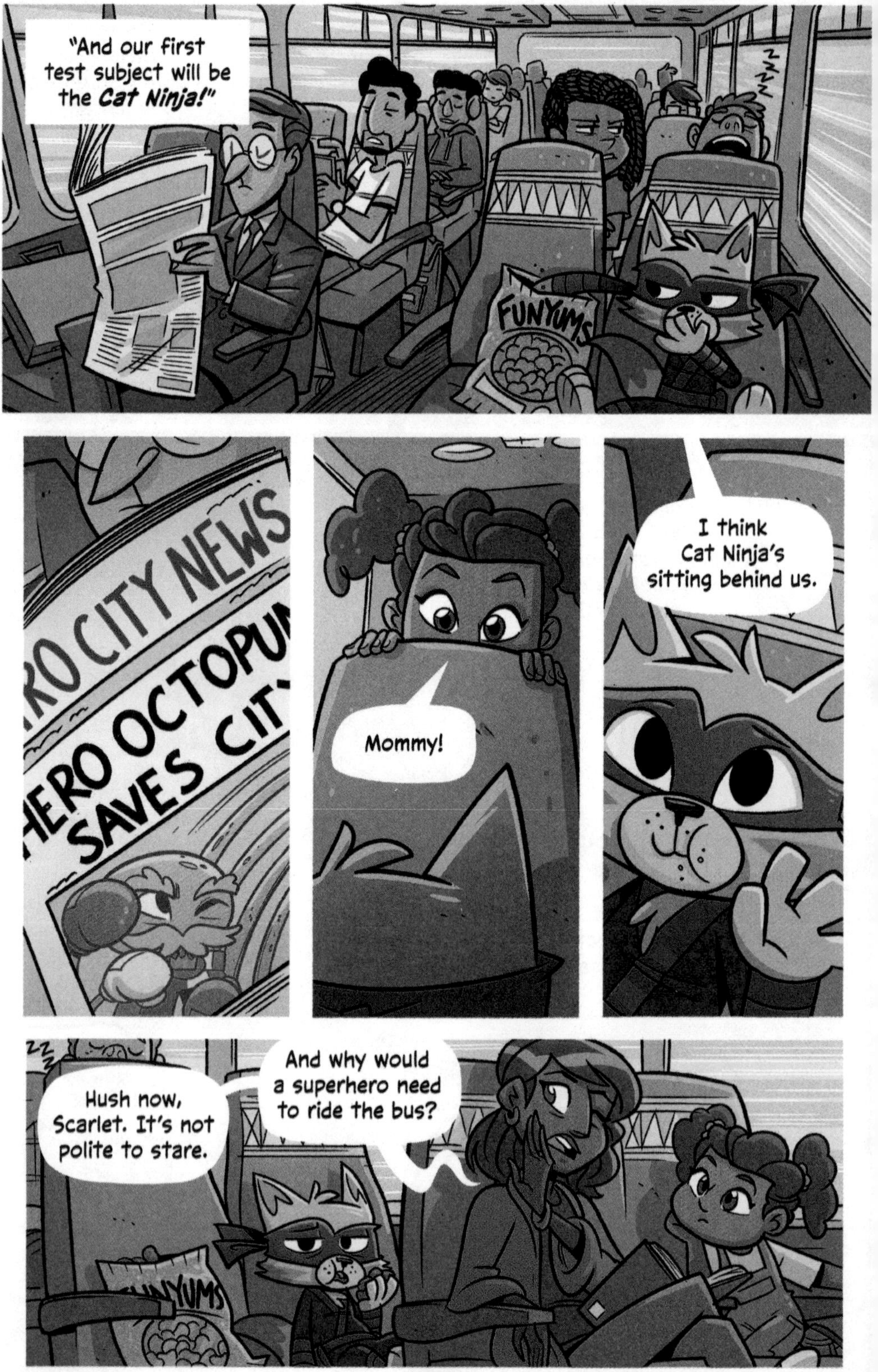
"And our first test subject will be the *Cat Ninja!*"
FUNYUMS
RO CITY NEWS
HERO OCTOPU
SAVES CIT
Mommy!
I think Cat Ninja's sitting behind us.
Hush now, Scarlet. It's not polite to stare.
And why would a superhero need to ride the bus?
FUNYUMS

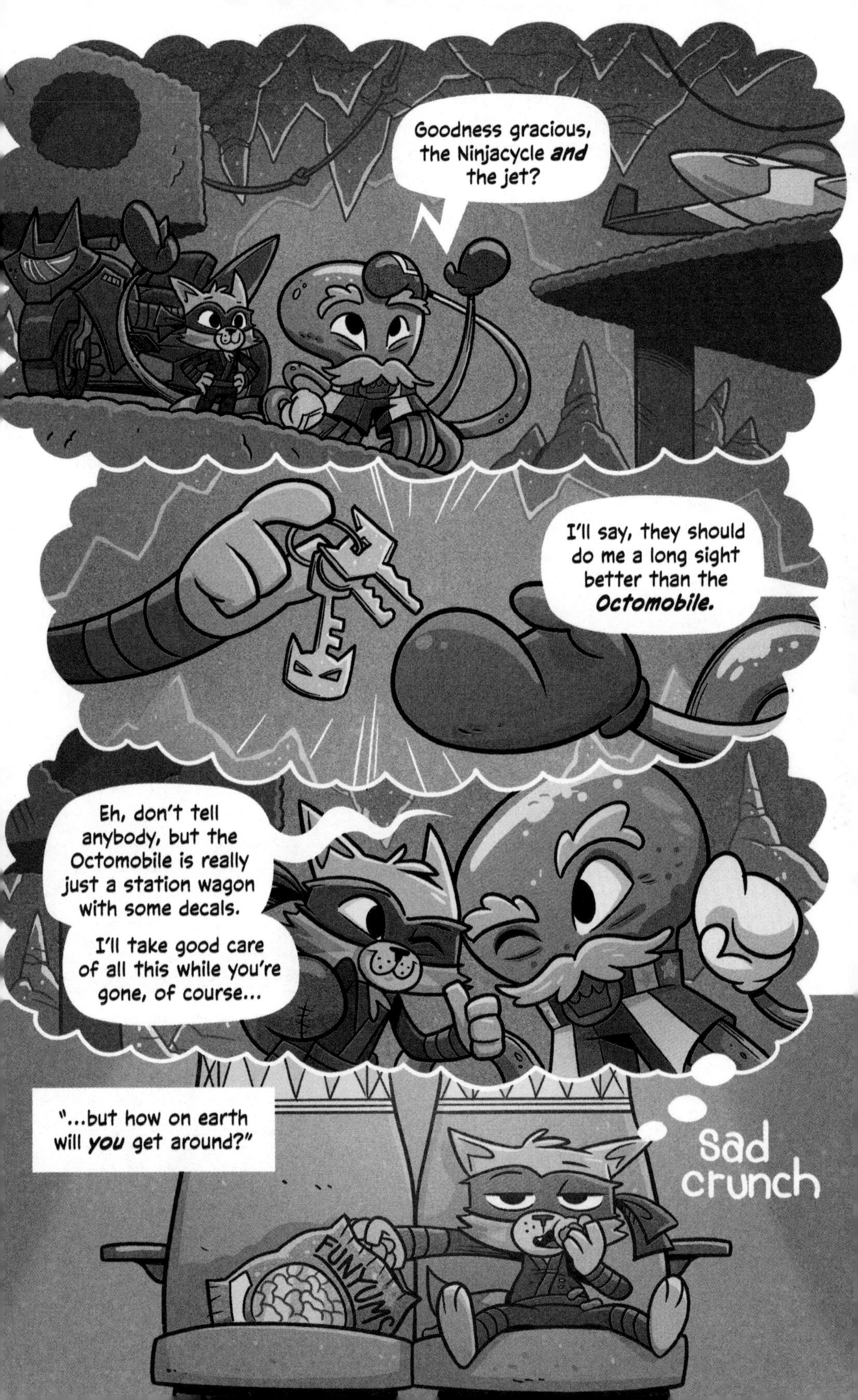

Goodness gracious, the Ninjacycle *and* the jet?
I'll say, they should do me a long sight better than the *Octomobile.*
Eh, don't tell anybody, but the Octomobile is really just a station wagon with some decals.
I'll take good care of all this while you're gone, of course...
"...but how on earth will *you* get around?"
sad crunch
FUNYUMS

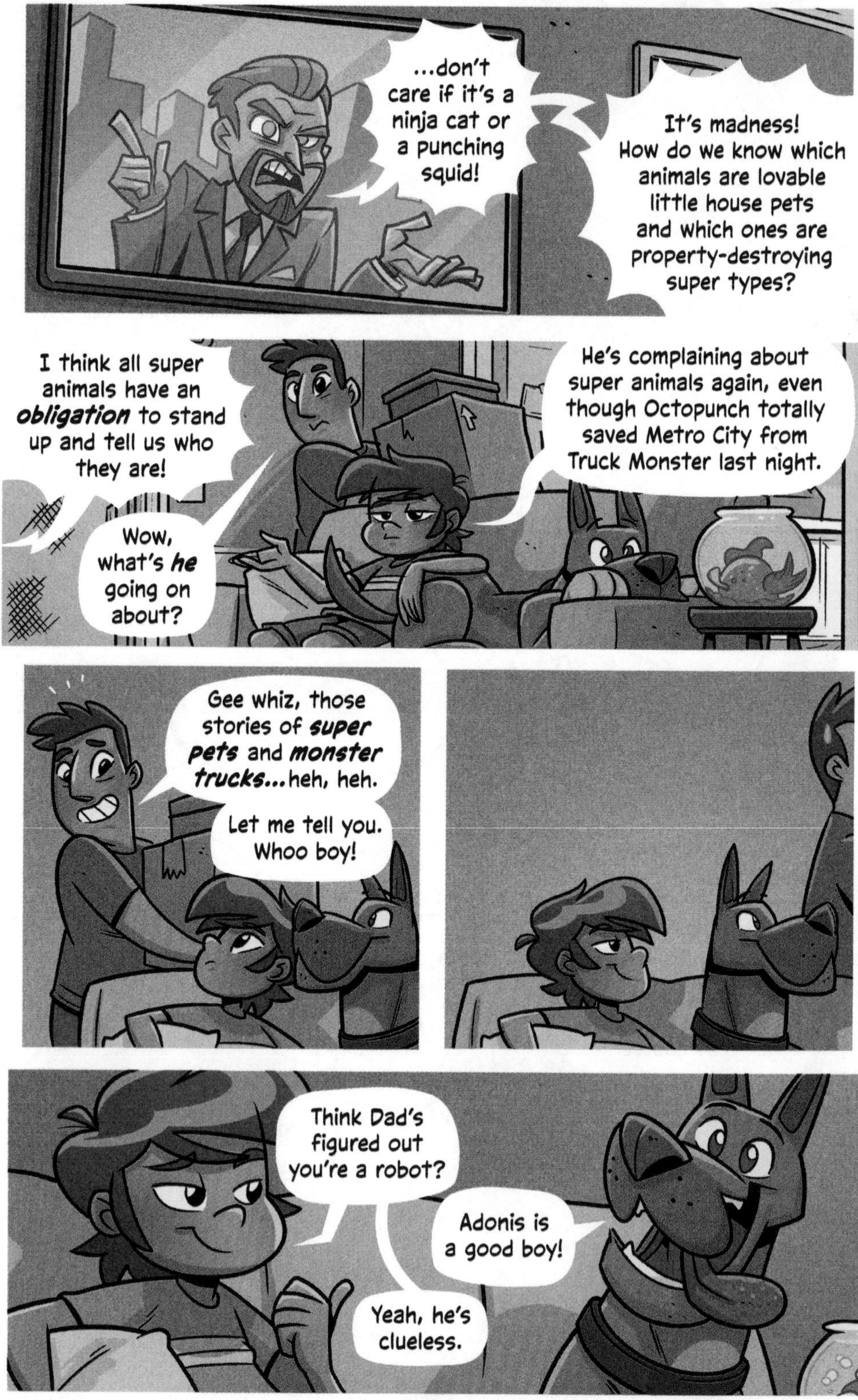
...don't care if it's a ninja cat or a punching squid!
It's madness! How do we know which animals are lovable little house pets and which ones are property-destroying super types?
I think all super animals have an obligation to stand up and tell us who they are!
Wow, what's he going on about?
He's complaining about super animals again, even though Octopunch totally saved Metro City from Truck Monster last night.
Gee whiz, those stories of super pets and monster trucks...heh, heh.
Let me tell you. Whoo boy!
Think Dad's figured out you're a robot?
Adonis is a good boy!
Yeah, he's clueless.

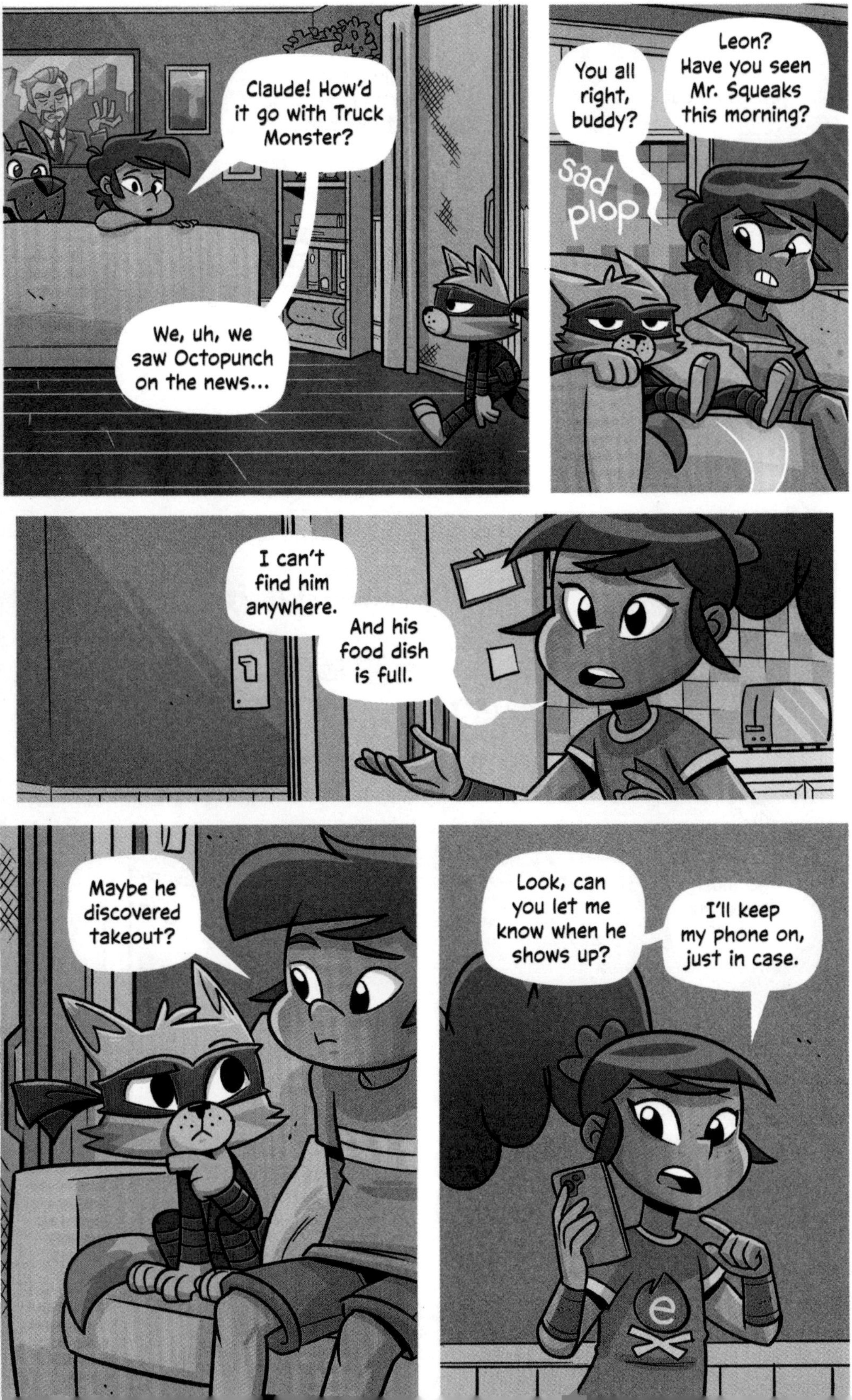

Claude! How'd it go with Truck Monster?
We, uh, we saw Octopunch on the news...
Leon? Have you seen Mr. Squeaks this morning?
You all right, buddy?
sad plop
I can't find him anywhere.
And his food dish is full.
Maybe he discovered takeout?
Look, can you let me know when he shows up?
I'll keep my phone on, just in case.

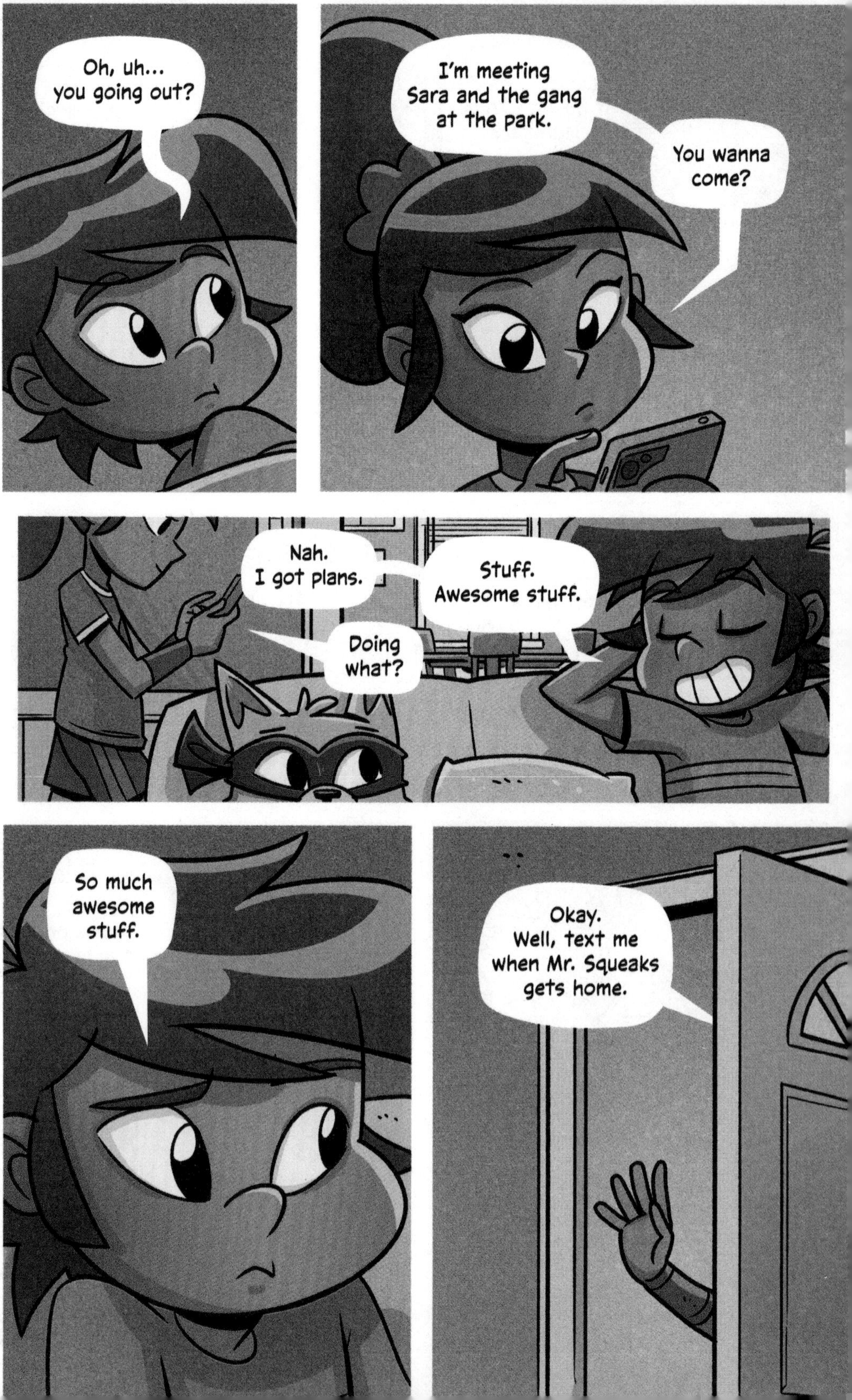
Oh, uh...
you going out?
I'm meeting
Sara and the gang
at the park.
You wanna
come?
Nah.
I got plans.
Doing
what?
Stuff.
Awesome stuff.
So much
awesome
stuff.
Okay.
Well, text me
when Mr. Squeaks
gets home.

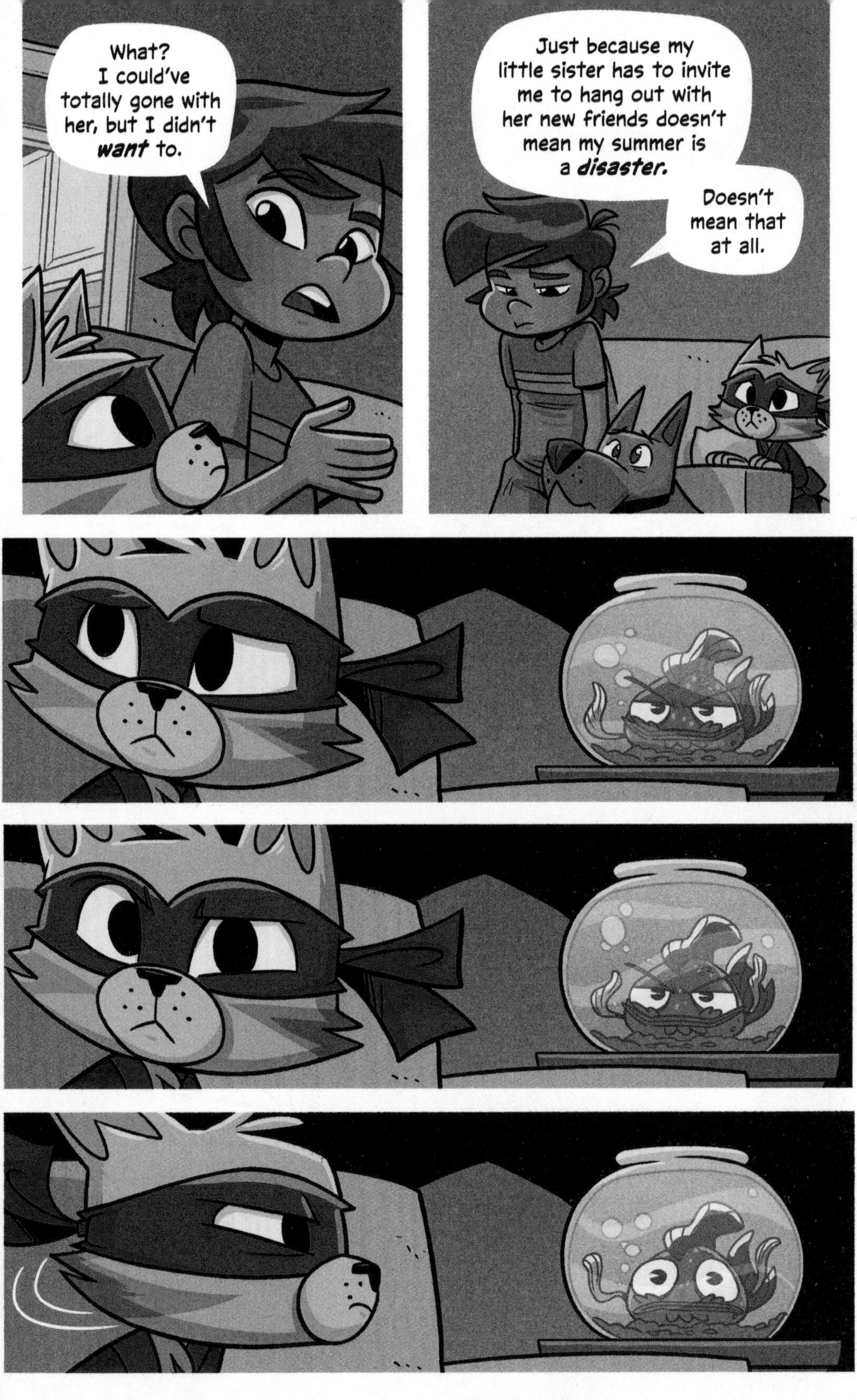
What? I could've totally gone with her, but I didn't *want* to.
Just because my little sister has to invite me to hang out with her new friends doesn't mean my summer is a *disaster.*
Doesn't mean that at all.

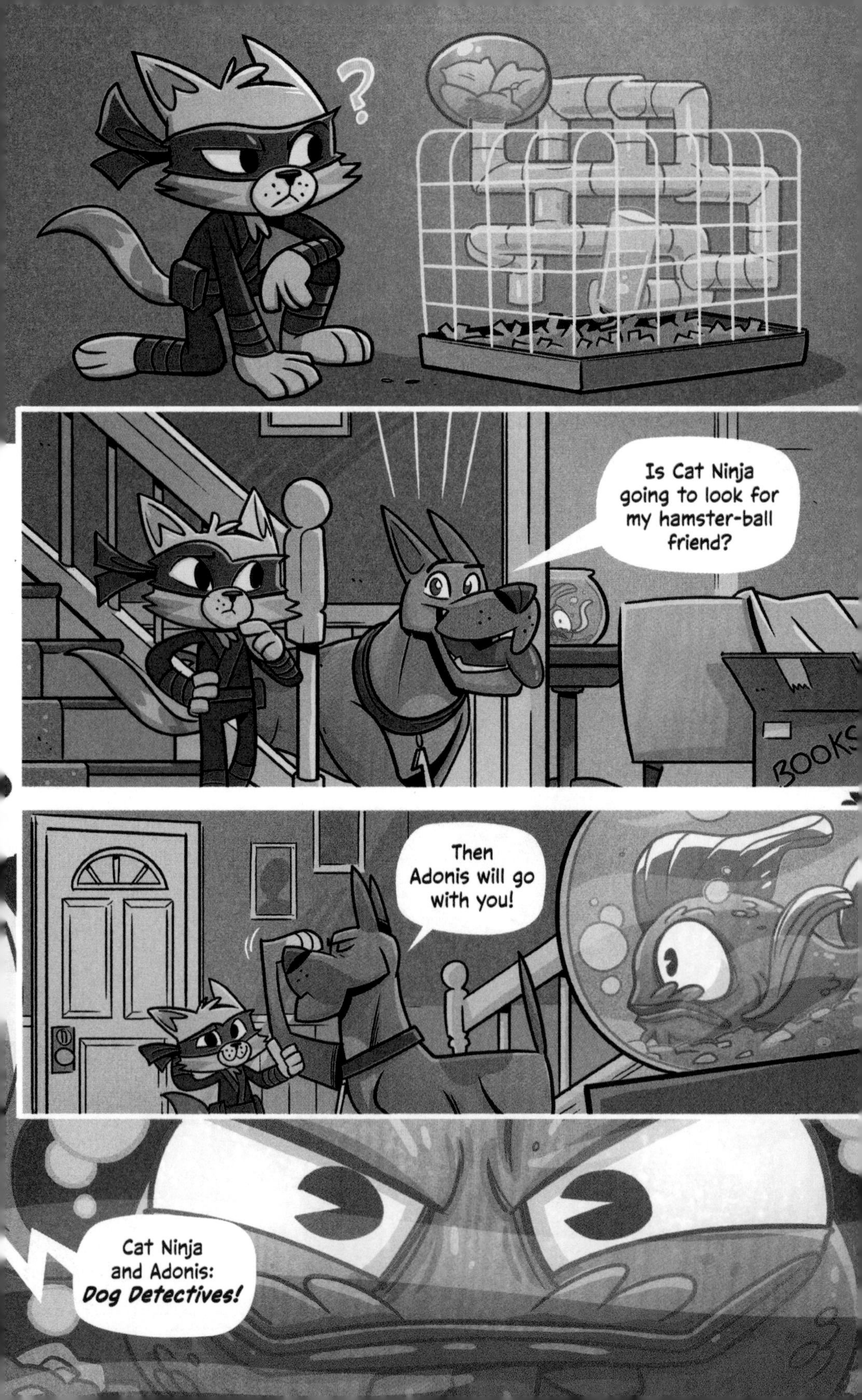

?
Is Cat Ninja going to look for my hamster-ball friend?
BOOKS
Then Adonis will go with you!
Cat Ninja and Adonis: ***Dog Detectives!***

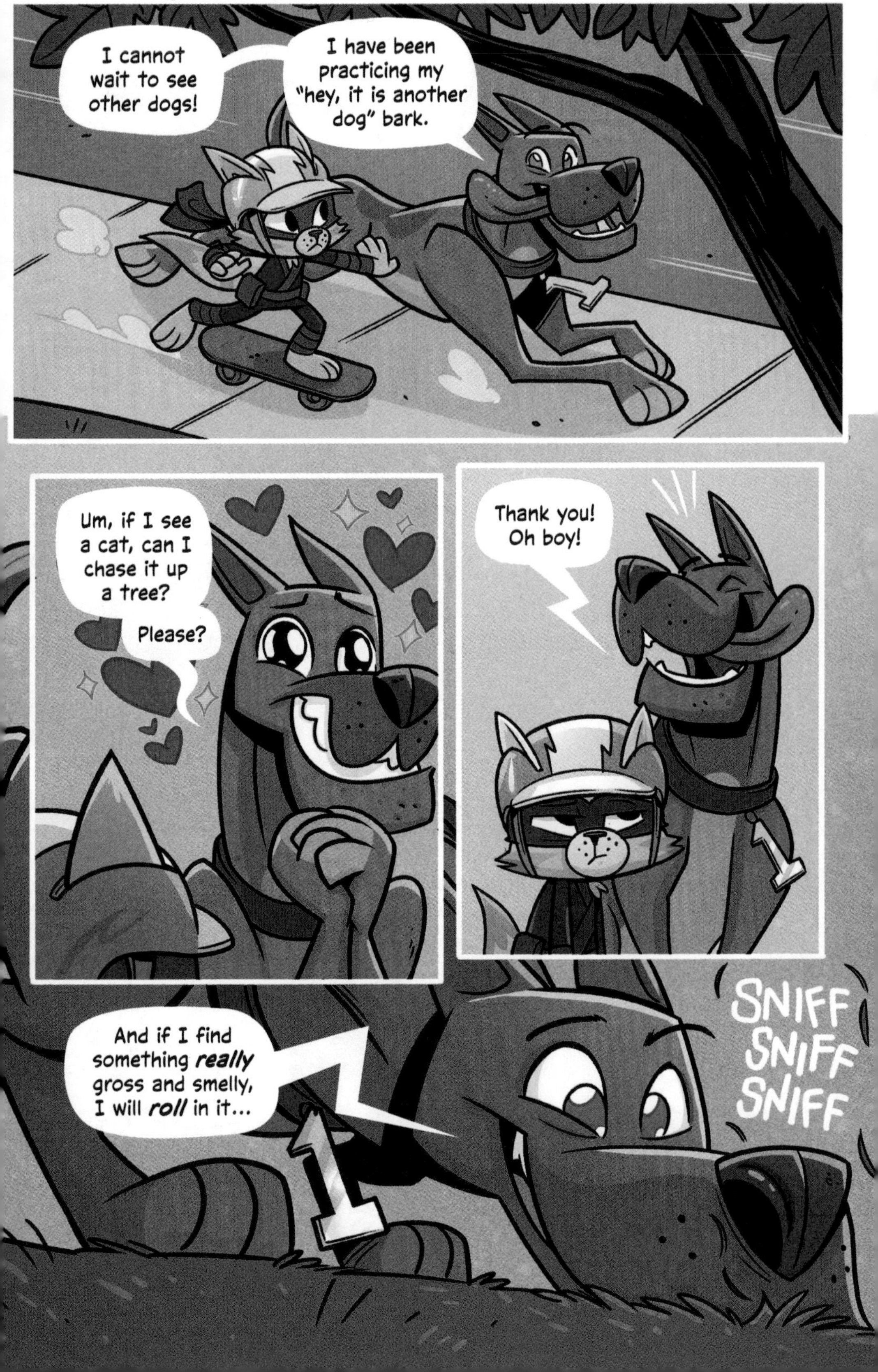
I cannot wait to see other dogs!
I have been practicing my "hey, it is another dog" bark.
Um, if I see a cat, can I chase it up a tree?
Please?
Thank you! Oh boy!
And if I find something *really* gross and smelly, I will *roll* in it...
SNIFF SNIFF SNIFF

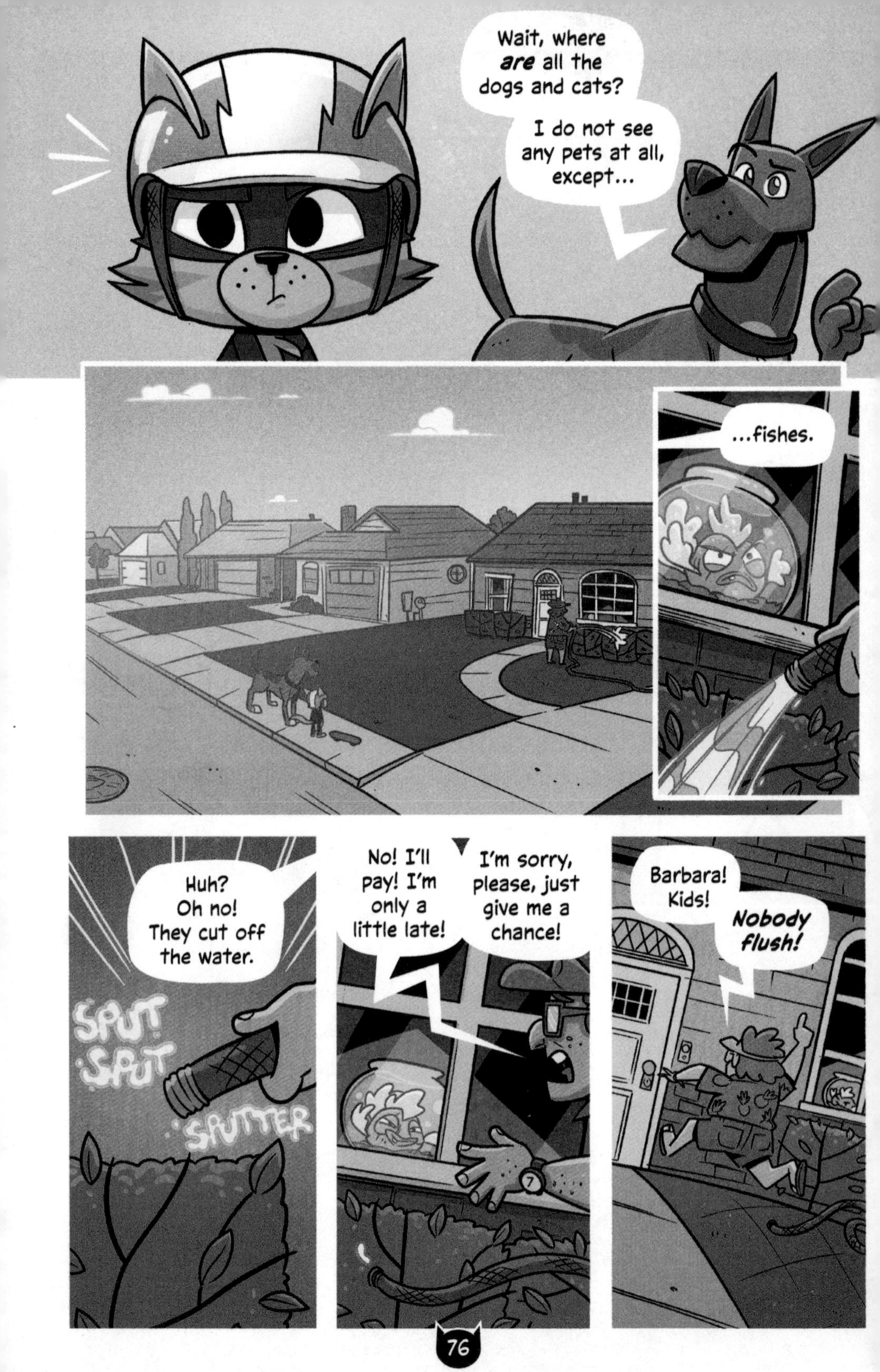

Wait, where *are* all the dogs and cats?
I do not see any pets at all, except...
...fishes.
Huh? Oh no! They cut off the water.
SPUT SPUT SPUTTER
No! I'll pay! I'm only a little late!
I'm sorry, please, just give me a chance!
Barbara! Kids!
Nobody flush!

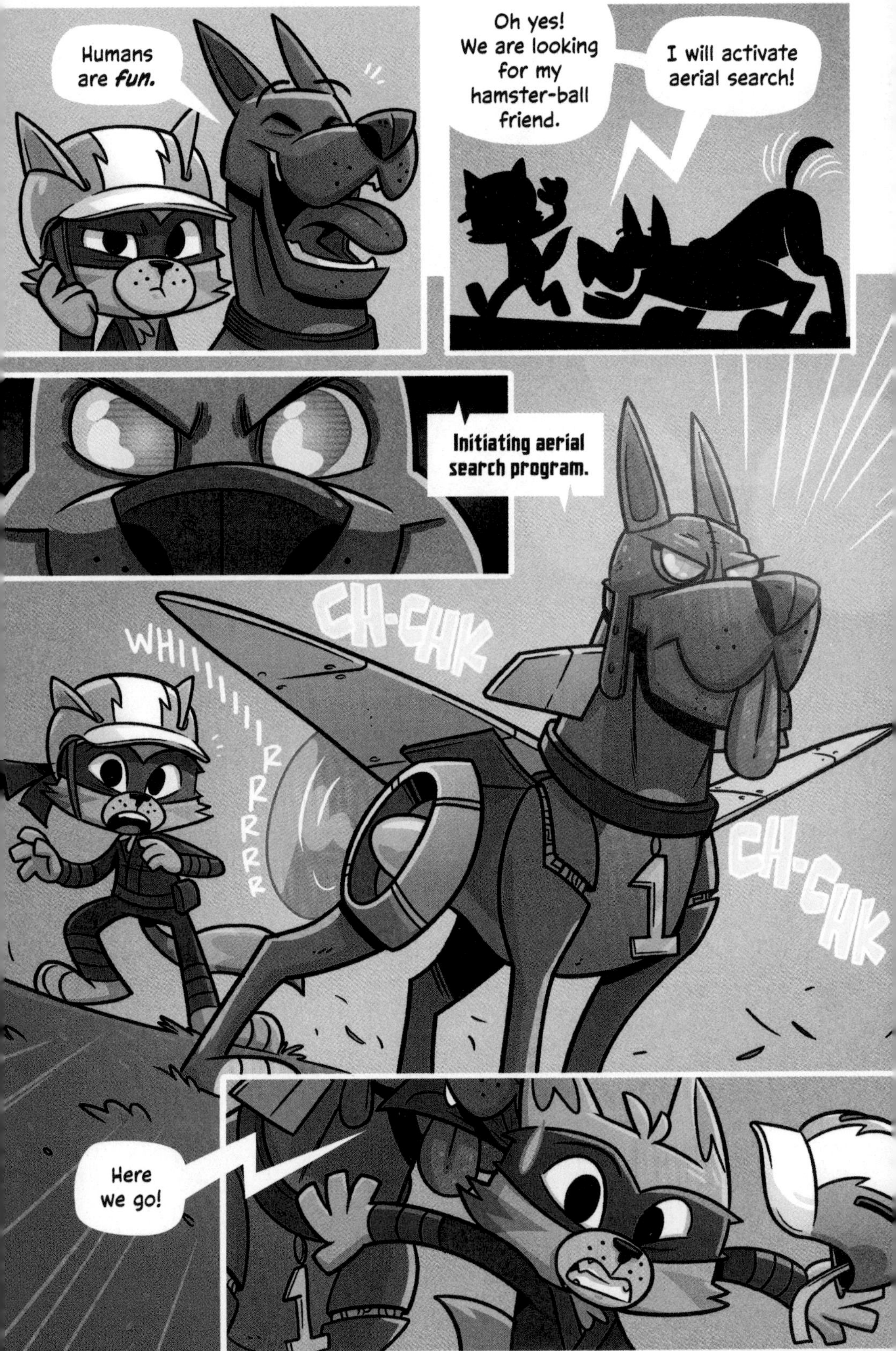
Humans are *fun.*
Oh yes! We are looking for my hamster-ball friend.
I will activate aerial search!
Initiating aerial search program.
CH-CHK
WHIIIIIIIRRRRRR
CH-CHK
Here we go!

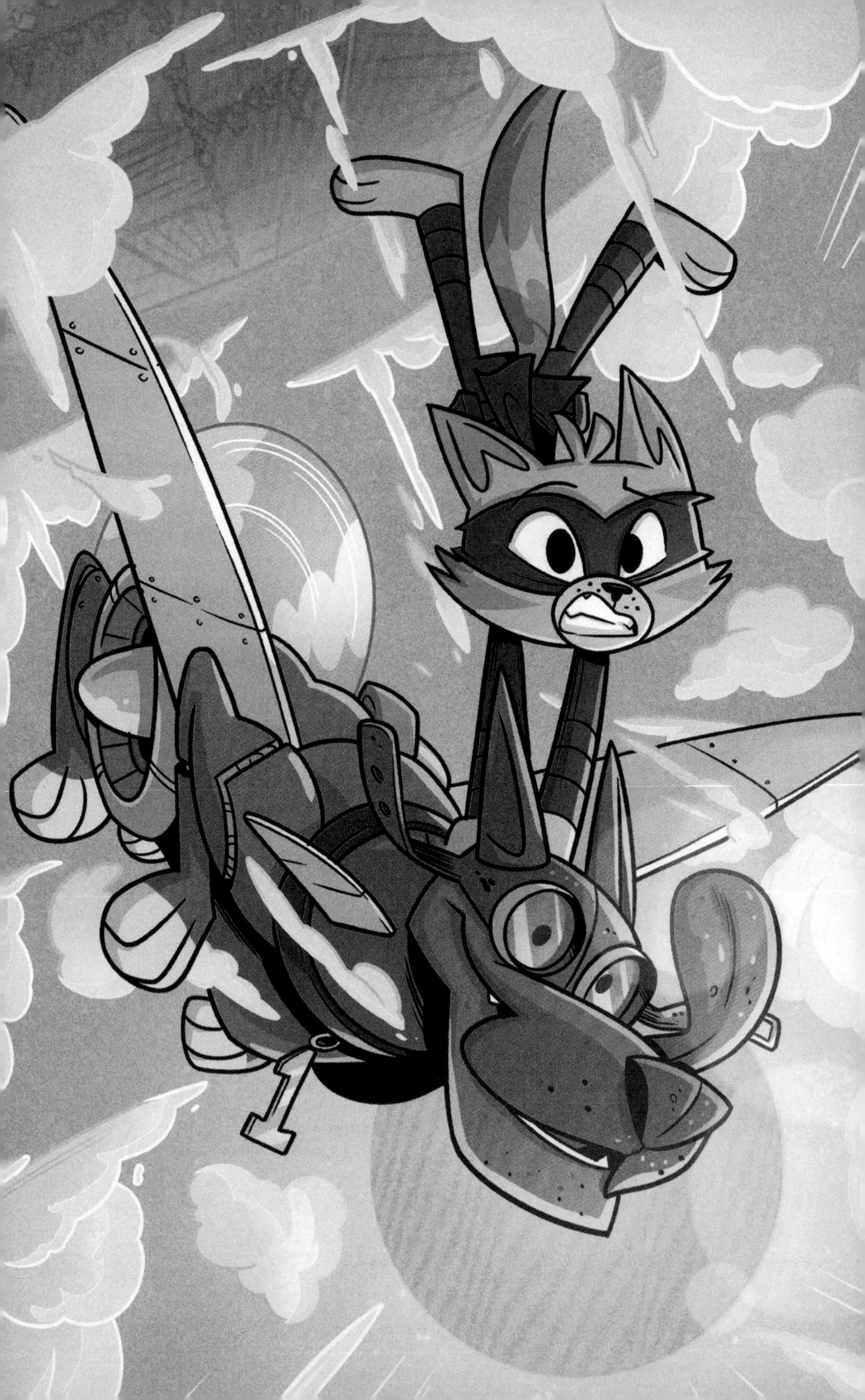

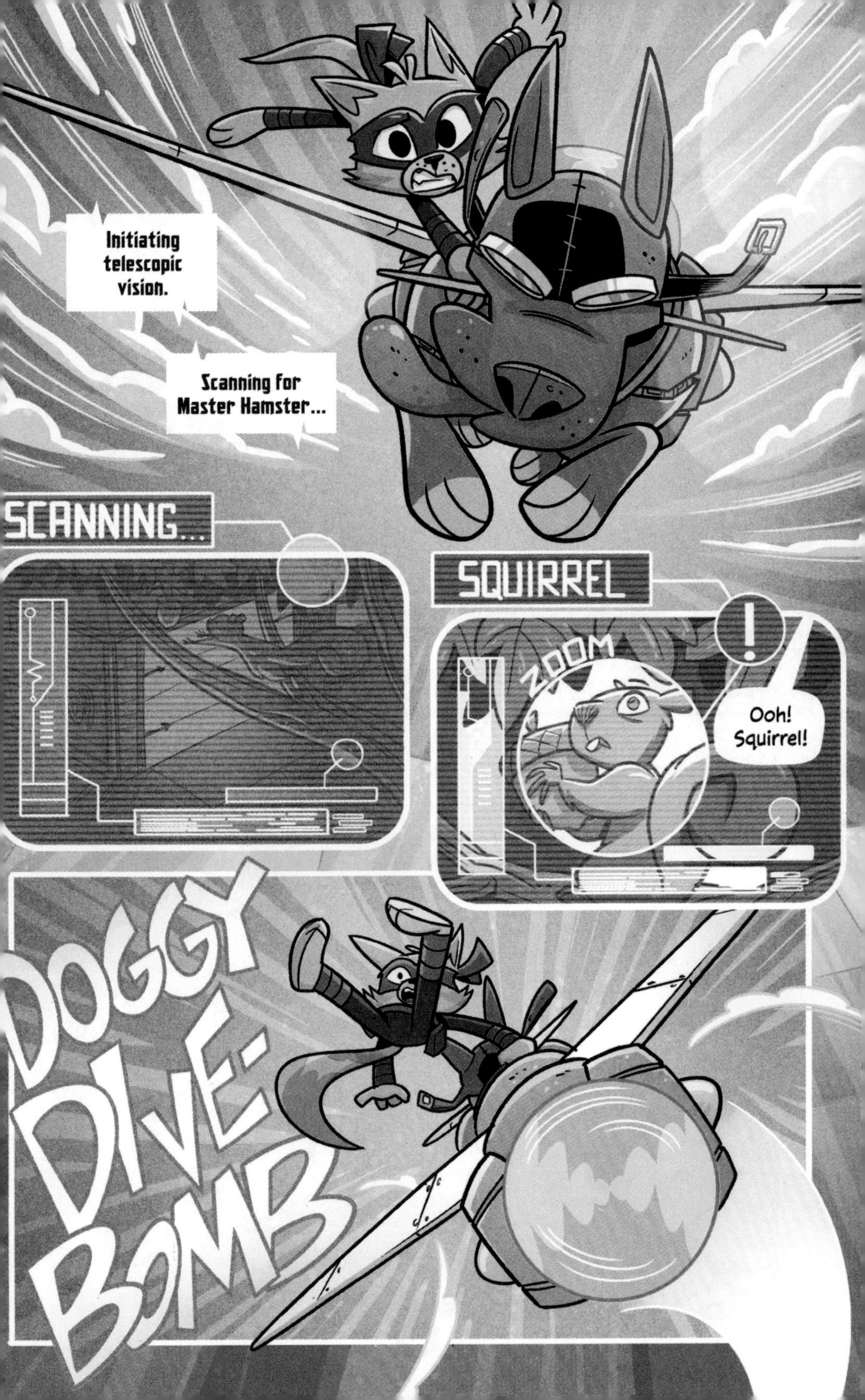
Initiating telescopic vision.
Scanning for Master Hamster...
SCANNING...
SQUIRREL
!
ZOOM
Ooh! Squirrel!
DOGGY DIVE-BOMB

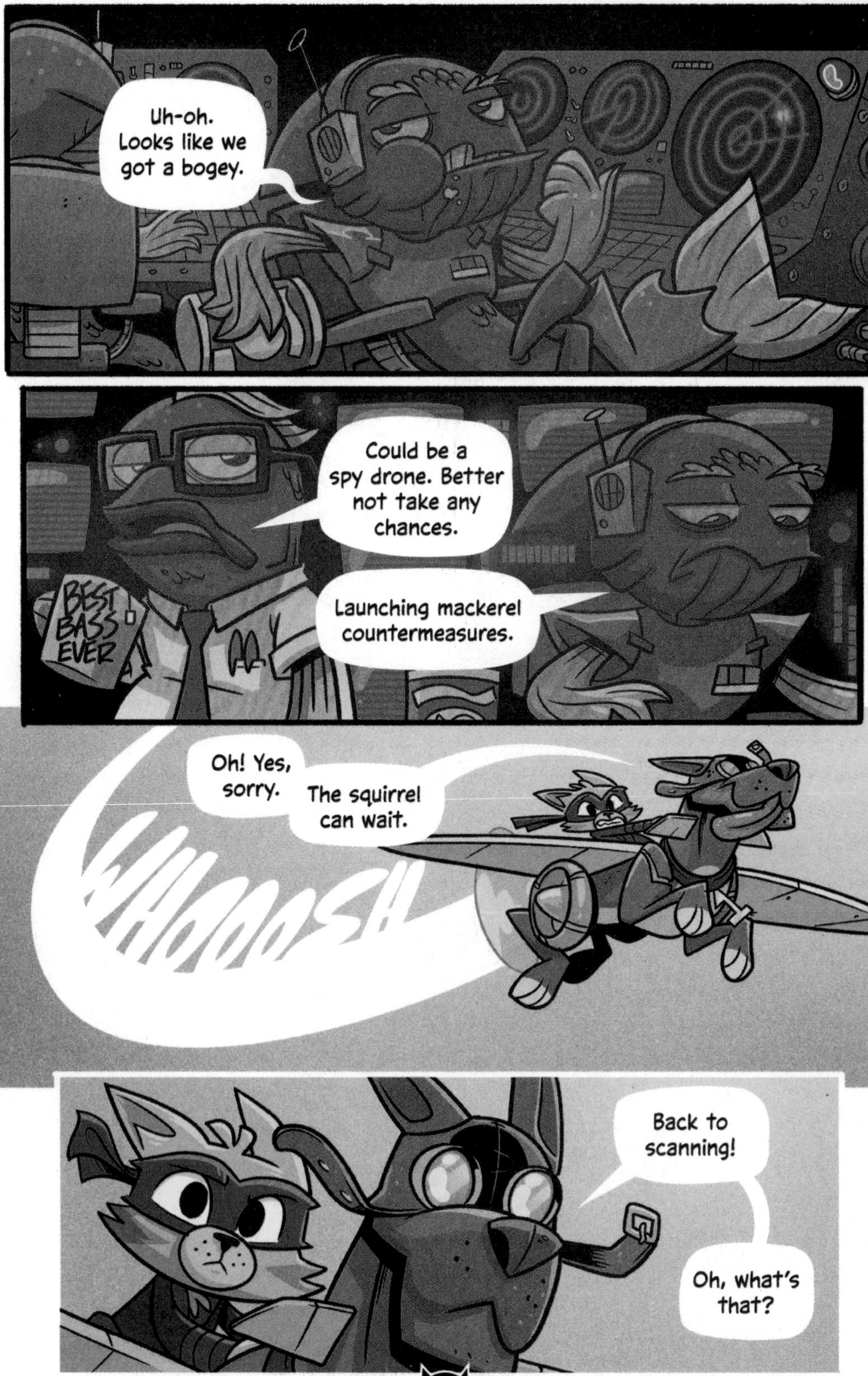
Uh-oh. Looks like we got a bogey.
Could be a spy drone. Better not take any chances.
Launching mackerel countermeasures.
BEST BASS EVER
Oh! Yes, sorry.
The squirrel can wait.
WHOOOOSH
Back to scanning!
Oh, what's that?

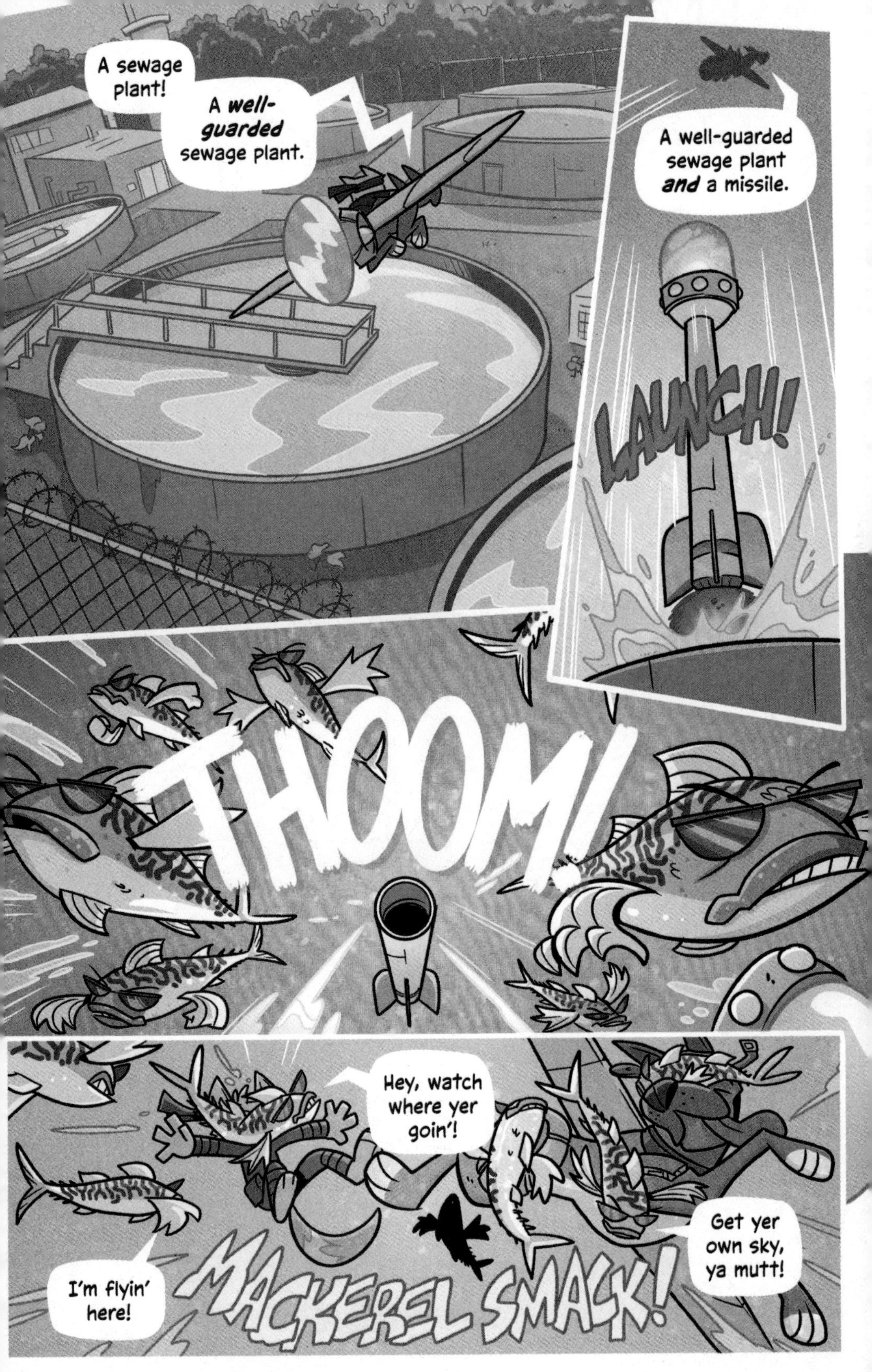
A sewage plant!
A *well-guarded* sewage plant.
A well-guarded sewage plant *and* a missile.
LAUNCH!
THOOM!
Hey, watch where yer goin'!
Get yer own sky, ya mutt!
I'm flyin' here!
MACKEREL SMACK!

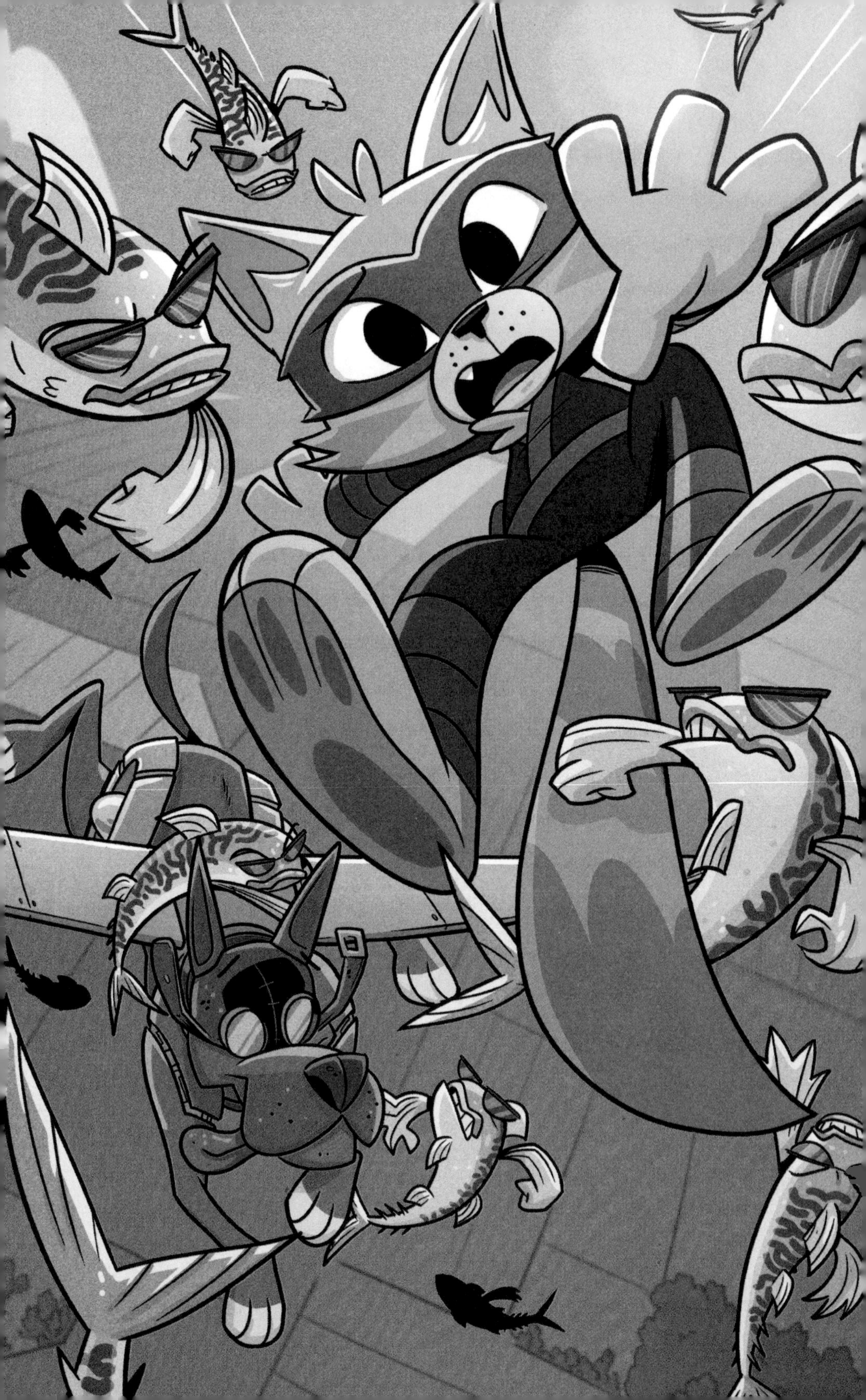

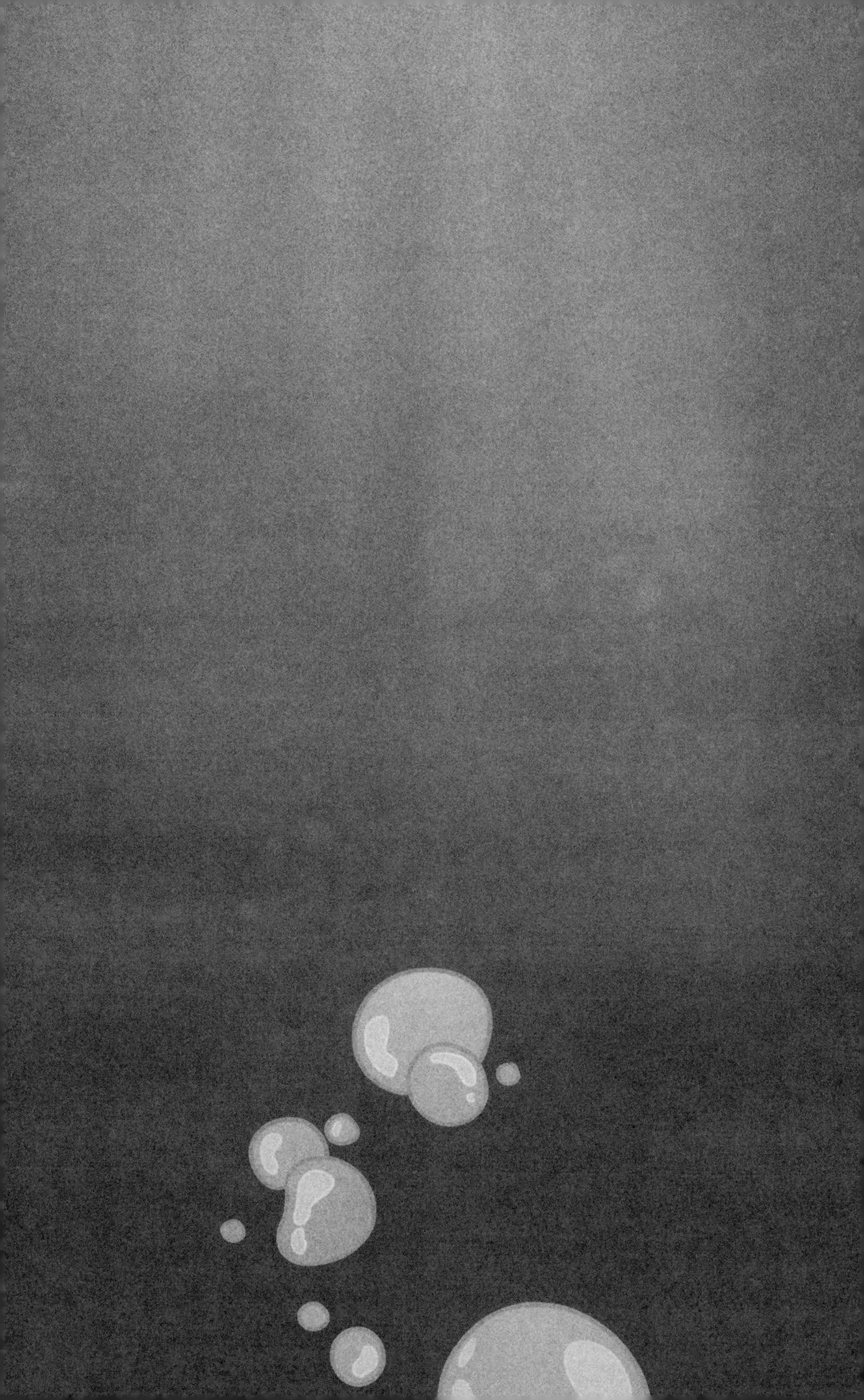

Chapter 4
As Quiet as a...Cat Ninja

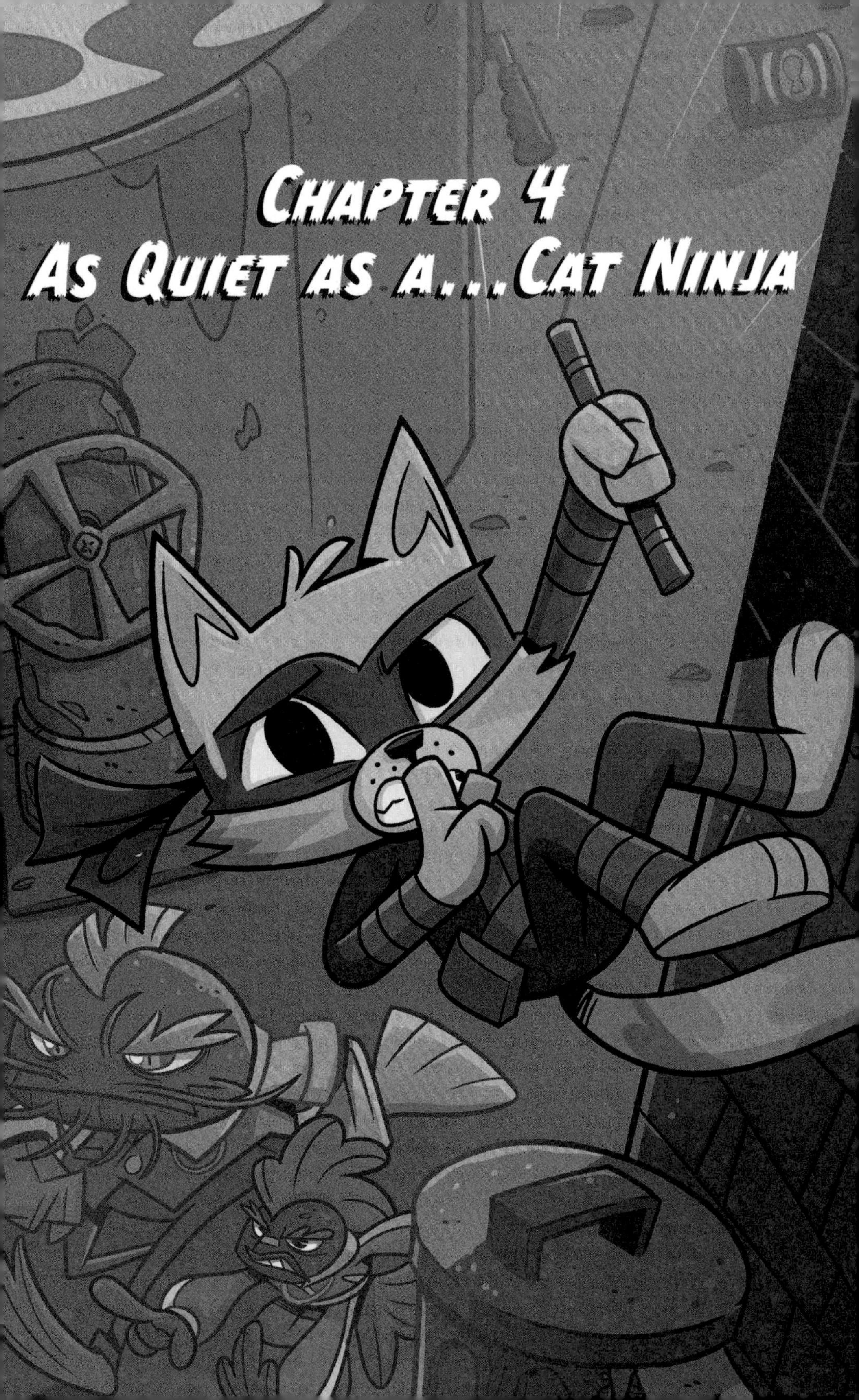

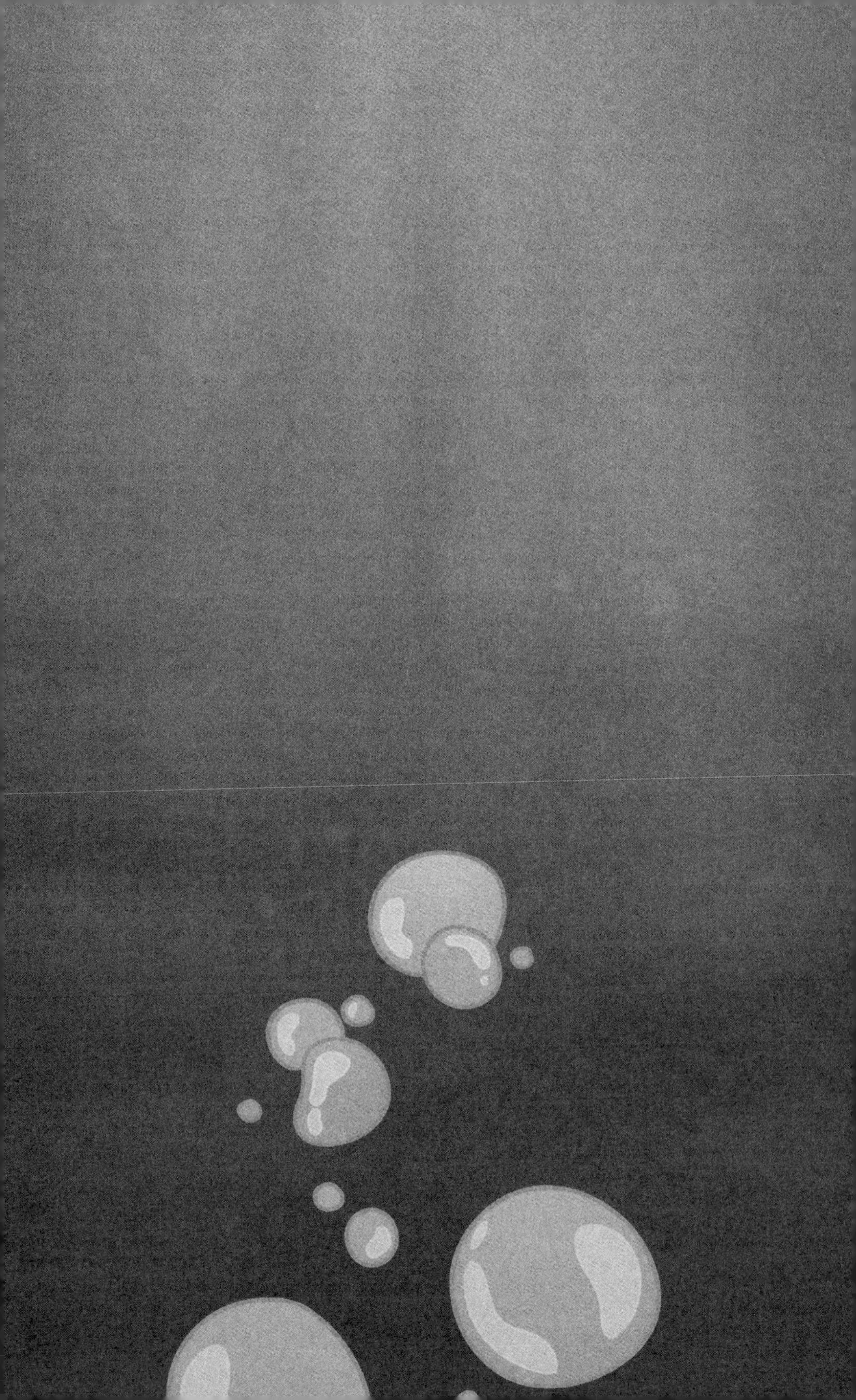

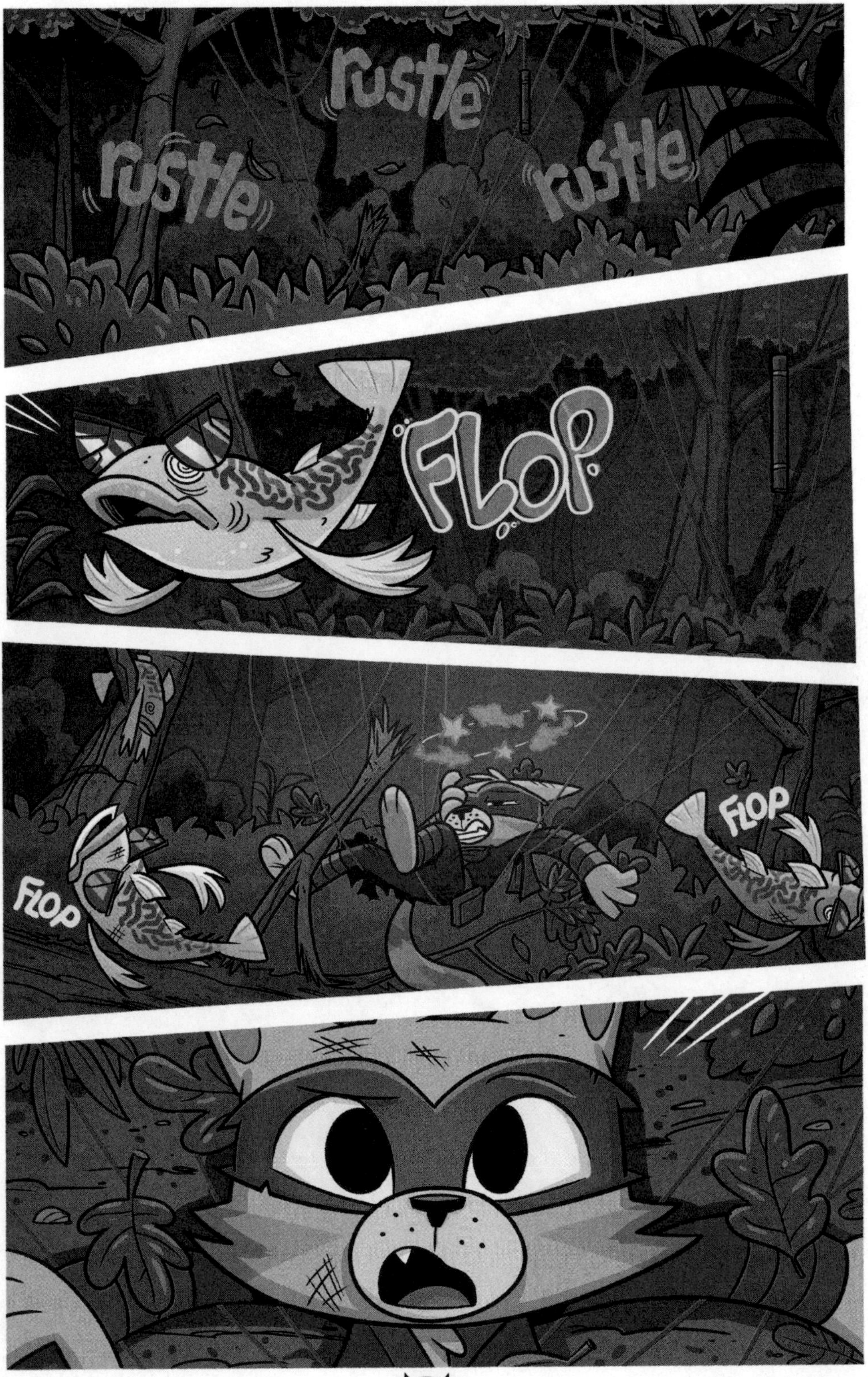

rustle
rustle
rustle
FLOP
FLOP
FLOP

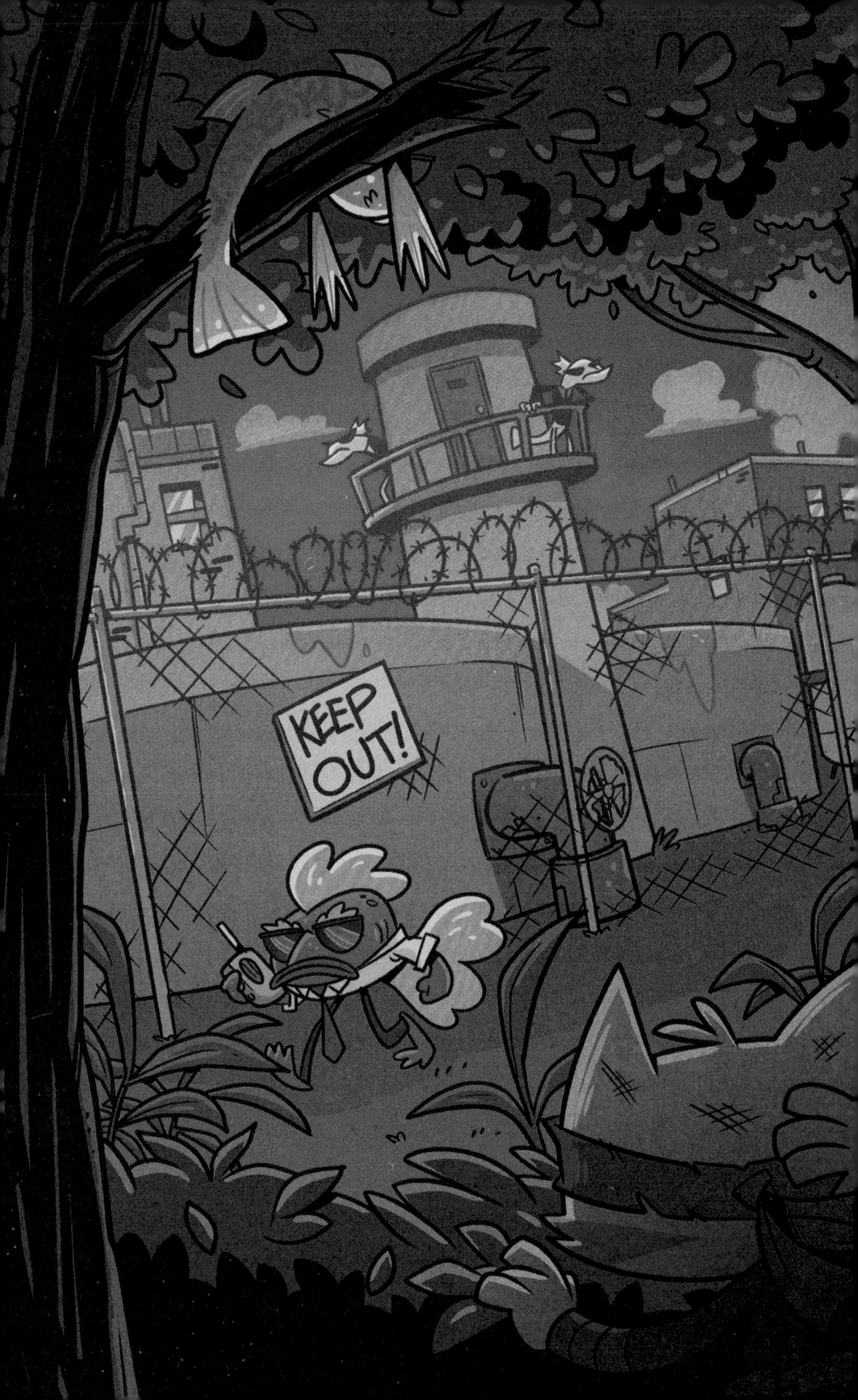
KEEP OUT!

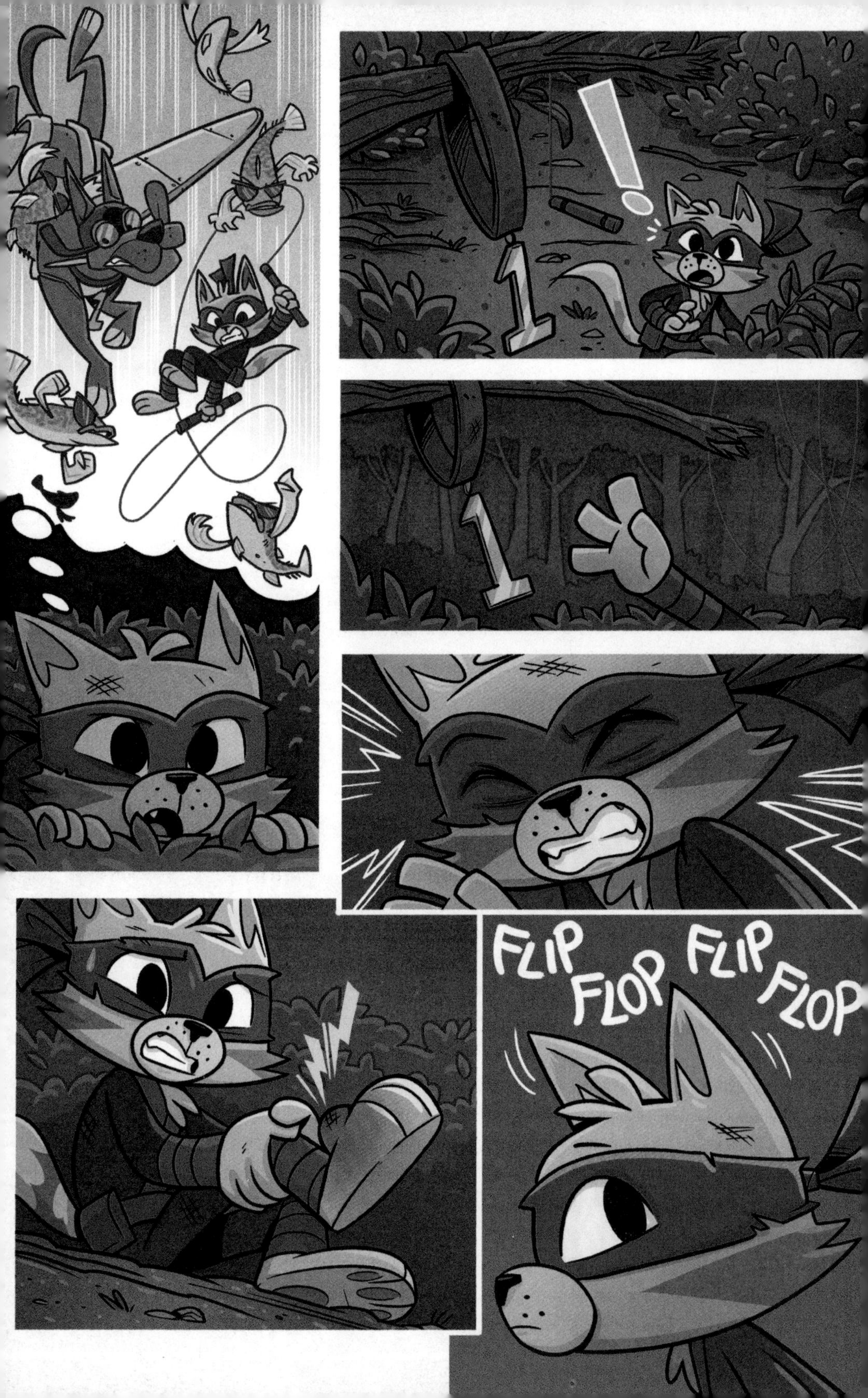
FLIP
FLOP
FLIP
FLOP

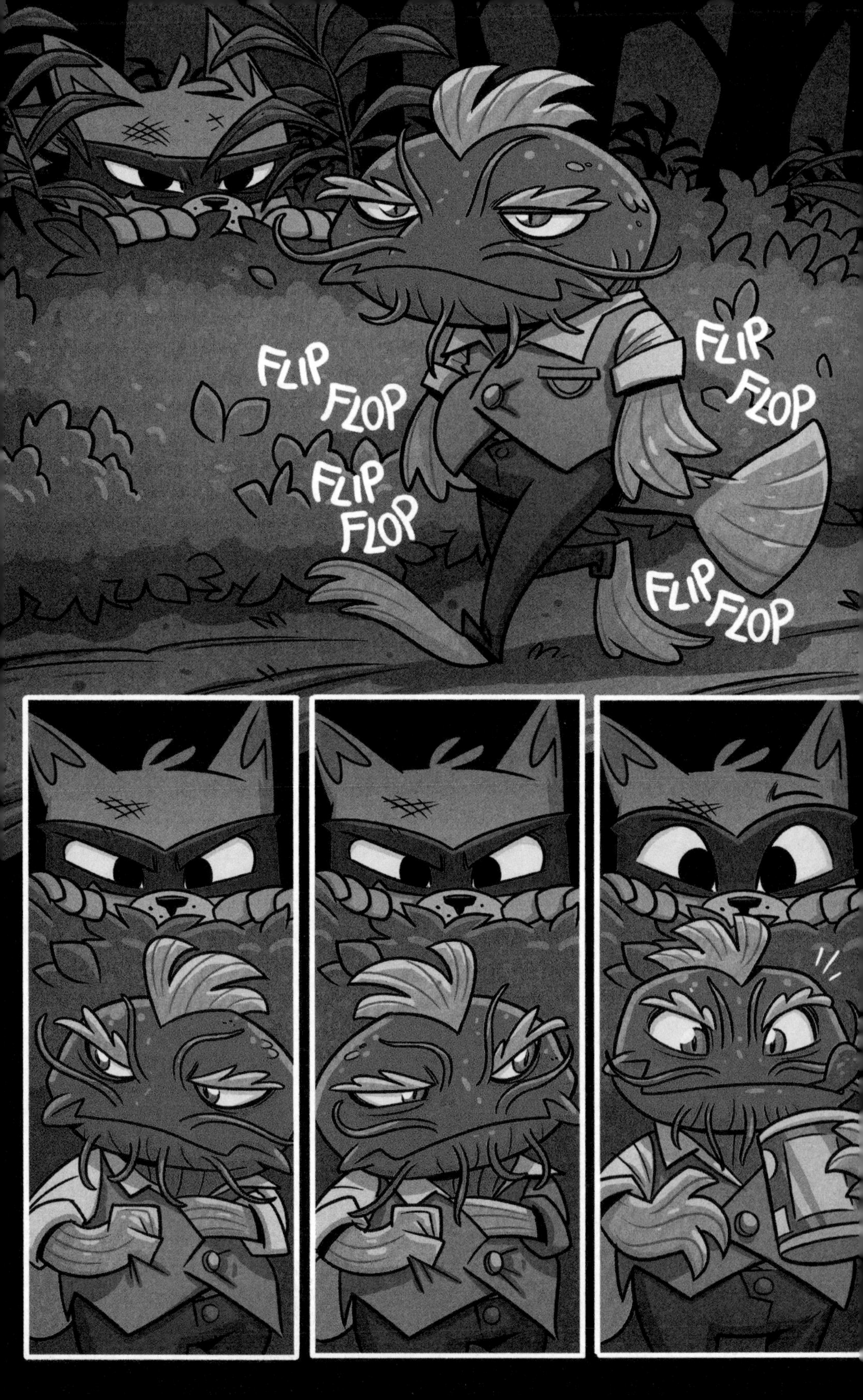
FLIP FLOP
FLIP FLOP
FLIP FLOP
FLIP FLOP

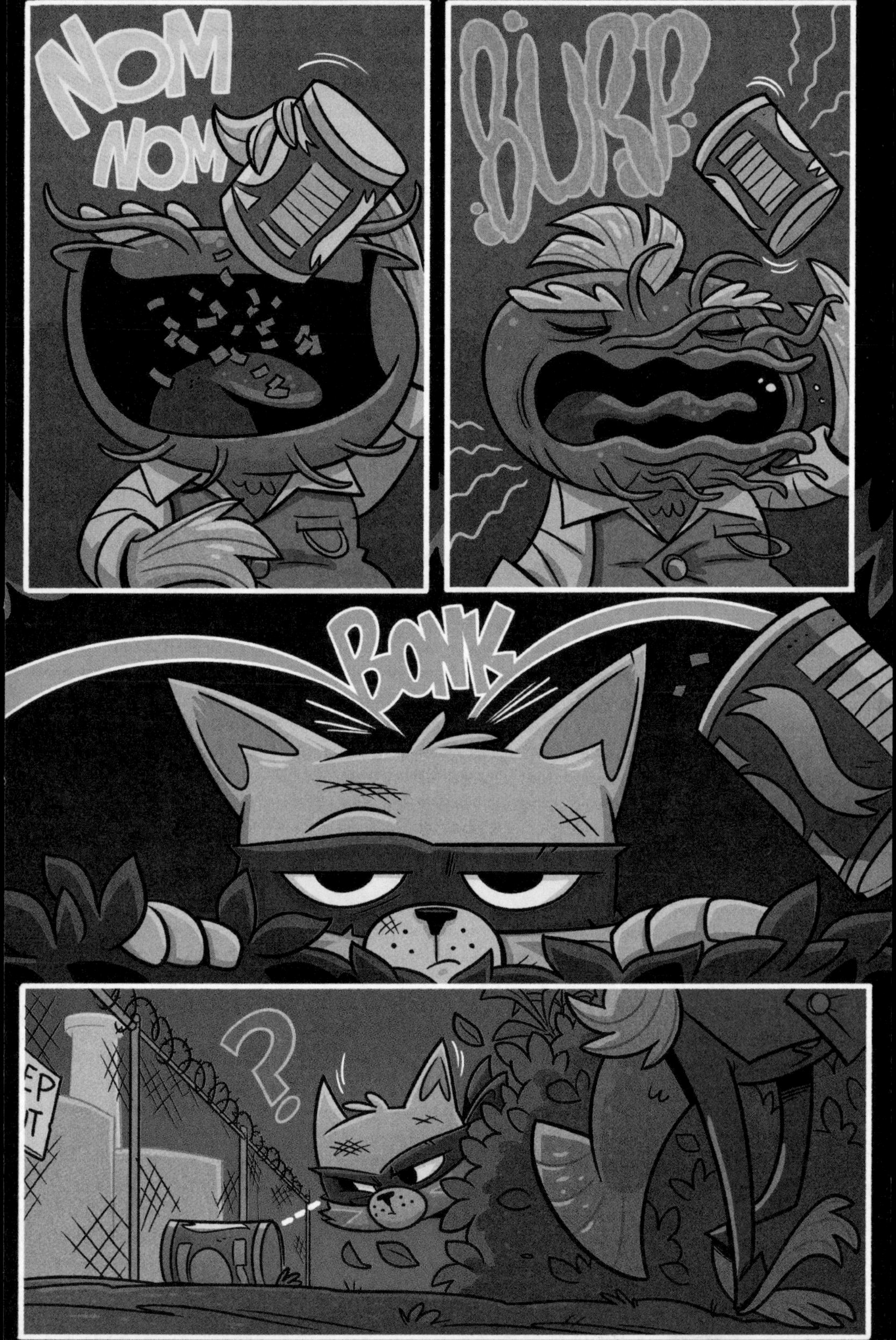
NOM
NOM
BURP
BONK
?

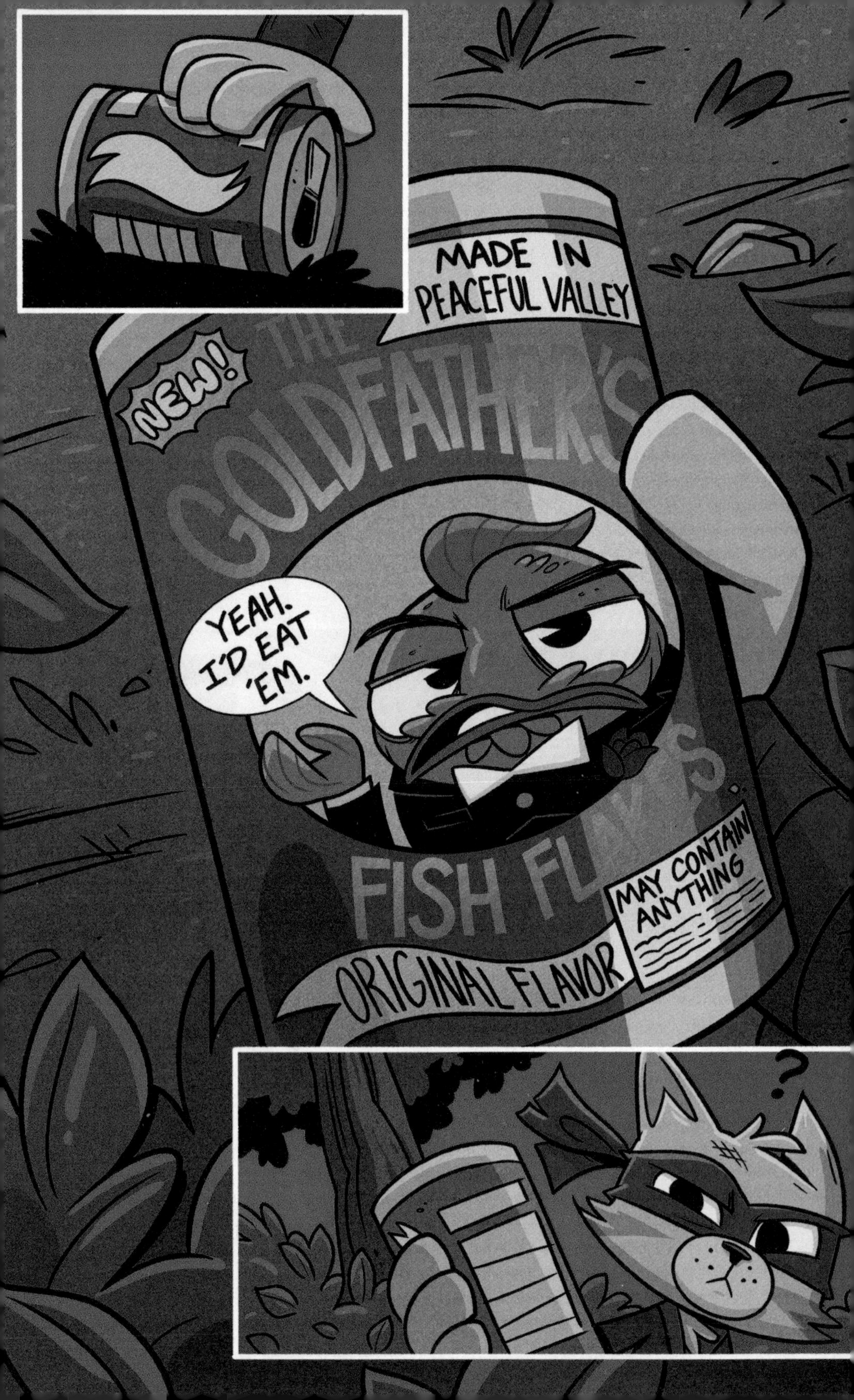
MADE IN
PEACEFUL VALLEY
NEW!
THE GOLDFATHER'S
YEAH. I'D EAT 'EM.
FISH FL
MAY CONTAIN ANYTHING
ORIGINAL FLAVOR
?

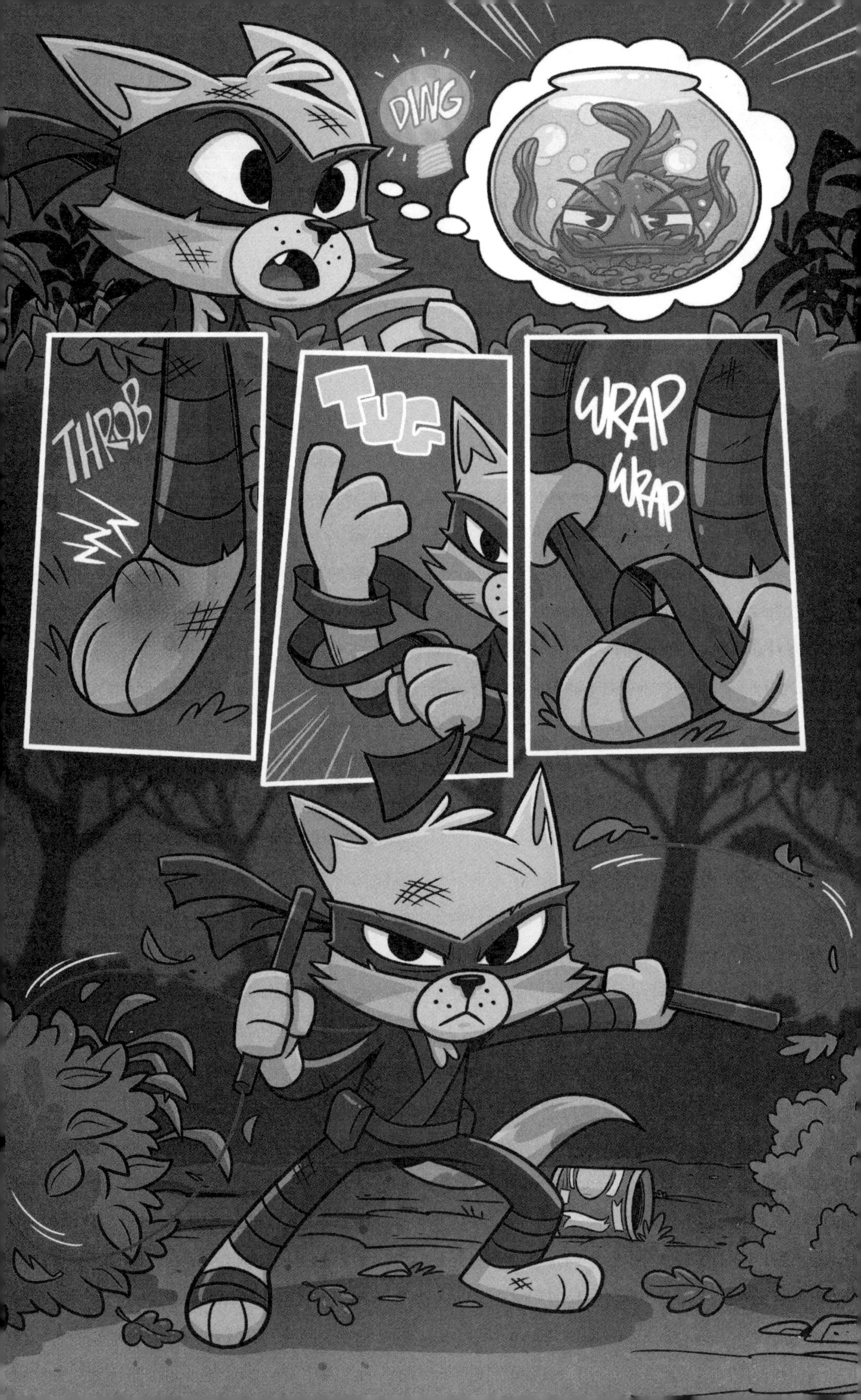
DING
THROB
TUG
WRAP
WRAP

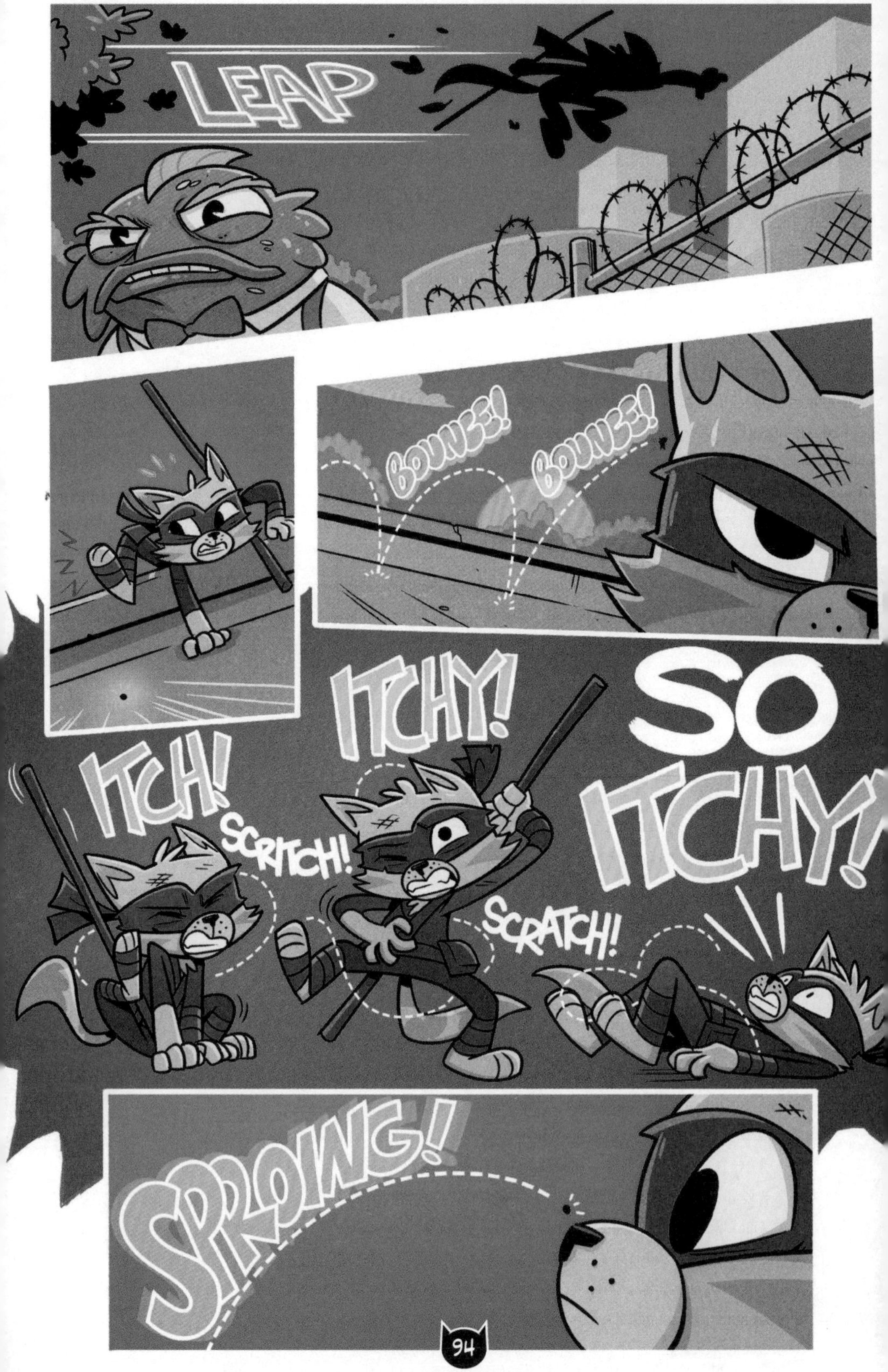
LEAP
BOUNCE!
BOUNCE!
ITCH!
SCRITCH!
ITCHY!
SO
ITCHY!
SCRATCH!
SPROING!

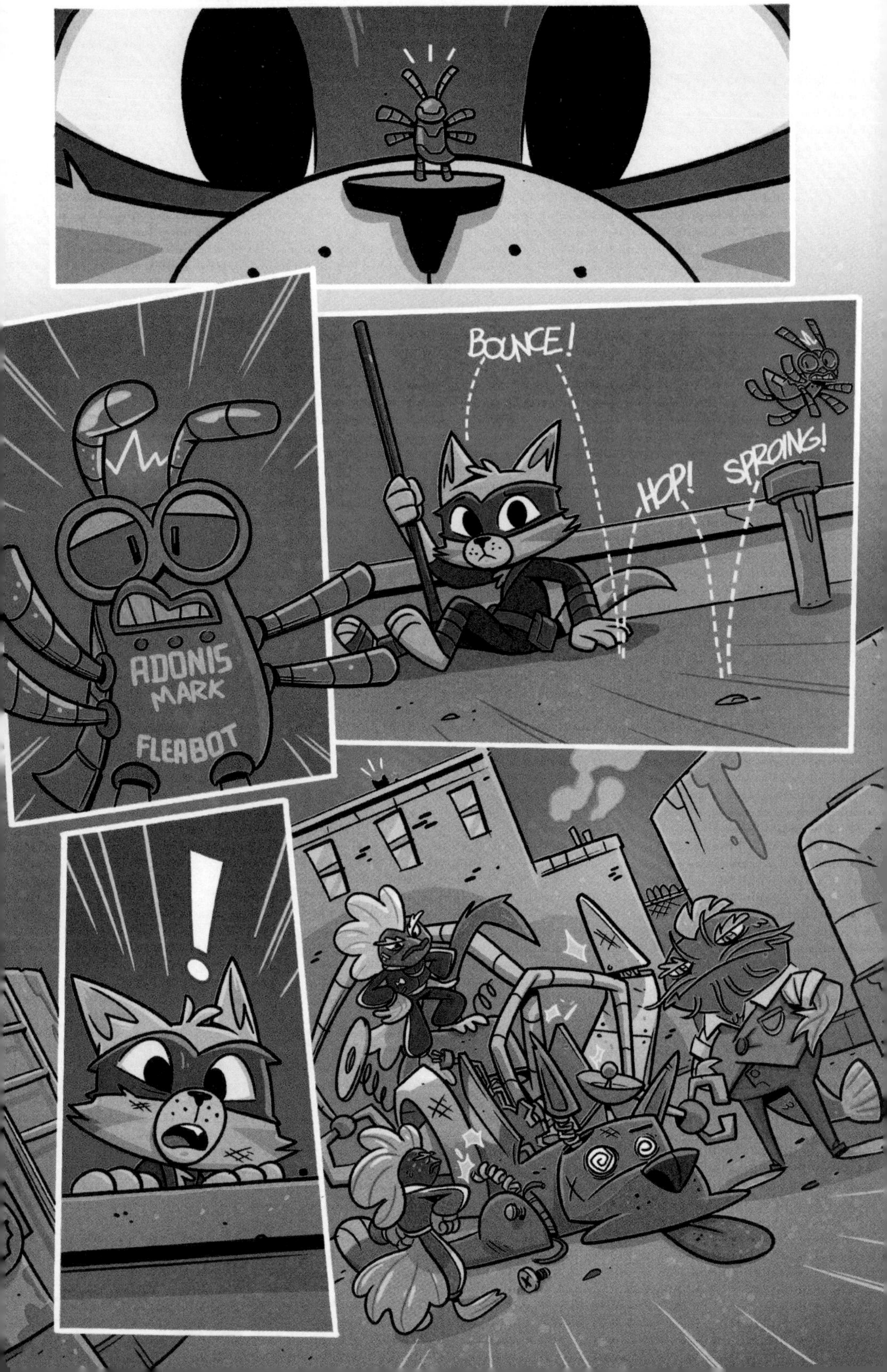
ADONIS
MARK
FLEABOT
BOUNCE!
HOP!
SPROING!
!

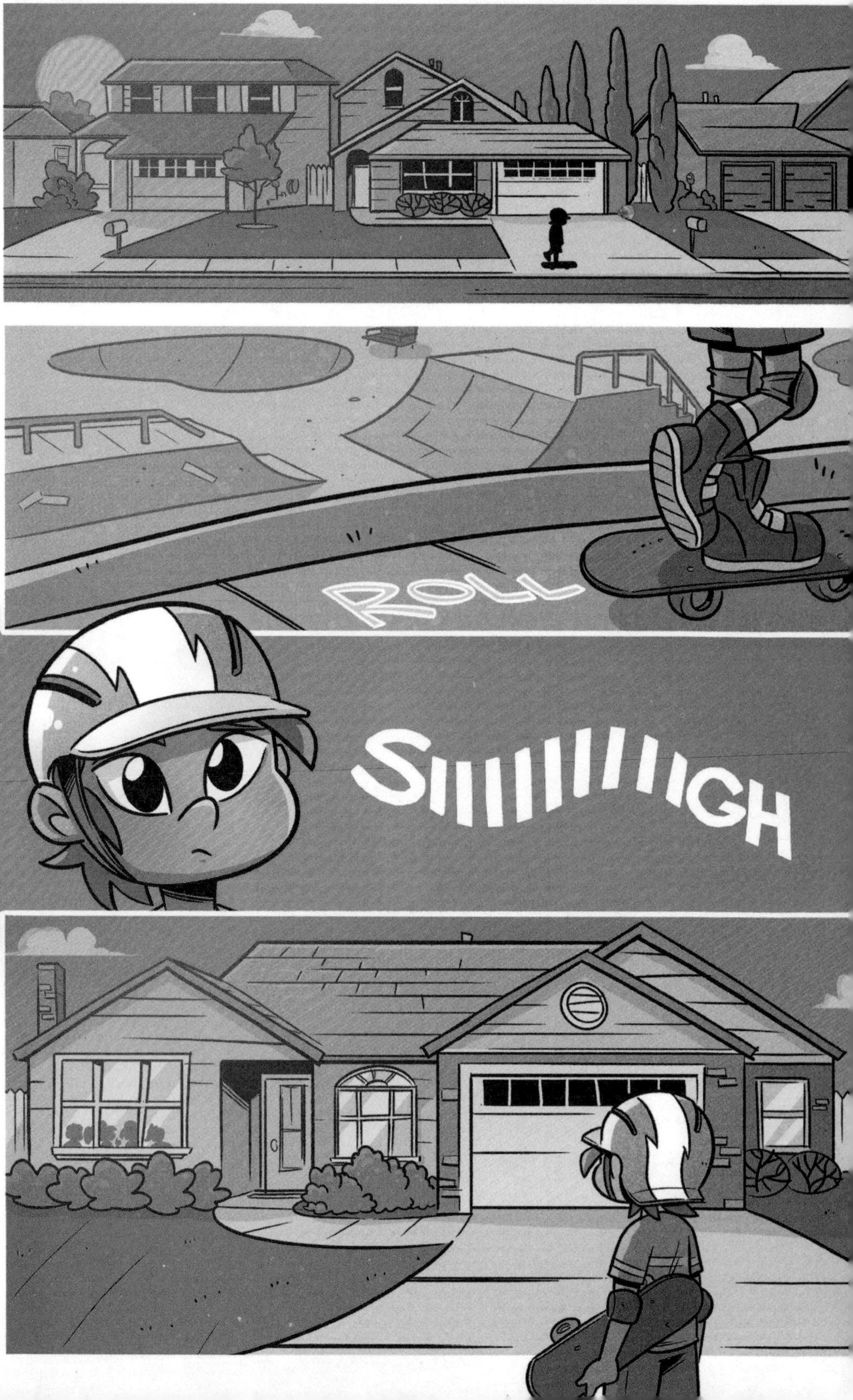
ROLL
SIIIIIIIIIGH

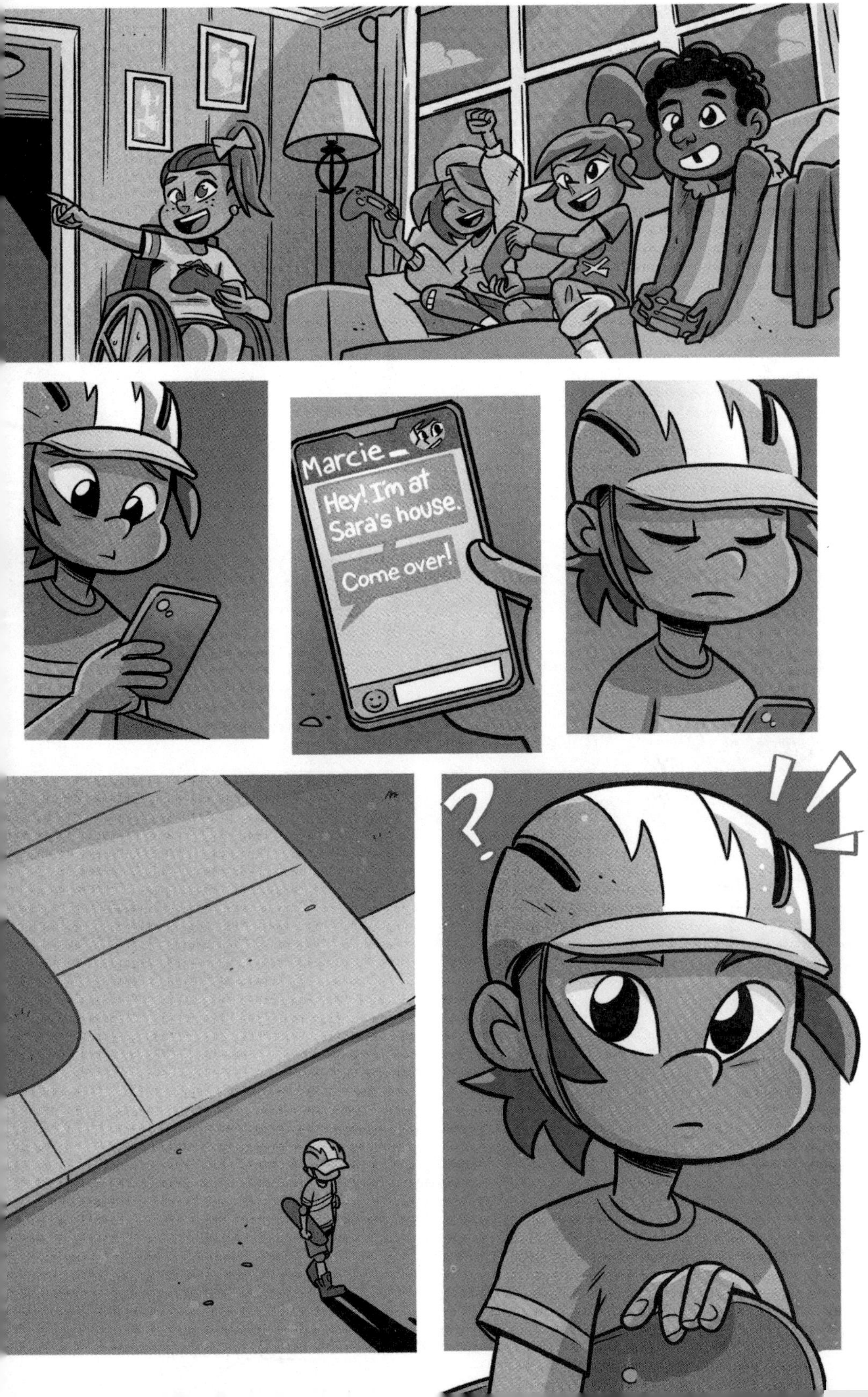
Marcie
Hey! I'm at Sara's house.
Come over!
?
!!

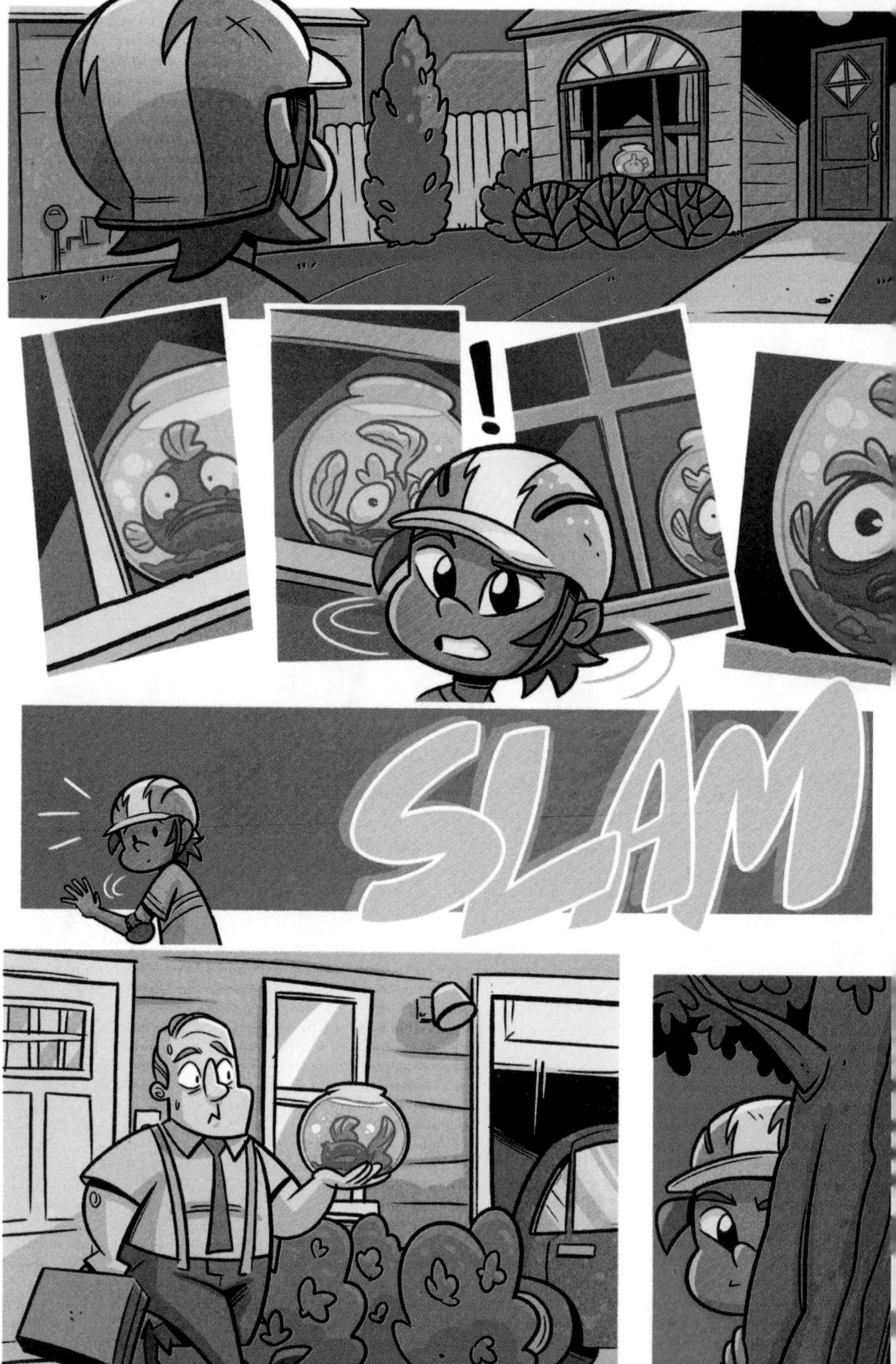
!
SLAM

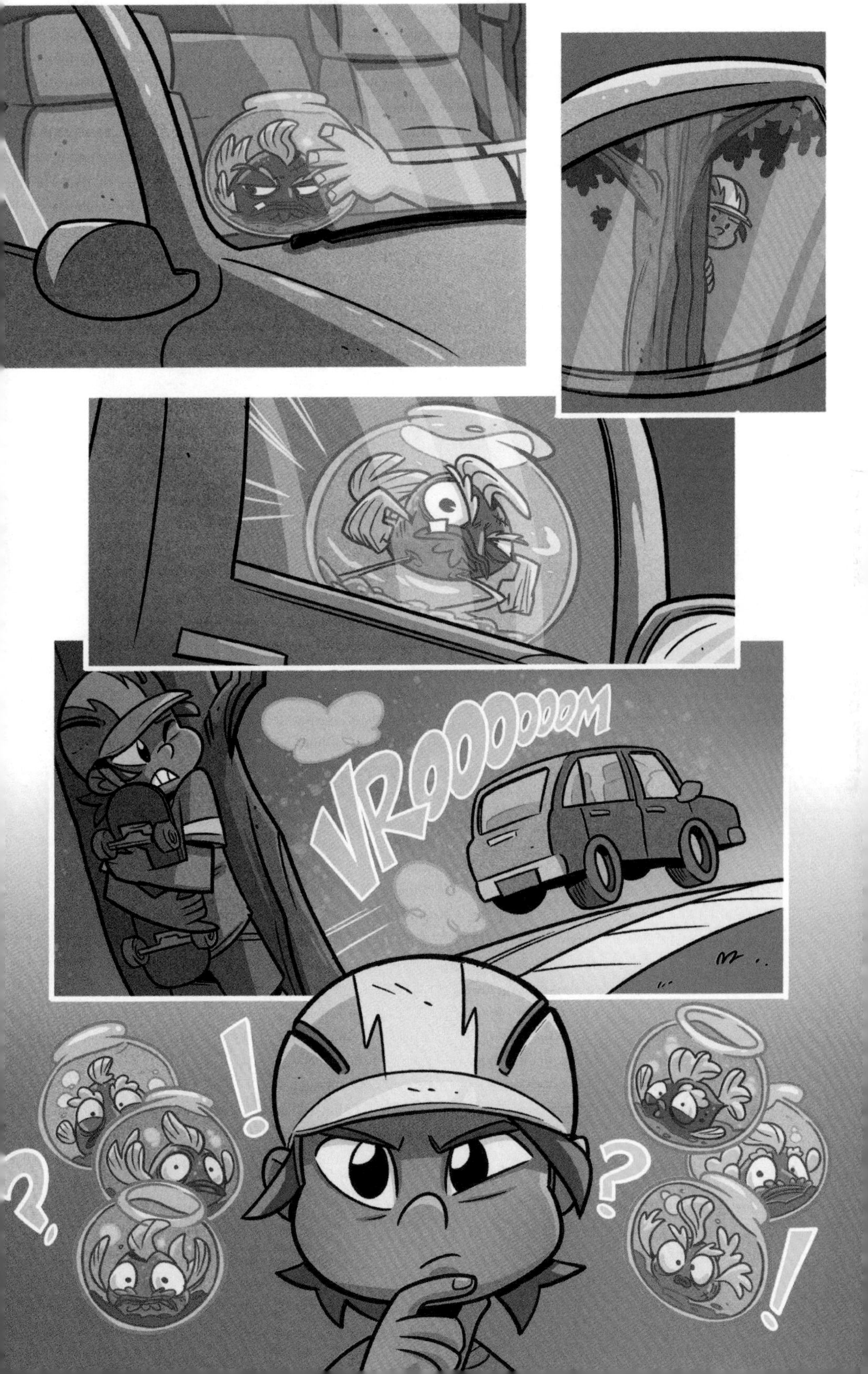
VROOOOOOOM

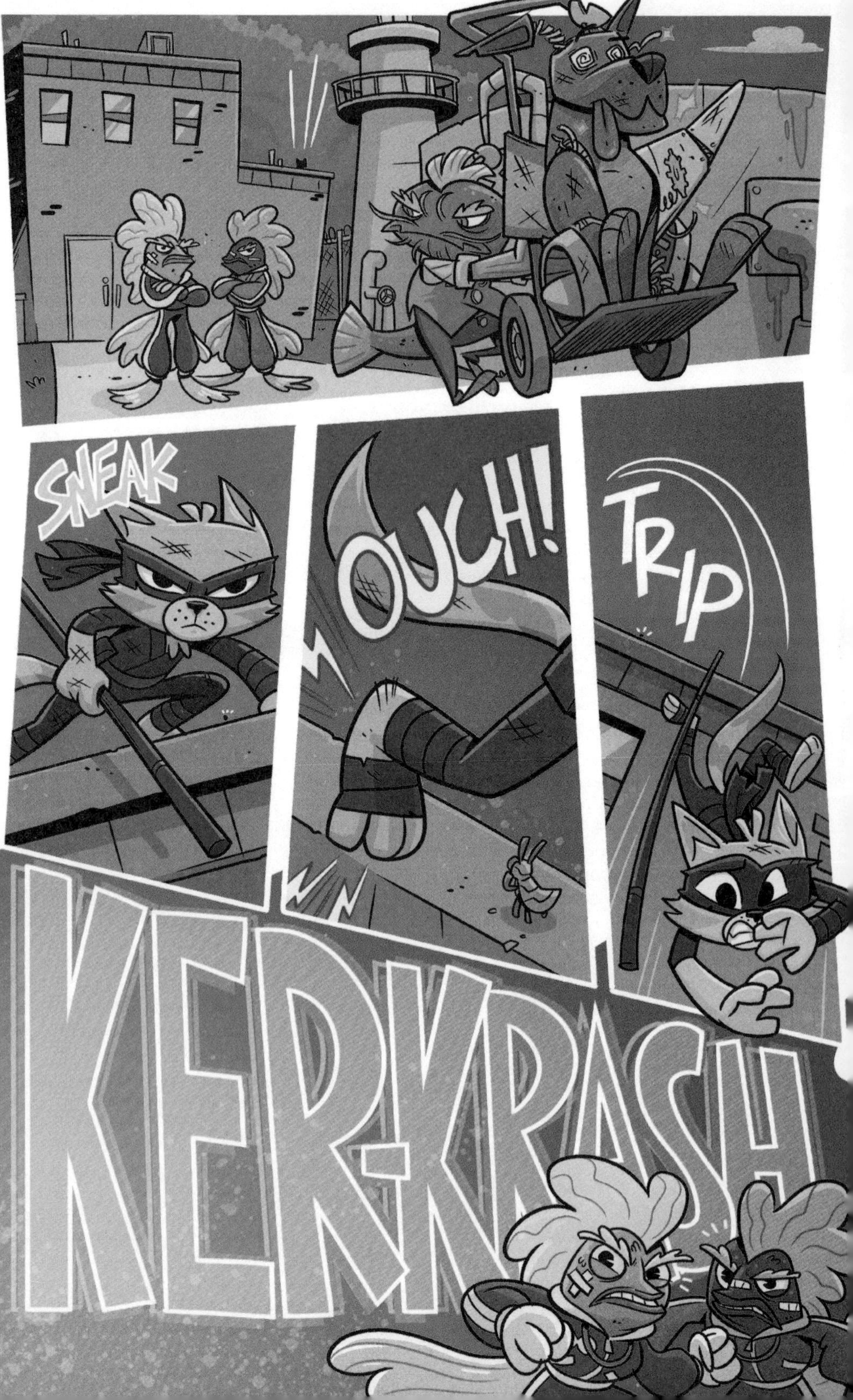
SNEAK
OUCH!
TRIP
KER-KRASH

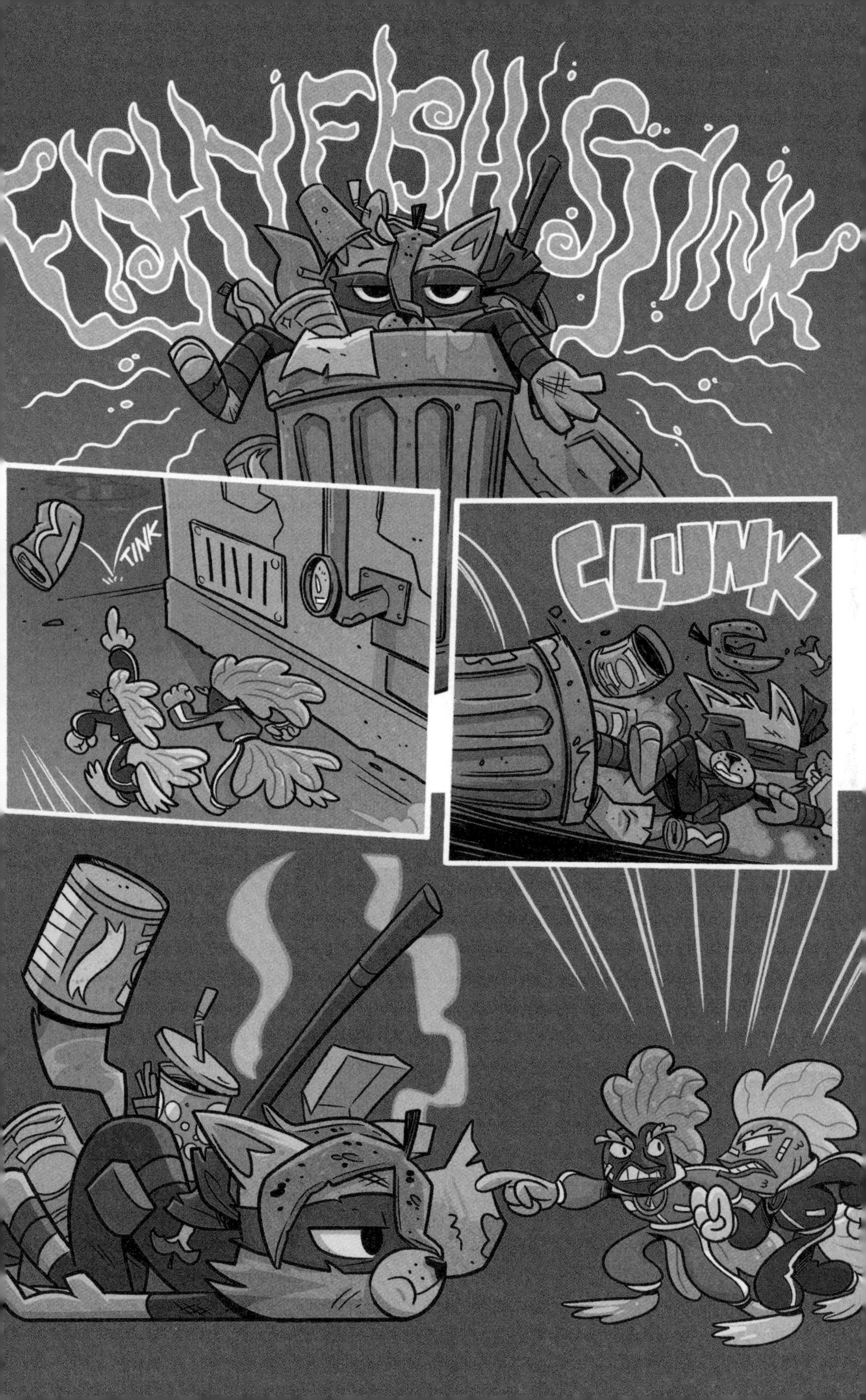
FISH STINK
TINK
CLUNK

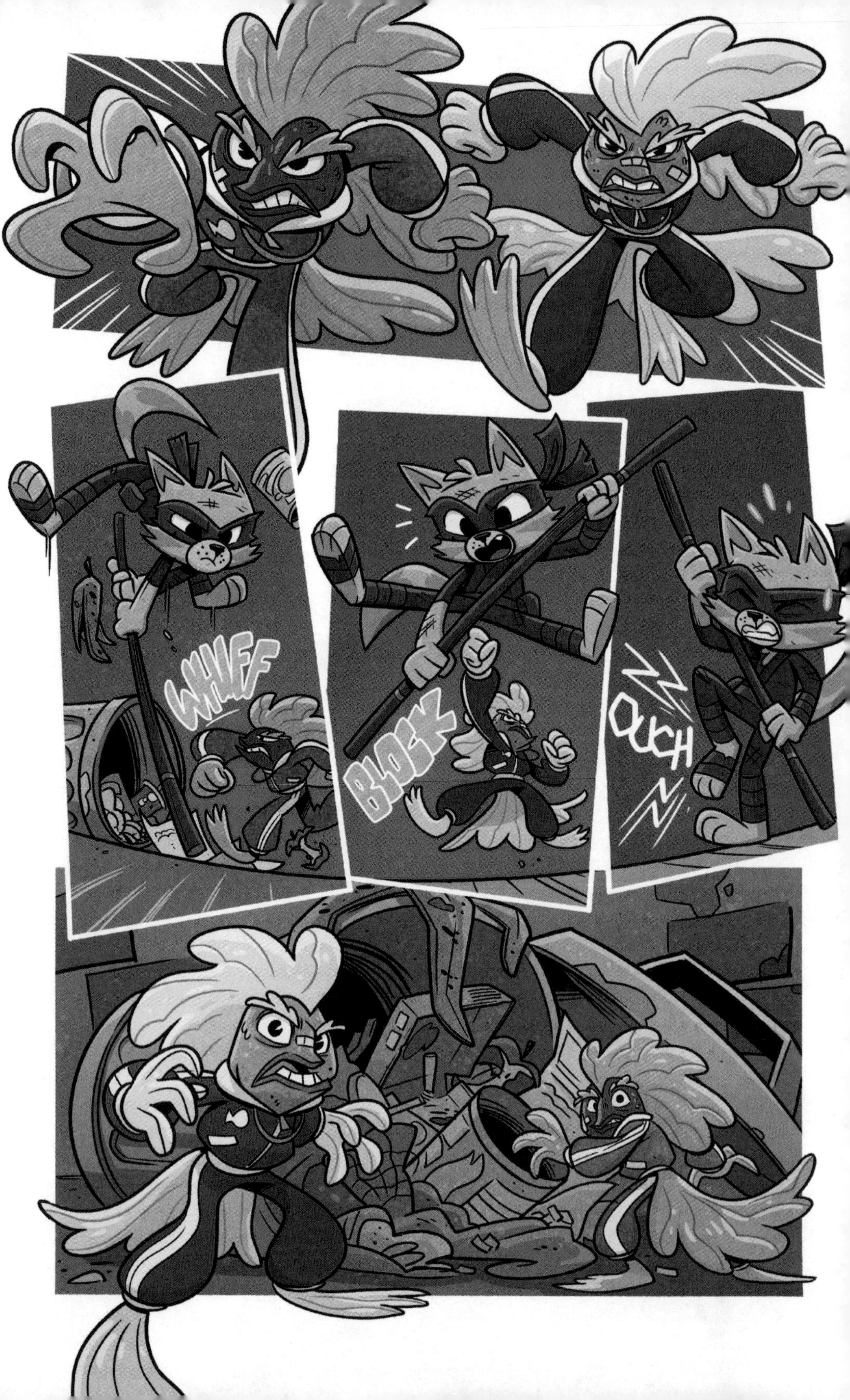
WHIFF
BLOCK
OUCH

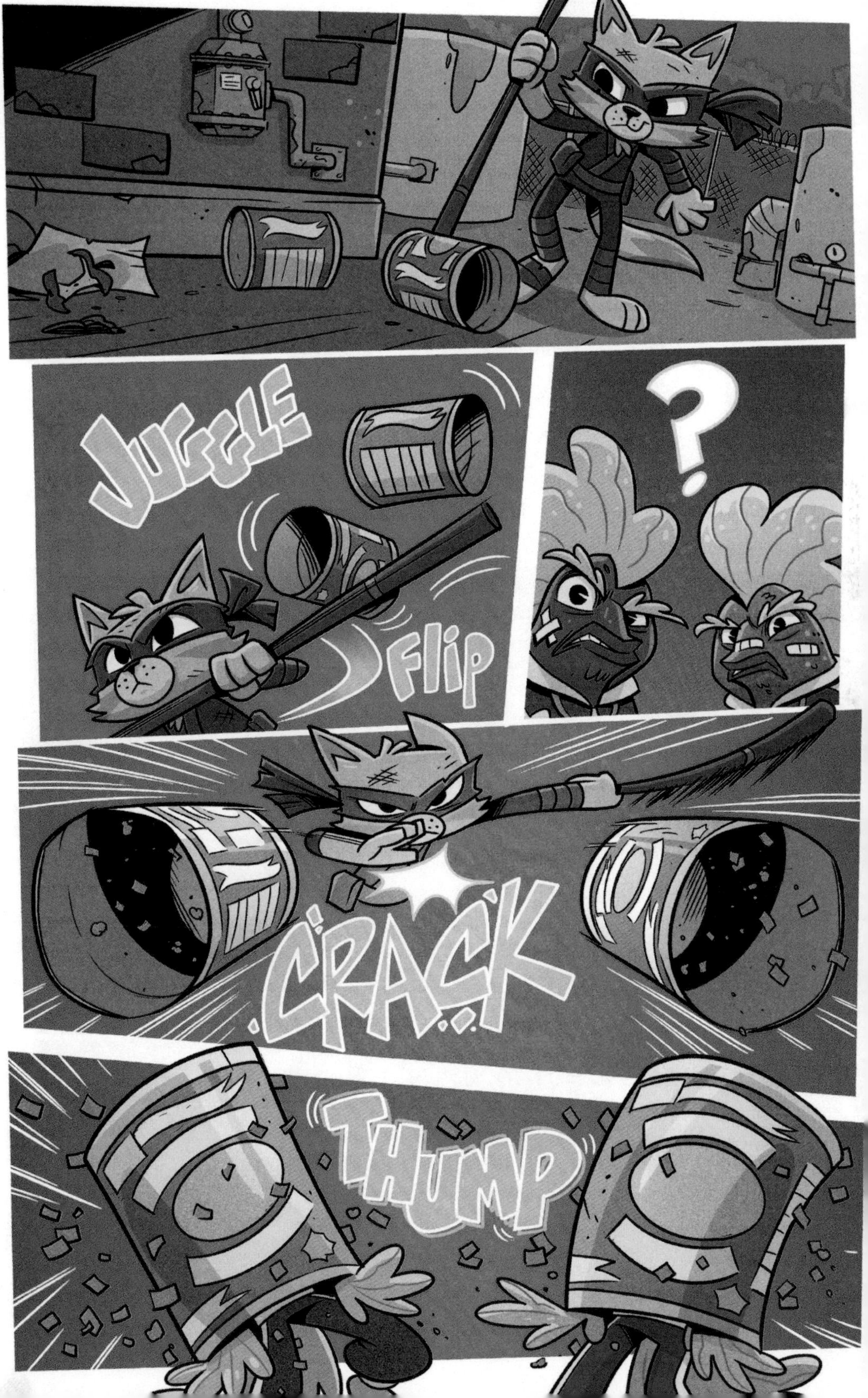
JUGGLE
FLIP
?
CRACK
THUMP

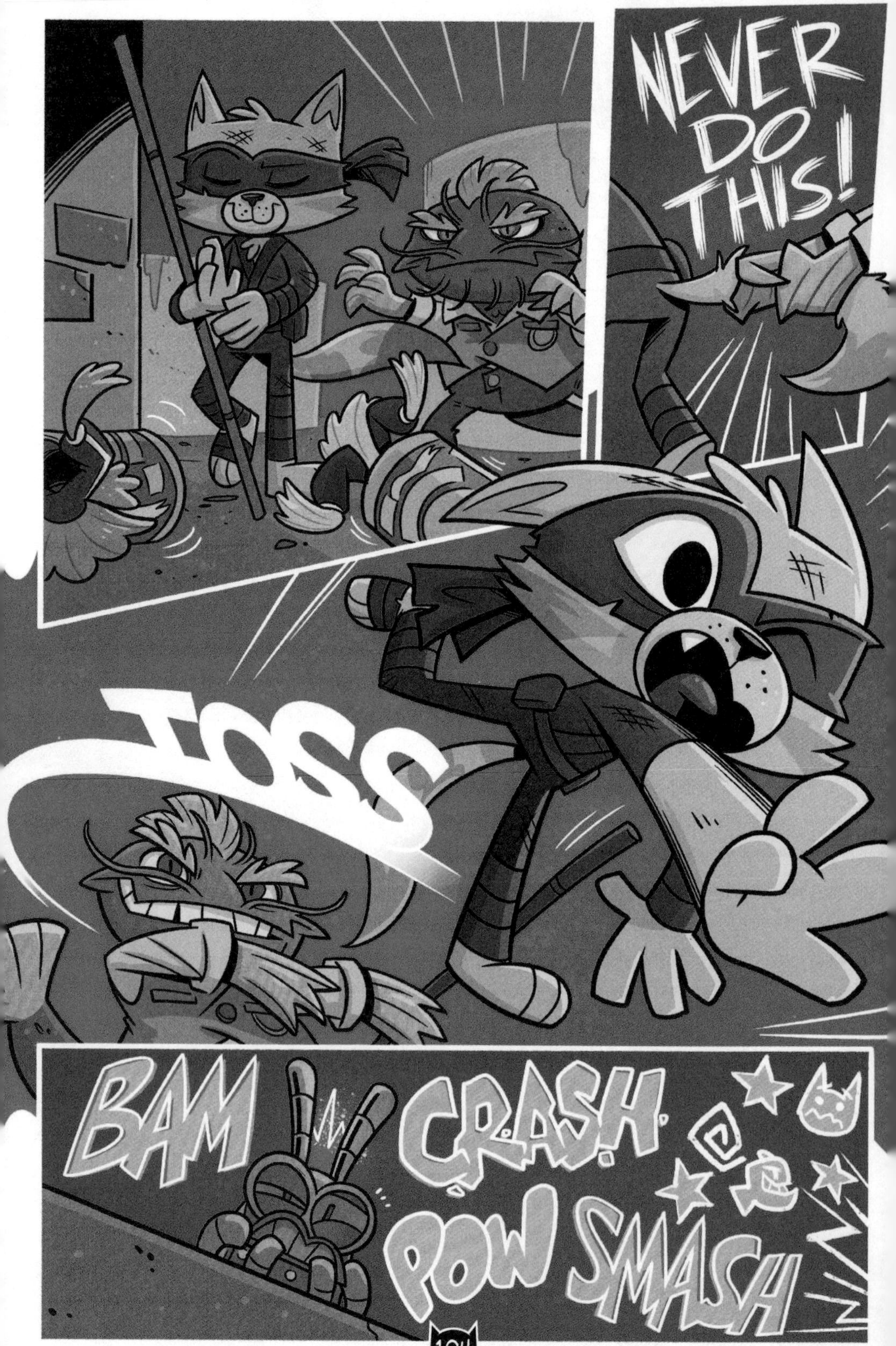
NEVER DO THIS!
TOSS
BAM
CRASH
POW
SMASH

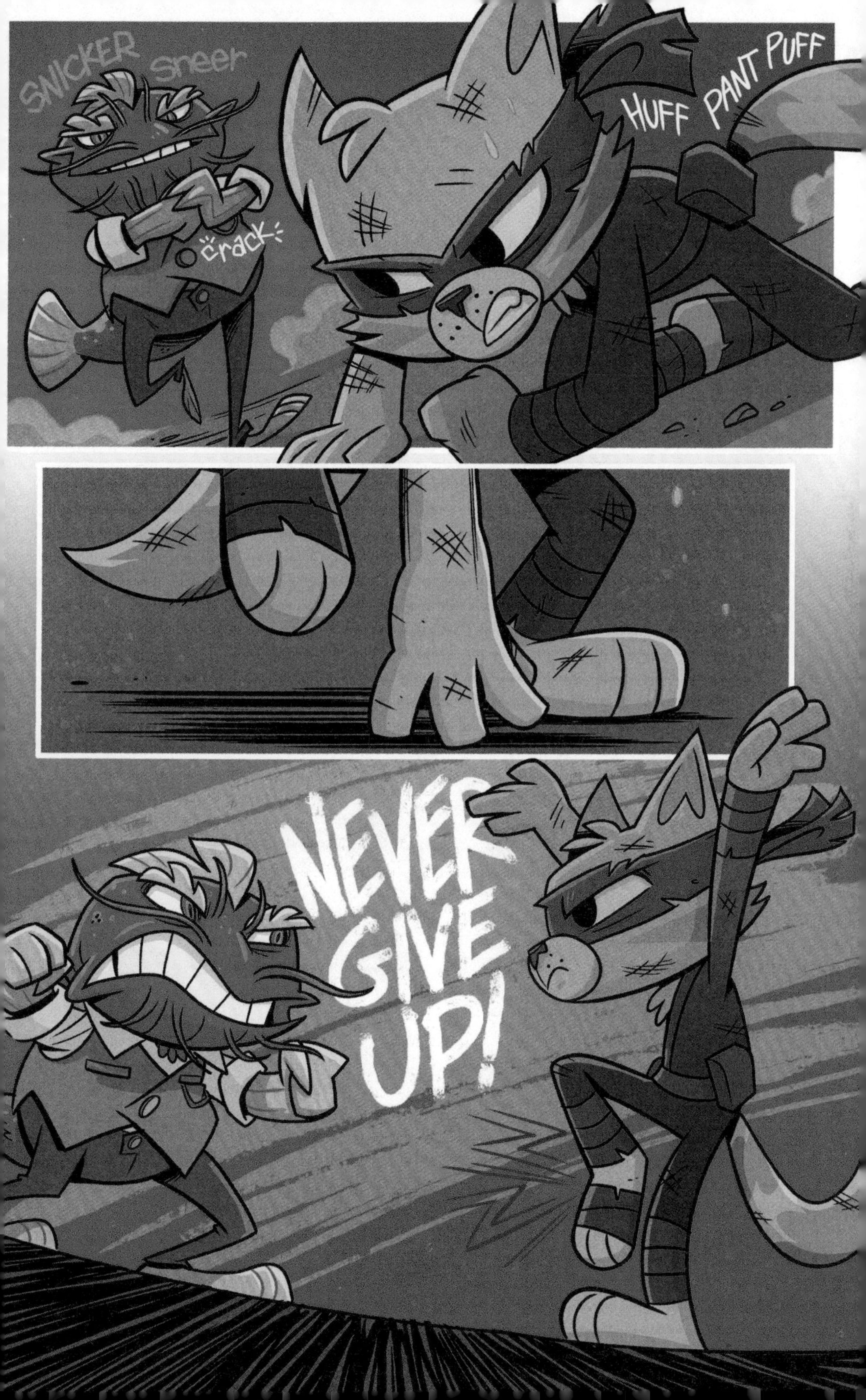
SNICKER sneer
HUFF PANT PUFF
crack
NEVER GIVE UP!

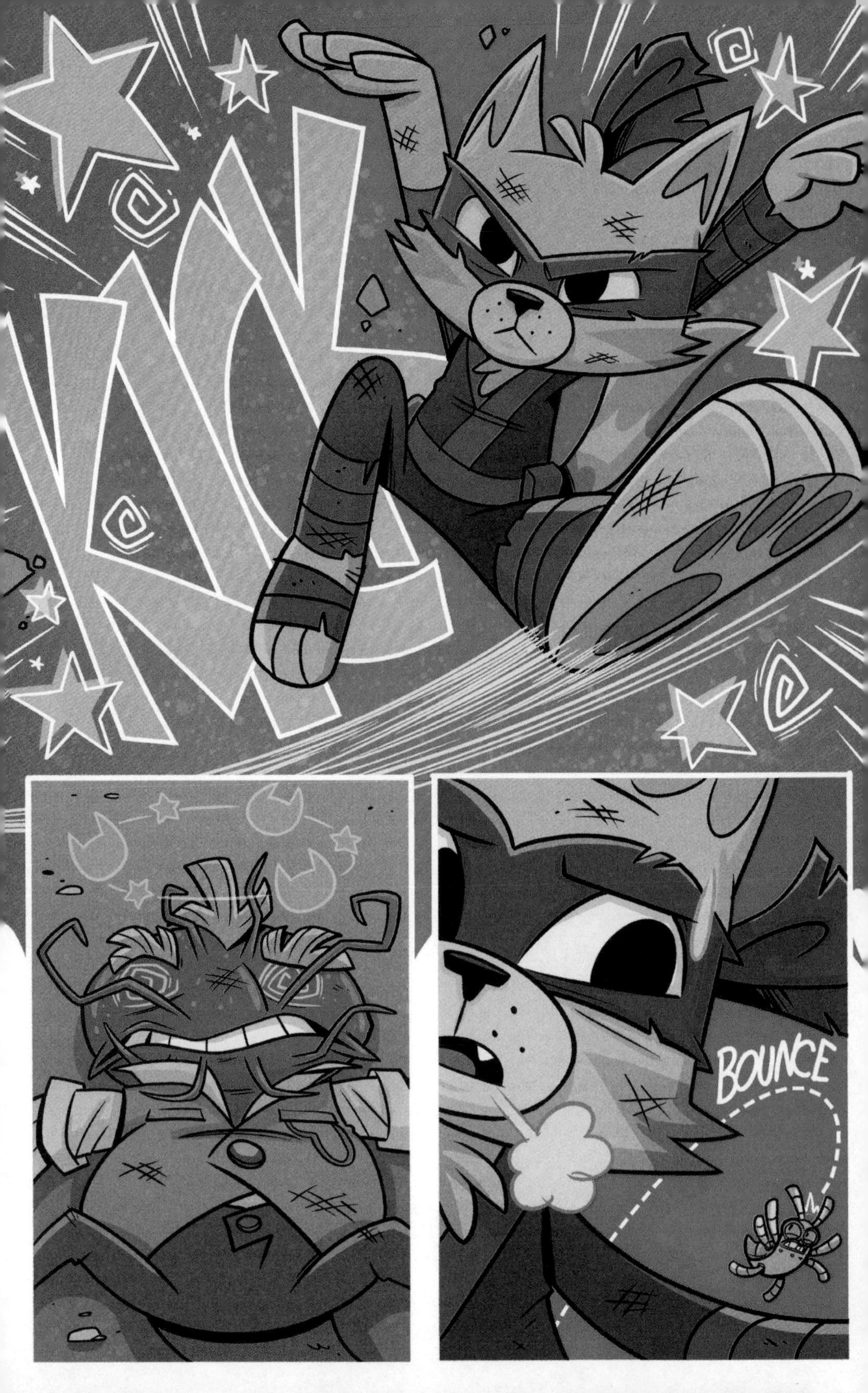
BOUNCE

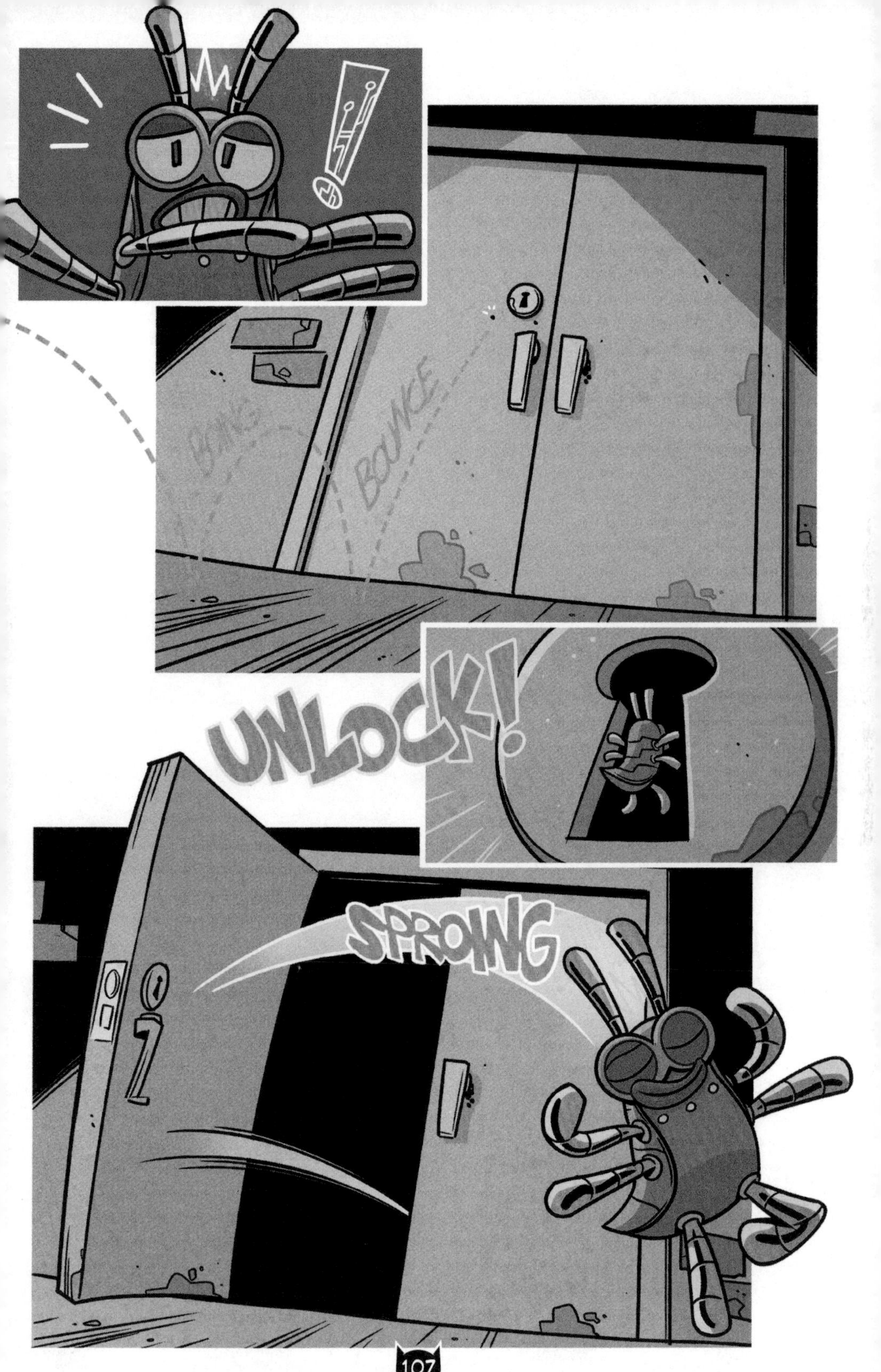
BOING
BOUNCE
UNLOCK!
SPROING

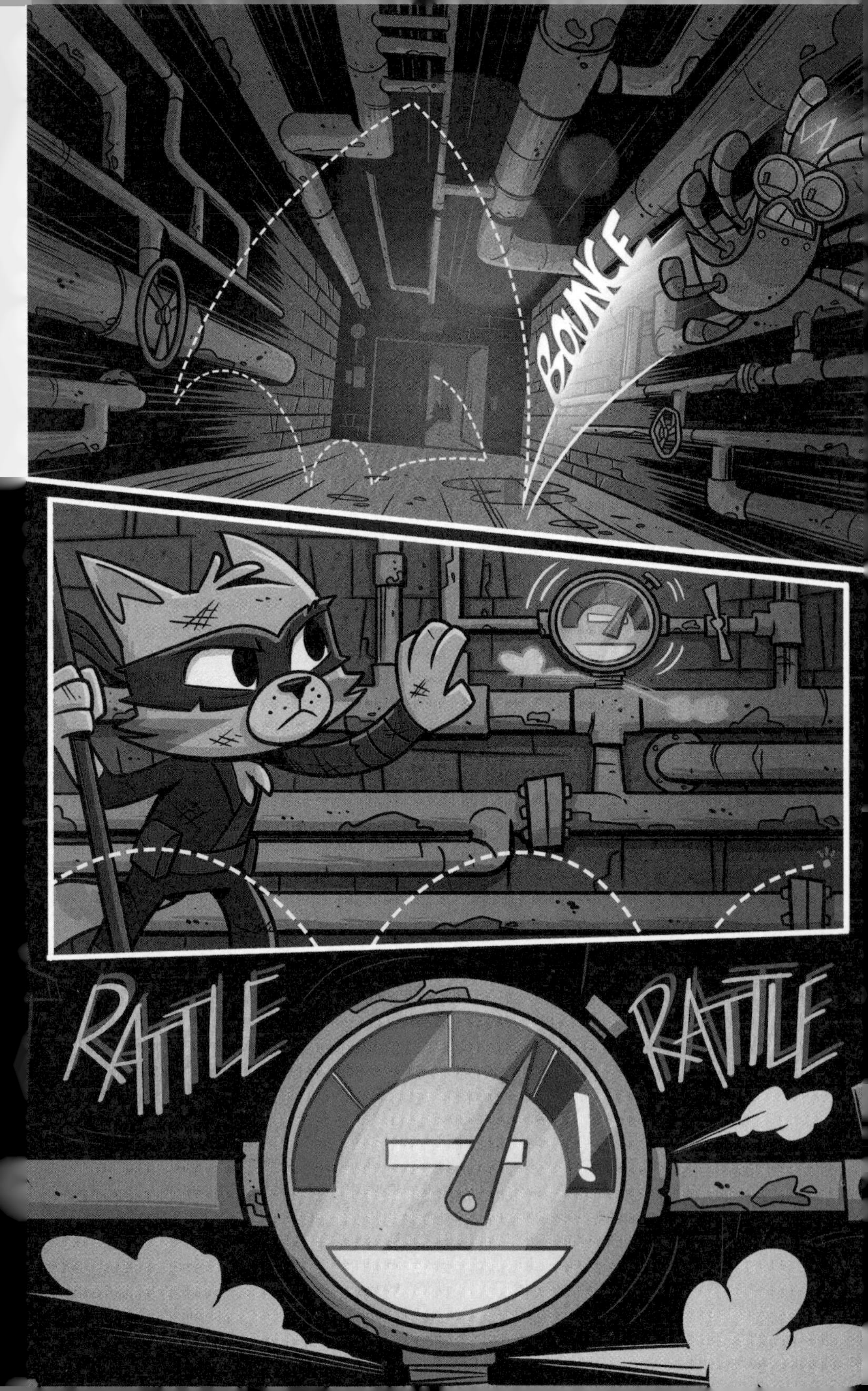
BOUNCE
RATTLE
RATTLE

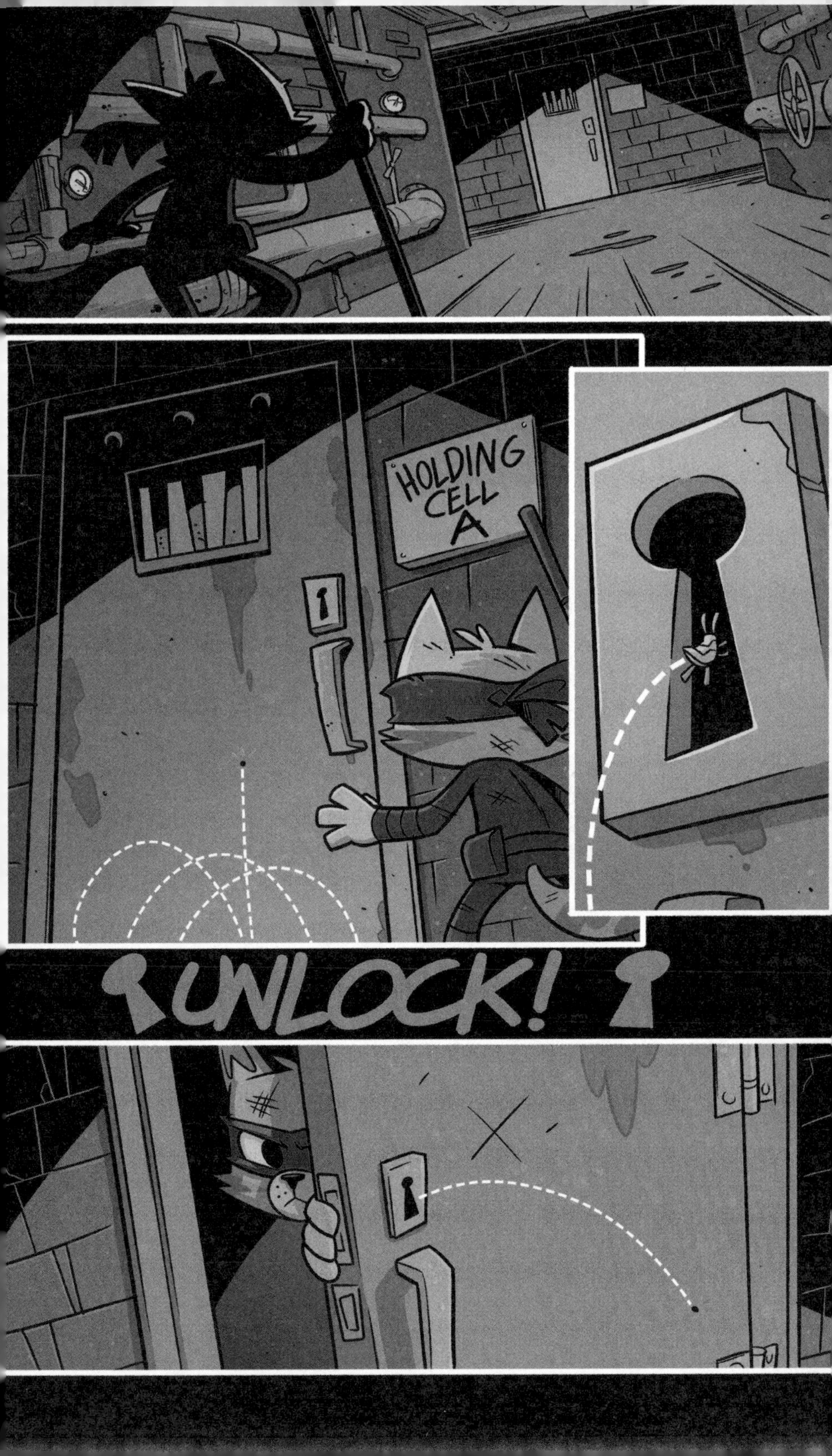
HOLDING CELL A
UNLOCK!

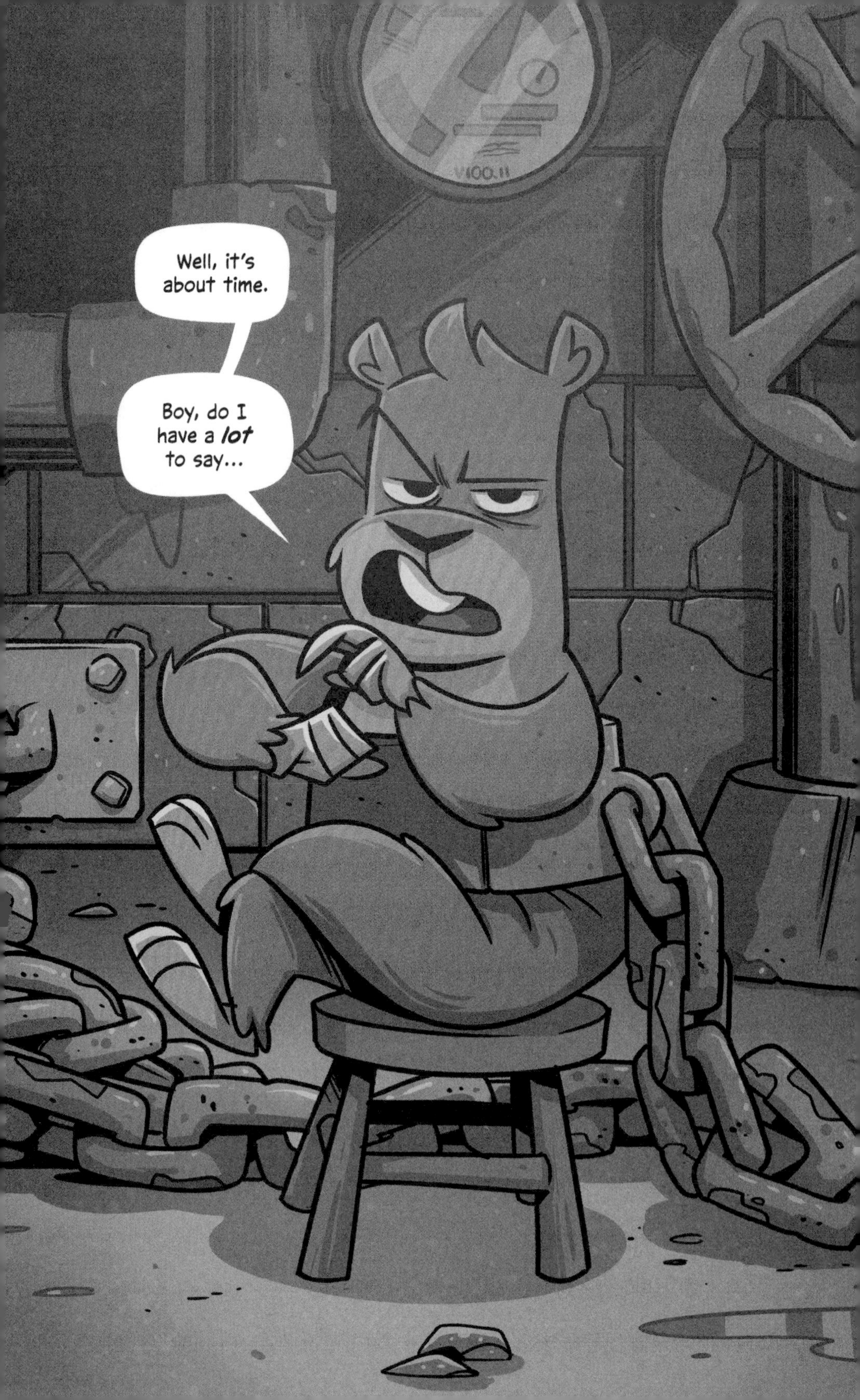
Well, it's about time.
Boy, do I have a *lot* to say...

Chapter 5
He Who Rules the Toilets Rules the World!

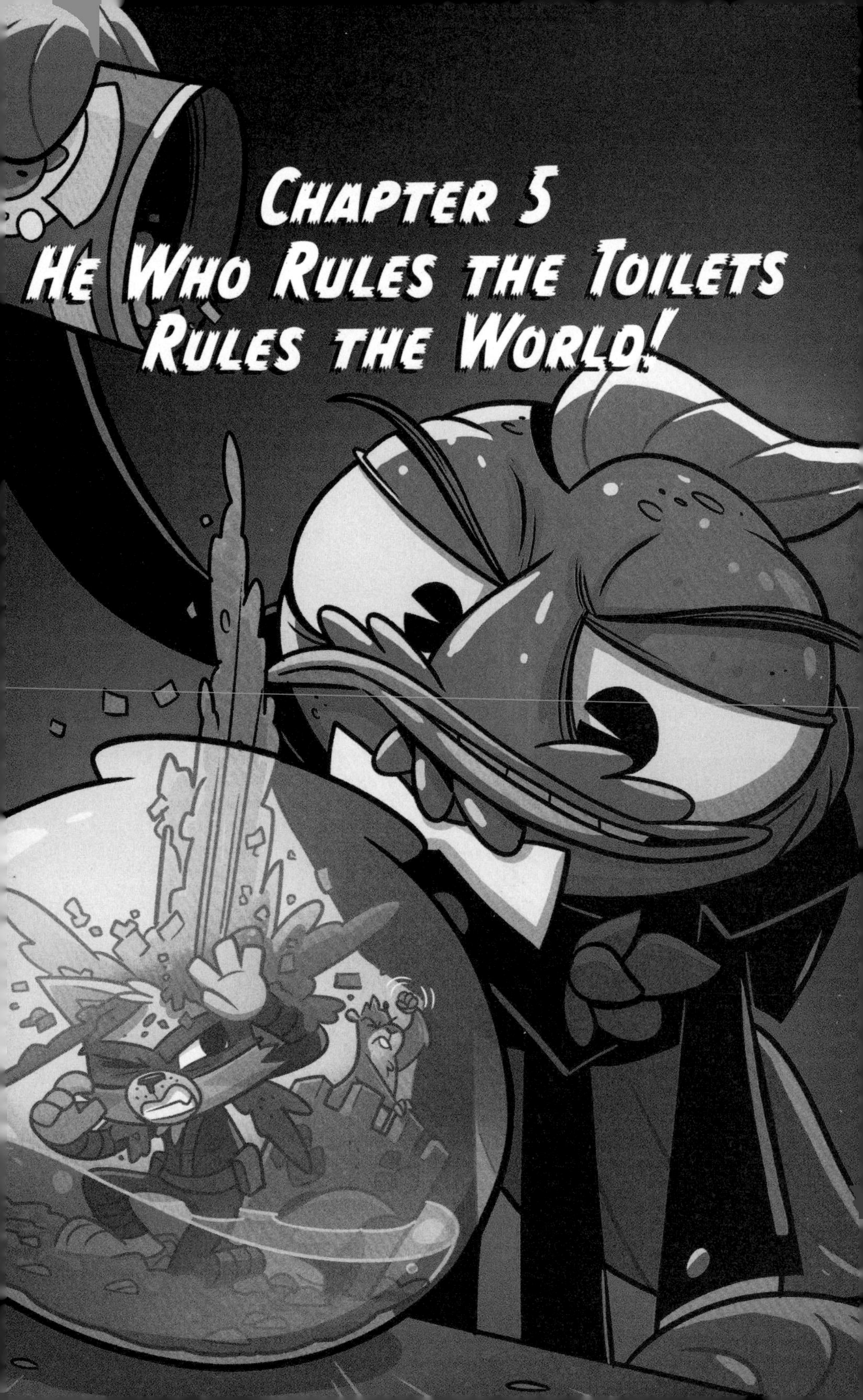

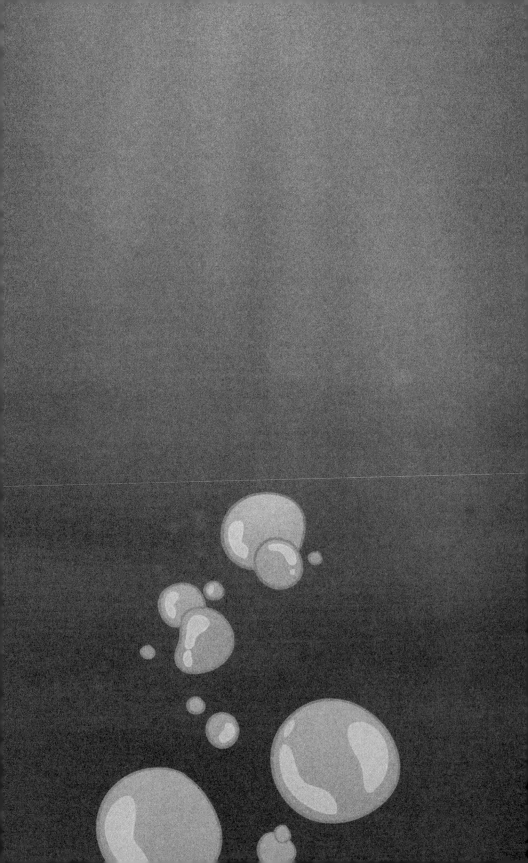

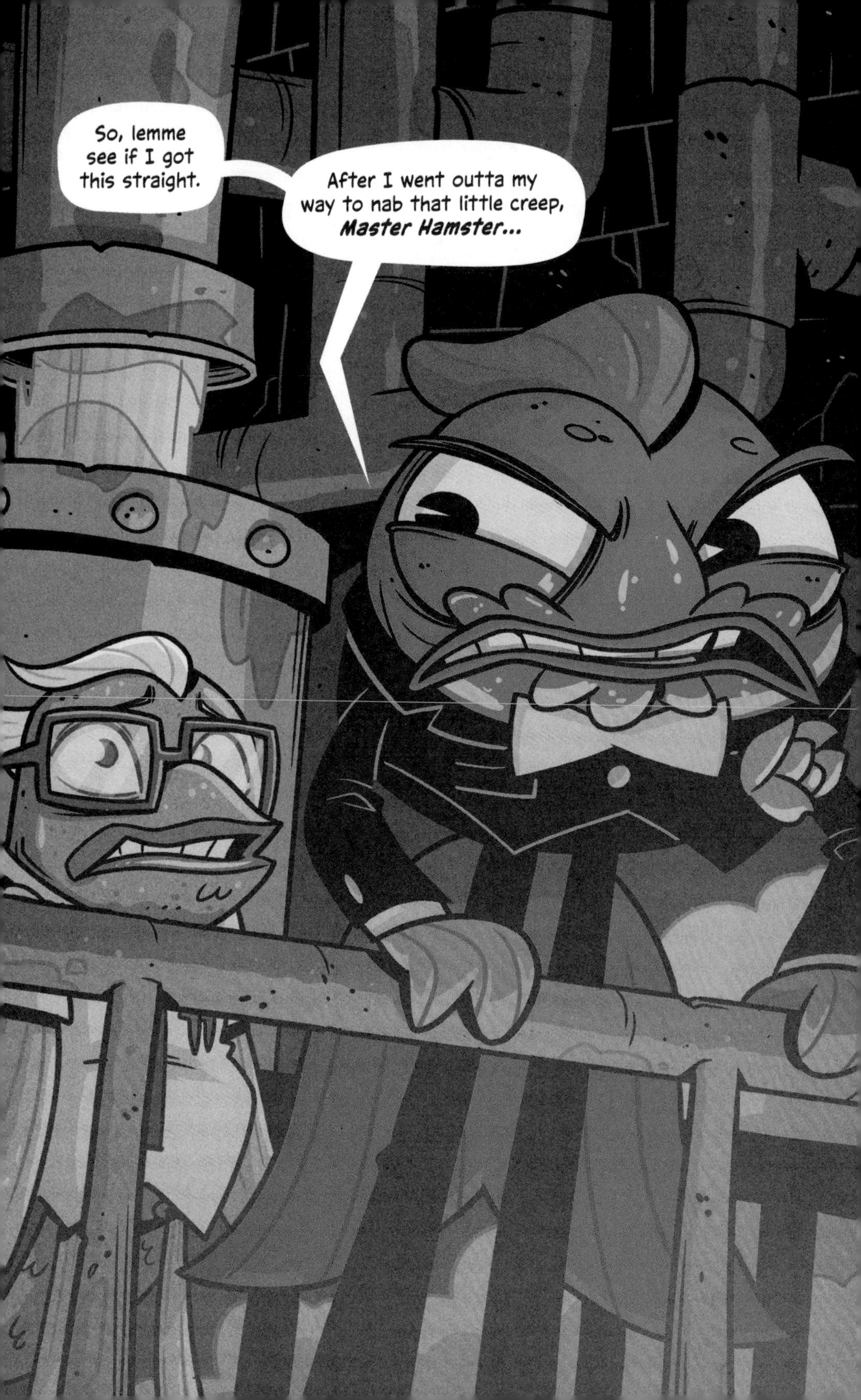
So, lemme see if I got this straight.
After I went outta my way to nab that little creep, *Master Hamster...*

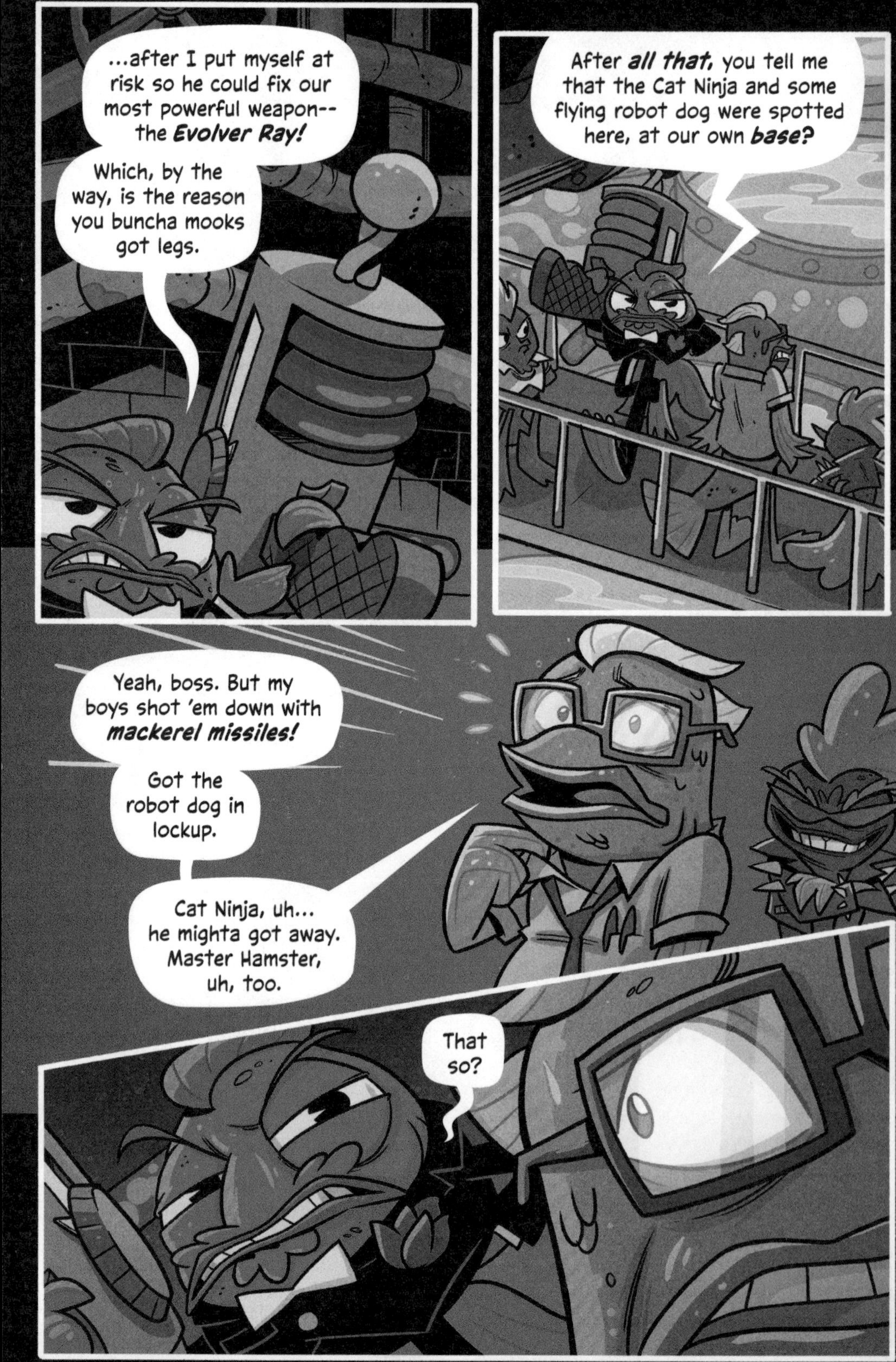
...after I put myself at risk so he could fix our most powerful weapon-- the *Evolver Ray!*
Which, by the way, is the reason you buncha mooks got legs.
After *all that,* you tell me that the Cat Ninja and some flying robot dog were spotted here, at our own *base?*
Yeah, boss. But my boys shot 'em down with *mackerel missiles!*
Got the robot dog in lockup.
Cat Ninja, uh... he mighta got away. Master Hamster, uh, too.
That so?

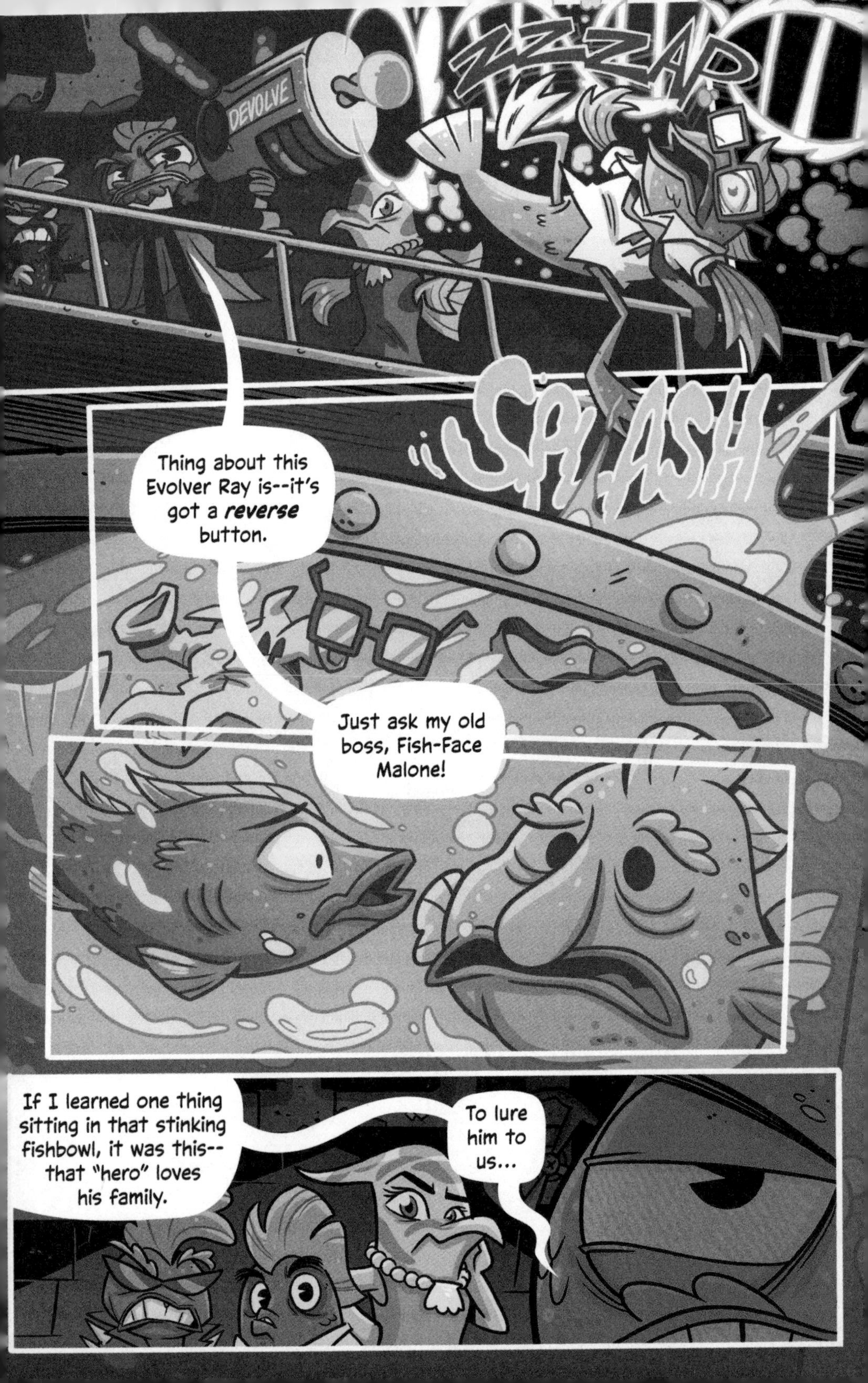
DEVOLVE
ZZZAP
SPLASH
Thing about this Evolver Ray is--it's got a *reverse* button.
Just ask my old boss, Fish-Face Malone!
If I learned one thing sitting in that stinking fishbowl, it was this--that "hero" loves his family.
To lure him to us...

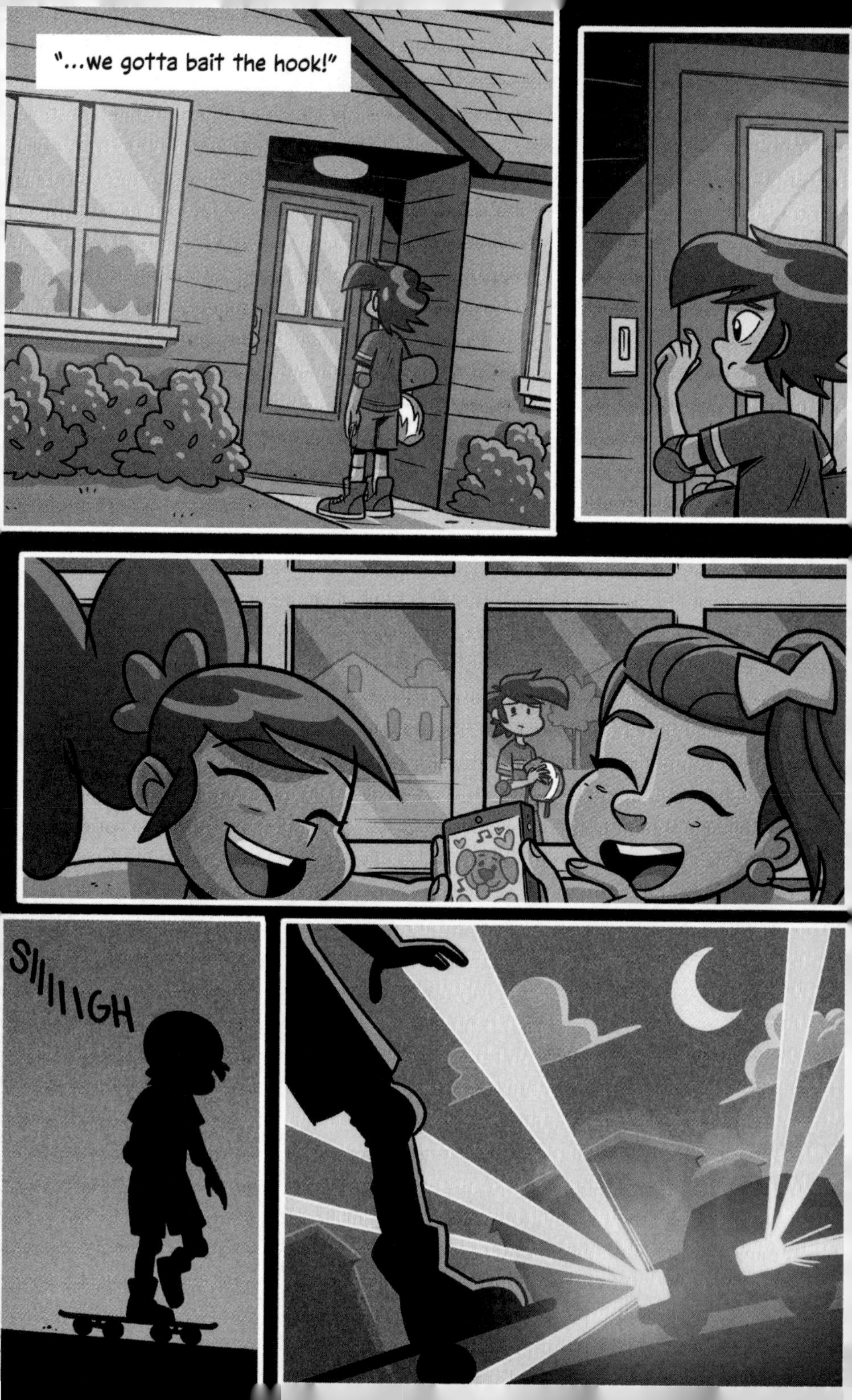
"...we gotta bait the hook!"
SIIIIIGH

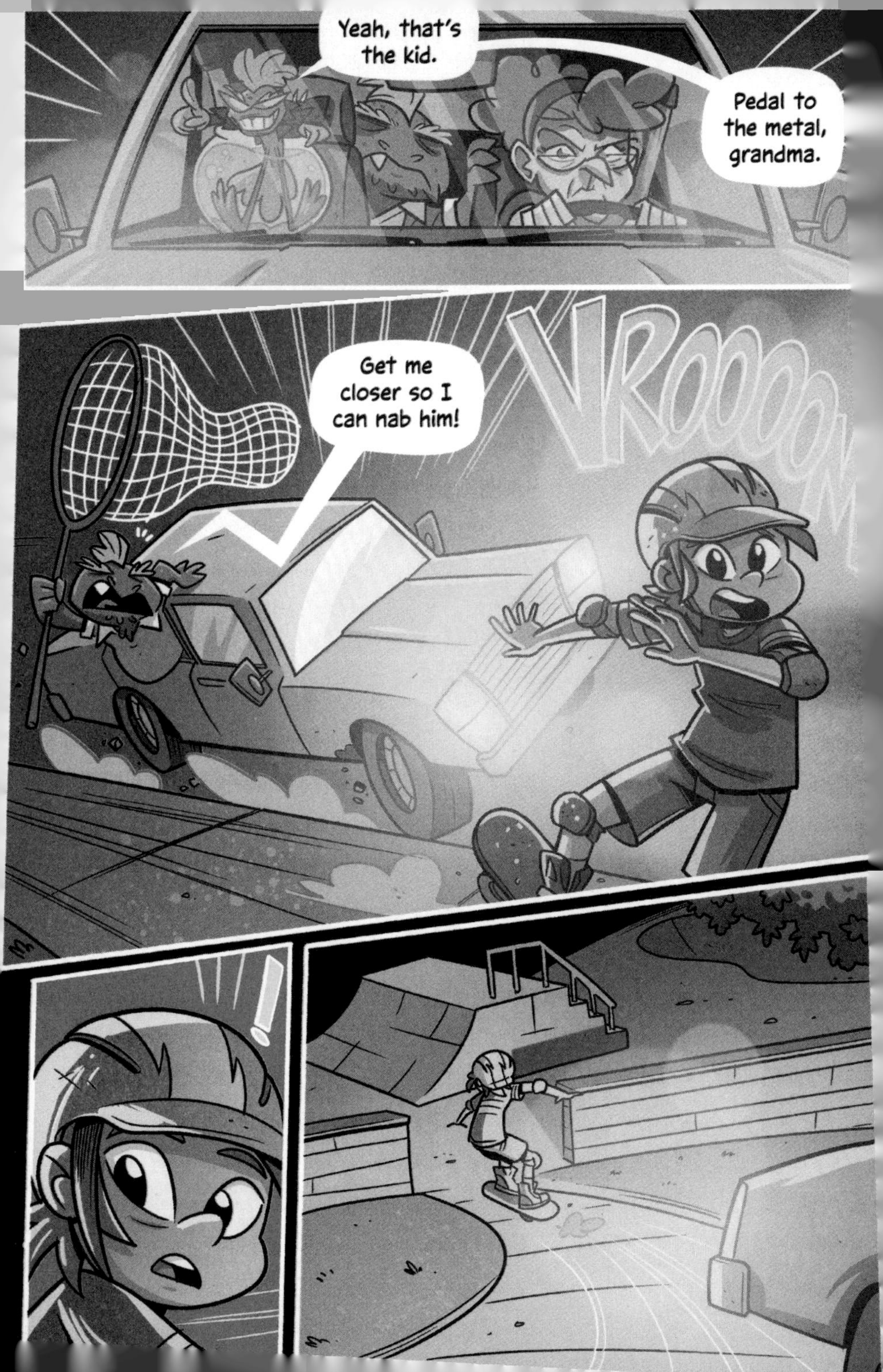
Yeah, that's the kid.
Pedal to the metal, grandma.
Get me closer so I can nab him!
VROOOOM

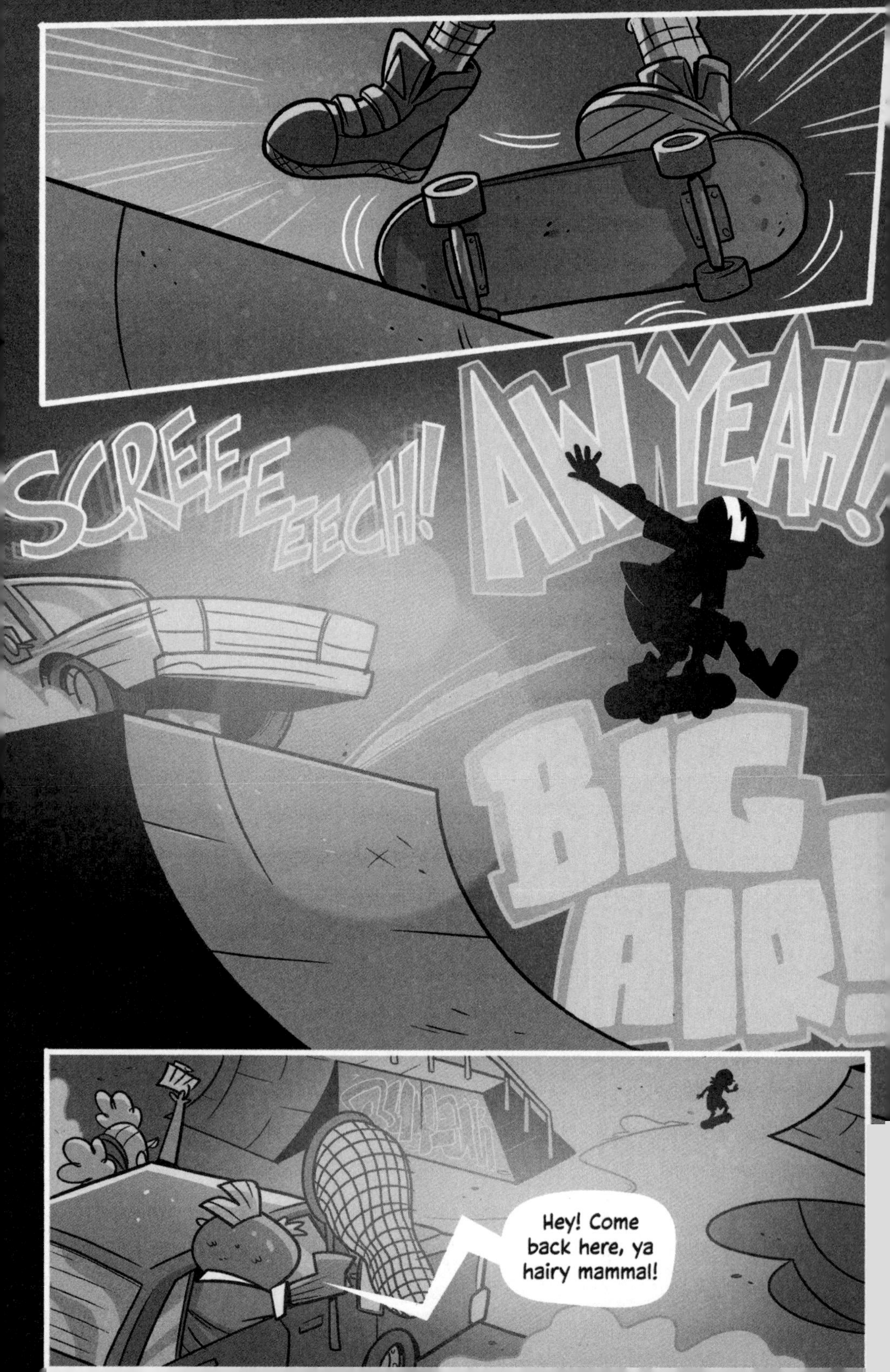

SCREEEEECH!
AW YEAH!
BIG AIR!
Hey! Come back here, ya hairy mammal!

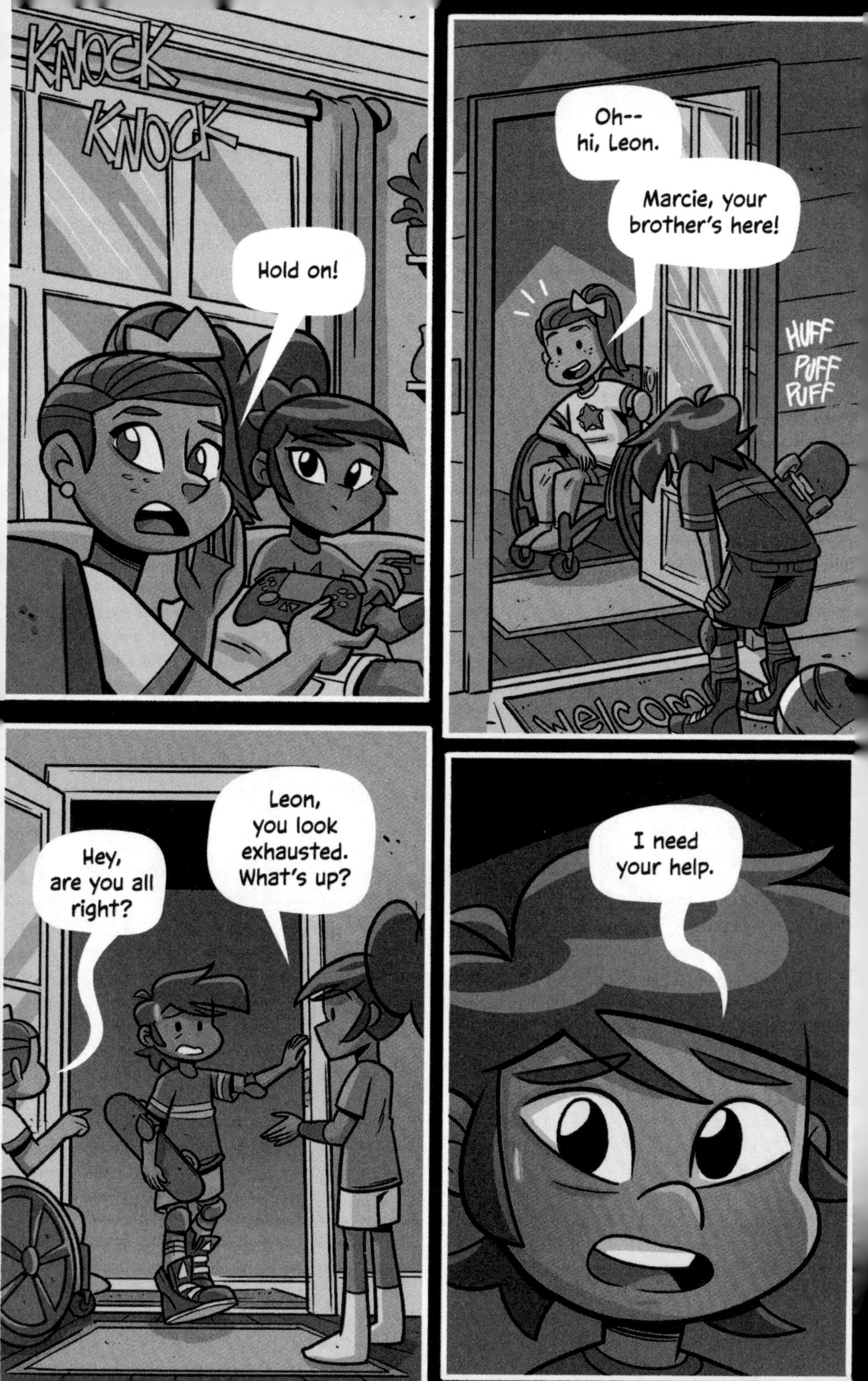
KNOCK
KNOCK
Hold on!
Oh--
hi, Leon.
Marcie, your brother's here!
HUFF
PUFF
PUFF
Hey, are you all right?
Leon, you look exhausted. What's up?
I need your help.

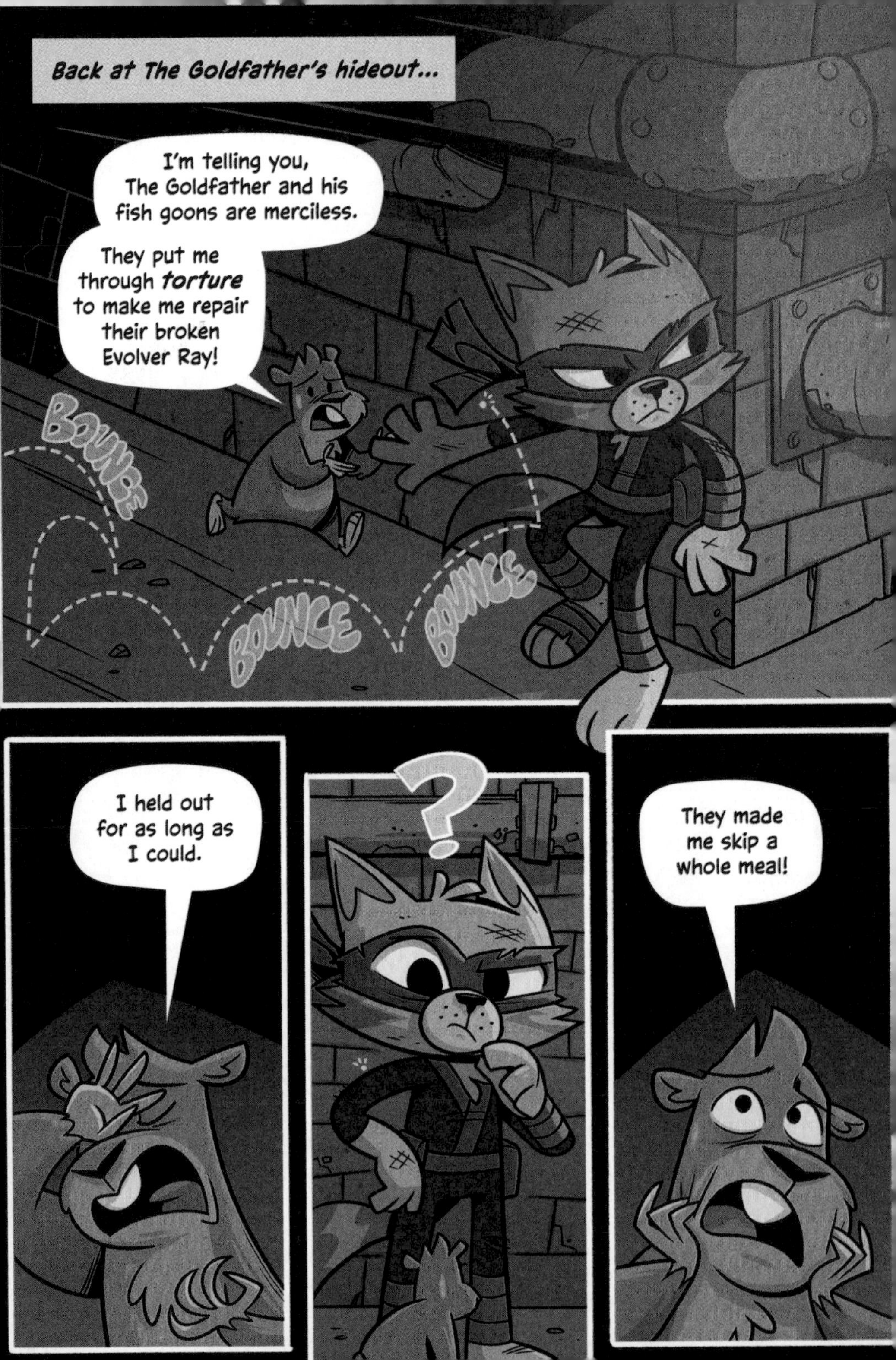
Back at The Goldfather's hideout...
I'm telling you, The Goldfather and his fish goons are merciless.
They put me through *torture* to make me repair their broken Evolver Ray!
BOUNCE
BOUNCE
BOUNCE
I held out for as long as I could.
?
They made me skip a whole meal!

It was **lunch!** My favoritest meal of the day!

I'm still **weak** with hunger.

WHUMP

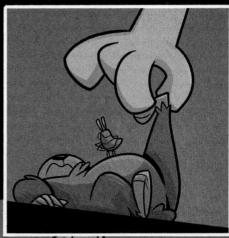

If I don't make it, give my hamster cage to Marcie.

Tell her not to get a new hamster, though! Keep it just as I left it. Like a **shrine.**

BOUNCE

BOUNCE

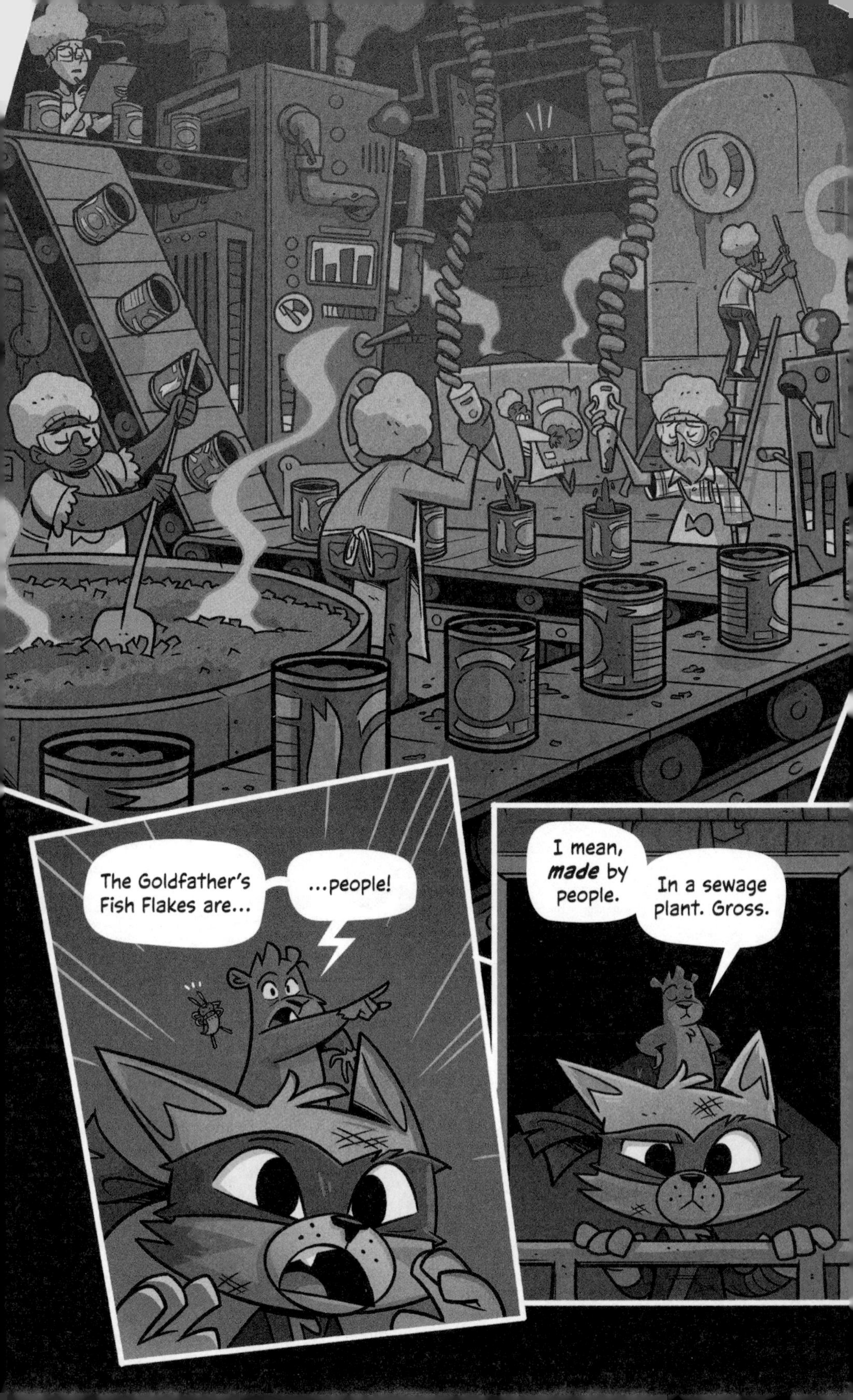
The Goldfather's Fish Flakes are...
...people!
I mean, *made* by people.
In a sewage plant. Gross.

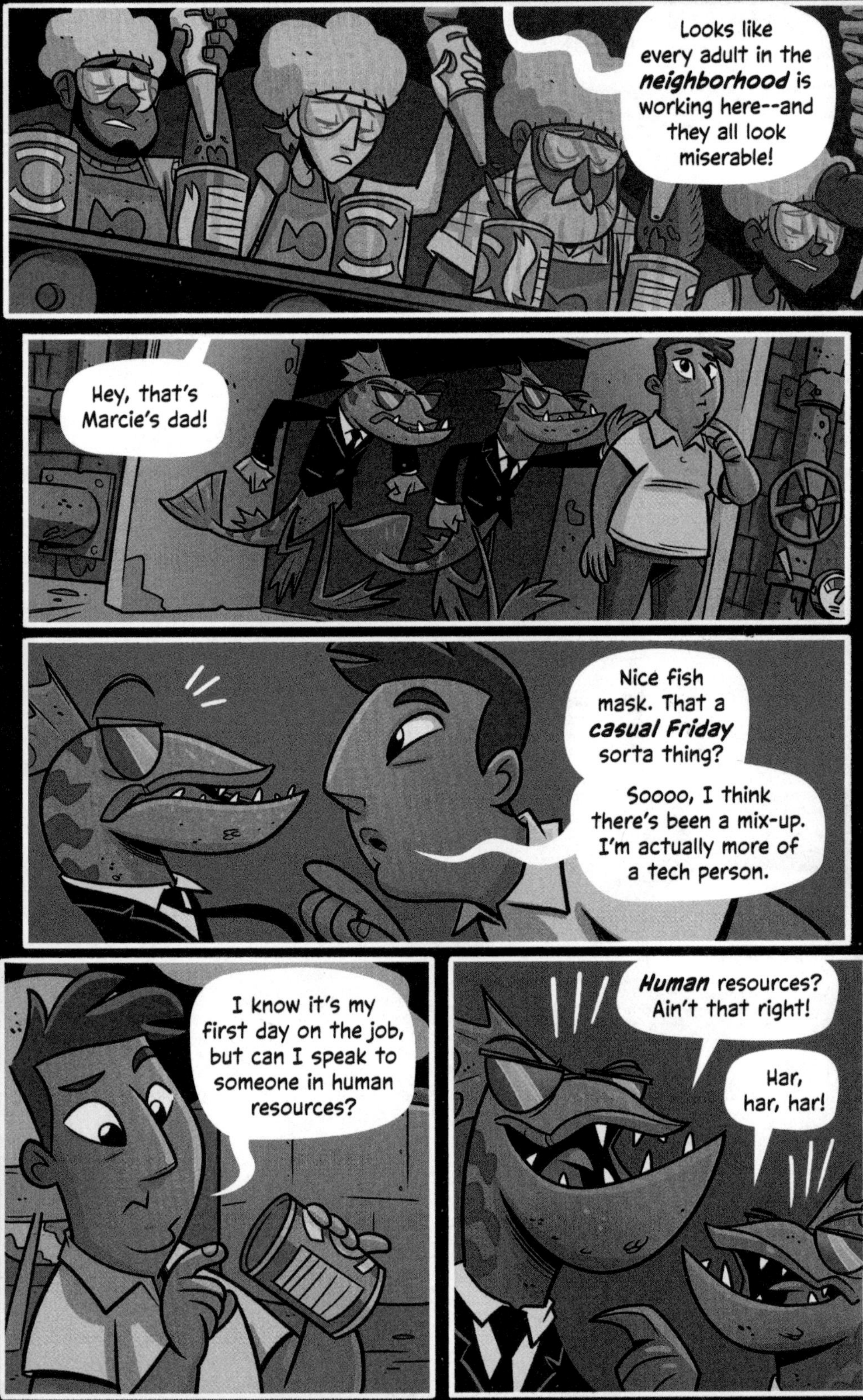
Looks like every adult in the *neighborhood* is working here--and they all look miserable!
Hey, that's Marcie's dad!
Nice fish mask. That a *casual Friday* sorta thing?
Soooo, I think there's been a mix-up. I'm actually more of a tech person.
I know it's my first day on the job, but can I speak to someone in human resources?
Human resources? Ain't that right!
Har, har, har!

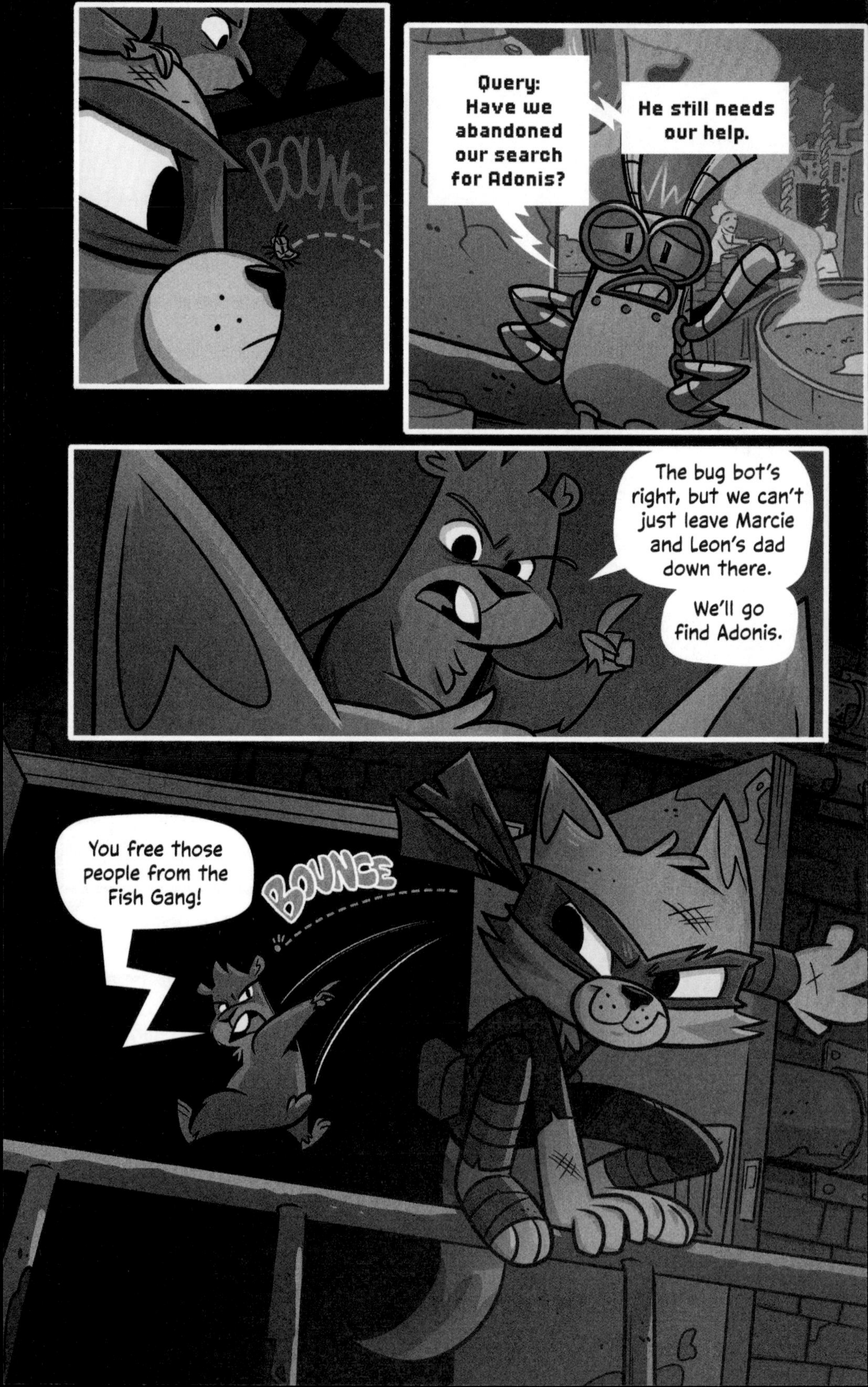
BOUNCE
Query: Have we abandoned our search for Adonis?
He still needs our help.
The bug bot's right, but we can't just leave Marcie and Leon's dad down there.
We'll go find Adonis.
You free those people from the Fish Gang!
BOUNCE

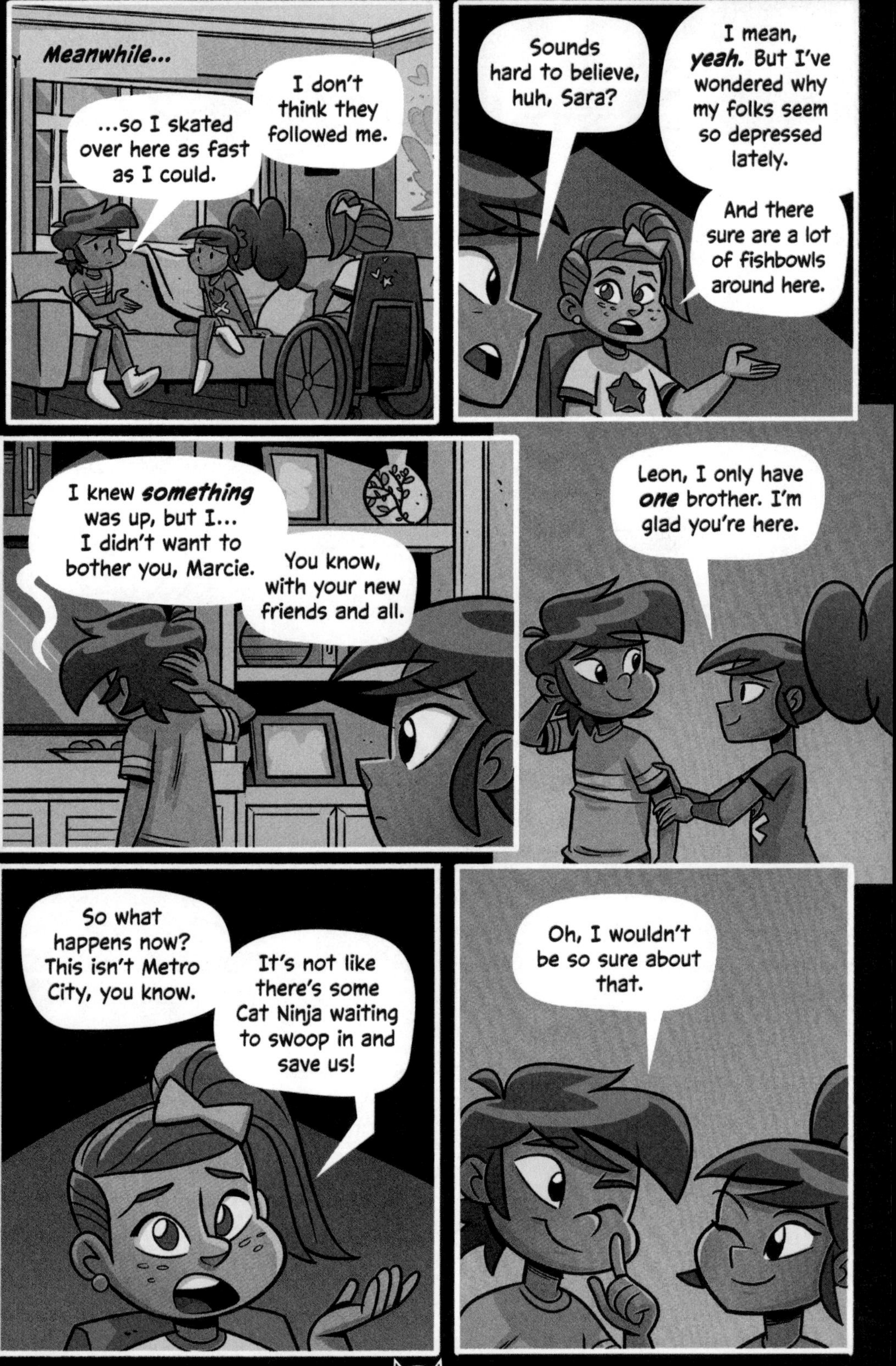
Meanwhile...
...so I skated over here as fast as I could.
I don't think they followed me.
Sounds hard to believe, huh, Sara?
I mean, *yeah.* But I've wondered why my folks seem so depressed lately.
And there sure are a lot of fishbowls around here.
I knew *something* was up, but I... I didn't want to bother you, Marcie.
You know, with your new friends and all.
Leon, I only have *one* brother. I'm glad you're here.
So what happens now? This isn't Metro City, you know.
It's not like there's some Cat Ninja waiting to swoop in and save us!
Oh, I wouldn't be so sure about that.

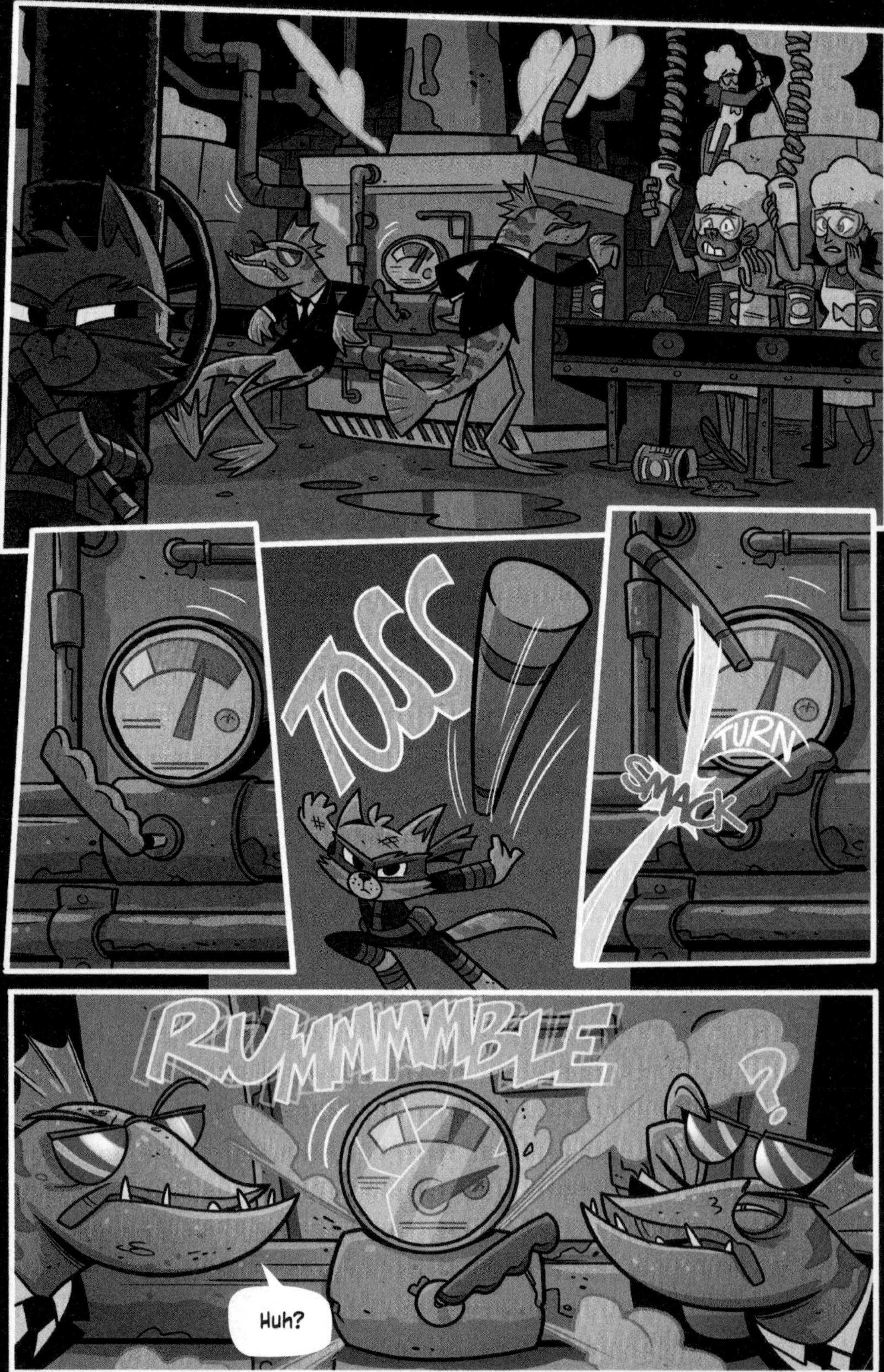
TOSS
TURN
SMACK
RUMMMMBLE
?
Huh?

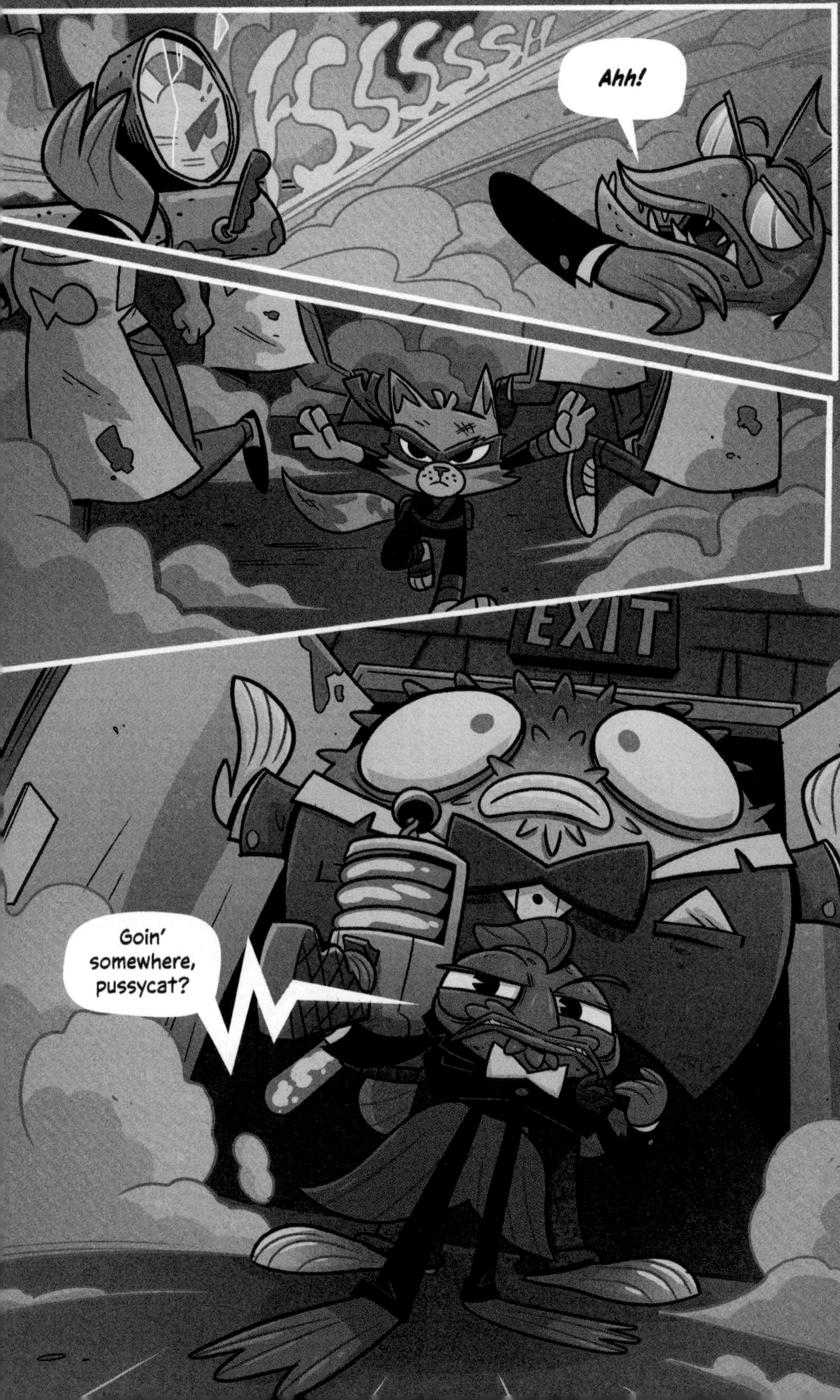

FSSSSSH
Ahh!
EXIT
Goin' somewhere, pussycat?

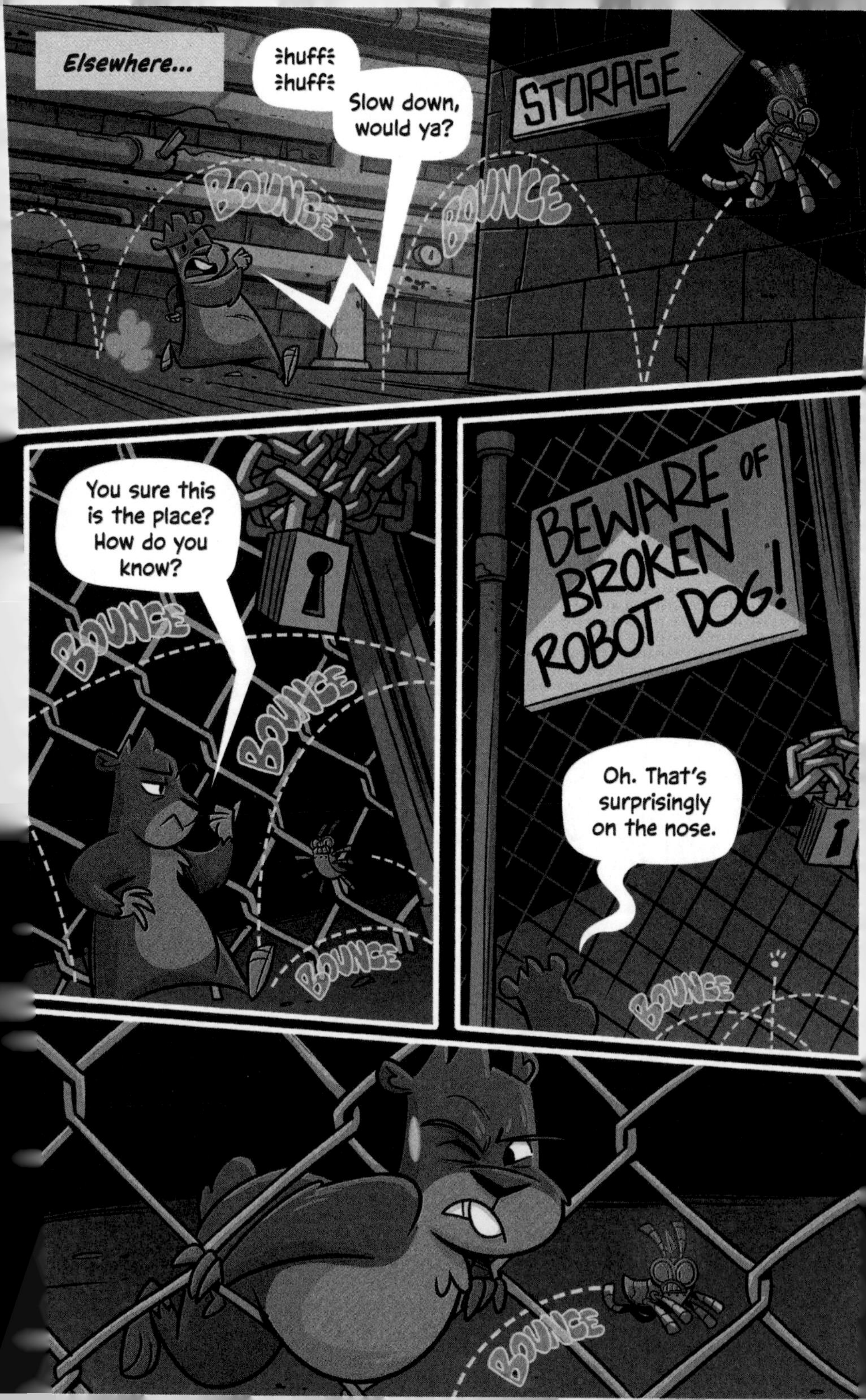

Elsewhere...
huff
huff
Slow down, would ya?
STORAGE
BOUNCE
BOUNCE
You sure this is the place? How do you know?
BOUNCE
BOUNCE
BOUNCE
BEWARE OF BROKEN ROBOT DOG!
Oh. That's surprisingly on the nose.
BOUNCE
BOUNCE

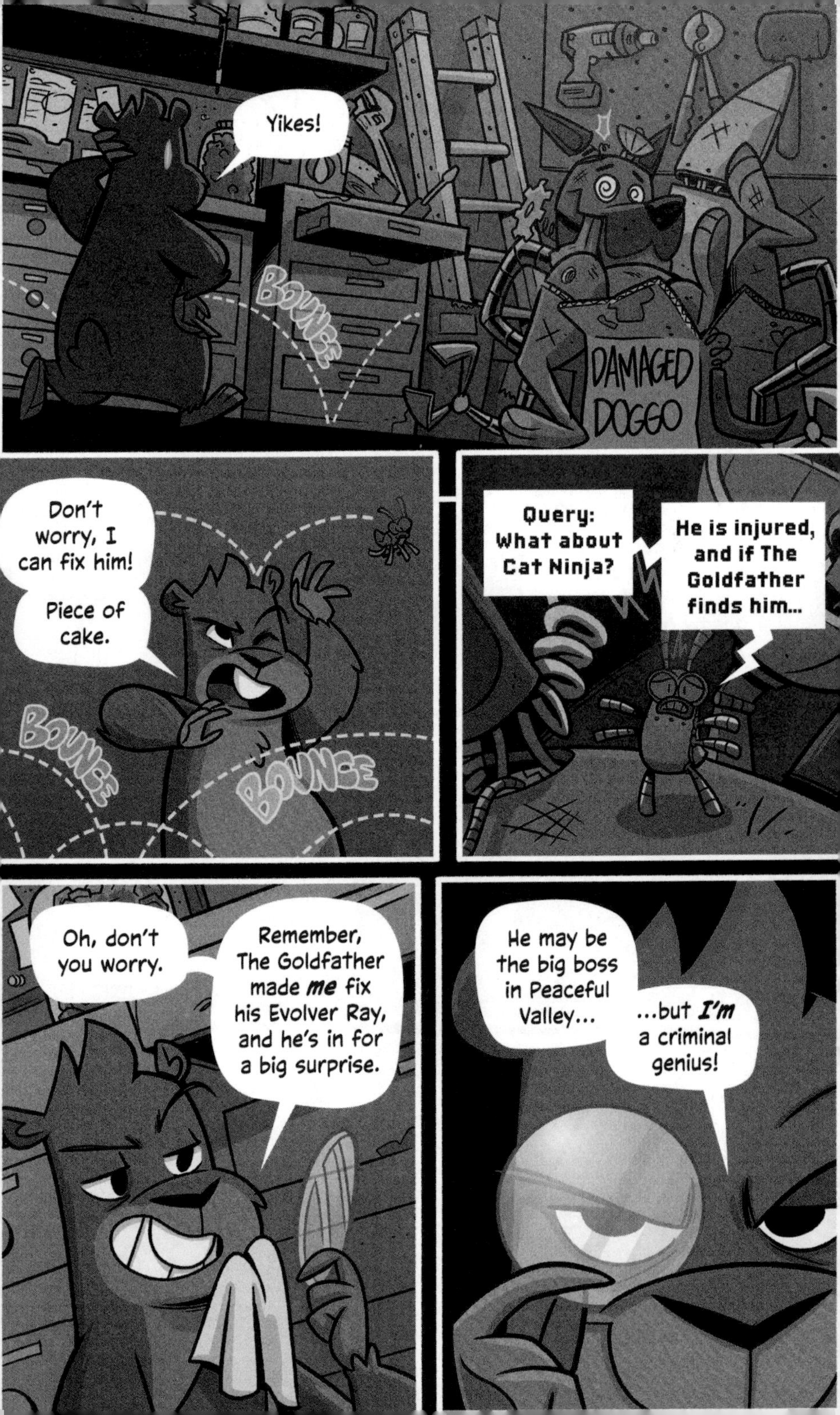

Yikes!
BOUNCE
DAMAGED DOGGO
Don't worry, I can fix him!
Piece of cake.
BOUNCE
BOUNCE
Query: What about Cat Ninja?
He is injured, and if The Goldfather finds him...
Oh, don't you worry.
Remember, The Goldfather made *me* fix his Evolver Ray, and he's in for a big surprise.
He may be the big boss in Peaceful Valley...
...but ***I'm*** a criminal genius!

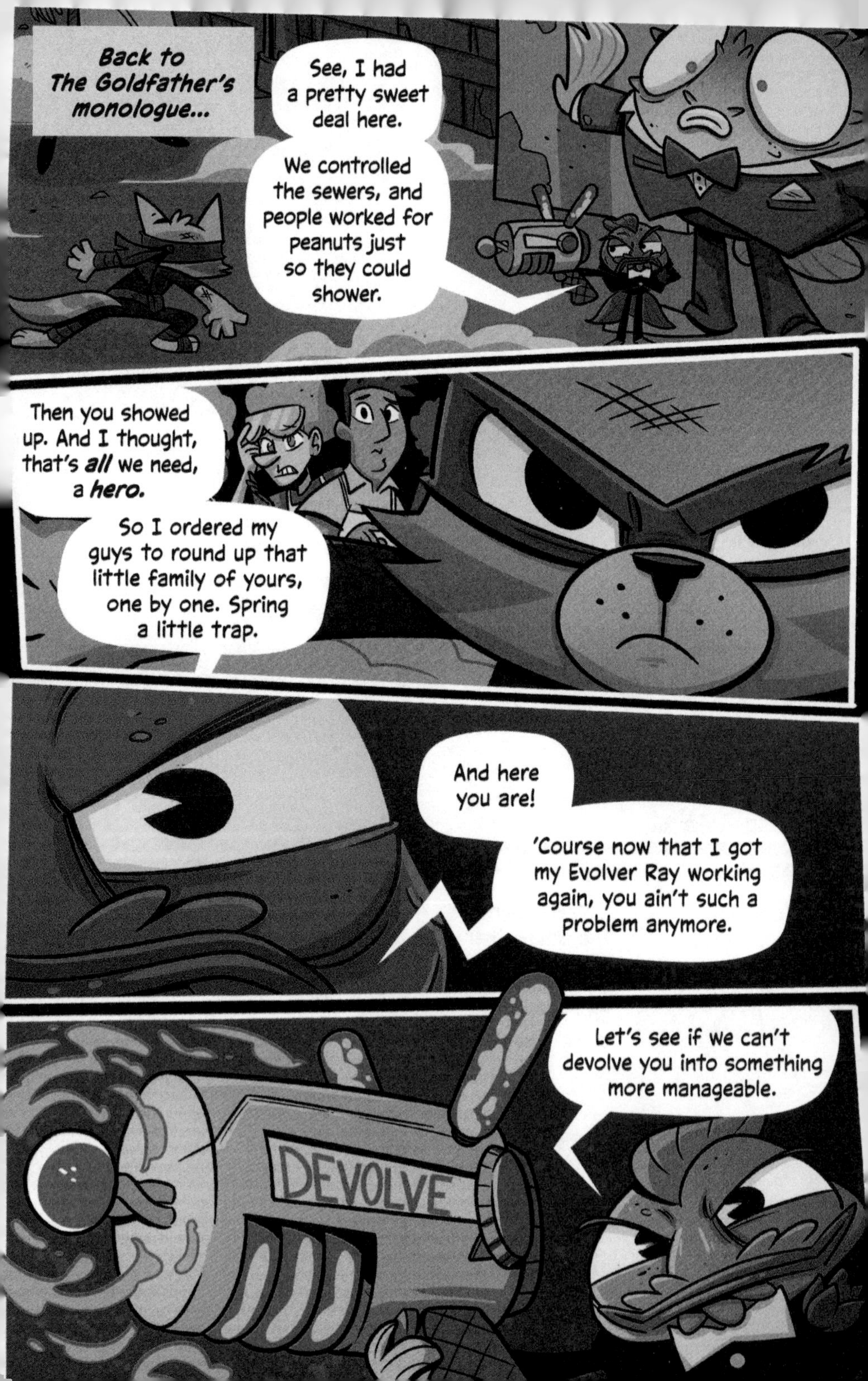
Back to The Goldfather's monologue...
See, I had a pretty sweet deal here.
We controlled the sewers, and people worked for peanuts just so they could shower.
Then you showed up. And I thought, that's *all* we need, a *hero.*
So I ordered my guys to round up that little family of yours, one by one. Spring a little trap.
And here you are!
'Course now that I got my Evolver Ray working again, you ain't such a problem anymore.
DEVOLVE
Let's see if we can't devolve you into something more manageable.

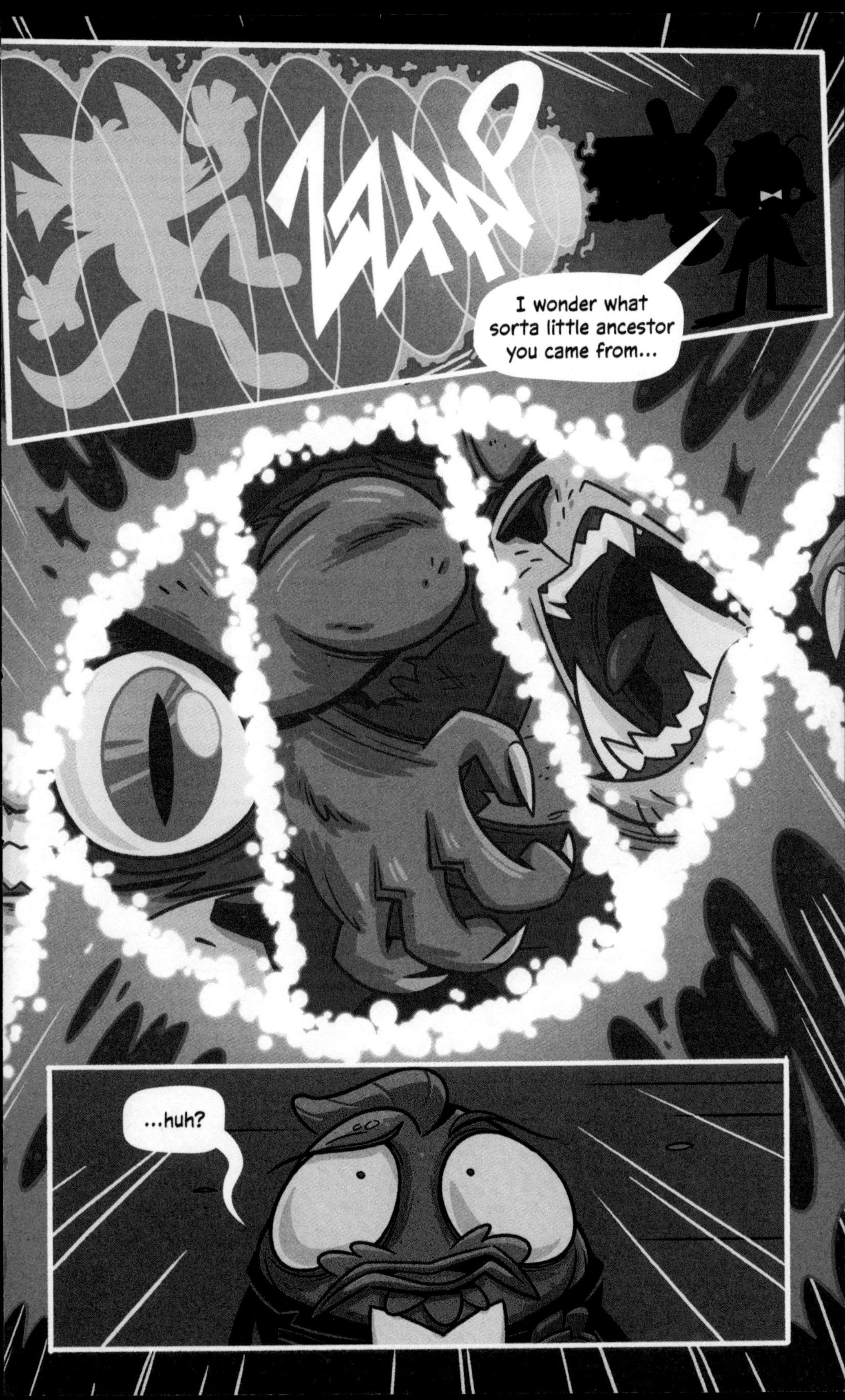
ZZAP
I wonder what sorta little ancestor you came from...
...huh?

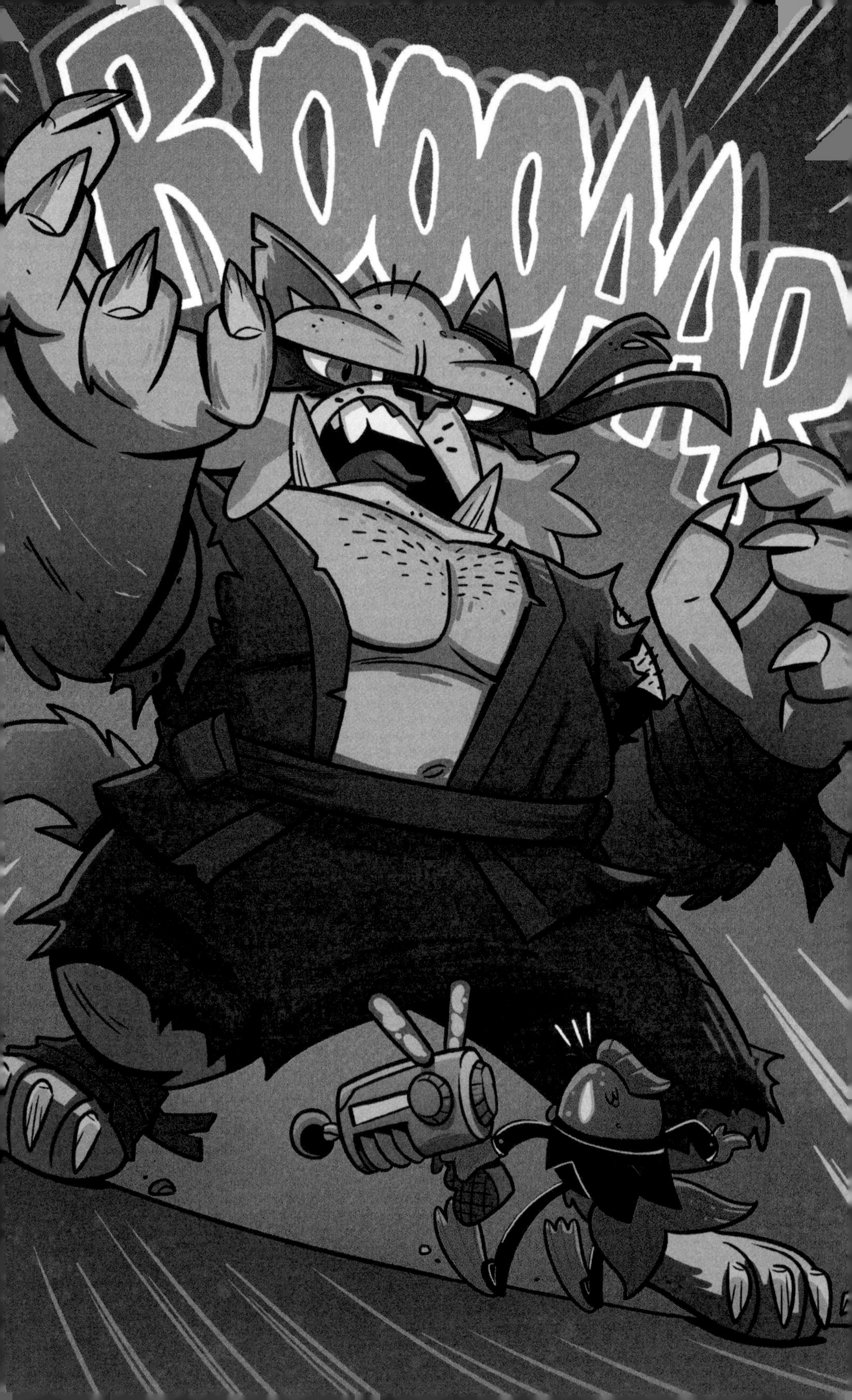
ROOOAAR

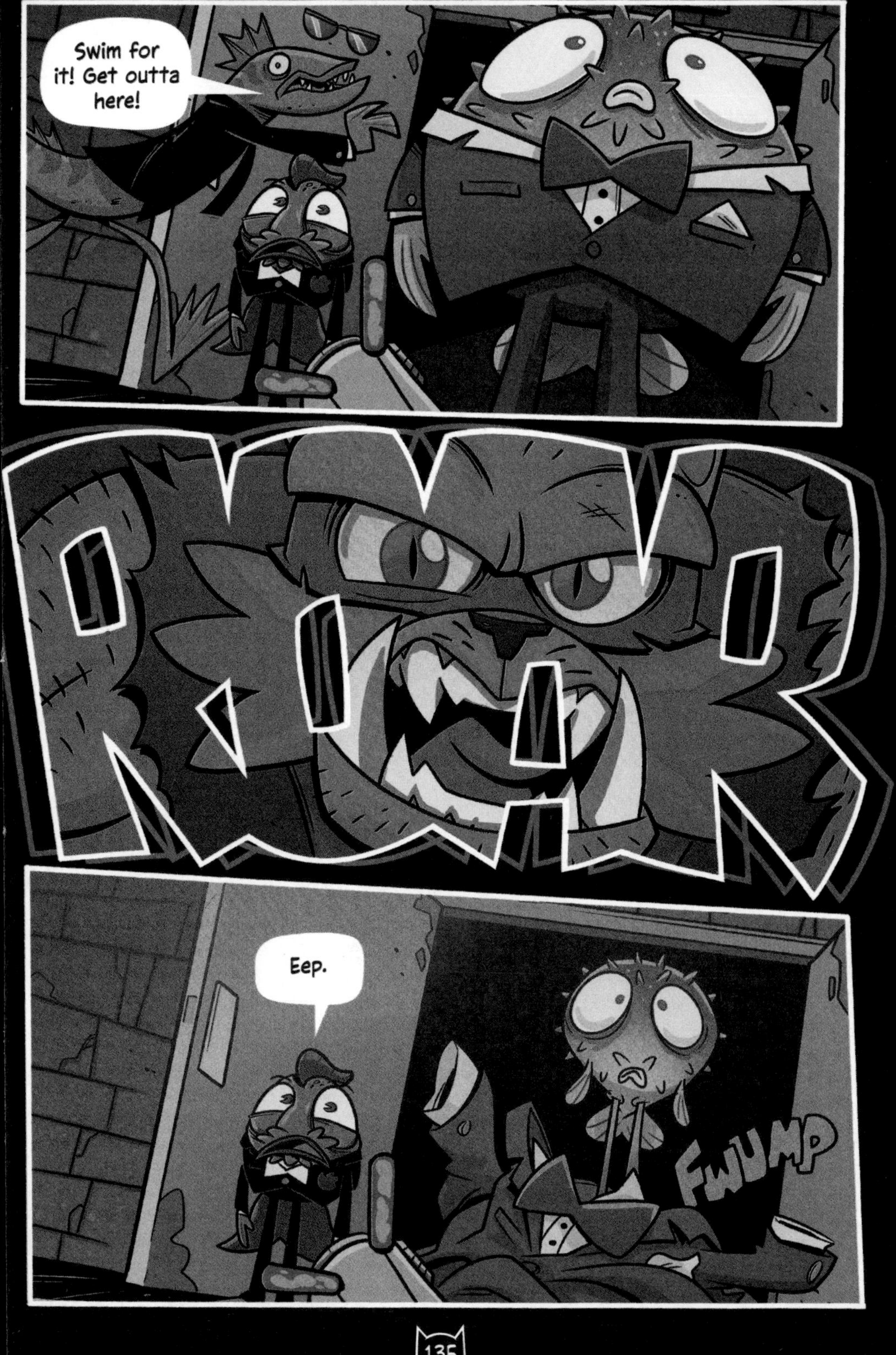
Swim for it! Get outta here!
ROAR
Eep.
FWUMP

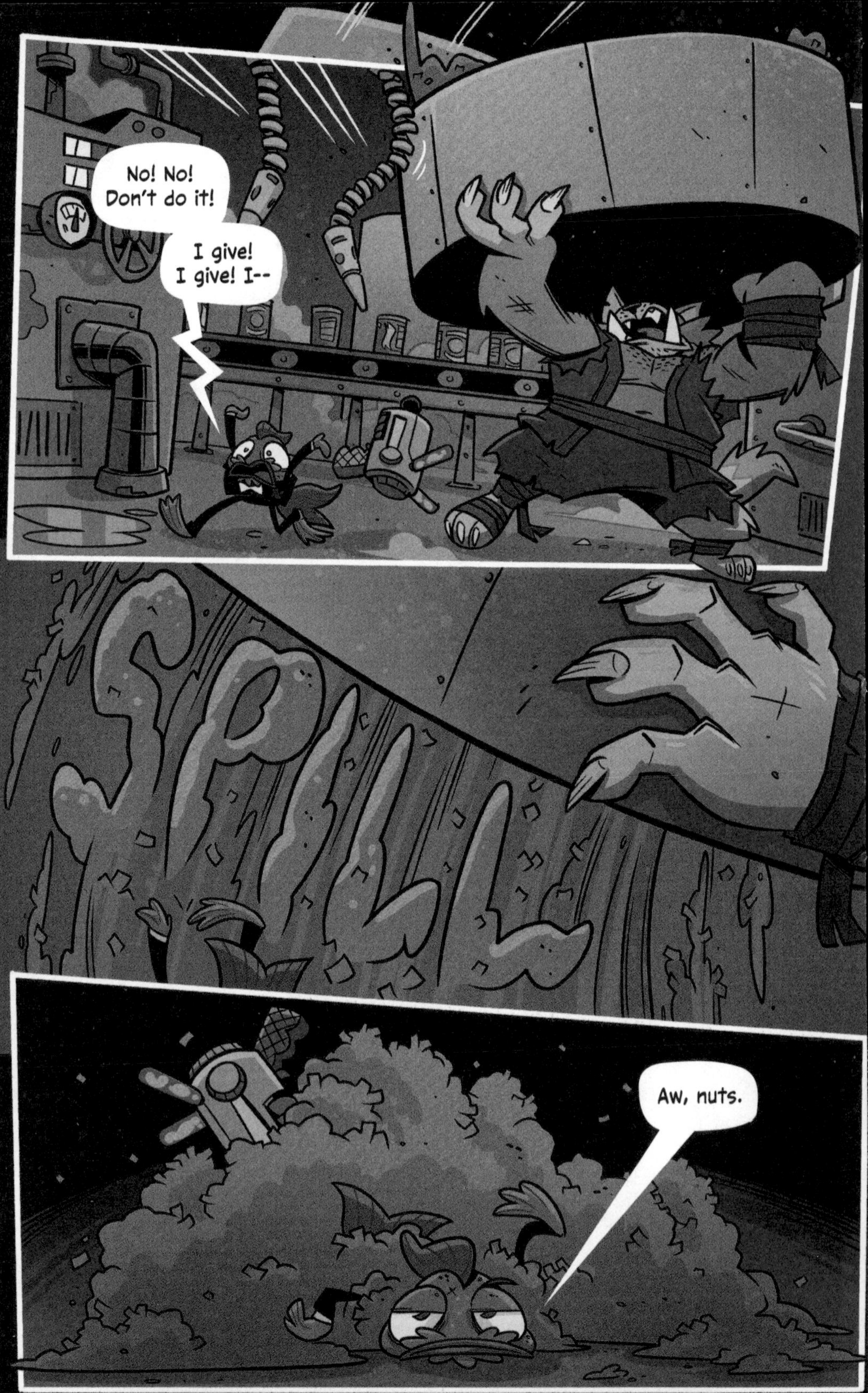
No! No! Don't do it!
I give! I give! I--
SPLLL
Aw, nuts.

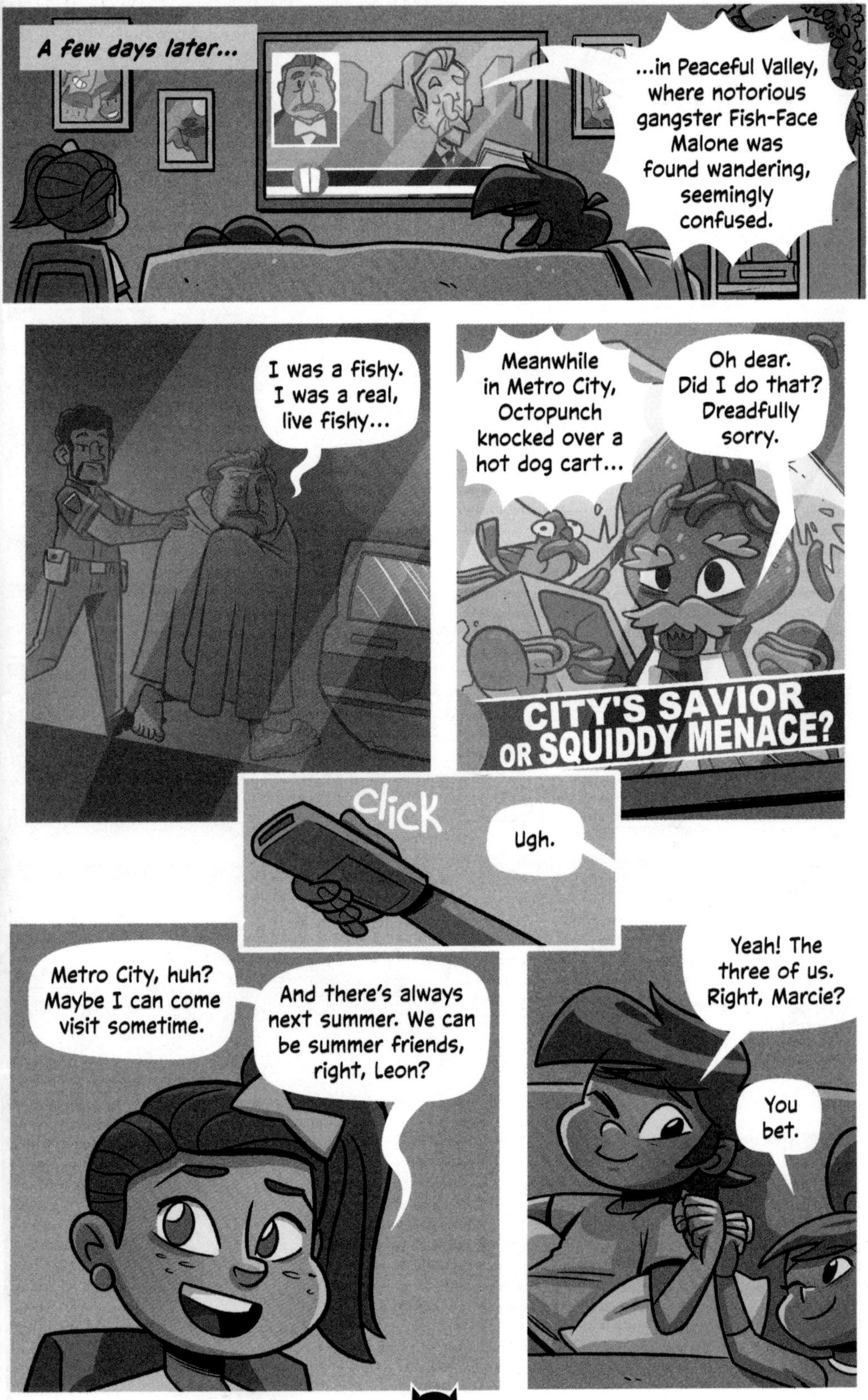
A few days later...
...in Peaceful Valley, where notorious gangster Fish-Face Malone was found wandering, seemingly confused.
I was a fishy. I was a real, live fishy...
Meanwhile in Metro City, Octopunch knocked over a hot dog cart...
Oh dear. Did I do that? Dreadfully sorry.
CITY'S SAVIOR OR SQUIDDY MENACE?
CLICK
Ugh.
Metro City, huh? Maybe I can come visit sometime.
And there's always next summer. We can be summer friends, right, Leon?
Yeah! The three of us. Right, Marcie?
You bet.

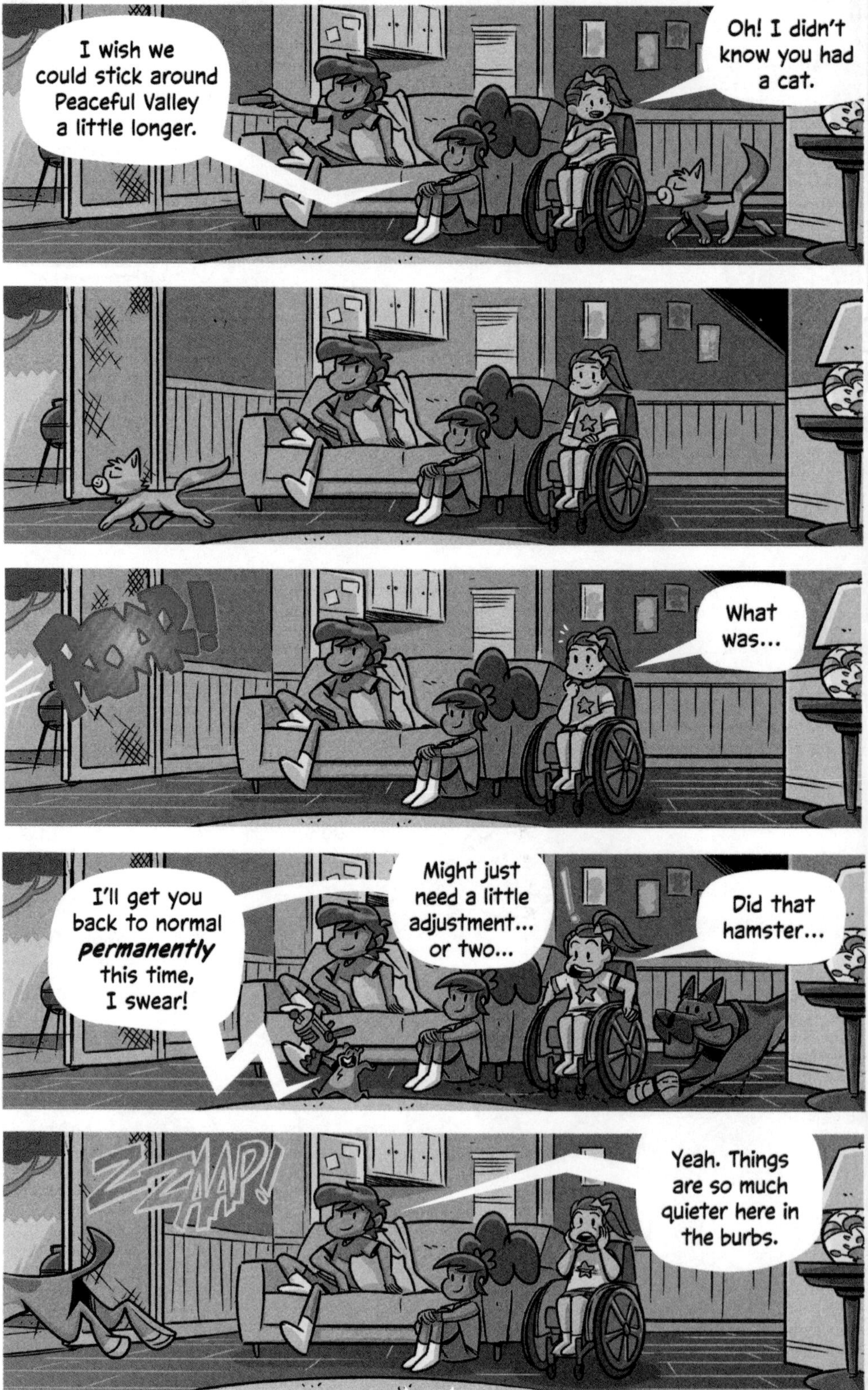
I wish we could stick around Peaceful Valley a little longer.
Oh! I didn't know you had a cat.
ROAR!
What was...
I'll get you back to normal *permanently* this time, I swear!
Might just need a little adjustment... or two...
Did that hamster...
ZZAAP!
Yeah. Things are so much quieter here in the burbs.

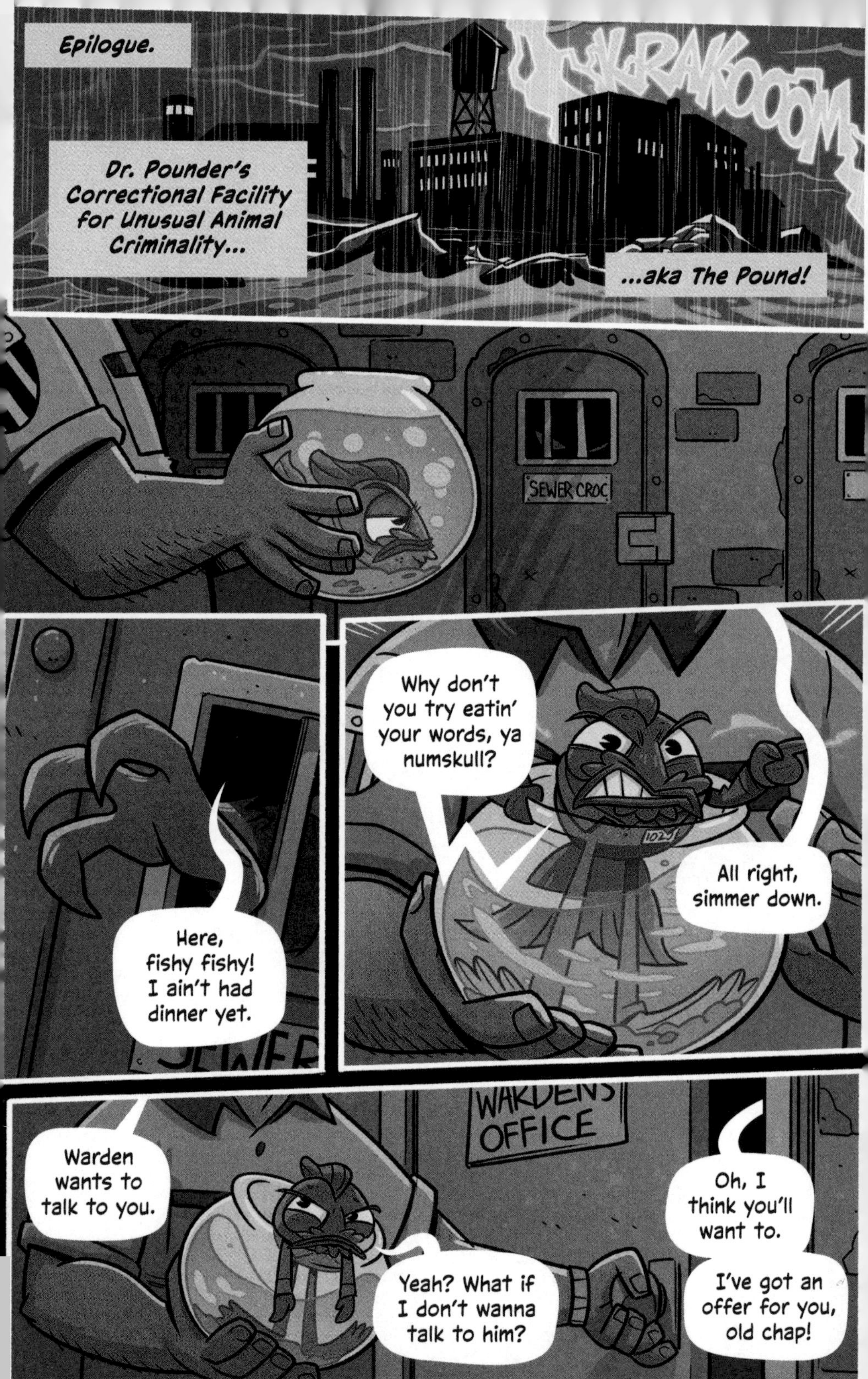
Epilogue.
KRAKOOOM
Dr. Pounder's Correctional Facility for Unusual Animal Criminality...
...aka The Pound!
SEWER CROC
Here, fishy fishy! I ain't had dinner yet.
Why don't you try eatin' your words, ya numskull?
All right, simmer down.
WARDEN'S OFFICE
Warden wants to talk to you.
Yeah? What if I don't wanna talk to him?
Oh, I think you'll want to.
I've got an offer for you, old chap!

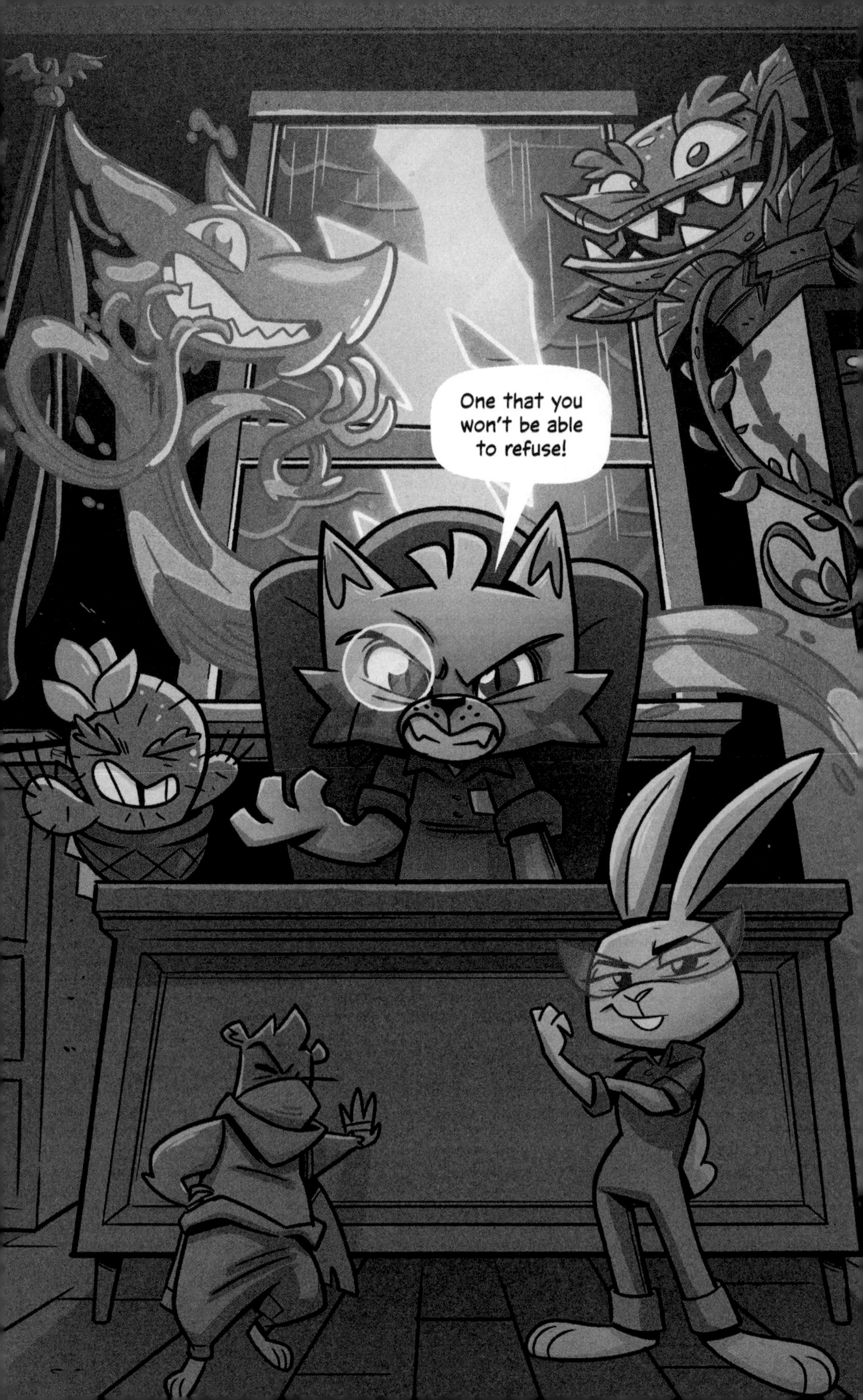
One that you won't be able to refuse!

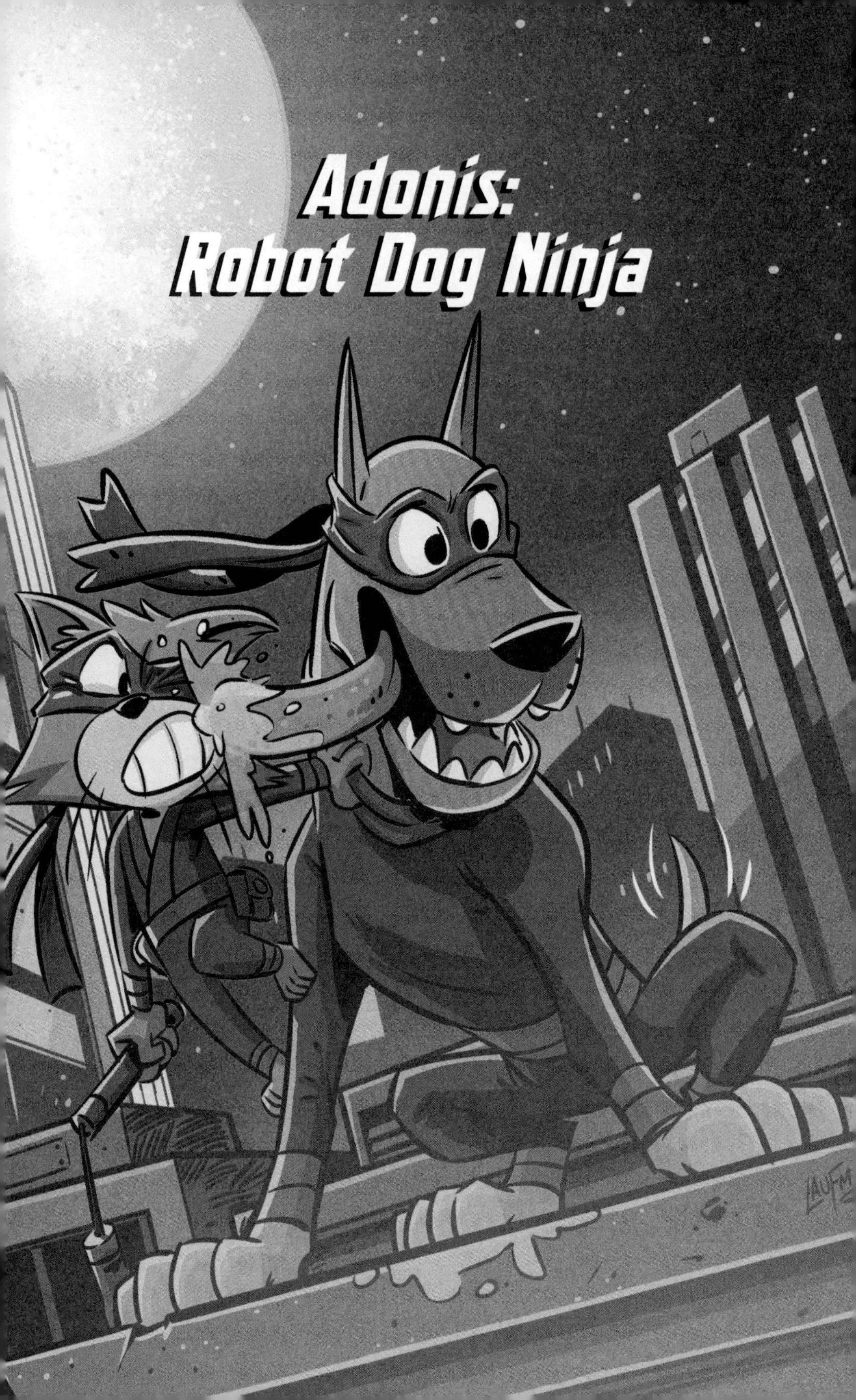
Adonis:
Robot Dog Ninja

Alejandro Arbona

Illustrated by
Derek Laufman

Colors by
Warren Wucinich

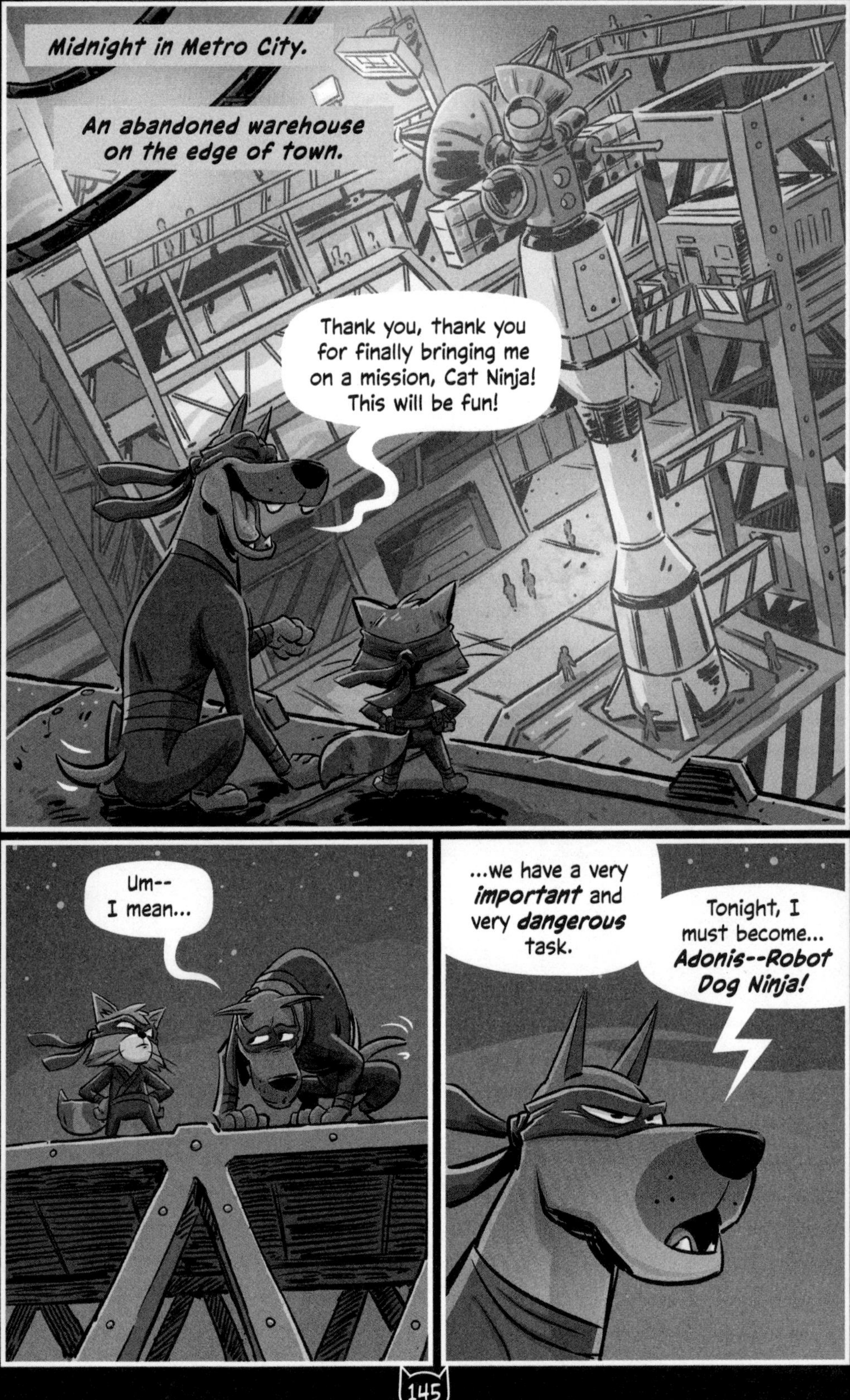
Midnight in Metro City.
An abandoned warehouse on the edge of town.
Thank you, thank you for finally bringing me on a mission, Cat Ninja! This will be fun!
Um-- I mean...
...we have a very *important* and very *dangerous* task.
Tonight, I must become... *Adonis--Robot Dog Ninja!*

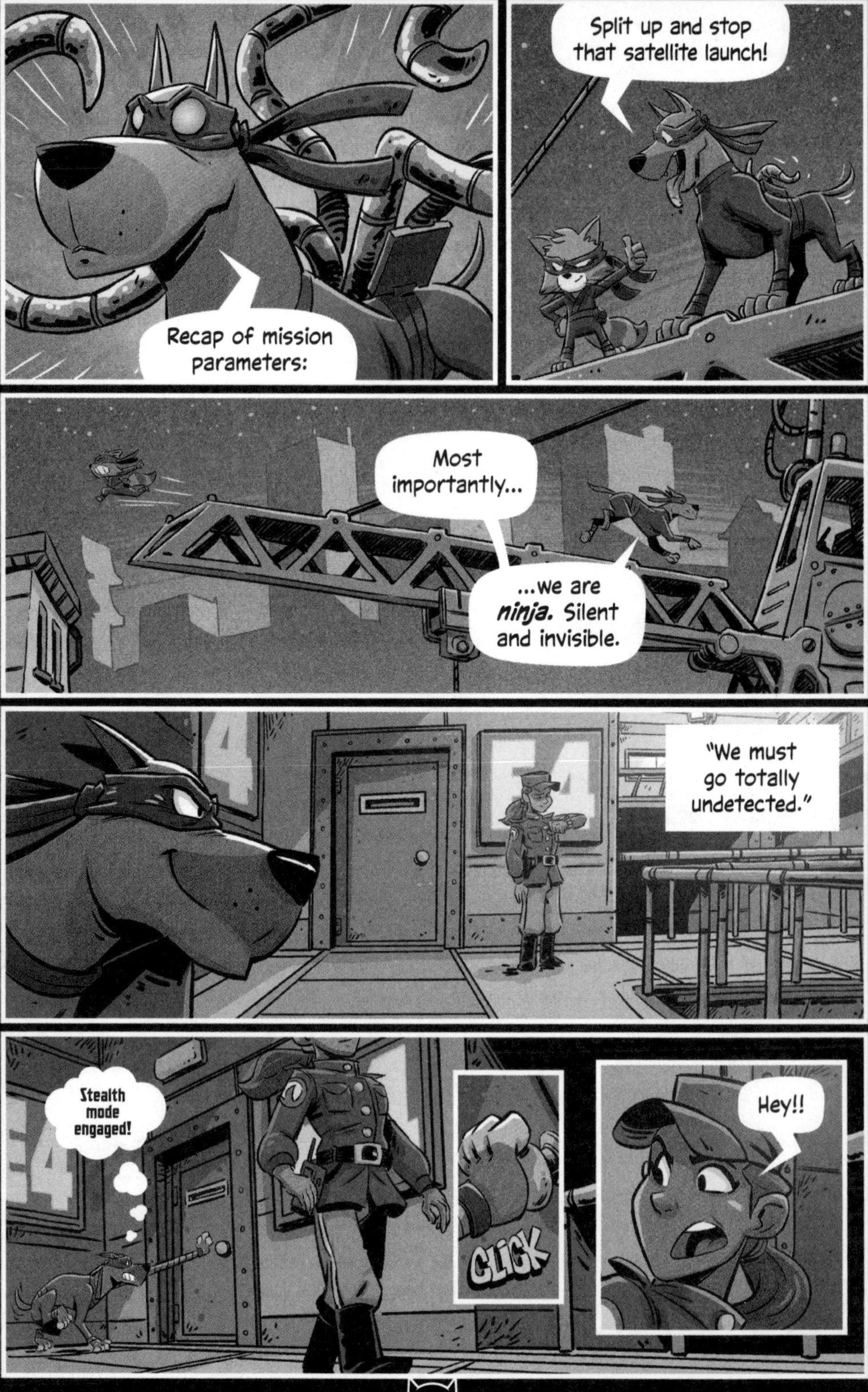
Recap of mission parameters:
Split up and stop that satellite launch!
Most importantly...
...we are ***ninja.*** Silent and invisible.
"We must go totally undetected."
Stealth mode engaged!
CLICK
Hey!!

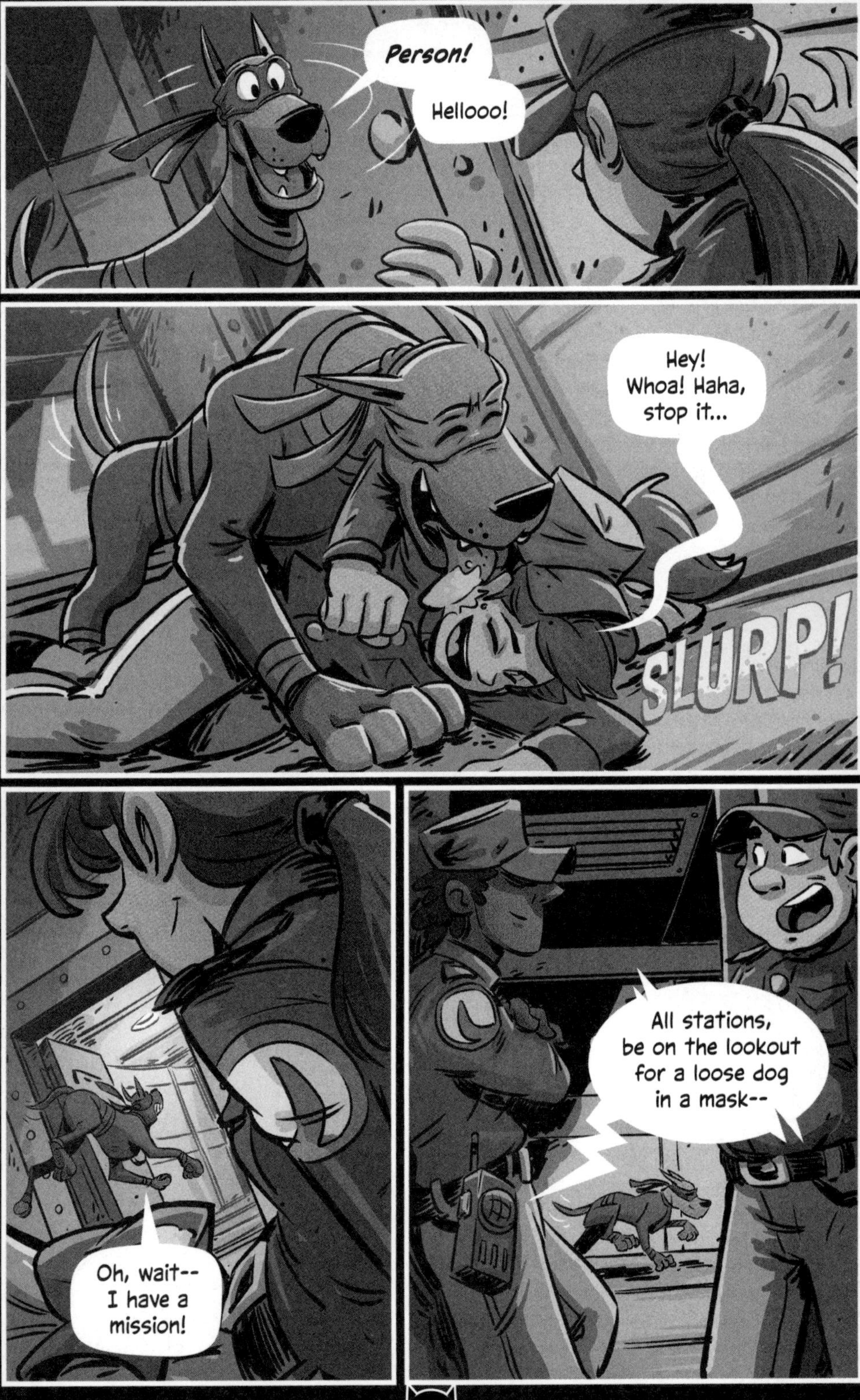
Person!
Hellooo!
Hey! Whoa! Haha, stop it...
SLURP!
Oh, wait-- I have a mission!
All stations, be on the lookout for a loose dog in a mask--

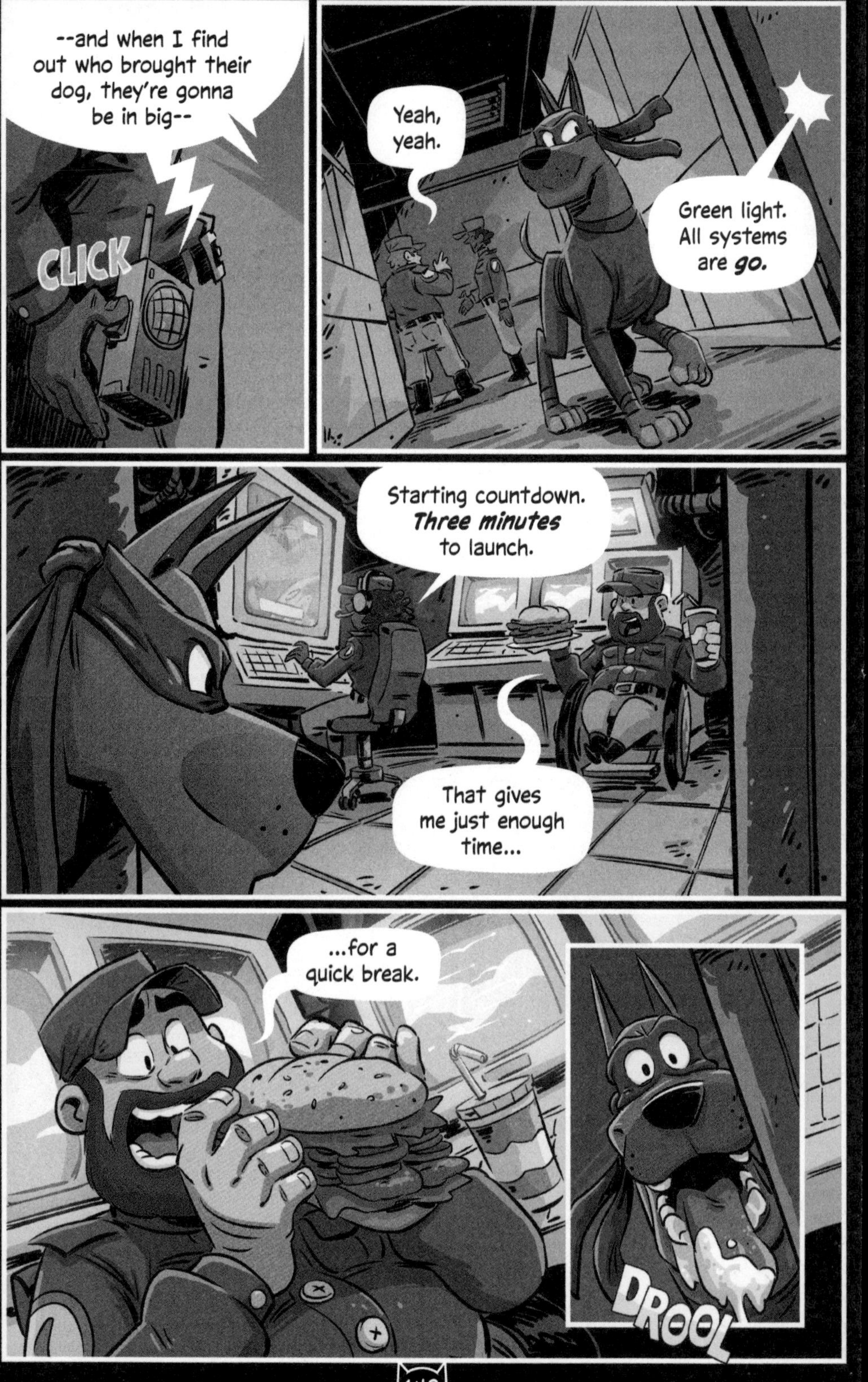
--and when I find out who brought their dog, they're gonna be in big--
CLICK
Yeah, yeah.
Green light. All systems are *go.*
Starting countdown. ***Three minutes*** to launch.
That gives me just enough time...
...for a quick break.
DROOL

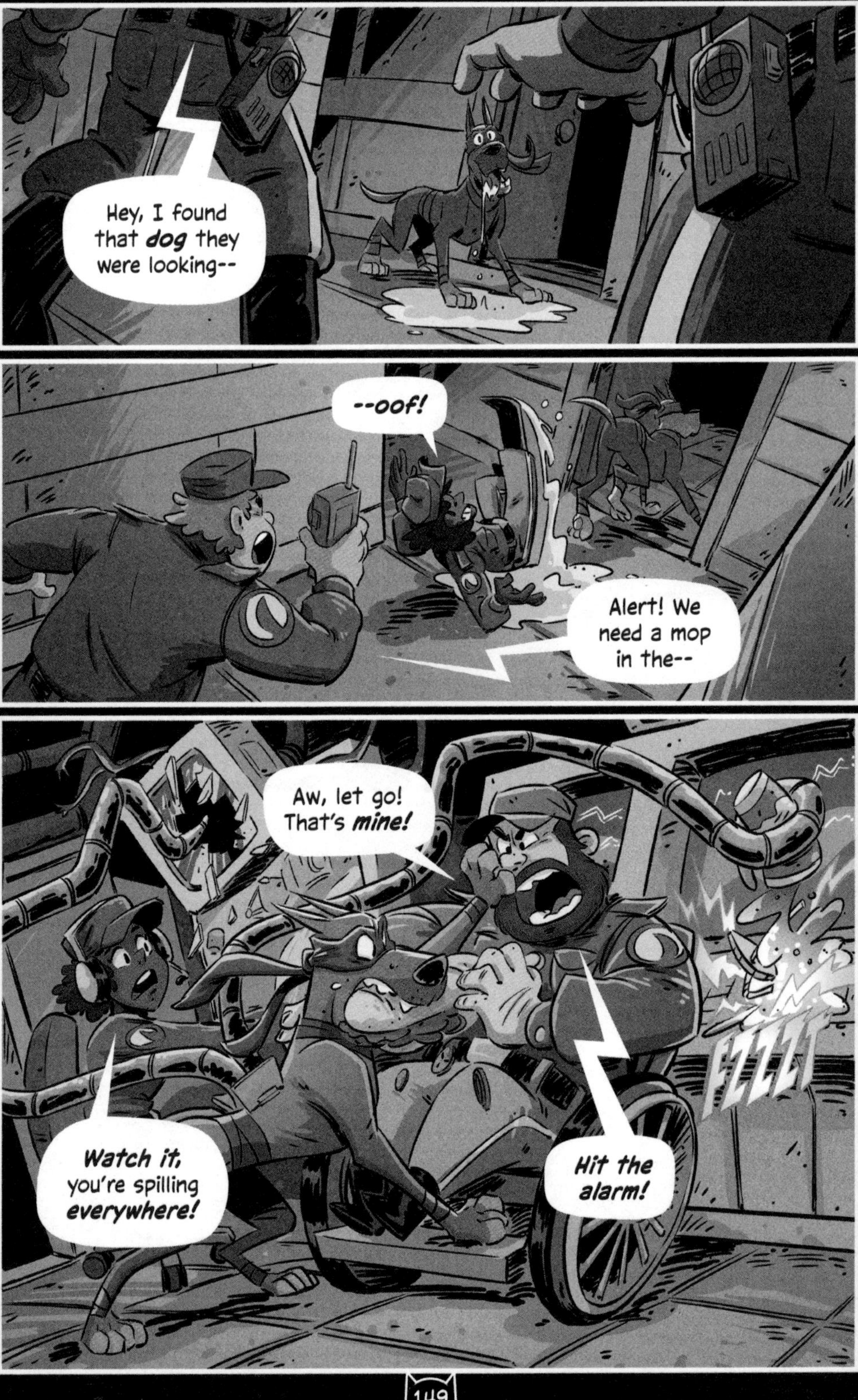
Hey, I found that *dog* they were looking--
--oof!
Alert! We need a mop in the--
Aw, let go! That's *mine!*
Watch it, you're spilling *everywhere!*
Hit the alarm!
FZZZT

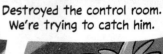

Did you say a dog?!?

Yes, sir.

Destroyed the control room. We're trying to catch him.

But you can still control the launch from here, sir.

Excellent. My satellite will fly above Mount Rushmore...

...and use its grow-a-tron laser to *embiggen* Abraham Lincoln's teeny-tiny nose!

Then the world will fear my name...

...*Rhino Blasty!*

You said it, boss!

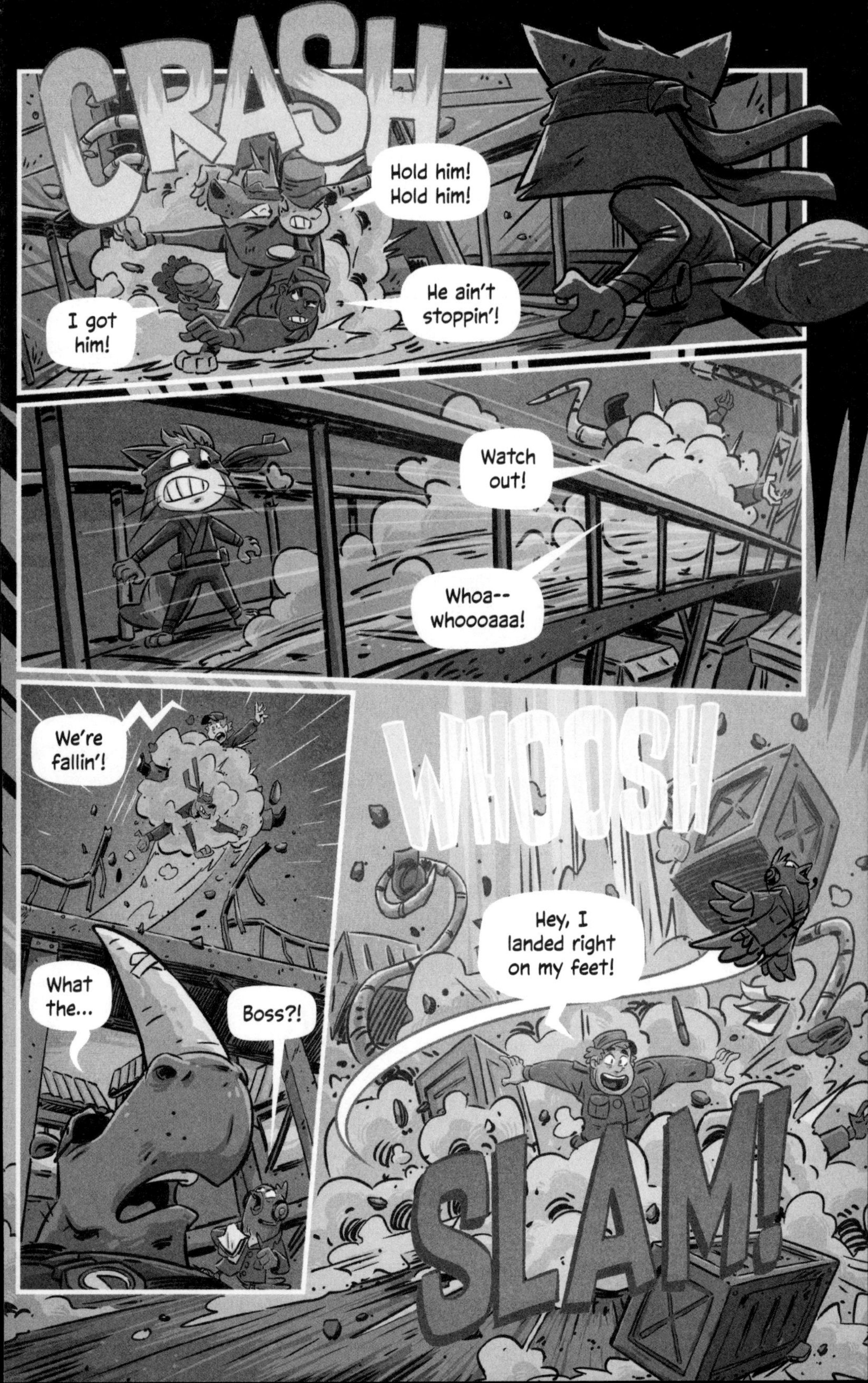
CRASH
Hold him! Hold him!
I got him!
He ain't stoppin'!
Watch out!
Whoa-- whoooaaa!
We're fallin'!
What the...
Boss?!
WHOOSH
Hey, I landed right on my feet!
SLAM!

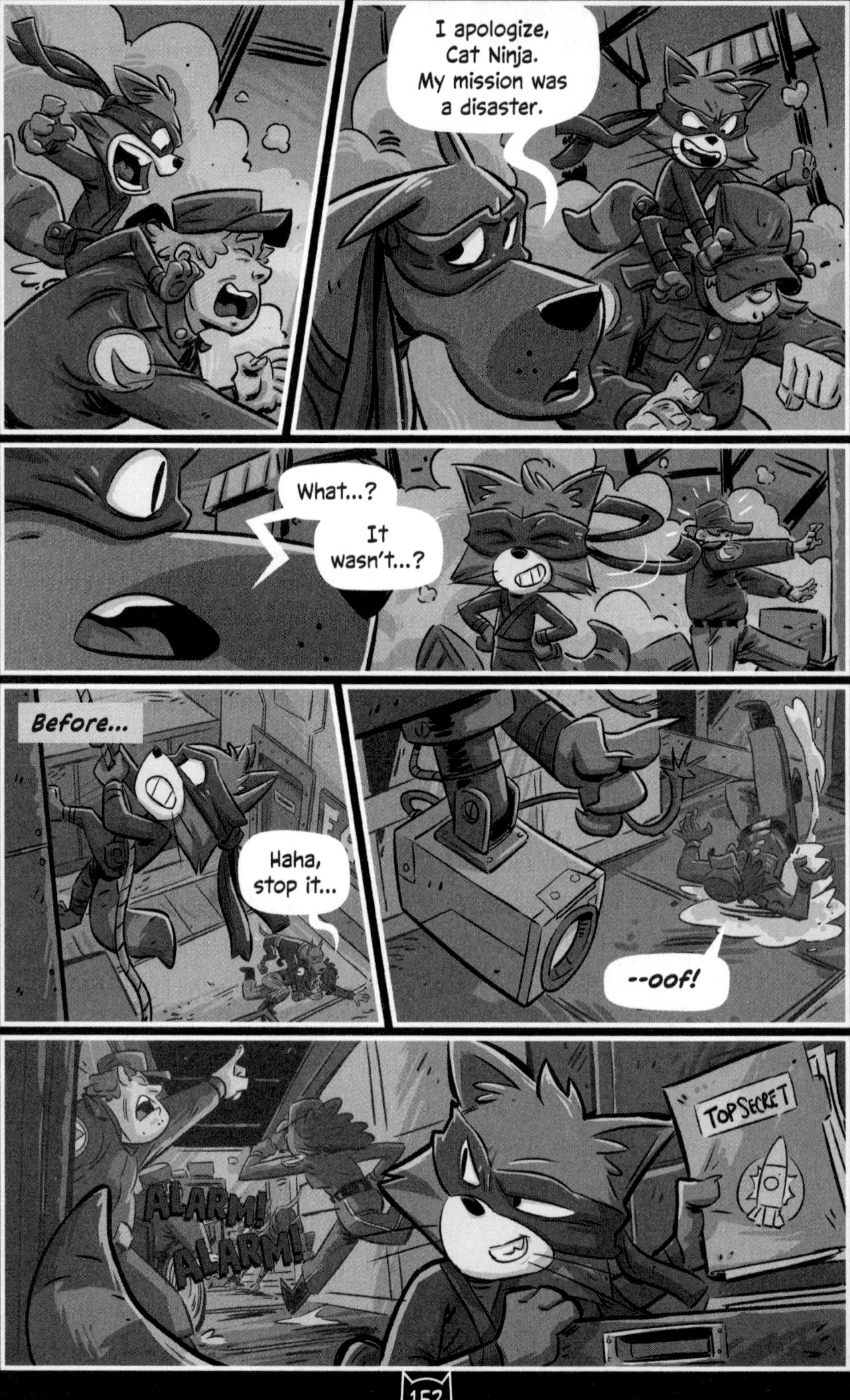

I apologize, Cat Ninja. My mission was a disaster.
What...?
It wasn't...?
Before...
Haha, stop it...
--oof!
ALARM! ALARM!
TOP SECRET

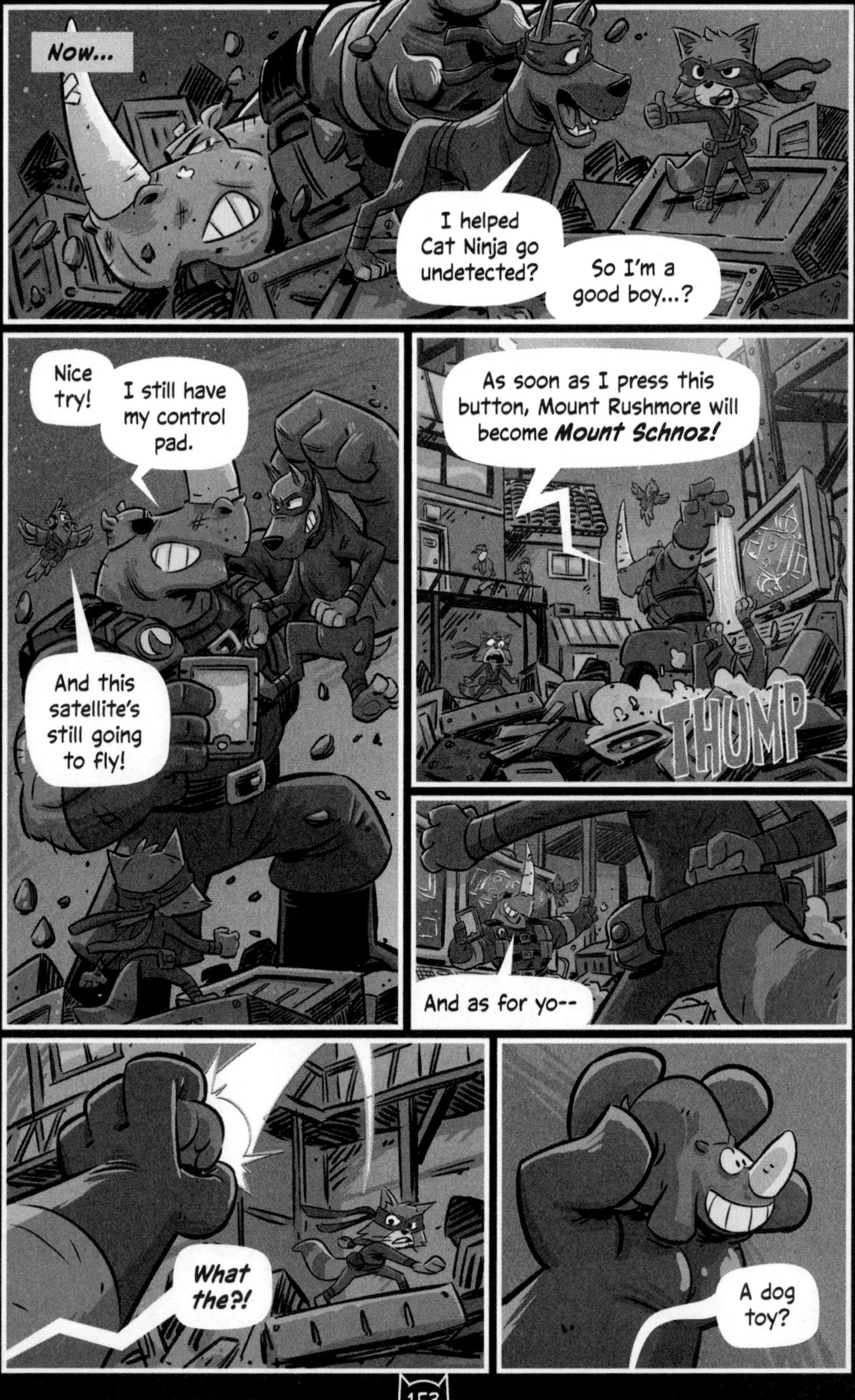
Now...
I helped Cat Ninja go undetected?
So I'm a good boy...?
Nice try!
I still have my control pad.
And this satellite's still going to fly!
As soon as I press this button, Mount Rushmore will become Mount Schnoz!
THUMP
And as for yo--
What the?!
A dog toy?

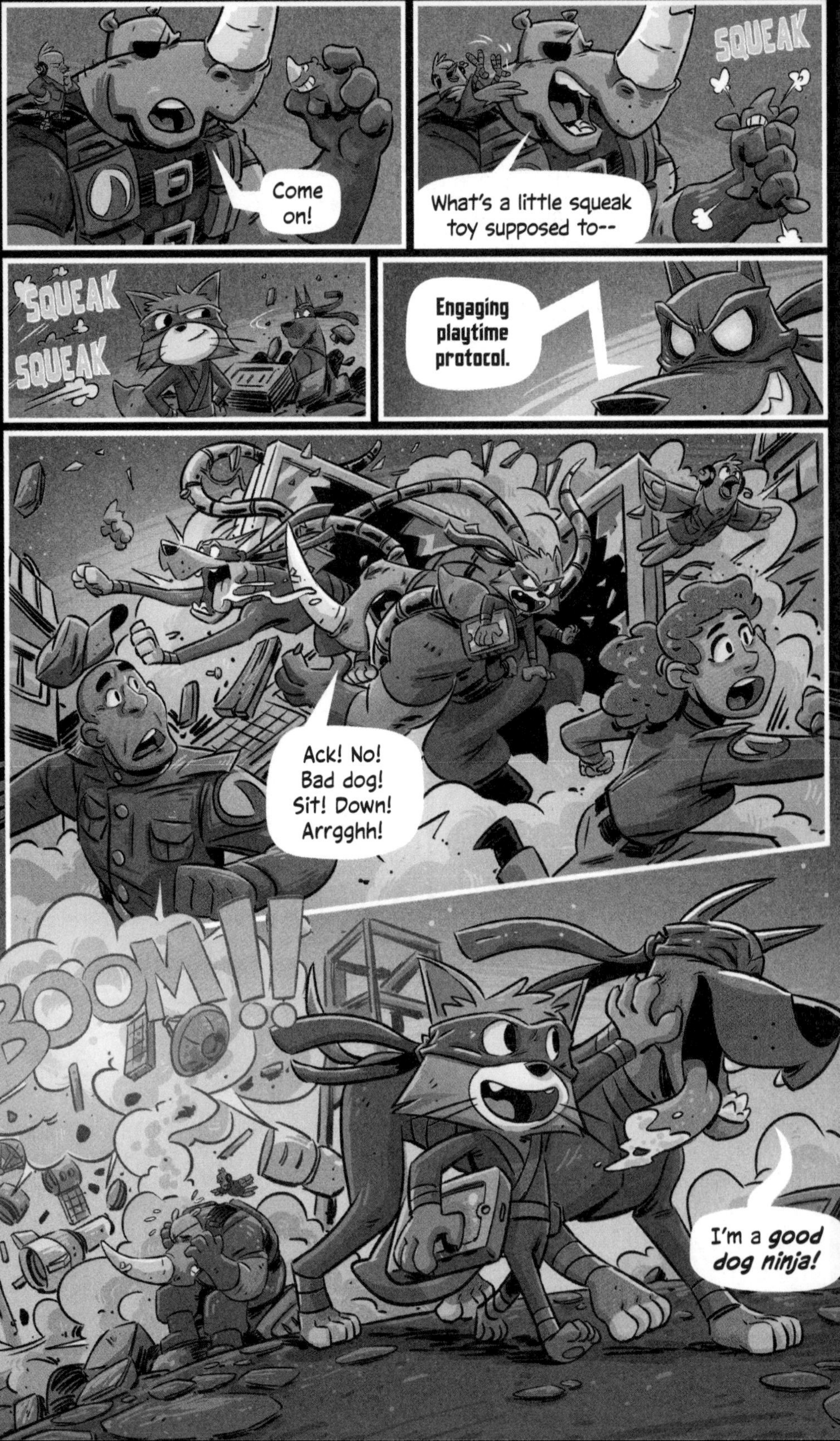

Come on!
SQUEAK
What's a little squeak toy supposed to--
SQUEAK
SQUEAK
Engaging playtime protocol.
Ack! No! Bad dog! Sit! Down! Arrgghh!
BOOM!!
I'm a *good dog ninja!*

About the Author

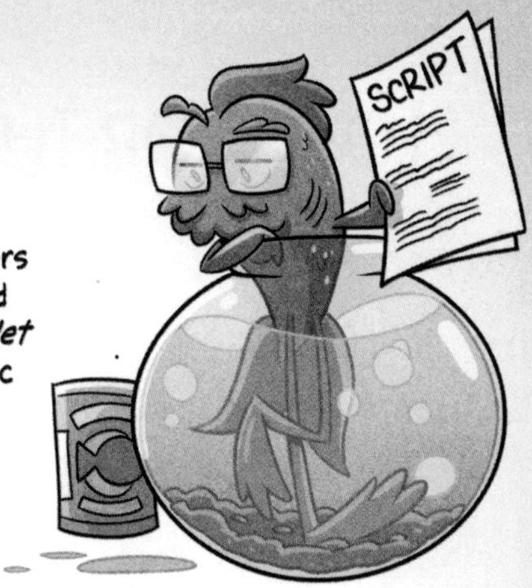
SCRIPT

MATTHEW CODY is the author of several popular books, including the award-winning Supers of Noble's Green trilogy: *Powerless, Super,* and *Villainous.* He is also the author of *Will in Scarlet* and *The Dead Gentleman,* as well as the graphic novels *Zatanna and the House of Secrets* from DC comics and *Bright Family* from Epic/Andrews McMeel. He lives in Manhattan, New York, with his wife and son.

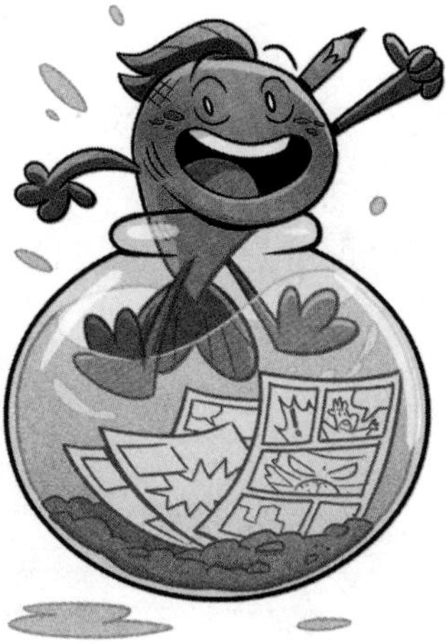

About the Illustrator

CHAD THOMAS is an illustrator and cartoonist living with his family in McKinney, Texas. He's worked on books such as *TMNT, Star Wars Adventures,* and *Mega Man* and also illustrates activity and educational books. He loves his family, comic books, and Star Wars and will let his children beat him in checkers, but never in Mario Kart.

About the Colorist

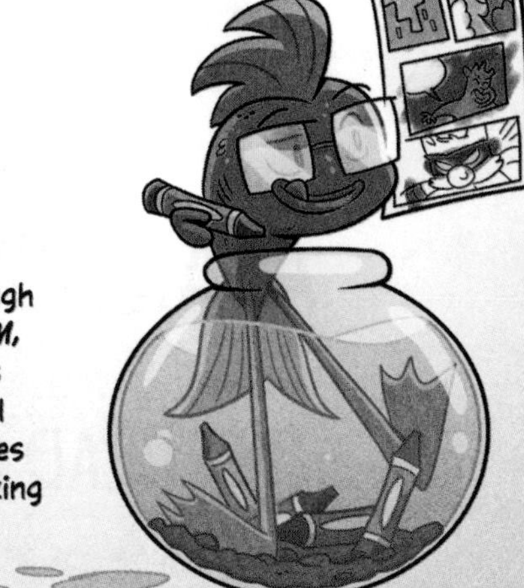

WARREN WUCINICH is a comic book creator and part-time carny who has been lucky enough to work on such cool projects as *Invader ZIM, Courtney Crumrin,* and *Bright Family.* He is also the co-creator of the YA graphic novel *Kriss: The Gift of Wrath.* He currently resides in Dallas, Texas, where he spends his time making comics, rewatching '80s television shows, and eating all the tacos.